indGame

NPCs

BOOK TWO IN THE INDGAME SERIES

indGame

NPCs

BOOK TWO IN THE INDGAME SERIES

ROD
R GARCIA

Enchanted Bubble Wand Press

an imprint of

EpiphanyMill Publishing

Text Copyright © 2023 Rod R Garcia

Cover Art Copyright © 2023 Rod R Garcia

Published in the United States by Enchanted Bubble Wand Press, an imprint of EpiphanyMill LLC. Star Valley, AZ

EpiphanyMill Publishing is a registered trademark and the bubble wand colophon is a trademark of EpiphanyMill LLC.

Visit us on the Web! EpiphanyMill.com

Library of Congress Cataloging-in-Publication Data

Garcia, Rod R

IndGame — NPCs / Rod R Garcia. — First edition.

ISBN 978-1-947691-15-5 (intl. tr. pbk.)

ISBN 978-1-947691-16-2 (eBook)

[1. YA-Fiction. 2. Science-Fiction. 3. Thriller-Fiction.]

I. Title.

Library of Congress Control Number 2023944982

The text of this book is set in 12 Apollo MT Std.

Book design by Rod R Garcia

Edited by E. M. B.

Cover design by Rod R Garcia

Printed in the United States of America

10 9 8 7 6 5 4 3 2 1

First Edition

For my parents:

Sandra J Gray

J Richard Garcia

and Elva Garcia

Thank you for the memories that shaped my world.

SPECIAL THANKS TO:

BETA READERS

Nicholas "The Professor" Jackson

Pat Muxie

COVER ART PHOTOGRAPHY

Betsy Ponce

COVER ART MODELS

Jake Ashton

Tyler Cox

Nico Pengin

A real friend is one who walks in when the rest of the world
walks out.

~ Walter Winchell

Prologue

My name is Packard Campbell. I play games for a living... or at least I did until my dad and I were involved in an accident that left me brain dead. He and Irene, one of his closest friends and colleagues, used an experimental procedure to, well, resurrect me. They used backups of my real and in-game memories that were stored in a quantum gaming database and rebooted me by loading me with cutting-edge medical nanotechnology called Nanops.

Obviously, that worked, or I wouldn't be here telling you this story.

As you might have already guessed, things didn't go exactly as planned... hence, the story.

You see, once they uploaded my memories, my brain had an awful time trying to sort out what was real and what wasn't. Memories of games and real life were jumbled up in my mind, like salt and sugar shaken together in a jar. And when I say games, I mean *games!* The Neural Reality system I'd been playing in for so long was something straight out of a Philip K. Dick novel. My dad designed it to put the player directly into the game and make their memories of past gameplay as real as any other memory.

If you've never experienced Marshal Blood *as* Marshal Blood, or saved the world as the *actual* Golden Sentinel, then buddy, you haven't played games.

Oh, I squirreled, didn't I? Sorry, I do that sometimes.

Salt and sugar, Philip K. Dick… oh yeah. By that point, my dad and I had three NPCs in our house, four if you counted the '65 GTO that seemed to have magically become an NPC. On top of that, Cool, the Elastic Giraffe — yep, the one from the Evolutants book series and the *Animehem* NR game — materialized sixty miles away at Arete Nanophysiology. Arete was Irene's facility where she brought me back from the dead.

In addition to Cool and Knightmare — yeah, the car has a name — Becky from *String Theories*, Clem from *Marshal Blood*, and my horse, Whisper, also from *Marshal Blood*, were in dad's house.

All in the flesh.

Through the magic of science, Irene verified the NPCs were as real as you and me. There were Nanops present in them, but they were flesh and blood. I'd seen them cry, get frightened and shoot at airplanes, and even get drunk off *one* beer. I probably wasn't ever going to talk about that last one in Clem's presence. Oh, hell, who am I kidding? I couldn't wait to razz him for that! Oh, they ate and peed, too. Becky and I saw Whisper do all that.

So, yeah, they were real.

Dad's freak-out when he realized Knightmare had become sentient was also real. He drove off in her in a fit of rage.

So, my life had been turned pretty well upside down. If I'm being honest, everyone's lives had been turned upside down. Dad, Irene, our friend Gunner, even Becky, Clem, Whisper, Knightmare, and Cool. They were all victims of circumstance. They didn't ask to be brought into our world.

I kept wondering how and when it might finally end. Little did I know — *by the way, nothing good* ever *follows 'little did I know'* — everything that happened up to that point was just the tip of a terrifying iceberg that made the Titanic's sparring partner look like a snow cone.

LEVEL FOUR
AREA OF EFFECT

1

What Doesn't Kill You…

"Is your dad ever coming back," Becky wondered aloud.

Dad had been gone for almost two hours, and I wasn't as confident saying he'd be back as I'd been an hour earlier. "I don't know," I finally said. "He was really freaked out."

"I was pretty hard on him in the beginning, wasn't I," Becky asked, her voice thick with guilt.

I flashed back to how I'd treated him when I woke up. "I was shitty to him when I first woke up from being dead, too." I stopped, realizing what I'd just said. "Not that you were shitty. You had a right to be upset and question what was going on."

She looked at me, her expression flatter than an old, warm soda. She clearly didn't buy my response. "You don't have to make excuses to make me feel better."

"Jest call a spade a spade, Marshal," Clem said from the couch. He was no longer slurring his words and was looking for his boots.

"We don't use phrases like that anymore, Clem," Becky said, shaking her head.

Clem snorted. "Jest like a woman to-"

I cut him off before he could alienate himself from Becky any further than he already had. "No, Clem. She's right. We don't say things like that anymore. You have a lot to learn about the world you're in. Your rhetoric was bad enough in the game world, but here? It'll get you, or Becky, or me killed. Besides that, it's just plain wrong."

Clem wasn't having any of my lecture. He looked like my words were hurting him, but not because he actually cared.

"Your head hurt," I asked.

"Like a rail worker's using it as a sledgehammer," Clem replied, wincing.

"Beer here is stronger than where you came from. You just drank the equivalent of four beers, in alcohol content, anyway." I left Becky on the couch and went to the kitchen to get Clem some aspirin. "Thanks for not peeing on my dad's couch," I called back.

"Some mighta come out t'other end," Clem replied.

I returned with the aspirin and a bottle of water to find Becky scooting farther away as discreetly as possible. I didn't know quite what to say. "You wha-"

"Only joshin' ya' there, Marshal. My britches are clean." He looked down at his pants and pursed his lips. "On the inside, anyway."

Becky looked mortified. "Can we just pretend we can't see him or something?" She shrugged. "I mean, it worked on me for a while, right?"

Clem cleared his throat.

I sighed. "As much as that might seem like a good idea-"

"Why're you takin' her side, Marshal?" It was Clem's turn to interrupt me.

"Look, Clem." My patience had worn about as thin as the elbows on dad's favorite sweater. "I'm on the side of everybody getting along, alright? My uh, my pa's gone missing and more of you guys are popping up by the minute."

Whisper whinnied softly in the kitchen.

"You should probably stay out of this, Whisper," I called out.

Whisper snorted and stamped a foot, but then settled down, having said her piece.

"Clem, all I'm asking is that you don't antagonize each other. Okay? What happens when you put a match to kerosene," I asked him.

He stared at me, blankly.

"I'm asking an actual question. Match? Kerosene?"

Clem looked super confused. "Uh, fire," he replied finally.

"Fire," I shouted. "No more putting matches to kerosene, alright?"

Clem looked at Becky, his face clearly saying, *'a little help here?'*.

Becky shook her head. "You got yourself into this one. Don't look to me for help."

Clem dropped his head, as if stricken. "I guess I'll take them aspreen now."

~

After Clem took his 'aspreen', and I showed him his boots and hat were safe, the three of us settled back onto the couch.

Becky looked like something was bothering her. "What's on your mind," I asked.

Becky's eyes found mine, and she offered a kind of half smile. "You really do know me," she marveled. "Don't you?"

I smiled and said nothing, not wanting to ruin the moment.

"What's an ennpeesee," she asked after a moment.

"Oh, uh..." I was blindsided by the question.

She looked even more concerned. "Is it bad?"

"Uh, no," I finally said. "It's not bad. I don't think it applies to you."

She wasn't going to accept a non-answer. "Well?"

I finally relented. "It's an acronym. It means non-playable character. Three letters: N. P. C. Basically, it's any character in a game, human or otherwise, not controlled by one of the actual players."

"You and your dad referred to Clem and me as NPCs," Becky said, her smile gone completely. "So, what does that make me? Scenery?"

"And right pretty scenery, at that," Clem added.

Becky scowled at Clem, and he wisely closed his mouth.

"Ew, Clem," she said, her nose wrinkling. "Just... ew." She looked at me, eyes pleading again. She was having the world's worst identity crisis. "What makes me any different from that lamp, or this couch?"

"No, we were wrong. You're nothing like an NPC," I replied, finally sure of what I was saying. "You're both independent of any system. NPCs have parameters. They have a certain set of phrases and responses, even limited actions and travel range." I took a deep breath before continuing. "But you guys are unique. You think for yourselves and make decisions outside the game scripting. There's no amount of programming that could make you do that if you were NPCs."

She mulled over my words, still looking unsure.

"Becky, until you and Clem came along, the only person who was even remotely real to me in this world was dad." I reconsidered that statement as it crossed my lips. "Okay, maybe Irene and Gunner too, but that's super recent." I grasped her shoulder gently. "You guys, my friends in the games, were my only real friends. Even though you were going through the motions according to a script, you were more real to me than the outside world, *this* world, could ever be." I looked at Clem, who was feeling some unfamiliar emotions and very unhappy about it. "But now, with you both here, acting on your own feelings and impulses? You're *not* NPCs. You're my friends. My *family*." I quickly looked at Becky. "Not like a sister or anything weird!"

Whisper blew a raspberry, clearly unmoved by the exchange.

"That includes you, Whisper," I shouted, probably a little too close to Becky's ear.

A satisfied whinny came back in response, and I knew all was once again well in the land of Whisper.

Clem cleared his throat again. He was either trying not to interrupt me, or hoping to not say the words he was thinking. Probably both.

"Uh, Marshal, I appreciate the sentiment. Uh..." Poor Clem was having actual feelings. "You, uh, clearly and well-deservedly have a great many friends. You've got Becky here, yer pa, Irene, Black Gunner Reeves, Whisper, that there jee-raff on the movin' picture contraption, and I've heard many other names mentioned in conversation that I cain't recall." Clem looked at the kitchen, maybe considering another beer before he spoke again. "You see, my wife and daughter died on the trail from Independence, Missourah, and I ain't warmed up to no one else since'n that time. I know I'm cantankerous and oft' times disagreeable, and I know I have many viewpoints and opinions that rub other folks wrong. But uh, well, yer my best friend, Marshal. Mayhaps my *only* friend. You've got Becky, Whisper, and t'others. I've got you."

Well, Clem might have succeeded at holding back the tears, but Becky and I were a little less stoic.

Becky lunged forward and hugged him, before backing off and grasping the front of his shirt in her clenched fist. Clem stared at her stupidly. I can't say I blame him. The reversal was a weird flex.

"If you'd be a little nicer, less judgmental, and try to consider other people's feelings, you might have more friends," Becky said through her tears. "And for the record, I'm willing to be your friend, too. I just need to see you trying." She let go of his shirt. "Okay?"

Clem nodded, flabbergasted. All the stoicism in the world couldn't hide that. "Agreed. But I ain't never had no lady-friends. I s'pect I'm goin' to say many offensive thangs, but I'll try, if'n y'all can be patient with me."

Can you say breakthrough? Because I swear, I felt like Dr. Phil at that moment, only with more hair. I mean, I knew it wasn't going to be that simple — spoiler alert: *it wasn't* — but it *was* the beginning of Clem's second official friendship.

~

As we were speaking, a loud clatter suddenly broke out in the kitchen. Whisper trotted around nervously, then someone shrieked.

Clem turned to me, cool as cucumber, and said, "I s'pect that's one of yer other friends poppin' in outta nowhere."

I went to get up from the couch and start towards the kitchen, but Clem grabbed my forearm. "You might wanna wipe them tears from yer eyes first. It's downright unmanly."

I wiped my eyes as I walked into the kitchen. Becky scolded Clem as I turned the corner. "That's the kind of thing we're talking about, Clem," she hissed.

"But it's true," Clem countered. "Ain't it?"

Once in the kitchen, I found Whisper backed up against our refrigerator, avoiding something, or someone, on the other side of the island. I patted her before investigating. "Good girl, Whisper. I've got this."

I poked my head around the side of the island, realizing a moment too late, if it were someone else like Clem, I might lose the top of my head.

Lo and behold, it *was* another gun-toting cretin. Though this one couldn't have hit me with a shotgun at point-blank range unless he was swinging it like a club. Kyle's aim was worse than a Stormtrooper's.

"Kyle," I said.

He looked up from his safe place in the corner next to our trash can. "Pack? Oh my God! It IS you!" He practically dove into my arms. "Where the hell are we," he whispered. "And why is there a horse in this kitchen?"

I grasped Kyle's shoulders and smiled. "You're safe, bro. I've got a lot to tell you, but let's do it in the living room, where we can sit down. I need to introduce you to a few more friends," I motioned towards the fridge. "Starting with my horse, Whisper."

Horses, it turned out, terrified Kyle. He crept around her gingerly, making his way to the living room door. "Your horse," he muttered.

"Dude," I laughed, "Whisper's as gentle as a puppy. She wouldn't hurt a fly." I nodded at her. "Go ahead, pet her."

Kyle stepped forward timidly, but when his spider-tingle didn't alert him to any danger, he reached out to pet her.

I turned to the living room to alert Clem and Becky to our newest arrival and clearly missed Kyle patting her on the hind quarters.

Turning back in what felt like super slo-mo, my mouth was an awkward oval as I shouted, "Noooooooooooo!"

But I was too late.

Whisper was gentle, but ticklish. Kyle found her sweet spot. She did what she always did, a reflexive kick with her back leg. And Kyle was suddenly across the room, embedded in the wall next to our dining room window. *Dead*.

2
Checkpoints

"Is he dead," Becky asked a moment later.

Clem checked Kyle's pulse. "As a door nail," he declared solemnly. "Friend of yers?"

"Yeah." I nodded slowly, scarcely able to believe what had just happened. "He was… a, uh, gunslinger, like you."

Clem dipped his head in prayer. "Well, rest his soul then." He reached out to close Kyle's eyes. But as he touched my friend's eyelids, he vanished. Kyle, not Clem. We weren't getting that lucky.

"'Tis the work of the Devil," Clem exclaimed, hopping back and eliciting a nervous grunt from Whisper.

I was surprised, to say the least. Both by the disappearance, and Clem's response. "Oh, come on, Clem. You don't belie-"

A shriek on the other side of the kitchen startled all of us. Whisper almost hopped onto the kitchen counter.

"Pack?" It was Kyle again. He seemed even more surprised than he had the first time. "Pack, is that you?"

"I thought we already went over that," I said, unsure of what was happening.

Becky squeezed my shoulder. "Did he just respawn, Packard?"

As much as I disliked the idea, it was the most logical explanation.

"Kyle!" I waved my hands at him, wanting him to focus on me. "It's me, Pack, and Whisper. Do you remember Whisper?"

Kyle looked at Becky and Clem. "I've never seen either of them. Which one is Whisper?"

"They're Becky and Clem," I said, nodding at them.

"I'd be Clem," Clem added, holding up a calloused hand.

Kyle nodded suspiciously. "Then Whisper is the horse," he asked, sounding uncertain.

I smiled. "Bingo. Do you remember her?"

Kyle shook his head. "Should I? Is this some kind of prank?"

Whisper farted. How could apples going in come out so awful?

"No, this isn't a prank, buddy," I assured Kyle, purposely ignoring Clem congratulating Whisper on the *potency of her winds.* "Let's go into the living room, where we can talk, okay?"

Kyle looked nervously at Whisper. "Is she coming too?"

"Gawd, I hope not," Clem exclaimed.

I shook my head. "No, Whisper won't be leaving the kitchen. Will you, girl?"

Whisper swished her tail, a clear sign of irritation.

"That means yes," I lied.

As Kyle gave her a wide berth leaving the kitchen, Whisper snorted, calling me out on my fib.

~

It was surreal, sitting on the couches with Becky, Clem, and Kyle. They were three of my closest friends from the gaming world, suddenly made real by... what? Nanops and memory files? I knew they were more than just a product of my memories or dad's programming, but if they were real, where had they come from? I thought about poor Gunner, trying to make sense of Cool, and wondered if we'd seen the last of the inexplicable arrivals.

It occurred to me that if more NPCs were to arrive, the meet and greet song and dance routine was going to get old really fast.

I handed my cell phone to Becky. "Record this for me, please."

Kyle was clearly not adapting to his new circumstances as well as Becky or Clem. "What's happening? Why are we recording?"

"Bro, what I'm about to tell you will sound crazy, but Becky and Clem can confirm it, one hundred percent." I nodded towards the kitchen. "Besides, when have you ever known me to have a horse... in my kitchen?"

Kyle laughed at that for a moment, before remembering he wasn't in Kansas anymore. He looked around nervously, his eyes scanning everything, like a drunken Terminator searching for its target. No, not *drunk*, I realized.

I patted his forearm before speaking. He was having a lot of trouble focusing. "Kyle, buddy, you with me?"

Kyle looked at me again, mostly recognizing me, but still incredibly anxious.

I squeezed his forearm. "Kyle, what were you doing before you showed up here?"

Kyle thought about the question, processing his experience. "I, uh, I was watching TV. *I Love Lucy*, I think."

"Okay, and where were you," I asked.

"Should I be recording this," Becky asked.

"No, thank you," I replied calmly, not wanting to increase Kyle's anxiety. "I'll tell you when." I gently squeezed Kyle's arm again. "Kyle, buddy. Where were you before you came here?"

"In our dorm," he replied.

"Is he high," Becky asked quietly.

"If he is, it wasn't on purpose," I said. "He's not into that." I returned my attention to Kyle. "Buddy, did you eat or drink anything?"

Kyle smiled again. "Laura, from the girls' dorm, said I seemed stressed. She brought over brownies and milk. I love brownies…" Kyle trailed off, looking at Becky. "Who's she? She's pretty." He let his gaze fall upon Clem's wind-weathered visage. "And he's not." Kyle looked up at me, not really frightened anymore, just tired and disoriented.

"As a kite," I told Becky with a sigh. "Hey, Kyle? Buddy, why don't you get some sleep, alright?"

Kyle nodded like I'd hypnotized him. Without even taking off his shoes, he put his head in Clem's lap, curled up like a baby, and was gone.

"I'm definitely recording this," Becky announced.

Clem, not knowing what 'recording' was, ignored the comment but looked up at me, stone-faced. "We're never speaking of this again. We clear on that, Marshal?"

~

Dad finally returned a little after 2 am. I'm not going to pretend I didn't give him a hard time for leaving us like that. He'd never done anything like that before.

"…and honestly, dad, it scared the hell out of me," I said, my face betraying my anger and frustration.

Becky nodded. "It *was* really scary, Mr. Campbell."

Dad hugged me, and then, completely out of the blue, he hugged Becky. "I'm sorry, kids." He motioned towards the garage door. "I got really frightened by what happened to the Pontiac. I know I could have, uh, *should have* handled things better." He held up a large grocery bag. "But I come bearing gifts."

"I had ev'rythang under control, Marshal's Pa," Clem said from the couch.

Kyle was still passed out in the fetal position with his head in Clem's lap. The crotchety sheriff had even placed a throw pillow under his noggin.

"Thank you, Clem," dad replied, raising his eyebrows at Becky and me. "I'm *so* lucky you were here." He set the bag on the coffee table. "Is that... *Kyle?*" He shook his head, accepting the madness way too easily. "Never mind. I'll be right back, I brought you something else."

Dad disappeared back into the garage and returned a moment later with... Elvis Presley? No, that wasn't right. Elvis had never been yellow with brown spots.

"*Cool,*" I whisper-shouted, trying not to disturb Kyle.

Cool wasn't nearly as subtle. "Pack Man! Your dad filled me in on the sitch, bro. This reminds me of the time Bookworm tossed Einstein and me into a King Arthur book!" He contemplated what he'd said. "Only this is waaaay different. I thought you died in the swamp, but your dad said that was only a game. He thinks I'm real but doesn't know how I'm here, and-"

Man, I thought *I* rambled. "Cool, bro, we have a lot of time to catch up." I hugged him before turning back towards the couch. "Cool, I'd like you to meet Becky and Clem."

Once again, Clem felt the need to clarify which one he was.

I smiled. There was no way these people, uh, you know I'm including Cool and Whisper, when I say 'people', right? Because, well... *people*... But there's no way they were just products of a game. None.

Cool grinned. His teeth were spectacular, like Michelangelo himself carved them from the finest marble. "Any friend of Pack Man is a friend of mine!" Cool pointed at Kyle. "Who's the snore machine?"

I laughed as dad emptied the contents of the bag onto the table. "The snore machine, eh? That's Kyle."

"Sorry kids, uh, and Clem," dad said. "If I'd known Kyle was going to be here, I'd have brought a box of Twinkies, too."

Becky replied before I could. "It's okay, Mr. Campbell. I think Kyle's had all the baked goods he can handle for one night."

~

The insinuation clearly flabbergasted dad. "Kyle's what?!"

"It appears he's the victim of the Devil's lettuce," Clem said ruefully. "Or, as the natives call it, pay-oh-tee. I s'pect he's on some sort of ancestral spirit walk right about now."

Dad looked at me. "Son, I never programmed anything like that. In fact, Kyle doesn't have any independent parameters outside time spent with you in the game. That's one hundred percent unique to him as an individual." Dad scratched his head. "And high? How-"

"And Clem was drunk," Becky offered.

"I wouldn't go so far as to say drunk," Clem countered.

"From only one beer. Because he's not used to beer from your world," Becky continued, ignoring Clem's objection. "Right, Pack?"

Dad looked at me for confirmation.

"Accurate," I replied.

Dad scratched his stubble and frowned. "If Kyle showed up, uh, impaired, and Clem got drunk-"

"A touch tipsy," Clem interjected indignantly.

"A touch tipsy," dad continued diplomatically, "then their physiology," he nodded at the others, "*your* physiology, is more synchronized with this world, reality, plane of existence... whatever... than Irene and I even realized."

"There's something else," I said.

Dad shrugged. He clearly expected nothing less than 'something else'.

"Kyle died," I said, not even sure if it made sense.

"But he's right here," dad said, confused.

Clem spoke up. "The young gunslinger, Kyle, popped into the kitchen from nowhere and shrieked like a wom-" He could see Becky waiting for his next word. "Much like a small child when he spied Whisper. I'm thinkin' he ain't never seen a horse before and didn't rightly know his actions were reckless. Young Kyle made a grave misstep, standin' directly behind Whisper when he patted her backside. Not in a *provocative* manner, mind you, but it must've tickled nonetheless because she kicked him clean 'cross the room and into yonder wall. I checked his pulse, and when I was fixin' to close his eyelids, he plum vanished!"

"He respawned where he first appeared," I added. "It was really weird. He didn't remember anything that had just happened when he reappeared."

"What do you think that means, Mr. Campbell," Becky asked.

Dad double facepalmed, holding the pose for a moment, even tossing his head back out of frustration for dramatic effect. Finally, he looked at all of us and said one word. "Checkpoints."

3

The Word Processor

Clem, who'd never heard of a video game, let alone played one, was unfamiliar with the term. He puzzled over it before repeating the word. "Checkpoints?"

"It's a place or thing in a video game that allows you to respawn there, instead of at the beginning of the game, if you die. Characters usually respawn at the last checkpoint they reached, dude." Cool clearly played video games, though I didn't know where, since we didn't have electricity in *Animehem*. Then again, he'd mentioned his friend, Einstein. Einstein was a Bili Ape, and one of the founding members of the superhero team, The Evolutants. He was probably the smartest creature alive, too... in that world, anyway. Maybe in *any* world. Remembering Einstein meant he had memories of things outside the games; things that happened in completely unrelated lore.

Dad nodded, looking impressed. "Solid," he conceded.

How had dad not picked up on the rest of Cool's statement? "Dad, did you catch what Cool said about Einstein, Bookworm, and King Arthur earlier?"

He thought about it for a moment. "Holy cow, kiddo! Agatha Christie has nothing on you. I didn't even pick up on that."

"It is almost three in the morning," I said. "I think you deserve a pass."

"Seriously though, son," dad said, looking stunned, "the implications are huge."

"What implications," Becky asked.

"What are imp-li-cay-shuns," Cool followed.

Dad took a deep breath. "We're going to have a long night. It's one thing to assume you'd know everything about the worlds I thought I created for all of you. It's something else entirely to accept that you can remember things that happened in worlds unrelated to the adventures Packard shared with you. What he's talking about is The Evolutants, a book series created by Edmund J. Gray. For Cool to remember that he'd need to have experienced it."

Cool's ever-present smile faded a bit. "So, you're saying I'm in another book?"

"Another reality, I think," dad said. "Given everything that's happening, who can say what the nature of reality even is?"

"Maybe Pack read the book Cool was talking about," Becky suggested.

I shook my head. "No. I got some Brave New Multiverse books before I was in the accident, but I never even had a chance to read the back covers, let alone the books themselves."

Dad shook his head again. "Becky, I know you're worried you might not be real, but everything points to you being no less real than Packard, me, or that lamp."

"Don't go there with the lamp, dad," I said. "The couch either."

Becky shot me a sideways glance dad chose to ignore.

"We were talking about checkpoints before Packard pointed out the rather important detail I overlooked," dad said. "Look, this is going to sound insane. As a rational human being- uh, no offense, Cool."

Cool blinked, unsure what should have offended him.

"As a rational person," dad sighed. The situation was beating his mind like a broom against a dusty carpet. "How can I accept the evidence that's been set before me? But it's still evidence. I can't deny it just because it doesn't fit my learned narrative. The Nanops did something miraculous and potentially dangerous. Irene and I have to figure out the repercussions of whatever actions we take, or don't."

"What were you going to say about the checkpoints," Becky asked.

"Oh, yeah." Dad was frazzled. "Thank you. This is hard for me to reconcile because I believe you, Clem, Cool, Kyle, even Whisper and Knightmare, are real. You're all sentient beings with a consciousness derived from somewhere other than here..." Dad drifted again.

"Your pa takes more side roads than you do, Marshal," Clem commented.

I was afraid that would trigger dad, but instead it made him smile. Then the smile broke into a quiet but genuine laugh.

"You're right, Clem," dad admitted. "About Packard and me both." He took another deep breath, maybe stalling, probably just thinking. Either way, when he spoke, he finally answered our question in a roundabout, dad kind of way. "It's difficult for me because what I'm proposing directly contradicts my contention that you're all real. At least on its face it does, but the reality is... There's that word again. *Reality.* We don't know what's happening. With competing theories all holding water, I suppose I have to embrace the idea that the Nanops can alter reality itself. I need to stop expecting things to work the way they're supposed to. As for the checkpoints, it's like I told Packard back at Arete. I think the Nanops are filling in the blanks, the gaps between this world and his mind. They're taking the world around us and somehow bringing his memories into reality. If that's true, and it sure appears to be, then it's not unreasonable to think they expect the world to adhere to the nature of the game world." Dad stopped again. "I have something to show you all, but first, I'd like to hand out a few goodies."

"Playing Santa again, dad," I joked.

Cool's eyes lit up. "You know Santa, Mr. Campbell? He's a friend of mine, too!"

Clem shook his head. "Father Christmas is a myth, son. Marshal was jest joshin'."

"I have a funny feeling Pack could tell us otherwise," Becky countered, as dad offered her a bag of trail mix.

"You like the kind with M&Ms, if I recall correctly," he said before offering a bottle of sarsaparilla and a bag of beef jerky to Clem, who graciously accepted the offering.

Clem looked at the refreshments like they were pure gold. "I ain't had sasparilly since before my family..." He trailed off, sighing deeply. "Uh, much obliged... Hal, was it?"

Dad looked sad for Clem but smiled anyway. "Yes, but Marshal's Pa is fine if you prefer it."

Next, dad handed Cool a bag of Doritos, the Cool Ranch flavor. Cool later told me he'd never tried the chips before. He just liked that his name was in the branding. He grinned and asked me to help open the bag.

After I helped Cool open his snack, dad passed me a bottle of Mountain Dew and a king-sized 100 Grand bar.

"If we're going to pull an all-nighter, I thought you might like this," he said. "There are a bunch of flavors of Lightning Rod energy drinks still in the bag if anyone starts to feel sleepy. Oh, and a box of kiwi-strawberry juice boxes for Cool."

Dad finally grabbed a huge handful of apples and disappeared into the kitchen to place them into the large bowl on the island for Whisper. "Who's a good girl," we heard him ask. Whisper whinnied happily, indicating that it was her. She was the good girl.

~

After dad returned from the kitchen, he bypassed us and went directly to the garage. We heard him fumbling around with boxes while conversing with Knightmare.

The car, uh, our... What the heck was I supposed to call her? Like everyone else in the room, she was far more than what she appeared to be. If I was going by the gaming world, as I was with the others, she was my friend. That suddenly made me feel like an asshole. I hadn't gone out to see her since she and dad got back. Once dad showed us what he'd gone to retrieve, and with his permission of course, I'd go visit her. Maybe I'd even introduce the others to her.

Baby steps, Pack, I reminded myself. *Baby steps.*

~

Dad returned a few minutes later carrying an antique all-in-one computer. He put it down roughly on the coffee table, almost tipping it with the weight of the unit. He finally positioned it, so we could all see it clearly from the couches.

"Please allow me to introduce to you, the Lanier Model 103, circa 1978." Dad sounded like he was introducing us to his oldest, dearest friend. In a way, I suppose that was true. "The Lanier was Grandma Campbell's first word processor," dad said proudly. "I never had the heart to get rid of it, since so much of our family's history was recorded on it, probably right in this very room."

It took a moment, but I finally recognized the machine. Let me tell you, the recognition didn't give me the same warm fuzzies it gave dad. I touched the keyboard tentatively as dad plugged it in. I shivered and drew back my hand immediately. Awful memories raced across the twisted landscape of my imagination.

Becky touched my arm gently, bringing me back from the brink of another memory meltdown. "Are you okay," she asked. "You look like you just saw a ghost."

Dad turned on the Lanier, oblivious to my concerns.

"More like a caveman," I replied.

Becky looked at me oddly before dad turned back to us.

Dad patted the top of the computer fondly. It was clear he'd never frantically tried to type in seven words, without making any mistakes, while being hunted by feral humans. "When I was creating the game *Regress,* I added this word processor as a checkpoint at a critical point in the play through. You have to type in a specific phrase to use it as a save point."

"It was a dark and stormy night," I muttered.

Dad grinned. "That was it!"

"I know," I said. "That game was the stuff of nightmares."

He frowned a bit. "Too much," he asked.

I shook my head. "Nah. The game was great. But seeing the old Lanier is bringing the worst of the memories back like a mental avalanche." I shrugged. "Just show them how it works. I'll be alright, I promise."

Dad stared at me for a moment.

"I promise," I repeated.

"Okay," dad finally relented, though it was clear he'd be watching me for a while. "Becky, since you don't have a sleeping teenager on your lap, why don't you try first?"

Becky regarded the old contraption the way a religious person would look at a rabbit's foot. "What does it do," she asked.

"It's a word processor," dad grinned. "Hopefully, if the Nanops are doing what I think they're doing, it'll be something more. Like an anchor to reality." He turned it towards himself. "Here. Just do what I do." He typed the words that still gave me the willies, *'It was a dark and stormy night'*, and hit ENTER. Dad looked confused for a moment, then he turned it back towards Becky. "You try it."

Becky couldn't hide her skepticism. "So, I type 'it was a dark and stormy night'? Like Snoopy?"

Dad nodded. "Exactly. It's case-sensitive. Capital I in 'It'."

"Of course it is," Becky muttered as she typed. "I mean, why wouldn't it be?"

"Exactly," dad replied, missing the sarcasm altogether. "Now just hit ENTER." He was super excited. If I weren't so nervous, it would've been cute.

Becky did as he instructed. The cursor dropped to the next row, only instead of merely flashing, as it had done when dad hit ENTER, two new lines of text appeared, flashing ominously in 1970s computer green.

COMMAND CONFIRMED

WELCOME REBECCA ROSE BRANSON

4

Saving the Day

After Becky — *I didn't DARE call her Rebecca* — reconciled the fact that a word processor made in 1978 seemed to know her by name, we moved on to Clem. Cool offered, but dad insisted we go in order of appearance… just in case.

Clem, with considerable effort, got out from under Kyle, who muttered something about the stinky old cowboy before Clem put the throw pillow back under his head. It looked like he momentarily considered placing the pillow over Kyle's face but decided against it. "That's gratitude fer ye," he commented as he moved to another spot on the couch. "Now, what do I do with this here contraption," he asked dad.

Dad turned the relic towards, uh… heh, the other relic. Please don't ever tell Clem I said that. Clem stared at the old word processor in amazement. "Do you even know what you have here?"

Dad shrugged. "What do you think it is, Clem?"

"A gol-durned goldmine is what it is," he exclaimed. "This here ee-lectronic printin' press could revolutionize the world of books and newspaperin'! You put this to good use, and you could be a right rich man, Marsh-uh... Hal!"

Dad grinned. "I'll keep that in mind, Clem. Thank you."

"Jest cut me in fer a slice, as I seem to be the impetus fer this here business venture." Clem spit in his hand, then extended it to dad.

Much to my surprise, and Becky's disgust, dad spit into his hand. He and Clem shook like there was real estate on the line. "Clem, my friend, if I ever turn this old thing into a business, you're on."

Clem seemed satisfied with the exchange and put his fingers over the keys, ready to type the next *War and Peace.* "Beggin' yer pardon, but you'll have to spell this out fer me. I ain't an educated feller like y'all."

Dad spelled the phrase out for Clem letter by letter, only having to restart once, as Clem didn't know how to capitalize a letter. Then, upon dad's instruction, Clem pressed the ENTER key.

COMMAND CONFIRMED

WELCOME CLEMENT STONEWALL PICKETT

"What's it say," Clem asked.

"It says your name," dad replied, omitting a few details.

Cool's face contorted comically. "Who's Stonewall?"

"Your *whole* name," dad admitted.

Clem narrowed his eyes at the machine. "If this thang warn't so valuable, I might be of the mind to fill it full o' lead."

"Stonewall is Clem's middle name," Becky whispered to Cool.

Cool's eyes widened. He clamped his mouth shut, recognizing the can of worms he'd opened.

Dad put his hands over the word processor in a mostly impotent act of protective bravery. "Remember, this 'thang' allows you to remember everything you've learned if anything should happen to you."

Clem turned his narrowed eyes on dad. "I really and truly don't want to end up like young Kyle here, so I know whens to keep my gun-" Clem suddenly remembered his gun. "Hey, you still ain't given me my gun back," he growled.

Dad nodded. "Yes, Clem, I realize that. Let's get this process done for the others, and then we can discuss your sidearm."

Clem looked at me, knowing I would be honest with him. I nodded.

"Alright," he conceded, but not sounding the least bit happy about it. "You do realize I'm still naked here?"

Of course, those were the words that woke up Kyle.

~

Kyle sat up, appearing confused and a bit frightened. "Who's naked," he demanded.

"I am," Clem said boldly. "That would be me, Clem!"

The added explanation caused poor Kyle to cover his eyes.

"It's only a figure of speech, Kyle," I chuckled. "You can open your eyes, bro."

Kyle opened his eyes slowly. Thankfully, he didn't seem as jumpy as he'd been a few hours earlier. That was until he noticed Cool, casually chomping on his Doritos.

~

Kyle rubbed his eyes, muttering, "I *knew* Laura's brownies tasted weird. Now I'm hallucinating." He waited for his eyes to adjust again and looked like he wanted to cry. "What the hell is that," he moaned.

Always everyone's friend, Cool held out his bag. "Chip?"

Kyle looked at the bag. In a strange, pathetic leap of faith, he reached out and took a handful of chips. "Uh, thanks?"

Cool grinned. I could see Kyle flinch when he saw those huge, potentially deadly teeth.

Cool was about the, well… coolest dude I knew. He was a great friend, a cunning warrior, quick with the dad jokes, and loyal to a fault. He was anything but dangerous. Unless you hurt one of his friends. Then he might use his hooves as clubs. But that's like, the rarest thing ever.

"He's a friend," I told Kyle. "His name is Cool."

"The eee-lastic, jee-raff," Clem added. "Durndest thang, ain't he?"

Kyle looked at me for a little emotional support. "Pack, what's going on? Who are all these people, and uh, giraffes?"

"Man, Kyle," I stepped forward and gave him a hug. "You had me worried for a few minutes, there." I motioned around the room, planning to make a quick series of introductions. "You've already met Becky and Clem," I started.

Kyle looked puzzled. "I have?"

Clem nodded. "You was on the pay-oh-tee, young gunslinger. High as a kayak, were the exact words, I believe," he offered. "Oh... and I'd be Clem."

"It's high as a kite," I interjected, "not a kayak, Clem. And I'm sure no one's going to mistake you for Becky."

"Gawd, I hope not," Becky muttered.

Clem's face contorted. "What's that supposed to mean?"

Becky opened her mouth to speak, but I continued my introductions before she could goad Clem any further. "Yes, Kyle, you met them," I said, "and yes, you were *high as a kite*. My advice for the future would be to avoid baked goodies from Laura."

Kyle nodded slightly, dumbfounded and utterly speechless.

I began motioning towards the others as I introduced them. "As you're already well aware, that's Clem. That's Becky, my dad, and Whisper is in the kitchen."

Kyle craned his neck suspiciously. "And why is Whisper in the kitchen," he asked.

"Because Whisper is a horse," I replied matter-of-factly. I suddenly hated how oddly logical my answer sounded.

Kyle nodded again, looking more like someone staring into the blank expanse of the abyss than someone meeting potential new friends. His words floated from his mouth on a wavering breeze. "Yeah, that makes perfect sense." His sanity was hanging on by a thread.

I reluctantly pointed at Cool, who held up his bag of Doritos and grinned. "You already met Cool... and Knightmare is in the garage."

Kyle's expression slipped into something between a smirk and a grimace. Would that be a girk or a simace? Oh well. It was an odd expression, even by Kyle's standards. "Next you're going to tell me that Knightmare is a talking car, and he's in the garage because there's no room in the kitchen, right?"

"She," I replied.

Kyle looked at me quizzically. "Excuse me?"

I nodded towards the garage door. "Knightmare is a she. I'll introduce you all to her later if it's okay with dad."

Kyle put one of the chips he'd gotten from Cool into his mouth and began crunching away thoughtfully. He finally shrugged, accepting his situation as best he could. "Well, either I'm still hallucinating, I'm dying somewhere, or this is real. Whichever it is, the chips are tasty."

Cool giggled and held the bag out to Kyle again. Kyle raised his eyebrows and took another handful of chips.

Dad waved Cool over to the word processor. "We need to keep this train moving. You're up, my friend."

Cool sidled up to the machine and morphed the leading edges of his front hooves into creepy little fingertips. He'd clearly been practicing.

"It was a dark and stormy night," he said as he typed the words.

Then he hit ENTER.

COMMAND CONFIRMED

WELCOME COOL THE ELASTIC GIRAFFE

Cool hooted gleefully when he saw his name pop up in that phosphor-green on black display. "I need a real last name, bros," he giggled.

"Pickett's a right nice surname," Clem offered.

Cool batted his eyes at Clem playfully. "Are you proposing, dude?"

Clem stirred uncomfortably, blushing. "Uh..."

Cool laughed again. "Just kidding, broski! I'll keep it in mind, though!"

Dad waved excitedly to Kyle. "It's your turn, Kyle."

Instead of sitting down at the word processor, Kyle turned to me, his eyes betraying his mind-blowing level of bewilderment. "Bro… I've known your parents since we were in kindergarten. What the hell's going on here?"

Becky put a hand on Kyle's shoulder. "Trust me, Kyle. Pack will explain what's going on soon. We've all been through the confusion. I promise you, if Clem can make sense of it all, so can you."

Clem looked like he was about to speak, but instead frowned and exhaled dramatically with an exaggerated huff.

Becky continued. "Mr. Campbell is Pack's dad… in this world, anyway." She nodded at the word processor. "Just type the phrase and see what happens. What have you got to lose?"

Kyle scanned the room, looking the rest of us over. He was having a really hard time accepting his current reality. He finally scooted towards the Lanier, but then paused again, glancing into the kitchen. "Wait. You said we were going in order of arrival, right?"

Dad nodded. "Yeah, and you're next."

Kyle shook his head. "No. Whisper was here before me." He looked towards the garage. "Daydream, too."

Clem and Becky corrected him in stereo. "Knightmare."

"Whatever," Kyle muttered. "They were here before me."

Dad and I locked gazes. His expression was beginning to match Kyle's. He looked helpless, frustrated, and teetered on a tightrope over a bottomless pit of desperation.

"I think Kyle's right. They need to do it too, don't they, dad," I asked.

Dad sighed. "And I skipped right over them," he lamented.

Becky chimed in, offering her two cents. "Cool's name came up fine, right? If the order mattered, then it probably wouldn't have recognized him." She shrugged. "Maybe you guys are overcomplicating it?"

Dad's frown softened a bit, and then took on the slightest cast of a semi-defeated smirk. "Well then, let's see if we can get Whisper to do this without breaking the Lanier, shall we?"

~

Dad reluctantly brought the old computer into the kitchen and carefully placed it on the floor, where Whisper could get to it.

"I can't believe I'm doing this," he muttered as he plugged it in.

A few moments later, the cursor on the Lanier's screen was flashing with rapt anticipation.

Dad looked like he'd just been tasked with opening a pickle jar only using a sledgehammer. "How the hell are we supposed to do this?"

"Maybe you're still overthinking it, Mr. Campb- uh, Hal." Becky looked uncomfortable. "Do you mind if I just stick with Mr. Campbell?"

I'm not sure dad even heard her last question. "What do you think we're overthinking," he asked.

Becky shrugged. "Maybe the ENTER key is all that matters?"

Dad, who was kneeling by the Lanier, looked up at Whisper and nodded. "I like that option far better than having her try to tap on individual keys," he admitted.

I felt like that would be too easy, but reality wasn't exactly behaving the way I'd grown to expect up to that point. "So, what? We type in the phrase for her and have her step on the ENTER key?"

"If it doesn't work that way, then we figure out a way to control the individual keys she steps on without damaging the computer," Becky shrugged. "It's good science, Pack. Mitigate the risk to a secondary test if the preliminary one doesn't yield useful results."

"'Zaktly what I was thankin'," Clem chimed in.

Becky grinned, despite herself. She raised an eyebrow, pretending to be impressed. "See? Even Clem knew that," she said.

Dad typed the phrase slowly, having to back off twice because his hands were shaking. Dad's hands *never* shook. I'd watched him soldering micro-components on motherboards without so much as a twitch. The day had really taken its toll on him. Not to mention, he was several hours past his normal bedtime.

"Let me get it, dad," I offered, kneeling beside him.

Dad scooted away but remained on the floor as a show of support.

I finished the phrase and looked up at Whisper. "Tcht-tcht."

She knew what the sound meant, but she eyed the Lanier as suspiciously as Kyle eyed her and remained rooted firmly in place.

I patted the Lanier gently. "Come on, girl," I chided. "The computer can't hurt you."

Whisper looked around the kitchen nervously. Dad knelt by me, Becky and Clem stood a few feet behind us, and Kyle stood in the doorway, clearly interested, but also terrified of my horse.

I placed my finger just above the ENTER key. "Just like squashing a scorpion... only soft. Okay?"

Whisper grunted. Her breathing was shaky, like dad's hands.

"I get you, girl," dad whispered.

"Jest trust the Marshal, Whisper," Clem added. "Like I do."

That familiar voice finally did the trick. Whisper looked up at Clem, uncertainty still simmering behind her big, dark eyes. The old sheriff nodded at the Lanier, as gently as a loving grandfather.

"Softly now, like the Marshal said. Jest like killin' a scorpion," he said, reinforcing my words.

And that was that. A little gentle coaxing from everybody's favorite bigot and Whisper set the front edge of her hoof against the ENTER key and pressed.

COMMAND CONFIRMED

WELCOME WHISPER FEATHERHOOF

Well, that was unexpected, I thought. "Featherhoof?"

Whisper cocked her head curiously upon hearing the name.

I looked from the computer to my horse. "Is that your name, girl? Whisper Featherhoof?"

She dropped her head slightly, affecting a show-worthy nod.

"I'll be damned," dad muttered.

"She was raised by Injuns a' fore comin' inta' yer care, Marshal," Clem offered.

"That's true," I replied, realizing that Whisper having a last name while Cool did not wasn't likely to be the weirdest thing to happen to me all day.

~

After explaining to Clem that we no longer referred to the original inhabitants of the Americas as Injuns, we finally convinced Kyle to sit down and type the seven infamous words on the worn-out keyboard.

As he pressed ENTER, it occurred to me that I'd never known his middle name. As a lifelong fan of the Terminator franchise, I was duly impressed.

COMMAND CONFIRMED

WELCOME KYLE REESE CONNER

Even dad was taken aback. "I'd like to be able to take credit for that," he said. "Honestly, I'm as surprised as you probably are, son."

Kyle looked at us sideways. I grimaced awkwardly, realizing he was still completely in the dark about everything that had been happening.

"Kyle, buddy," I said softly, "I promise I'll tell you everything in a few minutes. First, I want you to meet someone." I nodded towards the garage, making eye contact with dad. "If it's okay with dad, of course."

Dad smiled softly. He was finally calming down a bit. Thankfully, the off-the-cuff mention of Knightmare didn't put him back on edge. "She's as much a part of this as anyone else," he admitted with a shrug.

5

Knightmare

Knightmare, my other trusty steed, waited patiently in the garage, surrounded by unused camping gear, barely used yard tools, well-worn medical equipment, and sealed boxes of old Individual Gaming Corp data files.

I led the way as we stepped out through the kitchen door, followed by Becky, Kyle, Cool, Clem, and finally dad.

"Hello, Packard," Knightmare chirped, sounding genuinely pleased. "It's so nice to see you!"

Becky looked confused. "She can see you?"

"I am equipped with sensors that allow me to perceive my surroundings quite nicely," KM replied. "While it is not exactly *seeing* as you would understand it, my version of visual acuity is no less effective. Consider the star-nosed mole, atretochoana, sea urchin, Japanese swallowtail butterfly, Mexican Tetra, or Texas salamander. Not to mention, bats, dolphins-"

"I think she gets the point, Knightmare," I laughed. "It's nice to see you, too, girl."

"I apologize if I frightened you earlier," she said softly. "It was not my intention." She hesitated for a moment. "Your father was quite agitated, and we had important things to discuss."

"It's okay, KM," I started, but dad cut me off.

"It really wasn't okay," he said. "I reacted badly. While I did need to speak with Knightmare alone, I could've handled things better." He patted KM's fender and my shoulder at the same time. "I should be the one apologizing, not you, Knightmare."

"Apology accepted," KM chimed happily. "But our time together was productive, wouldn't you say?"

Dad patted her fender absently. "Yes, it was. I appreciate your insight."

Someone cleared their throat behind us. I looked back. With a series of pointed fingers, Becky, Kyle, and Cool immediately threw Clem under the bus.

Clem frowned. "Here and I thought we were all friends."

"Did you have something to add, Clem," dad asked.

"Well, y'all did say there was to be an introduction of sorts. I'm supposin' it was to this fine-lookin' horseless carriage here, in which case, I'd be Clem."

"Hello, Clem," Knightmare replied. "It is a pleasure to make your acquaintance. And thank you for the compliment. I am considered a classic. Perhaps we can go for a ride sometime. I am quite fond of the open road."

Clem nodded. "I'm a mite-bit partial to wide open spaces as well. A ride would be right nice."

Clem never ceased to amaze me. Of all people to introduce themselves to the talking car, I wouldn't have placed odds on the displaced cowboy. The next day, I discovered that Clem had just assumed all cars could talk. He got seriously offended when dad's car didn't strike up a conversation on our trip home from Arete. The offense became an honest-to-god grudge when the vehicle didn't respond to Clem's attempt to introduce himself the next day.

Dad patted my shoulder again. "Why don't you introduce the rest of the gang while you're at it, son?"

I took the cue and ran with it. "So, Knightmare, you've already met Clem. As you might have guessed, he's not from around here. Clem is a bona fide lawman from a place called Rotgut, Arizona, and hails from somewhere around the year 1894."

Knightmare processed that for a moment. "Are you saying that Clem is a time traveler, or that he is here as a result of the Quantum Nanops?"

Well, there was a term I hadn't heard yet. I knew I should have continued with introducing the others, but I was intrigued. Becky's expression said she felt the same. Another delay in the intros would be a small trade compared to the knowledge KM seemed privy to. "Quantum Nanops?"

"Yes. It is the name your father and I gave them during our outing earlier. If you would like to introduce the others first, I would be happy to fill you in on the details when you finish."

I took a deep breath. It sounded like dad had gotten some answers, and I was itching to be let in on the secret. I turned and made eye contact with dad. "Dad?"

He nodded. "Yes, son. It's important information, and I'll call Irene as soon as I feel it's humanly appropriate, but please introduce the others. I'm tired, and I'd really like to lie down for a few hours before finding out what's going to be thrown at us next."

"If'n you'd give me back my pistola, it wouldn't matter what life threw at us," Clem interjected. "I could shoot it right outta the sky a'fore it even got to us. I'm jest sayin'."

Dad sighed for the umpteenth time that night. "I know, Clem... I know. I appreciate your patience." Dad's response sounded about as sincere as a customer service rep for a cable TV company. All that was missing was a curt 'please hold'.

I looked back at Knightmare, suddenly feeling every bit as tired as dad just admitted to being. I pointed to my right, where Becky stood. "This is Becky. She's from right here in San Francisco, but like you and Clem, she's from another, uh... somewhere else..."

"Another universe," KM replied matter-of-factly. "May I assume that your other friend is also from another universe?"

I glanced at Kyle. He had the same deer in headlights look he had when Laura Hansen from the girls' dorm first flirted with him. I still owed him one hell of an explanation. "Yeah, everyone here except dad and me are from- Wait... *what?* Did you just say *another universe?*"

Knightmare began to respond, but dad cut her off. "Okay, so now you know Clem and Becky. The young man using Packard as a social interaction shield is Kyle. Yes, he is also from parts unknown, as is Whisper, a horse from Clem's world. She's in the house for now, but you'll meet her soon enough. I can't exactly keep her in the backyard, and confining her to the kitchen feels a bit cruel." Dad stopped and looked at me, his eyes silently apologizing for the interruption. "Oh, and you've already met Cool."

"Indeed," she replied. "He is quite entertaining, if not refreshingly childlike."

Cool shuffled his big metal hooves a bit. "Uh... thanks?"

Without skipping a beat, Knightmare turned her attention to Becky and Kyle. "I am quite pleased to know both of you, Becky and Kyle. I am Knightmare. Packard sometimes refers to me as KM. Since you are now all my friends, you may choose either, or both." After a brief pause, she added, "please extend my warmest greetings to my other new friend, the prisoner of the kitchen, code name: Whisper."

Dad flashed that defeated little smile again. The conversation was way beyond his pay grade. "She's not actually-oh, forget it." He looked at Kyle. "Please pay attention, bud. I know we still need to bring you up to speed, but this information is important to all of us, and will help you make sense of all of it."

I sighed. "Does any of this *actually* make sense?"

Knightmare beat dad to an answer, a fact that clearly relieved him more than he would ever admit. "Yes," she said. "For a short time, while my neural network was being fabricated and my AI system was coming online, I was in direct contact with the Quantum Nanop hive mind."

"Why are we calling them Quantum Nanops," I asked.

"When the Nanops were exposed to the quantum database containing your in-game memories, a forced evolution took place. The Nanops had been designed to heal, nothing more. To fulfil that requirement, they were programmed to learn and adapt as their situational demands changed. The database gave them something they did not possess prior to the upload: intelligent perspective. The Quantum Nanops have evolved and should now be considered a new life form. I have humbly coined the term technoorganism. Had I shared that with you yet, Hal?"

Dad shook his head. "No, you hadn't."

"I'm quite proud of it," she chirped.

Dad was looking shaky again. I assumed it was a brutal combination of extreme exhaustion and another dose of a very frightening reality. He was teetering somewhere between bravely

holding it together and running in circles and tearing his hair

out. "Do you want to tell the others what you told me about why

you're all here," he asked.

"Certainly," she replied. "The Quantum Nanops are

confused."

Becky wrinkled her nose. "Confused?"

Knightmare was silent for a moment, as if expecting further

questioning. "Yes, confused. Packard's brain was their sole source

of context as they were born into an unfamiliar world. They know

what he knows, fear what he fears, crave what he craves. To them,

Packard might as well be a god, and his memories a religious

text. The problem is this. When Irene and Hal merged the Nanops

with the quantum database, no parameters were set to clearly

differentiate between organic and artificial memories, so the

Quantum Nanops simply accepted *everything* in Packard's mind as

reality."

"I am so in the dark here," Kyle groaned. "And I'm starving."

I looked back at him. The deer in the headlights was gone. All that remained was a hungry sloth in a sliver of moonlight. Wow, I'm usually quick with a snazzy analogy. That was not my best work. Hey, I was tired, too. "Sorry buddy. Hang in here with me a few more minutes, okay? I'll get you something to eat and tell you what I can as soon as KM finishes explaining."

Kyle nodded numbly. "Okay, bro."

I returned my attention to Knightmare as Clem gently placed a calloused hand on Kyle's shoulder. "So, how does that explain you and the others?"

"I must admit," KM replied, "the physics are well beyond my comprehension, but as I stated before, I briefly connected to the hive. For one glorious moment, I understood. Then it was obscured."

"Understood what," Becky asked.

"The universe."

~

As Knightmare explained it, the Quantum Nanops, being unable to distinguish between real and artificial memories, determined that reality, more specifically *my* reality, was incomplete. They were trying to fill in the gaps with people and things that never actually existed in our world.

The Quantum Nanops brought my friends into existence to please me... to *complete* me.

Becky was looking upset again, her grip on who or what she was had been shaken harder than the poor New York snow globe Clem found in the living room. "So, what... I'm just an AI's interpretation of Packard's interpretation of me? Like a copy of a copy?"

"Not at all," Knightmare replied confidently. "When the Nanops linked to the quantum database, their initial goal was to heal Packard. However, once they completed the memory upload, the hive began to run calculations, create algorithms, and extrapolate data. In the time it would take for you to sneeze, the hive evolved far beyond the understanding of the universe as you know it. A few moments more, and it developed the ability to comprehend, view, and finally access the parts of the multiverse necessary to fulfill its perceived purpose."

Dad cleared his throat. "This is what you've been needing to hear, Becky. Clem, Cool, Kyle... It's important to all of us."

Becky reached down and absently squeezed my hand. A moment later, Kyle clasped my other hand tightly.

Knightmare continued. "I was brought here from another world," she said, pausing thoughtfully. "Or more accurately, the Quantum Nanops brought my consciousness here. However, I am what you in this world refer to as artificial intelligence. Therefore,

I could pinpoint the precise moment my consciousness was moved from one vessel to another. I experienced a brief period of displacement before being inserted into the vessel you see me in now. I also experienced a few microseconds of the completion of my vessel, during which I remained in contact with the hive."

Becky let go of my hand. "So, this isn't really my body, but I'm still me?"

"It is your body, down to the very last atom," KM replied, "but at the same time, it is not the one you inhabited prior to arriving in this world. It is not as much a copy, as you seem to fear, as a precise genetic duplicate."

Kyle suddenly caught his breath. "You're saying our minds are from a parallel universe, and our bodies have been created to, what... be vessels?"

"Isn't that what all bodies are," KM replied.

The garage fell silent.

Cool finally broke the awkwardness with a low, impressed whistle.

"Yeah, that's been rattling around in my head for the past few hours," dad muttered.

Clem beat me to the next question. "Are we it?"

"Please elaborate," Knightmare replied.

Clem thought for a moment, and though I was tempted to clarify the question myself, I decided it was his question to ask. He was beginning to grasp something even dad was struggling with. Who was I to interfere?

"Should we s'pect more of the Marshal's friends to jest pop in? Like young Kyle, here," Clem finally asked.

"The odds lean heavily in favor of that being the case," KM said.

I shook my head. The others were taking the news surprisingly well. Cool already seemed to have a solid grasp on the concept due to previous adventures. Becky was finally sorting through her more difficult layers of doubt. Clem was shockingly accepting of his circumstances. Really, though, what choice did any of us have? Accept reality as it was or lose our minds trying to deny it. I finally let my gaze drift to Kyle. He was looking around my garage curiously, processing the madness in his own unique way. "So, while the Quantum Nanops are out there Jerry Maguire-ing my life, what are we supposed to do? Wait for more?"

Dad sighed. "We'll come up with a game plan with Irene tomorrow. For now, I think everyone needs to get some rest. Why don't we all head inside? I'll bring in some sleeping bags, and we'll need at least one cot."

Cool stepped further into the garage. "If you don't mind, Mr. Campbell, I'd like to stay out here with Knightmare. Nobody should be alone right now, dude."

KM started to object, but dad nodded in agreement. "That's kind of you, Cool. I'll leave the garage door unlocked, so you can come in any time you want." Dad paused, suddenly looking uncomfortable. "You do use the bathroom, yes?"

Cool grinned. "Most assuredly so, dude. And let me tell you, they're-"

Dad put a hand up, stopping Cool before he could describe anything that could never be unseen by his mind's eye. He nodded curtly, clearly trying not to imagine the mechanics of the event. "Just... come in for whatever you need."

"Weren't we going to try the word processor out on KM," I asked as dad started pulling sleeping bags down from an overhead shelf.

"Yeah... yeah, we were," he replied. "Wanna bring it out and plug it in, kiddo? It takes a moment to warm up, anyway."

I did as he asked, sneaking into the kitchen to tousle Whisper's mane a bit before taking the Lanier back out with me.

As dad set up a cot next to KM and handed Cool a pillow and blanket, I watched the word processor return to life.

Dad handed Kyle three sleeping bags and gave Becky a stack of pillows, which they promptly took into the house and deposited on the couch. They returned just in time to find dad typing the now familiar phrase, 'It was a dark and stormy night'.

He looked up at me from the Lanier. "Any ideas, son," he asked.

I shrugged. "The edge of Whisper's hoof worked for her. Maybe press it with KM's steering wheel?"

Dad returned the shrug. He was beat. He looked like he would've let her drive up onto the keyboard if it would've let him finally go to bed. "A little help, then?"

Together, dad and I lifted the one-piece computer and pressed the ENTER key against the bottom of KM's steering wheel.

COMMAND CONFIRMED

WELCOME KNIGHTMARE PONTIAC GTO

~

"Hal, if you would prefer, in the future, I can access the Lanier's operating system remotely," Knightmare offered.

Dad and I had just set the hefty machine down on the garage floor. That beast must've weighed about sixty pounds! Dad turned to face Knightmare. "You can *do* that?"

"Certainly. My universal interface system allows me to communicate with computer systems reaching back as far as the mid-20th century." There was an uncomfortable pause before she spoke again. "Perhaps I should have shared this information before you went to the trouble of lifting it into my cockpit?"

Dad looked frustrated, but he reigned it in quickly. "Yes, Knightmare. I would appreciate you sharing any information that feels pertinent, no matter how insignificant it may seem, as soon as you think of it."

"Your blood pressure is slightly elevated, and-"

"We'll discuss boundaries tomorrow, too," dad said shortly, cutting her off before she could finish. He ushered Clem, Becky, and Kyle into the house before hefting the Lanier up one last time. "Good night, Knightmare. Good night, Cool." He lugged the Lanier back inside and set it back on the coffee table, telling the others he wanted to be ready in case more *friends* showed up.

Before I closed the garage door, I repeated dad's sentiment, wishing Cool and Knightmare a good night's rest. As the door closed, I could hear Knightmare explaining to Cool that she didn't require sleep, and she had plenty of facts and stories to keep them occupied until morning. For a moment, I thought Cool might regret volunteering to keep her company, but then I remembered who I was thinking about. Cool was one of the most thoughtful, caring, genuine souls I'd ever had the pleasure of knowing. But he was still going to be tired when daylight came. I told myself that offering him coffee, or a Lightning Rod energy drink, at breakfast would probably be a mistake.

~

I finally sat on the couch by Kyle and made good on my promise to fill in the rest of the blanks, including his previous appearance and untimely departure. Clem and Becky had already bundled up in sleeping bags and were both giving Kyle's earlier bout of snoring a run for its money.

As Kyle and I spoke, I fidgeted absently with the Lanier. The keyboard was as familiar as the keys on my cell phone, or the fingers on my own hand. I can't exactly say why I typed the phrase. I suppose I'd typed it so many times, it was just second nature. Before I knew it, those awful words were there. *It was a dark and stormy night.*

And then I pressed ENTER.

Damn second nature.

COMMAND CONFIRMED

WELCOME PACKARD DYLAN CAMPBELL

Dad was heading up to bed when the words appeared. I headed him off at the pass, feeling like a mule just dropkicked my head. "Uh, dad? What do you think this means?"

He came back down the stairs and peered at the screen. His expression dropped as he read the words. He suddenly looked sick. "Oh boy. Remember those implications I mentioned earlier, son?"

6

I'm Sorry, Dave. I'm Afraid I
Can't Do That.

My name is Hal Campbell. I know, I know, you're used to my son, Packard, narrating this story. Well, as much as we all love the sound of his voice, there are times when a different vantage point is important to the development of a tale.

This was one of those times.

I'm sure Packard was doing a fantastic job of bringing you up to speed, but believe me, there's no possible way he could have conveyed the strain I'd been under. I endured every parent's worst nightmare, then got pulled from the brink of despair by a miracle of science. Who knows what would have become of me if Irene and I had failed, but considering what was happening in our lives, I didn't know what success or failure even looked like anymore. We had opened a can of DUNE-sized worms, and my son was paying the price.

Granted, there were more people involved than just Packard and me. Irene was at the center of the whole mess with me, and then there was Becky, Clem, Kyle, a damned elastic giraffe, a talking car, and a horse in my kitchen. Not to mention poor Gunner, who had definitely not signed on for the abyss he'd inadvertently stared into. Yet here we all were, waiting for the other shoe to drop.

I'm happy to say it didn't happen that night. At least not as far as we knew. Things were happening elsewhere that would affect us later, but for the last few hours of that night, we had what I now think was our last semblance of peace, and our last shred of security.

Clem and Becky conked out the moment they crawled into the sleeping bags I gave them. Clem was so impressed with the newfangled bedroll, I forgot to remind him to take off his boots before climbing in. I considered waking him, but I figured he'd adapted to enough of our modern customs for one day. Clem would require baby steps.

Packard and Kyle sat on the couch for a while, my son keeping his promise to fill in the blanks for his interdimensional friend. I gave Whisper a few more apples and let her out to the backyard, where she relieved herself with a grateful grunt. I'd have to clean up before Mrs. Bumblesnaps complained about the smell. Her eyesight was on Mr. Magoo level, but she could track missing persons for the FBI with her sense of smell.

You already know what happened when I was heading up to bed. Packard just *had* to type that phrase. And I'll be damned if the word processor didn't know who he was.

I admit, it was easy to accept the machine recognizing NPCs from the games. As real as they were, I could still justify them being a product of the Quantum Nanops. But my *son*? How was I supposed to reconcile the fact that he was somehow anchored to a checkpoint? The system didn't recognize me. After he got his confirmation message, I typed the phrase in again, and again, and

again.

"Dad," Packard whispered, mindful to not wake Becky or

Clem. "Dad, it's not going to work. You don't have the Quantum

Nanops in you."

I sighed. He was right, but somehow continuously trying

felt like I could deny reality a chance at control. "I know, son," I

said, feeling positively defeated by the day. I stood up from the

couch, shaking from a combined lack of sleep and too much

caffeine. I looked from Packard to Kyle, and back to my son. "We

need to get some sleep, guys. We'll talk to Irene in the morning." I

dropped my head and walked towards the stairs.

"Dad," Packard called out, a little louder than I think he

wanted to. "Are you okay?"

"It's not me I'm worried about, son," I muttered before

trudging upstairs and falling onto my bed. If I had the energy, I would have cried myself to sleep, but instead I just spent an entire REM cycle plagued by nightmares that wouldn't get any better with daylight.

~

Morning came with a cruel jolt of adrenaline that felt like a heart attack but just proved to be anxiety, reminding me that the world was not okay.

I quietly slipped down to the kitchen, where Whisper and Clem, who had already rolled up his sleeping bag and was feeding his old friend an apple, greeted me.

"I reckon ye won't mind, but I filled the washbasin with water for Whisper," Clem informed me.

Whisper seemed surprisingly content for a horse who'd just spent the night in a strange room that was clearly not a stable.

"No," I replied, "I don't mind at all. Thank you for looking out for her." I absently reached for a coffee cup and took a coffee pod out of a decorative bucket on the counter. "Would you like a cup of coffee, Clem?"

The old cowboy, who was probably not any older than me, but had seen hard days on even harder trails, brightened at the mention of coffee. "Don't mind if I do! It's nice to know at least that hasn't changed." Clem watched me insert the pod into the maker and press a flashing blue button. "Is that how y'all make coffee now," he asked, trying his best to not sound surprised.

I handed him a second pod while the first one brewed. "These are coffee pods," I told him. "One cup of coffee per pod."

Clem shook the pod next to his ear. "Well, I suppose I shouldn't be too surprised, seein' as y'all have talkin' pictures, horseless carriages, and aeroplanes."

"Airplanes," I corrected, "and I must say, Clem, you're dealing with all of this remarkably well."

"I s'pose I am," Clem nodded thoughtfully. "I look at it this way. Either I take what I see at face value and learn to work with it, or deny what I see and accept that I've plum lost my mind. I don't know about you, but I'd rather think I'm sane in a crazy world, than t'other way around."

Clem surprised me with his logic. I'd always assumed he was as unintelligent as he was narrow-minded. After all, I wrote him that way. Considering his ability to adapt so fluidly to technological advances, ideological concepts, and social constructs, I realized I'd underestimated him sorely. He had to be observant and clear-headed to be the peer and friend Marshal Blood needed. The game was bloody and gritty. A simple-minded buffoon wouldn't survive that world, let alone be competent enough to back the main player through nearly impossible situations.

As the coffee maker finished brewing, I offered Clem some pumpkin spice creamer.

"I ain't so sure about the cream," Clem replied, "but if y'all have some sugar, I'm right partial to the sweetener."

I retrieved a bag of white, granulated sugar from the pantry and Clem's eyes widened.

He looked shocked. "White sugar? I don't need nothin' that fancy or s'pensive. Brown or even molasses would be fine."

"It's alright, my friend," I said, remembering how rare white, refined sugar would have been in his time. "Live a little bit."

Clem wisely took a sip of his coffee before committing to the sugar. He screwed up his face a bit, settling on an expression that was difficult to read. Distaste? Confusion? I assumed the latter, awaiting the comment that was sure to follow, considering the source. "This ain't like any coffee I've ever had," he said, staring into the cup. "It tastes fine, but there's none of the grit or crunchiness I've grown accustomed to. Not even a trace of eggshell to speak of."

Becky wandered into the kitchen behind Clem as he offered his commentary. "Eggshells," she asked, looking apprehensive. "Are we having breakfast?"

"I was jest commentin' on how smooth the coffee is in this here world," Clem replied. "No chunks of coffee beans, nor trace of eggshell to be found." He swished another sip of coffee around in his mouth a bit before swallowing. "And the water here is the clearest water I've ever tasted. No algae, dirt, and not the slightest hint of animal urine."

Whisper let loose a disapproving grunt, matching Becky's expression.

Becky put a hand in the air. "Forget breakfast," she said without skipping a beat. "Where are the others?"

"Cool is still in the garage with Knightmare," I replied. "He finally dozed off, and I didn't have the heart to wake him." I smiled despite myself. "He's the cutest damn thing when he sleeps. He's all curled up in a ball."

Clem smiled. He was equal parts confused and amused by our elastic friend. "Like a kitten," he said, nodding.

"No," I replied, considering what I'd seen when I peeked into the garage. "More like a ball of yarn."

Becky giggled at the thought, then turned to Clem, her face darkening again. "Urine. Why? I was hungry."

Clem looked at me and shrugged. "I think I'll take some of that sugar now. And mayhaps I will try that pumpkin cream. How does one go about milkin' a pumpkin, anyhoo?"

~

Once Clem had raved sufficiently about the mysterious merits of milking pumpkins, and how the pumpkin's cream was perhaps the most miraculous thang he'd seen since arrivin' in our world, I offered him and Becky breakfast. After the urine comment, Becky opted to ease into breakfast with a glass of orange juice. Clem requested another 'dee-licious' cup of 'pumpkin-creamed coffee' before eating anything.

As I fished a box of frozen waffles out of the freezer, I heard the shower in Packard's bathroom upstairs turn on. I suddenly realized it might have been a while since Becky had taken a shower, and that Clem, though he'd probably had his fair share of baths, had never even seen a shower. "Becky, I still have some of Packard's mom's clothes upstairs, and we have plenty of hot water. Would you like to take a shower before we leave?"

Becky smiled. "I appreciate the offer," she replied. "My clothes are fine, though. If I want a shower, I imagine I could take one in the ladies' locker room at Arete, right?"

I shrugged. I saw no problem with that. "I'm sure Irene wouldn't mind at all," I replied.

"Good then," Becky nodded. "Because those waffles look good, and Clem needs a shower and a change of socks more than anyone here."

~

I left Becky to make her own waffles and took Clem upstairs to my bedroom, where I picked out clean socks, a change of underwear, and a plain, white t-shirt.

Clem eyed the underwear suspiciously while I retrieved a large bath towel from the upper shelf of my closet. "I ain't accustomed to wearin' another man's skivvies," he said, shaking his head.

"Do whatever you want," I said. "But I think it's a safe bet you haven't changed the ones you're wearing in a good long time. Going commando doesn't sound very sanitary, considering the condition of your pants... uh, britches."

Clem frowned. "I know what pants are. There's no need to talk down to me. Though I ain't too clear on what you mean by 'calm ando'."

"It's nothing important, Clem," I said. I nodded towards the bathroom. "Follow me, I'll show you the shower."

Clem stood about six feet away from the shower as I showed him the bottle of liquid body wash and shampoo blend and placed a washcloth over the shower door handle. I pointed at the shower head. "The water will come out of here in a spray. Be careful though. It can get very hot... or cold." I motioned to the knob that controlled the water flow and temperature. "If the arrow points at the sun, the water will be hot. The snowflake means cold. Got it?"

Clem nodded dubiously.

"Good, then I'm going back downstairs to keep the breakfast and coffee train running. Do what you want about the skivvies, but please take the socks at the very least," I recommended.

Clem grunted and looked at the clothes in his hands once before sighing. "I s'pose yer right."

I left the room and headed downstairs, stopping at Packard's doorway. Packard was laying back on his bed, reading the Evolutants book he'd been putting off.

"You let Kyle take a shower first, eh," I smiled. "You're a good friend, kiddo."

He set the book down and grinned. "I heard you offer Clem some new skivvies. Maybe I learned how to be a friend from you?"

That put a smile on my face that could've rivaled one of Cool's grins. "Becky's downstairs having breakfast, if you want to join us."

As Packard stood to follow me, a commotion erupted in the master bath.

"It's on the sun! It's on the sun! IT'S ON THE SUN," Clem hollered.

Packard and I ran back towards my room, but Clem called out. "Never y'all mind… I done figger'd it out!"

~

Kyle came down a few minutes after Packard and I did. He'd washed and combed his hair and changed into an old t-shirt I'd gotten from a Six Flags amusement park years earlier. A group of Looney Tunes characters sat in the front car of an old wooden rollercoaster, hands in the air, anticipating the big drop.

"I hope you don't mind, dad," Packard said apologetically. "None of my shirts fit him."

I nodded at Kyle. "It looks better on you than it ever looked on me, kid. Consider it yours."

Kyle smiled. "Thanks! Are these some of the characters you made?"

I laughed. "The Looney Tunes gang? I wish! They're some of the best-known characters on the planet."

Becky looked up from a bite of waffle. "You mean you don't have them in your world, Kyle?"

Kyle shrugged. "Not that I know of. But I've always been more into video games than cartoons."

Becky took another bite of her waffle, and a swig from a large glass of milk. "Well, we don't have frozen waffles in my world."

Packard turned to her, shocked. "Seriously?"

Becky laughed. "No. I'm pretty sure frozen waffles are a thing everywhere."

As Becky took another bite, and Packard's waffles popped up from the toaster, I offered Kyle a couple as well. He graciously accepted, and asked if a cup of coffee would be out of the question.

"Thankfully, it's urine free," Becky said. Her voice sounded serious, but as soon as she said it, she laughed nervously. She'd clearly pushed the envelope further than even she was comfortable with.

Packard and Kyle turned to face her, both gawking like she'd just admitted to being a serial killer or something.

"She's been hanging around Clem too long," I offered in her defense. "Cream and sugar in your coffee, Kyle?"

Kyle seemed to rethink his request before finally saying, "cream only... please, sir."

The kids ate waffles and drank coffee, milk, and OJ, while Whisper and I stepped out into the backyard. She watered the small patch of grass before trotting back in through the back door. I looked at the pile of manure she'd dropped there during the night. Luckily, the early morning frost minimized the smell. Instead of cleaning it up, I decided to rake it out over the base of the rosebushes. A little fertilizer never hurt anyone.

When I returned to the kitchen, Cool had joined the group. Packard was graciously serving him waffles.

Much to my dismay, he had also brewed Cool a cup of coffee.

It was going to be a long day.

~

Clem spent nearly an hour in my shower. When he finally came downstairs, he looked almost presentable. He was back in his old, beige canvas pants, of course. His waist was a lot trimmer than mine, and his legs were a bit longer than Packard's. I couldn't imagine him agreeing to sweatpants, so his old trousers would have to suffice. Aside from the pants, though, he was wearing the new socks and t-shirt I'd given him. When he set the dirty pile of old underclothes on the kitchen counter, right next to Cool's plate of waffles, I saw that he'd accepted the new skivvies as well.

Cool picked up his plate and stretched his body away from the counter without missing a bite. You probably thought I was going to say *beat*, right? Anyway, I brushed the old socks and underwear into the trashcan next to the island and chose to ignore Clem's thoughtlessness. Instead of reeking of horse, gunpowder, and body odor, he smelled like tea tree oil and sandalwood. Heck, the man even combed his hair. It was hard to not be impressed with the transformation. He'd tucked his t-shirt neatly into his pants and put his gun belt firmly back in place. He clutched his old, blue button up work shirt and dirty, brown vest protectively, ensuring I didn't throw them out as well.

"I must say, Marshal's Pa, I could easily get accustomed to that stand-up bathing apparatus of yers." He rubbed his eyes, blinking rapidly. They were red and tearing up pretty severely. "I gotta warn ye, though, that there soap in a bottle is not meant to come in contact with yer peepers. It stings somethin' awful! Not so bad as lye soap, mind ye, but damned powerful nonetheless."

"I should've mentioned that, Clem," I said, realizing how much we took for granted every day. "I'm sorry."

Packard made a plate of waffles for Clem as I moved Knightmare into the driveway and relocated Whisper to the garage. I filled an old plastic kiddie pool with water for her and set a few more apples on my workbench, affording her easy access.

Clem reminded me that I would need to get something more in line with Whisper's dietary needs, or she'd end up with an upset stomach. The farts were bad enough, and I really didn't want her to be any less comfortable than she already was.

Finally, I filled an ice chest with bottled waters and energy drinks and placed it with a bag of snacks in KM's front seat.

As Kyle, Cool, and Clem finished their breakfast, Packard and Becky sat on the stairs, waiting for the next phase of the morning. I saw Becky run her hand along a folded metal platform at the base of the stairs. It was easy to miss, as it was stored neatly against a wall, but once you saw the grooved track that ran all the way to the upstairs landing, it was impossible to unsee.

"What's this for," she asked innocently.

Packard looked at the platform for a moment, another wave of painful memories washing over him. It was different from his gaming memories. These were harshly real. He laughed through his nose, but it was halfhearted at best, and more out of habit than humor. "That was for my wheelchair," he said quietly. "Since I got home from Arete, I almost forgot it was there."

Becky looked sad. "I'm sorry. I didn't mean to…"

"It's okay," Packard assured her. "The lift is not among my worst memories. Not by a long shot." He looked pensive, and I knew what he was thinking about, or more accurately, who. Victoria had become a ghost, whose memory haunted both of us daily. I'm talking figuratively here, not literally. She was just so ingrained in both of us, it was impossible to get through a day without missing her at least once.

Becky placed a hand gently on Packard's. "If you need to talk."

"I'm okay," he said, but smiled a cockeyed smile at her, silently letting her know he appreciated her offer.

"You two about ready to hit the road," I asked, surprising them both.

Becky immediately removed her hand from Packard's. "Uh, yes sir."

Packard turned to say something, but I felt I'd embarrassed them enough.

"Be sure to use the restroom, then meet me out front," I told them. "I'll wrangle the others together. We're burning daylight."

Becky scurried off to the restroom while Packard, already one step ahead of me, stepped out to hug Whisper before heading out to the driveway.

~

We put up the convertible top and got on the road a little after 9 am. Thankfully, the traffic was uncharacteristically light, even for a Saturday.

Clem, Kyle, and Cool sat in the back seat, while Becky sat up front, between Packard and me. I couldn't think of any modern cars made with a split front bench seat, but the configuration was perfect for our growing party of six.

I was about to turn on some music when Packard stopped me.

"I had another dream last night, dad," he said softly.

I knew where the conversation was about to go. "Was it a dream or a memory?"

"A memory," he replied. "Though it's so hard to tell the difference sometimes."

"Why don't you tell us about it," Becky prompted. Then she looked at me. "Is that okay, Mr. Campbell?"

I nodded. "Yeah, I was about to suggest the same thing."

Knightmare's voice suddenly chimed from the speakers. "Would you like me to take over driving, so you can listen to Packard's story?"

I wasn't used to giving up control that easily, but I wanted Packard to know he had my undivided attention. I took my hands off the wheel and placed them in my lap. "Yes, Knightmare, I'd like that. Thank you."

Packard looked out the window for a moment, clearly wrapping his head around the memories. He finally began talking, but didn't turn to look at us as he told his tale.

7
War is Hell

It was definitely a memory. I was on a moonlit battlefield, surrounded by soldiers from the past, present, and future, fighting for the survival of our timeline.

I was a part of the Chrono Corps, an elite unit made up of some of the bravest warriors to ever take up arms against an enemy force. The men and women on my team were unique and specialized, to say the least. Most people would assume that I, being from the future, would be better equipped to deal with the threat we faced. Just like a battle couldn't be won on sheer wits, fancy weaponry alone couldn't win wars. The twelve members of my unit were the foremost experts in their fields: tactics, tracking, demolition, reconnaissance, search and rescue, and counterterrorism. In addition to our extensive combat training, we'd all logged thousands of hours in the time-booth, honing our skills in swimming, diving, parachuting, survival skills, and emergency medicine. We'd been on offensive raids, suicide missions, and held the front lines against the worst Baron von Do-Over had to offer. To be honest, none of us actually knew our enemy's name, just the faces of the soldiers he constantly threw in our direction like spaghetti at a greased wall. I called him a 'he', but as Foster always said, our foe could have just as easily been a woman, or something from the distant future we couldn't even comprehend. He said labeling our enemy was dangerous and could cause us to make false assumptions about their endgame.

Foster was an operations sergeant ripped straight out of World War II. Literally. We were all recruited from different points in history, and we had all been killed in action in our respective wars, snatched from death's clutches by a strange twist of fate and repurposed to be humanity's last hope. Talk about second chances. Among other things, Foster advised our team leader, a woman named Kaori Sato, on technical and training matters.

Captain Sato was a tactical genius. She began her military career as a samurai and had been instrumental in winning the Battle of Torikai-Gata under Takezaki Suenaga. She was one of the bravest, most selfless, and honorable leaders I'd ever served under. It's safe to say, without Captain Sato, the world as we know it would have been enslaved several millennia ago, and most of us would never have been born.

First Lieutenant Kaveh Firooz was Sato's second in command. The loyal lieutenant served under Pantea Arteshbod as one of the 10,000 famed Persian Immortals. Historically, the Immortals had a checkered past, but Firooz was one of us now, and would never be deemed guilty by association. She specialized in rescue and reconnaissance missions, which was also one of my areas of expertise. That shared skill set resulted in our being paired off frequently for away missions.

I was the assistant ops and intel sergeant, directing our detachment's intelligence ops from the top down. I also assisted

Foster and replaced him when needed. As you can probably imagine, redundancy across the team was necessary for so many reasons. I was as much a uniquely qualified specialist as a trusted failsafe. I got my initial military experience in the early 25th century as a soldier in the United Terran Liberation Forces, and my mom received my dog tags and a letter of condolence in early 2406. My real tour of duty began the day I died.

Among those whose guilt by association had been washed away upon induction into our little unit was Weapons Sergeant Beauregard Montgomery, formerly of the Confederate States Army. Montgomery had been raised mostly barefoot in the backwoods of Alabama and was one of the most gifted trackers alive, anywhere, any time. He was as close to feral as I imagined a human being could be while still managing to function in society. Yet when the chips were down — in our line of work they frequently were — he was better protection than an entire wolf pack.

Speaking of redundancy, our second weapons sergeant was Titus Decimus, formerly of the Roman Legion. Aside from his broader duties on the team, his specialty was close range combat and battle tactics. He was as heavily scarred as he was muscled, and holding true to his hand-to-hand training, he was as aggressive as Sato was stealthy.

We had two engineer sergeants. Saoirse O'Doyle was an IRA trained demolition demigod. She'd been building, rigging, and detonating explosives since the tender age of nine. Considering she was somewhere in her mid-thirties, I'd always found it impressive she was only missing a couple of fingers. O'Doyle took Jacques de Montbard, a twenty-something year old Knight Templar, under her wing after his recruitment. De Montbard had shown promise when working with gunpowder and had the underpinnings of an architectural education. The latter made him quite adept at finding the sweet spots to place charges when bringing down structures. In short, O'Doyle knew how to make things go boom, and de Montbard knew where the booms did the most damage.

Our unit also had two medical sergeants. In truth, we all had medical training. *You could never have too many qualified field medics.* But former SAS operative, Grace Clarke, and Israeli Defense Forces specialist Shira Amar, were as close to miracle workers as I'd ever seen. Clarke, easily being the most empathetic member of the team, was the lead when it came to search and rescue. She wasn't anywhere near the tracker that ol' Montgomery was in a rural setting, but in an urban environment, she made me believe in good old-fashioned gut feelings. Once upon a time, Amar had been a soldier with one of the most heavily trained, dangerous units the world had ever known. However, before she lost her life on a covert mission behind enemy lines, she was one of the IDF's foremost hostage negotiators. It was no mistake that she became our go-to person for all things counterterrorism.

Rounding out our dirty dozen were two communications sergeants who could get a point across with a set of brass knuckles or a sharp blade just as easily as they could set up an improvised comms hub. Olga Vasilyev, who doubled as a tracker, but always smelled considerably better than Sergeant Montgomery, had been trained by the Russian Spetsnaz. Her nickname was Auntie Personnel, a play on words inspired by antipersonnel mines. I always teased her, telling her I was going to get her a t-shirt that said, 'FRONT TOWARD ENEMY'. God help the person who got close enough to read it while fighting her. Her comms counterpart was an honest-to-god Viking warrior. Sigurd Halldórsson also had Firooz's back for reconnaissance. Aw, hell, Halldórsson was a man for all seasons. Comms, recon, interrogation, and even the occasional Leeroy Jenkins level berserker rage.

We were a team to be reckoned with. Considering we'd each already faced our own days of reckoning, there was very little we actually feared.

While the Marines said 'Semper Fi', our motto was simply 'Stay Alive'.

~

There were other units involved in the fray, but we rarely overlapped missions. There was an old saying about too many cooks. I'm pretty sure the sentiment summed up why each unit was completely autonomous.

There were Mongols, Conquistadors, Rangers, and Thunderbirds. Soldiers from the French Foreign Legion fought alongside elite members of the Greek Hoplite Phalanx, and ruthless Swiss Mercenaries.

We may have been the textbook definition of ragtag, but we were also reality's last best hope for a good night's sleep.

If dealt with swiftly, chronflicts — yeah, you read that right — never impacted the actual timeline. Time is like superglue;

it doesn't set immediately. It starts fluid and continues to get stickier until it finally firms up and sets permanently.

There were times, however, when we couldn't nip the chronflicts in the bud. That was when things got complicated. The day I'm telling you about was one of those days.

The faceless enemy, whom we'd all given our own nicknames to, had been attacking key turning points in the timeline for more than a century. Our little unit was small potatoes in a long, distinguished line of temporal defenders. Most battles were won easily by being in the right place at the right time, pun definitely intended. We had the advantage of time-pings, alarms on a quantum computer that told us where the fluidity of time had been disturbed, as well as where the ripples had originated.

In ninety-nine percent of the incursions, we were able to trace the ripples backwards by a few days, arriving ahead of the enemy and stopping them before they could do any lasting damage.

Lately, though, the enemy had been getting the drop on us. We were constantly walking into traps. The ripples were accurate, and the anticipated forces showed up as expected, but there was always an additional team of enemies deployed that seemed to appear out of nowhere.

Those ambushes constituted the other one percent of our missions, and logic dictated it was only a matter of time before that percentage increased.

We arrived in Stalingrad on 20 August 1942. The time ripples originated from 23 August, so we dropped in early as usual. Per history, the German 6th Army troops and their allies fought the Soviet Union for control of the city of Stalingrad, now known as Volgograd, for almost six months. The Red Army eventually overpowered and destroyed the 6th Army, but the ripples told us something was about to change and dramatically alter the course of human history from the mid-20th century forward.

We knew that in 3 days' time, the 6th Army and elements of the 4th Panzer Army, supported by intensive Luftwaffe bombing, would reduce much of the city to rubble. We weren't there to stop that from happening. Our mission wasn't to judge or change history; our mission was to stop those who would manipulate history to create a timeline that suited their needs. We used the greatest resource available to us, the experience of tens of thousands of soldiers who had fought in countless battles since the beginning of recorded history.

As per standard operating protocol, we were all outfitted with our standard body armor and a variety of weaponry. The weapons we carried were a blend of regulation and personal choices. Each of us carried a CTP hybrid, a molecularly fused tungsten-diamond blade, pellets of fast-acting hydro-nano-acid, and a wrist-mounted plasma torch.

Some of us carried an additional weapon that linked us to our past. Honestly, those were the tools of the trade that most frequently saved our asses.

The entire unit chron'd in on the northern border of Stalingrad, but Vasilyev, Foster, and I went in as an advance scouting unit. Firooz, Montgomery, and O'Doyle were on scouting detail as well, posted within a quarter of a mile just in case things went drastically south. We always detached in groups of six, but sometimes split those numbers in half to look less conspicuous and reduce damage in case of capture. All twelve of us wore time-appropriate Russian outerwear that allowed us to blend in. Even though we all wore cochlear and vocal translator implants, Vasilyev took point as we made our way into the doomed city. She was the only native speaker and knew the subtle nuances that would help to seal our cover.

~

The three of us settled in at a corner table at a small sidewalk café called Bistro Blini. Upon entering, the aroma of freshly baked bread and the sound of Tchaikovsky playing softly in the background on a gramophone tantalized our senses. A sign out front advertised the day's specials as being borscht and pelmeni and reminded us that a glass of ice-cold kvass was the perfect way to combat the heat and humidity of a summer's day. Vasilyev had requisitioned a few Soviet rubles and kopeks before our departure, and politely ordered us each a glass of kvass and a slice of honey cake.

The server, a young woman named Galina, brought our order quickly, and with a smile that made me cringe when I thought about the absolute hell that was about to descend upon the city. There was a military presence there already, but the troops wouldn't be enough to repel the 6th Army in the beginning. Bistro Blini would soon be obliterated, like it had sat in the path of the lava flows of Vesuvius herself. Sometimes I wished I could warn people, send them away to a relative or something, but I also understood why that was the cardinal no-no of all no-nos. Time was a fragile thing. We were allowed to visit the bistro and interact with Galina only because she wouldn't be alive in a week.

"Beautiful day," Galina said, placing our order on the old wooden table. Those were the last words she said. A moment later, a gaping, red hole appeared in her shoulder. She had a moment to register surprise on her face before a second hole appeared in her abdomen, spraying Foster with a mixture of blood and our server's breakfast.

"Hit the ground," Vasilyev shouted, but we were already dropping. Reflexes are a powerful thing, and blood is a powerful motivator.

More holes blew through the wall behind us, and the chair Foster had just been sitting in exploded into toothpicks.

Vasilyev grabbed Foster's shoulder and studied him carefully. "Are you hit," she asked finally. "Is any of that your blood?"

Foster shook his head. "Negative," he shouted. "It's all hers!"

I unholstered my CTP and slammed in a cartridge filled with 4.6 mm copper pellets. Splintered wood and powdered concrete rained down on us like nuclear ash. "This was supposed to be a safe zone!"

Vasilyev nodded fervently. "There was no weapons fire in this sector for three more days!"

"Another trap," Foster grumbled, slamming a cartridge into his CTP, and placing a cigarette carefully between his weather-chapped lips. "I was looking forward to that honey cake, dammit." He leveled his gun sight at the front window and covered Vasilyev and me as we took cover behind a large concrete planter.

Once we were behind the planter, Vasilyev and I got into position, covering Foster's retreat. She fired at the street outside and shouted, "Foster, to us!"

The big, bearded man scrambled in our direction, but yelped in pain as he ducked behind the planter with us. I looked down and shook my head when I saw the side of his head was bleeding. Foster had been hit.

He put a hand to the side of his face, then took it away, covered in blood. He turned his head, so I could see the damage. "How bad is it?"

There was a lot of blood, but I breathed a sigh of relief when I saw that, aside from a bit of scarring, he would live. A bullet or shrapnel had nicked his earlobe. "Just a flesh wound," I shouted back.

Foster looked disappointed. His unlit cigarette drooped dejectedly. "Damn, I was hoping for a Purple Heart this time."

"Sorry, old buddy," I shouted back. "You've gotta look at my ugly face for a good while longer!"

Bullets whizzed by like angry mosquitos, tearing our surroundings to shreds. Shrieks and cries came from the kitchen, and what I assumed was an oven exploded in a ball of fire that made the summer heat feel like a tanning bed.

I looked back and saw that the entrance to the kitchen was far too exposed to be a viable retreat option. The open-air design to the café's front wall gave us zero options for advancement. The enemy had us pinned down like a high school wrestler in an Olympic competition.

I chanced a look around the side of the planter, and a spray of bullets forced me to pull back like a turtle into his shell. Before I ducked back, however, I saw there were at least six enemy soldiers advancing on the café. Not surprisingly, none of them was German or Russian. They all wore the easily recognized midnight blue and charcoal uniforms that our time-hopping enemies had boldly chosen. They'd gotten the drop on us again.

Our ear implants crackled slightly before a frantic message came through. It was Halldórsson. He rarely lost his cool over the radio. "By the gates of Valhalla! The ripples were wrong! Hear me now, the ripples were wrong! We be under fierce attack, beset by enemy fire! Make haste to the place of our arrival!"

I looked at Vasilyev and Foster. They both shook their heads. We weren't going anywhere.

I was about to respond when I heard shouting coming from the front of the café. A moment later, the firing ceased.

Foster put up his hands, signaling for Vasilyev and me to stay down. "It could be another trap," he said loudly.

We waited a few moments, sidearms at the ready, before finally standing in unison and taking aim at the café entrance, ready for our last stand.

We all lowered our weapons when we saw Firooz, Montgomery, and O'Doyle approaching, stepping over the bodies of half a dozen dead enemy soldiers. They'd all stripped off the Russian clothing, exposing their combat armor and weapons. Montgomery was scoping out the rest of the area, scanning for additional enemies.

O'Doyle waved at us, motioning for us to join them. "Haven't ye heard? Alpha team needs backup! What are ye doin' dawdlin' aroun' here for?"

The three of us ran from the demolished café, each having to hop over poor Galina as we did. She was barely recognizable by then.

As we exited the building, I spotted one of the enemy soldiers struggling to raise a rifle, pointing it at Montgomery's back. Without so much as a thought, I aimed and fired my CTP pistol. In a fraction of a second, the pistol chambered a copper pellet, converted it to plasma, and fired the round at the downed soldier. His body jumped and twisted with the impact of my round, and two others. I looked to each side and saw that Vasilyev and Foster had matched my move, second for second. The soldier's rifle clattered to the cobblestone street, his dead finger still lodged inside the trigger guard. The charges our CTP weapons fired were small copper slugs, essentially BB's. But passing through the laser-induced ionization chamber converted them to energy bolts that traveled more than ten thousand feet per second, creating impact damage comparable to .50 cal heavy machine gun bullets.

Montgomery, realizing he'd just come within a microsecond of being a dead man, spit a wad of tobacco on the ground next to the destroyed corpse. "I seen 'im. I jest reckon'd it's 'bout time y'all did some o' the work fer once!"

Firooz looked at Foster's bloodied face, grimacing. "How bad is it?"

Foster touched his ear gingerly. "I suppose I can cross piercing my ear off my to-do list," he shrugged. "I'll live."

Firooz nodded, not even remotely registering Foster's stab at humor. "Then we need to get to the insertion point, now." She circled two fingers in the air and pointed north. "Split into our two teams again. Vasilyev, your team will circle around and approach from the west. My team will approach from the east. Standard pincer movement. Now, go, go, go!"

~

The six of us ran together for half a click, passing through Lenin Square and hopping the trolley tracks, before my unit veered off slightly to the left and ran northwest into the woods. Firooz led her unit northeast, towards the Volga River. We could hear shouts and gunfire coming from the clearing where our remaining team was setting up base camp.

The shouts were frantic and told a tale that tried to get the better of my imagination. If we were going to provide proper backup to our teammates, then our heads had to be on straight. No doubt, no fear, no apprehension.

As we approached, we could see intermittent muzzle flashes coming from the clearing where we'd left Sato and the others. I focused on the flashes, zeroing in on their direction and spread. The latter would tell me who was firing, as the enemy didn't have CTP weapons. The spread of the CTP flash was slightly wider and flatter, and the trained eye could spot the difference at about forty meters. Montgomery taught me that, and the knowledge saved our skin on more than one occasion. Knowing *who* was firing meant knowing who was safe to fire *at*.

I shut off my com-link for a moment and listened to the voices as I watched the muzzle flashes.

Directly ahead, a phalanx of enemy soldiers was firing into the clearing. I could hear Halldórsson's booming voice yelling at someone to "stay down" and Sato shouting orders I couldn't quite make out over the weapons fire.

I slowed down to stay stealthy, being careful not to give my position away by snapping any tattletale twigs. Reactivating my com-link, I asked, "Vasilyev, Foster, can you hear me?"

They both responded that they could, and I told them what I'd made out. "I'm about thirty meters out. I'm going to close that to fifteen and lay down some fire. When they turn to focus on me, come in as planned and squash 'em from both sides!"

"Roger that," Foster called back.

"Affirmative," Vasilyev agreed.

A few seconds later, I found a well-fortified, easily defended position at the base of two ancient trees. Their trunks had grown away from each other, creating a tight notch that would be difficult to penetrate in the poor lighting of the waxing gibbous moon. "I'm in position," I whispered.

Foster responded first. "Alright, Big Wheel. I'm ready to prang these bastards! You in position, Vasilyev?"

She replied immediately. "Konechno! Foster, you talk too much. How do you Americans say? Roll up your flaps?"

What sounded like a dismissive grunt came back as a response, but I knew Foster's laugh when I heard it.

"What I wouldn't give for a pineapple, right now," he said.

He was referring to a grenade. We all carried a variety of grenades, but pineapples were our special, future-tech version, which used photoionization to convert copper pellets to plasma-based shrapnel. That would have been overkill, to say the least. One pineapple could destroy a battleship from the inside out.

"I know, I know," he sighed. "Overkill."

Vasilyev cut in, interrupting Foster's lamentations. "Are you ready, Campbell?"

"Cool hand Campbell, ready for-"

"By Foster's beard, would you mickleamunners just *do* something already," Halldórsson shouted over the com. I'd forgotten he could hear us.

I settled into the notch between the trees and began firing.

~

As well organized as our time hopping adversaries were, their protective measures were virtually nil. They had no body armor to speak of, not even hockey pads, and their weapons were little more than a hodgepodge of scavenged weapons from virtually every time-sector we'd clashed with them.

What they seemed to have over us every single time, were sheer, crushing numbers. Let me make one thing clear, time travel was extremely dangerous. I don't mean *where* we went, that's a given. I mean, *how* we got there. The temportals we used were only stable for a short period of time and could only handle a limited amount of mass before the quantum gravity at a given destination began to uh... cause mistakes. Things got put back together wrong. And when I say things, I include *people* in that group. It *wasn't* pretty, I can promise you that. I suspected that's why the enemy troops always had lower density clothing and less feature-rich weaponry. They always packed light because they bet on winning battles based on overwhelming numbers. That strategy hadn't played out too well for them for the better part of a century. Recently, though, we learned the hard way that, while their equipment was still inferior to ours, they'd made upgrades to their temportal-tech.

Heck, in the beginning, travelers couldn't even take anything metal with them. Something about the harmonic frequency required to create the wormholes caused anything metal to explode. Buffer tech got invented about twenty years after the advent of time travel and suddenly metal was no longer a problem. I suspected the enemy made a similar advancement in their version of the tech. They were masking the ripples, making it nearly impossible to get the drop on them. It would only be a matter of time before they resolved the density issue, and then we'd all be well and screwed.

I opened fire from the notch between the trees, taking down half a dozen soldiers before they realized the gunfire was coming from behind them. The entire rear detachment turned and began returning fire, shredding the surface of the trees, but not even getting close to hitting me. Staying behind one of the massive trunks, I repositioned my pistol in the notch and resumed firing. I heard angry shouts and pained shrieks coming from the confused knot of soldiers. A moment later, the pained shrieks outnumbered the angry shouts. Foster and Vasilyev had joined the dance, and they'd brought the mosh pit with them!

My two cohorts literally chewed through the group of soldiers, being careful not to hit each other in the crossfire.

I leapt from behind the trees and unleashed a barrage of plasma bolts that took the legs out from underneath the group still standing in the closest proximity to me. I rushed forward and continued firing until I was sure we'd taken out the last of the soldiers on our side of the fray.

More shouts erupted from further into the clearing. I suddenly saw Decimus burst forth from the battle, his custom-made tungsten-diamond sword raised over his head, and a hard-light shield clutched in his left hand. He turned again and began hacking and slashing at the enemy troops he'd just pushed past. He was screaming, but not out of pain or fear. Decimus was a warrior. He was screaming to let the bastards in front of him know that they were freaking doomed. Halldórsson pushed out of the battle just to Decimus's left. He held two soldiers by their throats and swung them at the other troops like rag dolls, knocking the startled soldiers aside before stomping on them like a crazed Riverdancer. Like I said before, he made Leeroy Jenkins appear restrained.

One of the luckier soldiers ducked the barrage of bodies and stomps and raised his gun, pointing it directly at Halldórsson's head.

Foster put a plasma round into the soldier's head, which disappeared in a wet spray. "Blow it out your barracks bag," Foster shouted, as he fought his way into the wall-to-wall enemy line.

I could hear Firooz, Montgomery, and O'Doyle on the com-link. They'd run into a similar knot of combatants on the other side of the clearing and were doing their best to thin the herd.

Sato suddenly pushed her way into view, her tungsten-diamond wakizashi in one hand and her CTP pistol in the other. She ducked a volley of bullets and returned fire with deadly accuracy. She swung her wakizashi in tight arcs, slicing through anything that dared get within a few feet of her. The former samurai moved forward and back, bobbing and weaving like a ballerina in a boxing ring. As she faced my direction for a few moments, I realized she had her eyes closed. I'd seen her do it in practice, using her other senses to guide her movements, but never in the heat of battle.

Foster slapped the back of my head, making me bite my tongue. "More fighting, less ogling, kid!"

I nodded, embarrassed, and slammed another pellet cartridge into my sidearm.

A voice called out from the northern edge of the clearing. We could hear it on the com-link as well, giving it a stereo effect. It was Clarke. She sounded panicked. "De Montbard has been hit! He's losing a lot of blood! Amar and I have him, but we can't treat him without some additional cover!"

Vasilyev pointed at the fray. "Foster, you and Campbell stay here and take these bastards down!" Before we could confirm, she ran north to help save de Montbard's life.

I had to duck as Halldórsson swung a soldier over my head. He gripped the hapless lackey by the ankle and used him against his own troops like a flyswatter. I almost told him to watch where he was swinging his toys until I realized he'd just taken down another combatant who was sneaking up behind me. The two soldiers' heads slammed together with a crack and an old rusty axe flew from my would-be assailant's hand. I picked up the axe and tossed it to Halldórsson, who always said it was better to keep fallen weapons out of the enemy's hands whenever possible. "Thanks, Siggie," I shouted. He hated that name, but that never stopped me from using it.

He growled at me as he let go of the dead soldier he'd been swinging and caught the axe. "Someday," he shouted.

"But not today," I shouted back.

Together, followed by Foster, Decimus, and Sato, we rushed into the thick of the opposing force and worked our way towards Firooz, Montgomery, and O'Doyle.

Decimus grabbed Sato roughly, pulling her towards him, burying her head against his chest. Thankfully, she'd opened her eyes, or he might have had her wakizashi shoved into his ear. He pivoted just as an enemy soldier unloaded a .45 into his back. The bullets ricocheted off the centurion's armor, killing the soldier and a few of the others standing near him.

Sato pushed away from Decimus, nodding through a grimace that any of her team would recognize as gratitude. She dove forward, hacking and firing, and we followed.

~

When we got close to the center of what was supposed to be our base camp, we all stopped and caught our breath. A massive temportal was in the clearing, and more combatants were pouring through.

"How long has that been open," I shouted.

"Too long," Sato replied. "It should have closed several minutes ago!"

"They've found a way to stabilize it," Decimus groaned.

Foster broke away as soon as we entered the destroyed base camp and headed towards some unopened crates.

Sato and Decimus began firing at the temportal, killing the enemy soldiers before they could get all the way through.

Sato shook her head at Foster as he rummaged through a second crate, then pointed at Halldórsson and me, nodding at the troops surrounding us. "You two provide cover while we create a bottleneck!"

"Ten-four," I shouted back. Then I turned my back to Sato and Decimus and began firing at anything that moved.

Halldórsson, who had a sidearm of his own, still insisted upon using enemy soldiers as a weapon. Most of them weren't even dead when he was doing it. They were like screaming, human bolos.

All hell was breaking loose in every direction, and it was all we could do to stay alive. Bullets pinged off our armor, but our heads were dangerously exposed. The helmets we normally wore during combat were in one of the crates. I suddenly realized what Foster was doing.

I could hear Foster's breathing in my earpiece, though considering I could hear my entire team all the time, I rarely focused on anything less than a shout for an assist or my name.

Vasilyev and Amar shouted to each other, protecting Clarke while she tried to save de Montbard's life. Firooz and her unit joined us at the destroyed base camp, their confused chatter about the massive temportal matched our own, almost word for word. We'd been in bad places before, but unless we could stem the tide of incoming soldiers, we were doomed.

I heard Sato gasp. That, my friend, is a *very* bad sign. I chanced a glance back at the temportal and almost dropped my gun. More than a dozen heavily armored soldiers who made Halldórsson look like a scrawny schoolboy stepped through and onto the battlefield, and more were on their way!

I suddenly heard Foster squeal with delight. He must've found something good. "My Red Ryder," he exclaimed happily, before running back to our position.

He joined us a moment later, holding the fully automatic CTP rifle he had lovingly crafted. It was one of a kind and put our pistols to shame. He'd affectionately named it Red Ryder.

"Really," I asked. "You risked all our lives for your rifle?"

Foster scrunched up his face, looking offended. "Nah, she was just a happy accident!" He held up his pistol and showed me what might have been the most beautiful thing I'd ever seen. "Who ordered pineapple on their pizza?" He'd plugged a beautiful yet deadly CTP grenade into a charging port on his pistol. As he spoke, a light near the port glowed a soft, reassuring shade of blue. A second later, Foster plucked the grenade from the charging port. The light switched to a deep, threatening red. He grinned at me as he tossed it right into the center of the temportal, hitting the ground as it flew.

I ducked, grabbing Halldórsson and pulling him down with me. I shouted into my com-link, "fire in the hole!"

Decimus leapt onto Sato. She wrapped her arms around the back of his head, protecting him from shrapnel.

A second later, a blast radiated out of the opening, shredding most of the soldiers in close range and sending the rest flying. The temportal slammed shut, cutting the remaining troops off mid-stride, and dropping the partial bodies right where they stopped.

I couldn't believe our good fortune. Foster saved the day with his pineapple and found his beloved Red Ryder in the process.

Then the armored behemoths began getting back up. Apparently, a temportal could cut them in half, but a CTP grenade that could take out a small fortress had no effect on them. We were screwed.

And then, before they could attack, the strangest thing happened. One moment my team was with me, and the next moment, they slumped to the ground, unconscious. All of them. A second later, the enemy troops dropped to the ground, too.

"Hello," I asked quietly. My earpiece crackled like the flames that surrounded me, but no one spoke. I was alone.

8
Science Friction

Packard finished telling us about his dream as we were approaching our exit. We had less than 2 miles to go before we reached Arete, so his timing was good. He finally turned to look at me.

Becky leaned back uncomfortably, pressing herself against the seat, clearly not wanting to block our line of sight.

"My dreams are basically just me reliving the games, right," Packard asked.

I thought about it for a moment. "Yeah, it definitely sounds like it."

He didn't look convinced. "Then why did I see everyone drop and go catatonic? That wasn't ever a thing in the game's narrative."

"Uh, Mr. Campbell?" Kyle spoke up from the back.

"Yes, Kyle?"

"Maybe his mind was actually there," Kyle offered. "Like my mind, uh, *our* minds are actually here?"

I shook my head. That didn't explain the combatants dropping suddenly. "No... I feel like..."

"He was watching their minds come here," Becky blurted out. She looked at me, her eyes huge. "Sorry for interrupting, sir." Her mouth hung open, as if she wanted to say something, but was processing the absolute horror of the concept.

"More imp-lee-cay-shuns," Cool asked from the back seat.

I sighed. I could see the security gate for Arete ahead. Where was I even supposed to start when we saw Irene? "Yeah, buddy... more implications."

~

As we approached the security gate, Cool flattened himself out and then, like liquid mercury, flowed to the floor, hiding at Clem and Kyle's feet.

The guard, a young woman named Jasmine, who typically manned the Arete building's front desk, approached the window. She and I had spoken on several occasions, so she knew me on sight. "Sweet ride, Mr. Campbell!"

Knightmare answered before I could. "Thank you."

Jasmine looked perplexed. She knew I hadn't answered, and KM's voice didn't exactly carry any bass.

"Sorry," Becky said from next to me. "I helped wash her, so I'm proud of her too. Polish and everything!"

Jasmine laughed. "Phew! For a second, I totally thought the car was talking to me." The young guard rolled her eyes. "I need to stop watching so many sci-fi movies."

In the back seat, I could hear Clem whisper to Kyle. "Don't all cars talk?"

Kyle laughed. "No man, not in my world, anyway."

Jasmine looked at them funny before turning her attention back to me. "Go on in, sir. I'll radio Gunner and let him know you're on your way in." She noticed Packard, sitting by the far window. "You're Mr. Campbell's son, right? How are you today?"

Packard nodded, but he, like the rest of us, had a lot on his mind. "I'm good, thank you," he said amicably.

Jasmine smiled. "I know you all didn't come to shoot the breeze with me. Gunner will meet you at the front desk."

We thanked Jasmine and drove along the wooded path that led to Arete's massive parking area.

"Sorry about the slip-up, Hal," Knightmare said as we pulled into a parking spot.

"No harm done," I said. "We're all adjusting to this new, uh… reality. We all have to be careful."

"Agreed," KM replied.

Clem cleared his throat as I turned off the engine. "Uh, Marshal's Pa, Marshal, Becky? Can one of y'all answer a question fer me?"

We all looked back to find Clem looking more puzzled than usual.

I nodded. "What do you want to know?"

Clem looked embarrassed. "Well, young Kyle here tells me that our peculiar friend Knightmare is the only talking car he's privy to. Might that be true?"

I had to keep myself from laughing. "Yeah, Clem. She's it. Cars from our world don't talk. They're just machines."

KM made a noise that sounded like an electronic huff.

"Except you, girl," I added. "You're special."

Clem spoke again before Knightmare could say anything else. "Well then, I might owe yer other fine automobile a bit of an apology," he said sheepishly.

Packard cocked his head and looked at our new friend curiously. "And why would you need to do that?"

If Clem was standing, he would have been shuffling his feet. "Well, I tried to have a word with her this mornin' while y'all were still sawin' logs, but she plum ignored me. So, I might have gotten a mite bit offended and show'd her my middle finger."

The uncontrollable laughter that followed was the breath of fresh air we all needed before heading in and facing reality, or what we thought we understood it to be, with Irene.

~

Gunner approached the thirteen-foot-tall glass doors that separated Arete's lobby from the outside world. They slid apart majestically, dwarfing the big man as he exited to greet us.

I opened my door and Cool slipped deftly from the floor, taking shape once again, but this time he was a perfect duplicate of Gunner only, *you guessed it*, yellow with brown spots. The Elastic Giraffe looked back at Clem, who already had one lanky leg extended from the back seat. He coughed, wrinkling his nose. "Dude! You have got to do something about those boots! Stuff 'em with dryer sheets or something!" He let loose another cough that might have actually been a retch. "Unless 'stinky feet' is your superpower… then *much respect*, bruh!"

Clem frowned at the comment, looking at his boots dejectedly. "These here boots was a gift from my dear ol' grandpappy." He scowled.

Cool turned to face him and flexed like a bodybuilder in the Mr. Universe competition. "Well, their smell is stronger than

Gunner, dude!" He turned back to find Gunner standing right behind him.

"Is that a fact," Gunner asked, raising an eyebrow thoughtfully.

Cool melted into a puddle at Gunner's feet, the only thing recognizable were his eyes and gritted teeth. An exact replica of Gunner's arm extended from the puddle. It got within six inches of Gunner's face and flexed. "Arm wrestle," the mouth in the puddle asked.

Gunner raised a sledgehammer of a hand and high-fived Cool's morphed appendage. A ring on one of the guard's fingers clinked musically as it struck the metal that made up Cool's shoe. "Nice to see you again, Cool," he smiled before extending a hand to Clem. "You too, Sheriff Pickett."

Clem just about blushed at the offered hand. "The pleasure's all mine, friend."

I watched as Packard and Becky shared an amused glance at the exchange. It appeared our little sheriff was growing up. Next thing we knew, we'd be taking him to the firing range for playdates.

Gunner waved at Packard and Becky. "Hey kids, who's your friend?" He nodded at Kyle, who had just pulled himself from the back seat.

Clem spoke up first, proudly proclaiming, "young Kyle, here, is a fledgling gunslinger. Much like me n' you."

Gunner looked impressed. "I see, a future lawman. Good to meet you, Kyle. My name's Gunner."

Kyle smiled and told Gunner that he was happy to meet him as well. He wasn't used to the reverence and respect Clem had bestowed upon him.

Gunner had already razzed me for my story choices in *Assassins Inc.*, so I let Clem's introduction stand. I patted KM's hood gently, and said, "and this is our other friend, Knightmare."

Gunner stared at the Pontiac, who remained suspiciously silent. "I saw this car last night. Is there something I should know?"

I patted her again. "It's okay to talk to Gunner," I assured her.

"In that case, I am delighted to finally meet you," KM replied. "Hal speaks very highly of you."

Gunner looked surprised. "He does?"

"No," KM continued. "I was merely making small talk. In fact, his vocal tones change when you are around. It is likely you intimidate him. Perhaps a fight would be appropriate to prove one's dominance over the other?"

Gunner looked at me, clearly uncomfortable, but still a bit amused. "No, that won't be necessary."

As we left KM and walked towards the huge doors, Gunner leaned towards me and quietly said, "Nightmare, huh?"

"It's spelled with a 'K', but yeah. The name fits at times," I replied.

Clem patted Gunner on the back. "She talks smart about a great many things, but she don't po-ssess the knowledge of human pleasantries, common courtesies, or the simplest of graces."

Gunner looked at me, his eyes widened, clearly not missing the irony in Clem's words.

When we entered the lobby, Irene was waiting on an overhanging balcony. Looking down at us, she scanned the growing party with unmasked dread in her eyes. She frowned before waving to us. "Come on up. I'll be in our usual meeting room."

~

We regaled Irene with everything that had happened since the previous afternoon, sharing every detail; Knightmare's frightening transformation, Kyle's appearance, *twice*, Cool's appearance at Arete, and the discovery of the checkpoint on the Lanier. We finished with Packard's memory of the game, as well as Becky and Kyle's combined theory about why all the other combatants suddenly lost consciousness.

"And I done scalded my tender bits with water from the sun before Marshal's Pa offered me coffee and clean skivvies," Clem added. "Also, I might owe his other automobile a sincere apology."

I shook my head softly. "Ah... there was that, too," I agreed. "So, Irene, what do you think?"

Irene appeared to be as done with the BS as I was. She looked at all of us, pausing one by one, dissecting us individually with her mind. "Did you bring the Lanier?"

"Yes, it's in Knightmare's trunk," I replied. "I can go get it if you'd like."

"Dad, that thing weighs a ton," Packard warned.

"I can go get it if you give me the keys," Gunner offered.

"Yeah," I conceded. "That's probably a good idea, if you don't mind."

"I wouldn't say words if I didn't mean them," Gunner said, taking the keys and heading out to the elevator.

"Damned fine lawman," Clem commented once Gunner was out of earshot.

Irene looked at him, puzzled.

"The Marshal and young Becky here had more than a few words with me," Clem explained. "I'm committed to tryin' to be a better person." He looked at Becky and smiled. "In fact, I made my second o-fficial friend last night."

Irene, clearly touched by the display, paused before speaking. "Well, Clem, that's as important as anything else I've heard since we all sat down. I'd postulate that you have more than two friends here at this table. Maybe even one outside this room."

Clem wiped his eyes. "Please excuse me, I think my hay fever's actin' up. And here I am without a handkerchief."

Packard passed him a box of tissues. "Think of those as disposable handkerchiefs," he said. "Hang onto the box. I do believe it's hay fever season, old friend."

~

Once Gunner returned with the word processor, I plugged it in and let Irene sit in front of it.

She placed her fingers tentatively on the keys, her index fingers hovering over the F and J. "So, 'it was a dark and stormy night'? That's what I type?"

"Capitalize the 'I' in it," Becky reminded her.

Irene typed the phrase and pressed ENTER without a moment's hesitation.

Nothing.

Irene looked back at Packard and the others. "Exactly what happens when you type the phrase?"

Packard stepped up next to Irene. "I can show you, if you'd like."

Irene rolled her office chair away from the table. "Be my guest," she replied.

Packard typed in the phrase. I found myself wishing I'd never heard those awful words, even from Snoopy. I winced when he pressed ENTER.

COMMAND NOT RECOGNIZED

PLAYER PACKARD DYLAN CAMPBELL IS ALREADY REGISTERED

WOULD YOU LIKE TO SEE A LIST OF ADDITIONAL CHECKPOINTS?

<YES/NO>

Several voices repeated the same question in unison. "More checkpoints?"

Before I could suggest thinking about it, Packard typed YES and hit ENTER.

ADDITIONAL CHECKPOINTS NOT YET AVAILABLE

PLEASE TRY AGAIN LATER

It was Packard's turn to look confused. "Additional checkpoints not yet available? What does that even mean?"

Everyone looked at Irene, who put up her hands in mock surrender. "Don't look at me. This is Hal's area of expertise."

I shook my head. "If you mean games, then yes. But if you mean checkpoints in the real-" I looked at our interdimensional visitors. "I mean, *our* world, then I'm just as much in the dark as you are."

Packard turned in his chair, his eyes wide. "Dad. The word processor is a checkpoint in *Regress*, but there's at least one checkpoint in every game you've made." He looked like he'd just stumbled upon the most terrifying secrets of the universe. "Is it possible the checkpoints from other games are here, but the word processor doesn't know it yet? Maybe the checkpoints from my friends' games are here because they are?"

I was feeling sick again. "The word processor isn't from any of their games, Packard. You just said it. It's from *Regress*."

Becky shrugged. "Then maybe someone from *Regress* is going to show up, too?"

Packard shook his head violently. "Oh, hell no. HELL no!"

Clem looked between us, and then to Kyle. "Any ideer what a re-gress is?"

Kyle shook his head, indicating that he did not.

Cool, who still looked like Gunner with jaundice, shrugged. "No clue either, bro."

"*Regress* is a super-violent horror game," I replied. "It's like a zombie apocalypse, but with feral, bloodthirsty humans."

I could see Gunner's wheels turning. He was silently judging me again. *Join the club, buddy.*

When he spoke, it had nothing to do with my most recent contribution to our predicament. "Well, aside from Clem and Knightmare being a little socially inept, I don't see any bad guys popping up," he said.

Clem's eyes narrowed at the comment, but he, like everyone else, was not looking for a fight.

Irene raised a finely plucked eyebrow. "Packard, I think Becky and Kyle might be right about what was happening at the end of your dream about the time-war game. And I don't think we've seen the last NPC to join us in our world."

Packard shifted in his seat, looking down at his knees as he spoke. "But it wasn't just my unit that dropped. The enemy soldiers fell, too."

Irene nodded. "Yes, I know. I think we need to be prepared for the fact that not all our visitors will arrive with the best of intentions."

"Speaking of visitors," I said, trying to change the subject a bit, "you really need to meet Knightmare."

Gunner grinned, despite the grim shadow that had descended upon the room. "That car's something else."

In a rare moment of what people unfamiliar with Irene might have mistaken for rudeness, she dismissed Gunner's comment and turned to me abruptly. "So, you say the car, Knightmare, is genuine artificial intelligence?"

I answered without an ounce of hesitation. "I've seen enough chatbots and programmable logic to know the difference. KM is light years beyond any AI available today."

Irene pursed her lips, thinking. "Do you think she'd be agreeable to some tests?"

"She's a little on the brutally honest side, but I'm sure I could talk to her," Packard said. "I've still got questions about what you said a moment ago, though. If that's okay."

Irene smiled gently. "Please, ask anything."

"What makes you think that just because my friends from the games have shown up, my enemies will too?"

Packard looked nervous, like when Vic Parker used to pick on him. He always hesitated to tell me because he feared Vic would retaliate.

"I don't know that for certain, Packard. The mass loss of consciousness in your dream might have been just that, *a dream*. It's possible your memories are malleable when they're experienced as dreams. However, if they are pure memories, and that incident never actually occurs in the real game, then Becky and Kyle's hypothesis could hold water." Irene looked at me for a second opinion, raising an eyebrow curiously.

I sighed. "Look, I don't want that to be the case any more than anyone else here. I'm scared to death of what's happening. The fact that I'm responsible for it has Boy Scouts practicing their knot tying on my intestines. But as a scientist... of sorts... I wouldn't be very responsible if I didn't explore all the possibilities, simply because some of them frighten me."

Packard slumped forward, dropping his elbows to the massive table. "So, you're saying that Blowtorch Man or Alistair McBain could just pop in for brunch."

Becky caught her breath. "Or the monsters from Laboratory 311?"

"Or Injuns," Clem asked.

"Native Americans," Packard and Becky said in unison.

"Well," Clem nodded, "that does make more sense than Injuns."

Irene retook control of the conversation. "Yes, as implausible as all those things sound, they're all possible." She took a swig of water before continuing. "We've opened Pandora's Box, that's for certain. Hal, based on what Knightmare told you about her connection to the Quantum Nanops, I have a working theory as to why your games seem to be based on real people and real events existing in the multiverse."

I felt the knots in my abdomen tighten, but morbid curiosity won the day. "Do tell."

"Have you ever heard of quantum clairvoyance," Irene asked.

I shook my head. I had not.

Irene nodded. "The quantum clairvoyance hypothesis states that everything in existence contains the information of everything else that exists. Every single atom holographically and energetically contains the information of the entire universe. The structure of the universe, the universe itself, *understands* itself. It's a potential scientific explanation for telepathy, clairvoyance, precognition, even connected souls. I believe you are a quantum clairvoyant, but to an exponential degree. Your ability's reach goes beyond our universe. I think you can see the multiverse. What you call a vivid imagination might be a powerful trans-dimensional flavor of quantum clairvoyance."

I considered my creative process. I'd wondered for years how I came up with the stuff I did. My parents, Victoria, colleagues, even Packard, would constantly comment on how unique my thought process was. But to me, it was just another day at the office. My head had always been my head. I'd lived with the thoughts and visions my entire life. I didn't know any other way to think. "That could explain a lot," I said finally.

Surprisingly, Clem asked the question undoubtedly on everyone's mind. "So, how do we stop them? The nannie-thingies?"

Kyle, who'd been even more quiet than usual, suddenly looked concerned. "Can we stop them without hurting us?"

Cool, who had also been uncharacteristically silent, turned to Kyle. "Bruh, that's what heroes do. We face danger, protect the innocent, stop evil nannies, and stuff. We risk life and limb, and sometimes face death."

Clem nodded. "It's a lawman's duty. I'd risk my life fer any of y'all."

Kyle shook his head. "Look, I'm not a real lawman, I'm just a kid. I don't have any skills or anything. Right, Packard?"

Packard grimaced uncomfortably. "Uh, yeah, that's kinda true..."

"Nobody's talking about anybody dying here," Gunner cut in, his deep voice causing Kyle to sit back in his seat nervously. "Clem just wanted to know if there's any way to stop the nannie-uhh, Nanops. I understand your concern, Kyle, but we need to let Irene answer the question. Okay?"

Kyle nodded as if Gunner had just scolded him.

Irene stood up and walked over to where Kyle was sitting and gently placed a hand on his shoulder. When she spoke, she was back in Morgan Freeman mode. She calmly directed her words of wisdom at Kyle, but spoke to everyone at the table. "Kyle, we know you didn't ask to be here. Neither did Becky, Clem, Cool, or any of the others that have been, well... appearing in this world." She removed her hand and walked over to a coffee maker against a far wall. As she continued, she popped a coffee pod into the top, and pressed the brew button. "I promise you, Kyle, my goal, and Hal's too, will be to figure out how to prevent the Quantum Nanops from bringing any new-"

Gunner raised a hand and interrupted Irene as politely as he could. In the time we'd known him, I'd never seen him interrupt anyone, especially not Irene. "Uh, Irene, I'm sorry about the interruption, but I think you should hold that thought for a moment." He held up his phone, though none of us could see what he was looking at. "I just got an alert, and we need to turn on the news."

~

"This is Belinda Sommerset with ABC 7 news, reporting live from San Francisco, where something is happening on the 83-acre lot that was once the home of the famed Candlestick Park. What exactly is happening on the coastal property is anyone's guess, but from where we're standing in Bay View Park, it looks like the old stadium, which was demolished in 2015, is magically rebuilding itself out of thin air."

The overdressed reporter, who looked like she'd been on her way to a red carpet event when the story broke, stepped aside, giving the cameraman full view of the mysterious happenings roughly a thousand feet away. It was exactly as she'd said. A massive structure, which resembled the former stadium that had stood on the land in the distance for more than fifty-five years, was somehow being pieced together. The new structure grew silently, seemingly from dust and particles that flew in from all sides.

Becky breathed out loudly, her breath shuddering. "Are those the Quantum Nanops?"

"I... uh... yes, Becky," Irene said. The thin veneer of Morgan Freeman calmness that had been there just moments before was gone. She forgot about the coffee she'd been brewing and stepped towards the 75-inch television screen mounted on the boardroom wall. "I think they are."

I felt like someone had just knocked the wind right out of me. My entire body went numb, and my mind felt like it was being forced through a sieve. "What have we done?"

Irene looked at me, eyes wide. All color had drained from her face. "Hal, Gunner, would you join me in the lab, please?" As Gunner and I stood, Irene looked at the others. "Kids, Clem, I need to talk to Hal and Gunner about something. We'll be back soon. Okay?"

Packard and the others nodded, though the three kids looked terrified. Even Clem and Cool looked unnerved, which shook me even more.

"We'll be right back," I assured them, before following Irene and Gunner down the hall.

~

Gunner and I followed Irene, who was walking at a considerably faster pace than usual, down an artificially lit corridor, past the nanoperating room, and into one of the many labs that existed within the inner sanctum. When we crossed the threshold, she closed the doors behind us and crossed her arms. She was in business mode.

She sighed, looking like she held the weight of the world on her fragile shoulders. "We need to decide what to do about them."

Gunner looked unsure of which 'them' Irene was referring to. "Them?"

Irene sighed again, clearly frustrated, frightened, and emotionally drained. "The Quantum Nanops, the NPCs, Packard, the building growing in the middle of a vacant lot in San freaking Francisco... *everything*!" She turned away from us, struggling with a rare bout of anger.

"Oh... I see," Gunner replied sheepishly. She was the only person I knew who could fluster him.

I waited for her to turn back and assessed her eyes before asking my own question. She was doing her best to quell the anger welling up inside, but I had to ask. "Any ideas? And not to beat a dead horse, but can we do this without hurting our visitors?" I paused, thinking for a moment. "And Packard? He seems to be governed by some of the same laws as the NPCs now. Any action we take could impact *my son.*"

That seemed to resonate with Irene's sensibilities. "I'm aware of that, but right now, we need to focus on stopping the spread of the Quantum Nanops, then we consider our next move."

Gunner cleared his throat before speaking. "I know we want to stop the Quantum Nanops in their tracks, but we need to consider the comfort of the others. We have three people, a cartoon giraffe — *I can't believe I just said that* — a horse, and automotive artificial intelligence who don't belong in our world and didn't ask to be here. I know you said we won't keep them prisoner, so I'm not suggesting we do that, but they are our responsibility. We should set up a place where they can at least be safe and reasonably comfortable until we figure out how to get them home. I don't know how big your place is, Hal, but I can't imagine it's big enough for everyone, and the horse has got to be an added complication. Not to mention, unless there's some reason to believe otherwise, that thing growing in San Francisco leads me to believe that we haven't seen the last NPC to show up. You mentioned they might not all be on the right side of the law. That makes me nervous as hell."

Irene clearly agreed. She took a deep breath before responding. "Yes, this has become a situation we never could have imagined. I think, for security reasons, they're going to need a place to stay that isn't your house, Hal. There are news agencies looking into the stadium land, which means local authorities and government agencies won't be far behind. We need to be ready to step in and take responsibility for this, but that would likely mean surrendering both of our facilities to the government in the process. If we do that, we won't stand a chance at stopping the Quantum Nanops. Government scientists, with no working knowledge of our accidental creation or the root source, would be ill-equipped to hammer out a solution. This is up to us." She walked to a large whiteboard on the wall and began scribbling notes. "Gunner, you'll oversee setting up living facilities for our guests. Arrange for a truck to retrieve the horse from Hal's home as well. As you stated, we might have more guests showing up, so set up the living environment in a location that can be flexible and easily repurposed. One of the warehouses that has close access to the gym showers and cafeteria should do. For security purposes, we'll have to keep personnel in that area restricted to a few of your key team members, so choose wisely. Hal and I will need to attack the situation from two ends: the Nanop aspect, and the quantum database."

"I'll need to head up to indGame headquarters in San Fran to access the database," I told her. "I'd like to take Packard with me, but we should talk to the others and gauge their frames of mind first. Honestly, if it helps keep our visitors calm, it might be best for Packard to remain here. I have a strong feeling he won't mind."

Irene jotted down some notes next to my name on the board.

Gunner turned to me, his expression and tone reminded me of a coach getting his prizefighter ready for a big bout in the ring. "I'd call ahead to your facility and increase security immediately. We don't know when or where new NPCs might pop up, but your team should be on heightened alert. Let them know we're hoping our visitors will be friendlies, but that may not be the case."

I nodded. "Is there a car I can use? I feel like KM should stay too. Does that make sense?"

They both nodded.

"You can use one of the security runabouts," Gunner replied. "They're EVs, so just remember to recharge it when you get to your facility. I'm going to call Jasmine at the gate. I want her on high alert as well."

Gunner walked about fifteen feet away and pulled his 2-way radio from its belt holster. "Unit nineteen, this is unit one. Come back."

Gunner's conversation became muted as he walked further away, so I turned back to Irene. "Any additional thoughts before we go talk to Packard and the others?"

She looked so sad at that moment, like she'd failed the world. Honestly, I felt the same way. "I think we both know this is not going to end well for any of us, Hal," she said.

Gunner returned, looking panicked. His next words superseded anything else Irene might have said. "They're gone!"

Irene caught her breath and dropped her dry-erase marker to the floor.

We both asked, "who's gone?"

Gunner shook his head. "Packard, Clem, Becky, the car, all of them. Jasmine said they left about two minutes ago. Packard said something about grabbing lunch. They must be headed for the stadium!"

I felt my head begin to swim. If Gunner and Irene hadn't gotten me moving at that moment, I might have fainted.

We sprinted down the hall to the boardroom, only to find it empty.

My son and the others were gone.

They'd even taken the Lanier.

LEVEL FIVE

WHAT'S THE WORST THAT COULD HAPPEN?

9

Roll 1 for Initiative

As soon as Dad, Irene, and Gunner left the room, Kyle went off. He was in panic mode. If there was anything I knew about panic from my years of interacting with NPCs, it was that it's more contagious than the most virulent virus.

Kyle paced back and forth as he began his rant. "Well, that went from being an all-inclusive, transparent conversation to, 'the grown-ups need to talk, and the kids aren't invited to the table', real fast!"

Clem screwed up his face a bit. "Yer forgettin' I'm a grown-up, young Kyle."

Becky put her hand on Kyle's shoulder, hoping to stop his pacing. "He's being figurative, Clem. He means they left us out of the conversation intentionally because they're talking about us… because we don't belong."

Clem and Cool both looked confused, but Clem voiced his confusion first. "Why is that a problem? They're the experts on whatever's hapnin' here, not us."

Kyle, still pacing, turned to Clem. "Because they're trying to figure out what to do with us, that's why!" He looked at Cool, whose emotional state was as pliable as his body. "We're a part of the problem, a fly in the ointment. Do you know what I'm saying?"

Cool nodded nervously. "Yeah, but I don't think Mr. Campbell or the others want to hurt us, if that's what you're thinking, dude. Besides, the Pack Man here is his son. They wouldn't hurt him." Cool looked at me, beginning to consider Kyle's paranoia. "Would they?"

"Of course they wouldn't," I replied defensively.

"But they also know you'd defend us if you went with them," Kyle shot back. "And like it or not, you're more like us than them. I mean, the word processor knew who you were, and you said you've got those, uh, Quantum Nanops in you, right?"

I knew Kyle was wrong, but I also knew there was no way to convince him otherwise. We were just going to have to wait until dad and the others came back and set things straight.

Kyle stopped in front of the Lanier. "We need to get out of here, now!" He unplugged the old word processor and tried to lift it, but realized he'd underestimated its weight. He turned to Cool. "Can you carry this?"

Cool reached out and carefully scooped it up like a claw in one of those toy-retrieval games. "No problemo, Kyle."

I couldn't believe what I was hearing. "Wait! What the hell are you guys doing," I asked loudly.

Kyle sidestepped to the door leading out into the hall. "We're leaving, bro. Or at least I am. You guys can do what you want, but I'd rather we stick together. Strength in numbers, you know?" Kyle's voice shook nervously. He wasn't used to standing up for himself, or making big decisions... any decisions, really. He was making up for lost time in a big and dangerous way.

I looked at Becky for some help, but she looked like she was ready to follow Kyle and Cool out the door. "Becky? What are you doing?"

She looked at me, her eyes full of that same panic I saw the day she'd materialized in our world. "Pack... we, uh... I don't know. I think we should go somewhere we can talk and put our heads together before we let the people who caused this decide our fates."

"That's my dad we're talking about, Beck," I replied. "He'd never hurt us."

Becky shrugged. "I know you want to believe that. I do too, but we can't risk it. We'll call him when we get somewhere safe, alright? We can hear what they have to say and decide what to do then. You have your cell phone, right?"

I nodded. "Yeah… but-"

Kyle bolted out the door. Cool watched him run to the elevator, and then looked back at me. "He's gonna be all alone, bruh."

Clem made his way to the door despite my obvious misgivings. "Like hell, he's gonna be alone. I don't think your pa would hurt us, nor would Irene or ol' Gunner, but Kyle's running' like a rabbit in a foxhole. Even if nobody else is goin' with him, I intend to." Clem pushed through the large office door and hot-footed it down the hall, calling after Kyle.

Becky tilted her head and looked me in the eyes again. "I promise we'll call your dad." And then she was out the door, too.

I shook my head. "I can't believe I'm saying this, but we're going with them, Cool."

Two minutes later, the Lanier was back in Knightmare's trunk, right next to the ice chest containing Clem's pistol. Another minute, and we were heading towards the security gate and Gunner's friend, Jasmine. Cool was once again on the floor, complaining about how bad Clem's feet stunk.

"If they smell so gol-durned bad, put yer head over by young Kyle's feet," Clem snapped, clearly tired of the criticism.

Jasmine looked at us suspiciously when we pulled up to the gate, clearly expecting to see dad behind the wheel. "Where's your father," she asked. Her eyebrows drew together, wrinkling her forehead comically, like a Shih Tzu puppy.

I smiled, trying not to come off as sus, but feeling like a kid who'd just been caught with his hand in the cookie jar. "We're just heading out for lunch," I replied. In a moment of pure inspiration, I asked her, "want us to bring anything back for you?" I sincerely hoped she'd say no, as I really didn't want to get her hopes up, only to leave her hanging.

She smiled, disarmed by my offer. "Nah, I've got a bag of trail mix in the guard station but thank you for asking." She pressed a button inside the shack, raising the flimsy wooden arm in front of us. "Enjoy your lunch," she called out as she waved us through.

A terrible pang of guilt washed over me as we pulled away from the gate and headed towards the 101. I'd defied my dad and maybe just cost Jasmine her job. I was an asshole.

Kyle leaned forward as Cool formed himself into a perfect duplicate of Clem, who did his best to ignore the unnerving transformation. "Where are we going," Kyle asked.

I shrugged, feeling guiltier than I could ever remember feeling. "Since we're out, we should go to the spot where the building is growing. If more of my friends from other worlds are going to show up, I figure that's as likely a place as any for it to happen."

Becky looked impressed. "That's solid deductive reasoning there, Einstein."

Cool leaned forward, placing his head right next to Kyle's excitedly. "You know Einstein?"

Becky turned, confused. "Uh, no. He died in like 1955."

Cool looked panicked. "He *what?!*"

"She's talking about a different Einstein, Cool," I assured him. "One of Cool's teammates on the Evolutants is named Einstein," I told Becky. "He's nothing like the Einstein from our world."

Cool grinned. The Clem face looked ridiculous with that enormous set of teeth. "He's the smartest dude alive, in our universe anyway, and he can fly!" Cool thought about it for a moment. "Oh, and he's a monkey."

"He's a Bili ape," I said.

Becky nodded. "Sure, because Cool's a giraffe. That makes sense."

Cool's grin widened. "Exactly!"

"Are you sure leaving your dad behind was the right thing to do, Packard," Knightmare suddenly asked as we veered onto the on ramp for the 280 north.

Kyle spoke up immediately. "Darned right it was! They were trying to decide what to do with us!"

"Based on my knowledge of Hal, Irene, and Gunner, I calculate a ninety-seven percent chance they would have offered us refuge and security," KM replied.

Becky looked at me, her eyes apologetic. "I'm sorry if we pushed you into leaving. It's easy to get caught up in the moment."

Kyle sat back, still feeling vindicated. "We did the right thing. Besides, if more of your friends show up, we need to be there for them. Right?"

"That's the only thing I'm going to agree with you on, Kyle," I said. "Otherwise, what we did was irresponsible and rude."

"Well, at least Clem agrees with me," Kyle huffed.

"I ain't never said no such thang," Clem countered. "I jest didn't want to see ya' out here on yer own."

Kyle stirred in his seat a bit. "Uh, well thanks, then," he said softly.

"We will arrive at the former home of Candlestick Park Stadium in 37 minutes," KM announced. "Police scanners indicate a roadblock at Harney Way and Hunter's Point Expressway, just three hundred feet from the reported phenomenon. Utilizing the dirt access road following the water's edge would bypass the roadblock with minimal additional time. Shall I plot a course including the revised directions?"

"Please," I replied. "And thank you, KM. The wheel's yours, girl. I hope you know how much I appreciate you."

"And I, you," KM replied as she merged onto the 85 north.

We were less than 40 minutes away from what I expected to be an important piece of my destiny, so I took a deep breath and closed my eyes.

10

Max Axe

The multiverse is a dangerous place. I should know, I've been there. Okay, so maybe not everywhere, but I've seen a lot of it.

There are more layers to the multiverse than a Chipotle bowl. Some of them are bright and colorful, while some are dark and depressing. Some of them have developed vibrant life, and others exist cold and barren. The physics of all the universes existing within the multiverse, as they relate to each other, obey a similar set of laws that you would find across an individual universe. The laws of gravity, spacetime, matter, entropy, inertia, and more, are mutable depending upon where you are in the universe. They can have profound effects upon each other, given the presence or absence of factors that the unique laws rely upon to even be necessary.

Science talk. Sorry, my mom's an astrophysicist, so I picked up her love for all things astrophysics and techie. In simple terms, think of two mirrors angled against each other, so you can see an infinite hallway of sorts. Then imagine each successive mirror in the reflection as a layer of the multiverse. The closer the reflection, or *universe* in our case, is to the originating mirrors, the more like your universe it is. But as you get farther away, the reflections become hazy, dark, and sometimes play tricks on our perception. The more realities you skip over, the more differences you'll find between your universe of origin and your destination.

Have I blown your mind yet? Well, hang on to your butts, because the best is yet to come.

My dad is a musician. Between him and my mom, they discovered how to manipulate spacetime using harmonics. I grew up watching them conduct time based studies, spatially based research, and finally multi-phasic-interdimensional experiments.

It only seemed natural that I would follow in their footsteps. Instead of following, though, I inadvertently paved the way for the next phase in their experiments, the human trials. I became an unwitting pioneer in the field when I plugged my guitar, Max, who I'll introduce in a minute, into one of the harmonic dilation modules. It worked nicely at first. The wormhole I created was stable, and I could manipulate it easily by pressing and plucking the strings. It was cool as hell, until it wasn't.

So, here's where things went wrong. In my defense, I never could have foreseen what happened next. I accidentally destabilized the wormhole when I tapped my tuning fork on Max. The next few moments were a blur of motion and sound. Before I knew it, I was lying on top of Max in a dark, muddy field in the rain. A pair of dad's titanium drumsticks lay next to my head and the tuning fork was a few feet away, sticking out of a puddle, glowing like green neon.

I tried to reach for the tuning fork, but my equilibrium was totally off-kilter. I rolled over and puked instead.

~

After I regained my sea legs, I gathered my drumsticks, tuning fork, and Max. I had to find shelter from the rain. The steady pitter-patter of droplets was turning into a genuine downpour. Max was not made for that type of abuse. To be honest, neither was I.

Sheets of rain blew past me like angry, wet swarms of hornets, and I shielded my face with my forearms. I looked down at my black leather jacket. While the leather was technically waterproof, if exposed to enough of the deluge, it was going to stink like a wet dog the next day. My knee-high leather boots were a bit of a blessing under the circumstances, as wet socks are *never* okay.

I turned in a slow circle, looking for any sign of shelter or civilization. On my second go, I spotted the tiniest flicker of light in the distance. I took my phone out of my pocket. After turning on the flashlight, I pulled my hoodie, which I wore under my leather jacket, up over my head. With my phone shielded by my jacket sleeve, I ran towards the light.

I traveled at least two hundred yards before I was even sure I was actually seeing a source of light. It flickered continuously. At first, I assumed the falling rain was tricking my eyes, but as I got closer, I recognized the light to be a fire, and a big one at that!

I continued to run forward, keeping my light trained on the ground in front of me. Wherever I was, it looked nothing like my hometown of Seattle. It looked more like pictures I'd seen of Ireland, or the Scottish Highlands. I sprinted through a muddy bog, overrun with thick grass and ancient-looking trees with gnarled branches that seemed to be begging for a handout in the worst, most terrifying way. Rocks the size of shopping carts and moss-covered tree limbs littered the landscape, making my trek to the beacon of light perilous at best. I tripped more than once, but the bog was damp, and thankfully my jeans and pride were the only casualties.

I ran for what seemed like several minutes before I was finally close enough to see the source of the fire. It was a lone one-story building. As I got closer, I could hear shrieking and yelling.

A few feet more and everything became clear, despite the steady downpour.

A group of about six men were tying a young woman to a post at the center of a woodpile. One of them shouted to the others when he saw my light. "It be another of them," he called out. "Another devil! It carries the light of Satan in its palm!"

"Get it," one of the other men, who was busy manhandling the screaming woman, said loudly. "We'll burn them together!"

I stopped dead in my tracks when I heard the exchange. *Burn?* "Oh, hell no!"

My would-be assailant had a rope in his hand, and he let a short length of it drop as he ran towards me. The moment he swung it in an arc over his head, I realized there was a metal hook the size of my boot attached to it.

He swung the hook directly at my face. If I hadn't slipped in the mud, he would have reeled me in like Charlie the Tuna! I stood back up and put my phone back into my pocket. "No Satan here, guys! Just a lost kid!"

The hook swung again, missing me by less than an inch, and the man advanced once more.

I can't really say what I was thinking, but as if by reflex, I grabbed Max by the neck and swung! My attacker ducked, but quickly discovered just how slippery the mud was where I was standing. He slipped backwards, pinwheeling his arms like a kid on a balancing beam. A moment later, he hit the ground and his head struck one of the moss-covered logs littering the surrounding land with a loud crack. I stared at the man, my jaw slack with disbelief. I was no biologist, but the angle his neck was twisted at looked very wrong.

One of the other men lashing the poor woman to the wooden post shouted, "he's killed Alaric! The devil killed brother Alaric!"

I held Max over my head, not caring about what got wet anymore. "What don't you people understand about *not a devil*!"

They didn't care about anything I said. Satisfied that the young woman was well-secured to the post, the remaining five men came after me.

If they were scared of a devil, then it was time to give 'em hell! "Back," I shouted, swinging Max like a battle flag. "I didn't have to hit your brother with my axe to kill him. It's a... uh, magical axe! And I can cut you down from right here!"

The men stopped and looked at each other, eyes widening in the light from the building burning behind them.

"Prove it," one of the men shouted defiantly.

Another man slapped my challenger across the face. "Damn you, Daegal! Never challenge a devil, lest ye be stricken down, or possessed!"

That gave me an idea. "I choose the one known as Daegal as my champion! He will fight you men on my behalf! He is now my puppet, and I, his master!"

All the color drained from Daegal's already vitamin D deficient complexion. "What are you talking-"

A large stick swung at Daegal's head. He blocked it, reflexively swinging back at his assailant.

"Excellent, Daegal! Now finish them," I hollered.

One of Daegal's companions swung a stick at the back of his knee, dropping him to the ground. Daegal scrambled away, getting to his feet and facing his companions, stick held out defensively before him. Oh, how the tables had turned!

"Now leave," I shouted. "All of you! Before I turn you all into my minions and make you, uh, e-eat each other's shoes! Yeah!"

And that did it. The men disappeared into the distance, tripping over every log and rock in their path, but still taking every opportunity to pick up sticks and stones and hurl them at Daegal as they ran. It was like an old Three Stooges moment, but scary, and with fire and hooks on ropes.

I suddenly realized the woman was screaming at me. I moved closer and heard her say, "my father! My father is inside!"

I ran to the door of the burning building and kicked it in. Fire erupted in a whoosh. It probably would have killed me if not for the torrential rain and the fact that I was soaked to the skin and covered with mud.

I dropped to the ground and crawled towards the doorway. There was a man lying a few feet inside. He wasn't moving, but he didn't appear burned. There was a hole in the ceiling above him, which allowed the rain to drench him right where he lay.

I put on my sunglasses and tightened my hoodie, leaving just enough room to see out of, but covering my nose and mouth with the wet fabric. Then, without really thinking anything else through, I crawled in to retrieve the man.

Though I was rain soaked and covered in denim and leather, the heat felt like taking a shower on the sun. I took hold of one of the man's ankles and pulled. A few moments later, I dragged him across the threshold, gasping for air and grateful for the cold rain. My lungs burned as I drew in air, and I knew I'd damaged them during the rescue. The question was, how badly.

~

When I rolled over, I saw the woman had finally freed herself. She ran over to where her father and I were sprawled out in the gloriously cool mud.

She reached under her father's head and shoulders and raised his face to her cheek, cradling him gently, rocking and weeping. If you've ever wondered if you can tell the difference between tears and rainwater on a person's face, I can tell you, proof positive, it's not hard.

Then, something miraculous happened. Had I not seen it with my own eyes, I never would have believed it, so I don't blame you if you don't... though it *would* help to usher the story along if you did. The woman, who didn't look any older than me, began to glow. It was a soft, hazy, whitish-blue emanation, more like a bioluminescent mist than artificial lighting or sunlight. Wisps of the mysterious light wafted off her like smoke and surrounded her father like a writhing, radiant cocoon. She extended her free hand to me. Without an ounce of trepidation, I extended my own, allowing our fingertips to touch. Our fingers intertwined, and I watched in detached amazement as the glowing mist crept from her fingertips to mine and quickly surrounded me as well.

For the barest of moments, it felt like my lungs were outside my body, taking in oxygen and what felt like sunlight. And then it was over. Her hand released mine and the soft blue mist surrounding me vanished. She continued to cradle her father, however, and the beautiful blue cocoon pulsed rhythmically. She hummed softly and rocked on her haunches.

As I watched her, I realized it no longer hurt to breathe. At that moment, I knew what she was doing. She was trying to heal her father.

~

Several minutes passed. I could see her eyes begin to flutter. She was getting tired. I was just about to say something, you know, suggest that maybe her dad was gone, when he suddenly gasped for air like a fish out of water!

The girl breathed a faint sigh of relief and almost fell backward. I reached out and steadied her before she collapsed. The glowing light enveloped me once more, causing me to shiver uncontrollably. I let her lean against me and reached out with my right hand, keeping her dad's head from slipping off her lap and into the mud.

Lightning crackled overhead, causing my muscles to tingle. My thoughts lit up like the wall of monitors from *The Matrix*. Images I'd never seen and languages I'd never heard flooded my mind like so many raindrops. I suddenly heard the girl's voice among all the others, gently coaxing me to focus on her alone. "…to me," she was saying. "Follow my voice to me."

Then my world went black.

~

When I finally regained consciousness, I was in a bed in a small, damp-smelling room. The building appeared to have been constructed out of stones and wood. The ceiling was unfinished, giving me a full view of the crisscrossing beams that held up the stained, wooden roof. I tried to move, but my body felt like I'd just fallen off my skateboard and into the path of an oncoming train.

"Don't try to move," the girl's voice instructed from across the room. "You're not ready for that yet." She crossed the room in three strides and smiled at me. "Welcome back to the land of the living."

"Thanks," I croaked. "I'm sorry if you've already told me, but where are we and who are you?"

The girl shook her head. "Nay, I've not told you anything yet. But there are no secrets here. You're in Lower Cairnshire. My name is Revna."

"Why did you bring me here," I asked before remembering her dad. "Is your father okay?"

"Thanks to you, he will be," Revna smiled. "You saved both our lives, so I owed you at least this much." Her smile faded. "You're no devil though, I can tell you that."

"I might be," I countered. "You don't know me."

Revna's smile returned. "You're no more devil than I am. And I'd bet a gold coin against those odds… if I had one." She glanced at a corner by a stone hearth, where a modest fire was crackling. My clothes were hanging across a clothesline a few feet from the fireplace. On a chair about four feet from the flames were Max, my drumsticks, my tuning fork, and my phone. "And that instrument is no more an axe than this shack is a castle. I'll tell you what you are, though."

"I'll bite," I said. "What am I?"

"You're equal parts brave and insane. Don't get me wrong, I appreciate that about you. My father and I would be wet piles of ash if it weren't for your quick thinking." Revna walked over to Max. "It may not be an actual axe, but it is a finely made instrument. Perhaps the finest I've ever seen." She picked Max up gently and brought him to my bedside. "I hope you don't mind, but I had to channel some of the Blue into your instrument."

She might as well have been talking in riddles. "The Blue?"

"You know, the healing energy we shared. When you kept me from falling over, you got more of the Blue than you should've, and the lightning channeled one of the Blue's spirits right into you." She patted Max. "I had to act quickly to get the spirit outta you. And I needed someplace to put it… so it went into your axe that isn't really an axe."

Did I hear that right? "You put a spirit into my guitar?"

"Better than in your head," she countered. "Wouldn't you agree?"

"I certainly do," a melodic voice agreed.

I looked around the room again. "Was that your dad talking?"

"Nay." She smiled and shook her head slowly. I think she assumed I was being deliberately obtuse. "It was your, uh, git arr? Is that what you called it?"

I looked at Max. He was clean and dry, and polished to a shine. I tilted my head curiously. "So, you're telling me you channeled a spirit into Max?"

"Aye." She smiled, looking as confused as I felt. "Is that not regarded as normal where you come from?"

"Uh… no…" I replied, wondering if I was hallucinating.

The third voice spoke again. "I can confirm. This instrument has never hosted a spirit. Furthermore, the materials used in its construction are not of this Earth."

Revna's eyes widened. "Where are you from, friend?"

I tried to sit, but found my body less than cooperative. "Seattle… Washington?"

Revna's eyebrows raised. "I've never heard of such a place. Is it far from here?"

I thought about what had happened in the last hour, probably more, since I had clearly been unconscious for a while. Nothing made sense. I was playing guitar in the lab, and sciencing with my tuning fork when… what? What actually happened? The only thing I could think of was the wormhole. But if I'd come through one, then where was I? And how was I

supposed to get home? "I think I'm a very long way from home,"

I said finally. I looked at the chair where my things were

sitting. "Would you mind handing me my phone?"

Revna looked at the chair curiously. "Fone," she asked.

"It's the flat, rectangular, shiny thing," I replied.

My host retrieved my phone and handed it to me. "It looks

like polished, black glass," she commented, making conversation.

I pressed a button on the side and the screen lit up,

illuminating the room better than the fireplace. Though I still had

eighty-one percent of my battery life, without a place to charge it,

that would go fast. I checked my signal and found I had zero

bars. In fact, the words 'No Network' had replaced the bars

altogether. I'd never even seen that happen before. I looked up at

Revna, who was staring at my phone's screen like it was a UFO or

something. "Do you have an electrical outlet and maybe a charging cable?" I already knew the answer to my question. I was fairly certain I wasn't in Kansas anymore.

Revna stared at my phone as she answered. "I don't know what those are, friend." She finally tore her gaze away from my hand. "Are you a devil?"

The question shocked me. "Wha- no! I'm just a kid who shoulda taken a left turn at Albuquerque."

Revna looked at me suspiciously, unimpressed with my attempt at humor. "I ask again, are you a devil?"

I turned off the phone screen and shadows cast by the firelight resumed their dark dance on the surrounding walls. "I'm not a devil. I promise. I'm a lost kid, and I'm afraid I'm a really long way from my home."

She nodded at my phone. "If you're not a devil, explain that... thing."

"It's a cell phone," I replied. "Where I come from, we use these to talk to each other and research things. I also use it to take pictures, listen to music, and watch videos."

Revna had no clue what I was talking about. "Vid-yos?"

"Uh… moving pictures," I replied. "I'll show you some if you'd like."

She nodded at the offer, and I turned the screen back on. I pulled up a video of my mom and dad I'd recorded at Christmas. "Come look," I said, beckoning her to my bedside.

Revna watched the video, slack-jawed.

I knew the scene well, as I'd posted it on social media a few months earlier. Dad had bought mom tickets for a European riviera cruise, and I'd caught her reaction on film. "That's my mom and dad," I told her.

When the video ended, she looked up at me, shaken. "How is that possible?"

I shrugged. "I don't know how it works, to be honest. I'm a musician." Then inspiration struck. "Say, would you like to hear my music?"

She nodded, still trying to make sense of my phone.

"You know, where I come from, we don't have, uh..." What had she called it? "The Blue. We don't have healing magic or the ability to channel disembodied spirits, either."

Revna looked stunned. "Then how do you heal your sick and injured," she asked.

"We have doctors," I told her. "And the doctors have machines that assist them. They're nothing more than tools, but I suppose to someone who'd never seen them, they could look like witchcraft... like your 'Blue' looks like witchcraft to me."

She considered what I'd just said. "And what would you say if it was?"

"Was what," I asked.

Revna shook her head, looking frustrated. "Witchcraft. What would you say if it was witchcraft?"

I shrugged again. "I'd be surprised, curious even, but not scared."

"It is witchcraft," Revna said softly.

I thought about it for a moment. "Is that why Daegal and his merry band of arsonists were trying to burn you and your father?"

She dropped her head. "Aye. But da isn't a witch. Only me."

I wasn't sure what to make of her admission. "And you were grilling me about being a devil," I asked finally.

Revna's expression darkened. "Witchcraft calls on the good spirits of the Blue to help and to heal. Sorcery calls forth bad spirits and devils for the most wicked, evil purposes! The two practices are nothing alike," she replied angrily. "Nothing!"

"Okay," I said softly, "like I said, I know as little about your world as you know about mine. What do you say we stop making assumptions and get to know each other instead?"

Revna sighed. "Aye. I am sorry about my questions, but you and your belongings are strange to me."

While we talked, I pulled up my music catalog on my phone. There were several hundred songs by almost as many artists, but there was one musician in particular I wanted her to hear. Me. On my world, my fans know me as 'The Bohemian Renegade'.

11

Max Axe
Verse Two: The Bohemian Renegade

What can I say? I freaking love music. I've tried my hand at every instrument I could get my fingers on. According to some major players in the industry, I've got a long, lucrative future to look forward to in music! Well, that was until I opened a wormhole and catapulted myself into a parallel universe. Now all I want for my future is to get home. But that story is for later. I don't want to get too far ahead of myself.

Like I said, my fans call me 'The Bohemian Renegade'. It's my stage name. My family calls me Packard, but pretty much everyone else I'm close to calls me Bo... you know, short for Bohem- ah, you get it, right? I never cared for the mansplaining thing.

Anyway, not really thinking about how fast my phone battery would go, I scrolled through several of my songs before settling on a musical masterpiece I called 'Snake in the Grass'. I could've played 'She', 'Leave it to Me', 'You Had Me at Goodbye', 'The Ballad of Unicycle Sam', or any of my hundred and one other songs, but Snake was a good all-around showcase for my skills.

Revna's expression was worth the wait. She caught her breath as she listened to my version of magic. From my blazing guitar work to my throbbing percussion and dark keyboard-driven overtones, I had her hooked from the first note to, well, almost the last. Her dad came in before the song could finish.

Revna turned guiltily, like he'd caught her doing something wrong. "Da, I wasn't expecting you back so soon."

Her father looked at my phone through narrowed eyes. "What have ye there, son?"

I turned off the song and looked at Revna, but her smile had faded into a blank, solemn mask of long-practiced sobriety. "It's my cell phone, sir. You might have guessed, but I'm not from around here. I brought it with me, from where I came from."

The man, clearly no stranger to hard labor, folded a pair of huge, grime-smeared arms in front of him. Thick scars, which looked like cables placed just beneath his skin, crisscrossed his forearms and the backs of his hands. "From the pits of the Horned One," he asked, his nostrils flaring.

I wanted to say something funny, you know, like about Seattle being the pits, but I was sure it was neither the time nor the place to try my hand at standup comedy. Instead, I simply replied, "no sir."

"Then throw that accursed devilry into the fire," he growled.

I knew I shouldn't have argued, but what was this, Florida? "What? This phone cost me more than a thousand dollars!"

"And it'll cost ye your life if ye don't," he shouted. "Now do it! It's a well-known fact, a devil cannot remain on this mortal plain without its totem! One of three things is about to happen: ye'll refuse and I'll kill ye where ye stand, ye'll comply and vanish along with yer devilry, or ye'll watch that demon stone burn alongside me an' my daughter and I'll humbly recant my claim."

About a minute later, I begrudgingly accepted his apology. The exchange took place outside, however, in a much colder, wetter setting than the small stone building. We had to vacate the home because of the toxic gases released when the lithium-ion battery caught fire. Noxious plumes of carbon dioxide, carbon monoxide, and hydrogen fluoride — yeah, I did well in chemistry — poured into the room faster than the crooked chimney could expel them upward. We were lucky the battery didn't actually explode.

We watched as the thick smoke billowed out of the chimney in gray and white clouds. Strands of muted colors that looked like I'd thrown Skittles into the fire with my beloved phone rode the rising tide of smoke. The colors prompted Revna's father, who'd finally identified himself as Darbinyan, to proclaim the phone accursed, though he also accepted I was an unwitting carrier, and thus innocent of devilry and malicious chicanery.

Though I was suddenly phoneless and standing in the rain covered in nothing but some sort of hairy animal skin, I took the concession as a small victory. As sad as I was to see my phone burn, it was indeed a small price to pay for my life. *Not today, Horned One... not today.*

We relocated to a large, semi-open building adjacent to Darby's home to escape the torrential rains. Upon stepping inside, a surprisingly intense level of heat assaulted my senses. I wondered why we hadn't come into the larger building first, but after a few minutes inside the hot, stuffy room, I understood. Darby explained that he was a blacksmith, and the large room was his shop. He apologized, telling me that he had to keep the shop hot and stuffy to help keep the metal pliable and easy to work with. At the center of the shop was a large, open, stone hearth. A tall, lanky, dark-complected kid, barely older than me stood at the mouth of the massive forge, sweating profusely as he worked an impossibly large bellows, stoking the fire, and coaxing the flames ever-higher.

Around the edges of the shop, hammers, tongs, anvils, chisels, and files of various sizes and shapes hung from the walls and lay scattered across workbenches.

In one corner of the shop, I spotted a hefty, belt-driven grinding wheel. A bucket of what looked like water or oil lay a few feet away.

"Torsten," Darby shouted, "come here and meet our guest!"

The young man let the bellows, suspended by three lengths of heavily corded rope, swing away from the forge, safe from potential damage. He ambled over to us in a few long strides, and extended a strong, grimy hand. His smile was genuine, and I wasn't going to let a little soot get in the way of a potential friendship.

"I'm Torsten," he announced, his voice deeper than I might have expected.

"Bo," I replied, easily matching his smile. Then I turned to Revna and Darby and repeated my name. "Bo. Since nobody asked before demanding I burn my phone."

Revna gritted her teeth in a clearly uncomfortable grimace, while Darby shuffled his feet and defiantly mumbled something about the Horned One.

Several hours passed before we were able to reoccupy the stone home, and by the time we did, everything inside reeked of the toxic smoke. My clothes were going to smell like chemicals for a very long time, but as sad as I was about their condition, my heart sank when I saw Max.

While he wasn't burned, the thick, oily smoke that had been swirling close to the fireplace had discolored his entire body. Short of stripping down several layers of his beautifully lacquered paint job, I didn't think anything would ever get him clean.

Then I saw the worst of it. Max's neck and pickguard had warped, and his fretboard had developed cracks.

I must have cried out when I saw him because Revna, who was standing behind me, put one of her hands on my shoulder and the other on the opposite bicep.

"I'm sorry," she whispered. "I'm so sorry."

I turned and looked her square in the eye. "If it wasn't for your dad's superstitious crap, I'd still have my phone and my guitar! Now all I have to my name, besides my clothes, are my drumsticks and a tuning fork!"

Darby stepped through the doorway when he heard my raised voice. "What's going on in here," he demanded.

Revna put herself between her father and me. "The smoke and heat damaged Bo's axe, uh, git arr." She nodded back at Max. "It's our fault, da. If you'd just trusted him-"

"What reason did I have to trust him," Darby shouted.

Revna finally raised her voice. Based on Darby's expression, I gathered the response was rare. "What reason did he have to save our lives? What reason did he have to fight those men on our behalf? What reason did he have to crawl into a burning stable to pull you from the brink of the pit?" She placed the tip of her index finger firmly on his chest. "You were dead, da. Dead. I was as good as dead. But Bo risked his life to save us both. You tell me what reason!"

Darby's face dropped for a moment. When he looked back up, he had a half-cocked grin plastered across his old, weathered face. His eyes twinkled mischievously, and he nodded. "That's my girl," he whispered before his grin became a full-blown smile only a proud parent could understand. "That's my strong girl." He craned his neck so he could see me. "She's fierce, isn't she? Believe me, I've seen her stand up to men bigger and stronger than me and kick their arses to boot. But standing up to me? I've been waiting to see what would finally bring that on." Darby reached out and hugged his daughter. "I'm proud of ye, daughter... so damned proud." Then he looked around her at me again. "And I'm sorry about yer axe, son. The devil-stone, nay, not at all sorry. But yer instrument... aye, I'm truly sorry. If ye'll allow me to, I can fix it."

I sighed and looked back at Max, my heart breaking all over again. "No offense, but you're a blacksmith. How would you know how to repair a guitar?"

Darby nodded. "I can understand why ye might doubt me, but my shop is quite advanced, and I'm more than adept at smithing, woodworking, and even some of the finer arts. Not to mention, I'm no stranger to stringed instruments."

The disembodied voice had been quiet for hours, but apparently Darby's offer struck a nerve, or would that be a chord? "Good Sir Darbinyan, if I am to continue to inhabit this vessel, it should be in suitable condition. Therefore, I offer a vote of confidence in your skills. I would humbly ask, however, if moving forward you might refer to me by this instrument's given name, if my carrier would allow it?"

Darby and Revna looked at me curiously.

Revna nodded at me. "That would be you, Bo. You're the carrier."

I was surprised, moved, and frankly a little overwhelmed by the suggestion. Though I didn't have the same blind faith in Darby, I couldn't argue with Max. "Uh, Max, yeah... I could call you that. But what about your name?"

The voice was silent for a moment. When it finally replied, it sounded confused. "My... name?"

"The spirits don't have names," Revna explained. "They have no need for them where they come from. On our plane, however, their carrier gets the honor of bestowing a name upon them. It's rare, but not unheard of, for a spirit to choose their own. But the carrier makes the final decision. What say you? Will you let the spirit choose the name?"

I was unable to process any real, coherent thought at that moment, though I couldn't think of any reason why I shouldn't continue to call my guitar Max. "I've never known a spirit before, and, uh, I've only ever called my guitar Max anyway, so... ok." I spoke directly to my guitar, unsure of where else to look. "But only on one condition. You have to call me Bo."

~

Following that surreal exchange, Darby gently retrieved Max from the old chair, and cradling him like a baby, took him to his blacksmith's shop. While he and Torsten went to work on my poor guitar, Revna and I turned to face the sooty mess the burned phone had created. Though my clothes reeked of smoke and battery chemicals, they were completely dry. I had Revna turn around while I changed back into them. I won't lie, I wasn't at all sad to be free of the old animal skin.

Revna wanted to air out their home, but the continuing torrential rains limited what we could do to counter the malodorous residue. After more than an hour of wiping, scrubbing, and dusting, Revna looked at the bed I'd been sleeping in earlier and smiled. "Fight fire with fire," she said matter-of-factly.

I was stunned. "The smell will go away eventually," I said. "You don't have to burn the place."

Revna laughed. Clearly my take on her phraseology amused her. "We're not burning the house," she replied, pulling a small, wooden box out from under the bed. "We're just going to burn some incense."

~

I really don't know what I expected when Darby said he could fix Max, but I think I was expecting it to take a few hours.

Boy was I wrong.

I spent three long days cooped up with Revna in that one room shack, with nothing to do but play UNO. *Oh, yeah*, I was lucky enough to find an old UNO deck in my inside jacket pocket. I can't even tell you how the deck got there, but without my phone or guitar, or even anything to write music on, the cards saved my sanity. Revna was a quick study, and before long, I was getting skipped, reversed, and drawing more cards than I remembered actually being in the deck. I didn't mind losing, though. It was a fun way to pass the time.

Eating, sleeping, and singing my songs for Revna monopolized the balance of the days. I stretched my legs a bit by making dreaded trips to the spider-infested outhouse and occasionally retrieving ingredients for our meals from the root cellar, which was thankfully too cold and damp to appeal to the local spider population.

Close to the end of the third day, Darby returned with a burlap wrapped package and a mischievous gleam in his eyes. "Break out the ale, daughter," he grinned. "It's time to celebrate my finest work ever."

Revna promptly disappeared down a ladder into the root cellar and returned with a small cask of what I could only assume was ale. I know I was underage, but I'd been drinking rancid rainwater for three days and had stools looser than a politician's moral code. *Anything* would be a welcome change.

While Revna poured three tankards of the bitter-smelling liquid, Darby set the burlap package on their heavy, butcher-block table.

"Go ahead, son," he prompted. "Open it."

I reached for the burlap wrappings and began to pull them away excitedly. Darby put a hand on a section of the material, warning me to be careful, *lest I cut myself.*

I looked at what I knew to be Max, hidden underneath a layer of the heavy, woven material. I was confused, to say the least. "Cut myself?"

Darby nodded, grinning. "Trust me. Start with the neck."

I did as he said and pulled the material down from the neck. What lay before me was nothing short of art. The 1958

Gibson Explorer that had come through the wormhole with me was still there in spirit, no pun intended, but so much of Max had been upgraded. I ran my fingers down the back of the neck, feeling the smooth, flawless wood on the backside as my thumb ran between the first and second strings, tracing the fretboard. I felt the new nuts and frets that Darby had lovingly inlaid at precise intervals. He had polished the tuning pegs and posts and reintegrated them into the new headstock. The old Gibson decal was gone. The original strings had also been reintegrated and ran down beyond the burlap folds that still covered the mystery that was Max's body. I pulled the final folds open and gasped when I saw my old friend's most significant upgrade. While Darby had placed the bridge, saddles, and pickups back into the body, he mounted a new metallic pickguard, covering most of the surface, in place of the old white one. The pickup switch, jack, and volume and tone knobs had been sunken in to accommodate what appeared to be a new tremolo arm. But the one thing that positively took my breath away, was a two-foot-long, crimson-hued, curved axe blade that spanned the entire length of the lower half and the boxed end of Max's body! Max looked like Gibson guitars had gone into the executioner's blade market.

I looked at Darby, unsure of what to say.

He grinned knowingly. "Now Max is truly an Axe," he declared loudly. "Go ahead, pick him up, but mind yer fingers. The blade'll take the wings off a gnat in flight."

"I can vouch for that," Max said proudly. "He's already done it twice."

I took Max's neck and carefully lifted my old friend. Darby had replaced the old leather strap with a length of shimmering black hide. It hung loosely as I shifted my guitar in my hands, adjusting my grip. "You've put on weight," I said, not even hiding my surprise.

Darby's grin broadened. "The neck and most of the body are now a solid slab of Lignum Vitae, the strongest wood known. I keep a small supply on hand for axe and mallet hafts, as well as the gear-shafts for my grinders. It's heavy, but I've found it to be more resilient than most metals. The thicker body, iron blade, and internal mechanics also add to the weight, but ye'll get used to it."

He lost me with the last phrase. "Internal mechanics?"

"Oh, aye," he said, grinning. "Just pull on the lever. Ye'll see."

I placed my hand on the tremolo bar and gave it a gentle tug. The huge, crimson blade, which I suddenly realized was mounted in two parts, retracted deftly into a set of long slots that ran along the front and lower edge of Max's body, completely obscuring them from view.

Darby nodded at Max. "There were metallic connections under the surface far beyond my understanding, so I left them in place, but made no attempt at reconnecting them. Max is strong, durable, dangerous, and dare I say, playable, but ye'll have to tend to the odd mechanics yerself. A series of small iron gears controls the movement of the blades, so unless something gets inside and mucks up the works, or ye forget to add a bit of lubricant, they'll work for a good long time."

Torsten, reeking of body odor and heated metal, entered the room while Darby was explaining. Revna retrieved a fourth tankard and poured him a healthy serving of ale.

Torsten pointed at Max with his tankard, splashing the floor with droplets of sweat and ale in the process. "Did you tell him about the dragon bones?"

I must have looked more bewildered than usual because all three of my benefactors laughed at my expression.

Darby reached out and ran a finger along one of the frets. "They're dragon bone, son. Every last one of 'em. Sure, they're rare and coveted on the shadow market, but considering ye saved my daughter's life, and my miserable own, I figured it was the least I could do."

"They're magical, too," Torsten said, looking very pleased with their work. "As are the blades, which were cooled and folded in undiluted dragon's blood, also quite rare."

I knew they told me Max was tough, durable, and all, but I felt like I was holding a nuclear warhead or something. "Dragon's blood?"

Revna looked confused. "Do you not have dragons where you come from?"

I shook my head. "Um… no. No dragons, spirits, Blue healers, none of that."

Revna shook her head. "Then what do you do for fun?"

"I played Max," I replied. Those simple words felt like the first sane thing I'd said in days.

Revna smiled. "Bo does have a nice singing voice," she told the others.

"Play us a tune," Darby prompted. "Something to commemorate the occasion!"

I cradled Max carefully. "I don't have a pick, and Max hasn't been tuned."

Revna pulled a length of lanyard out of her top, revealing what looked like a slightly oversized guitar pick hanging from the end. She removed the lanyard from around her neck and handed it to me. "Consider it a gift, for saving our lives and teaching me the Oooo No."

Darby looked at us suspiciously. "Oooo no?"

Revna shook her head at her father. "Grow up, da. It's a game, played with cards."

Darby blushed and shuffled his feet a bit while tending to his tankard.

I looked at the pick she'd handed me. It shimmered like the inside of an abalone shell. "Wow, thank you. I suppose now you're going to tell me this is a dragon's scale?"

She nodded. "I thought you didn't have dragons where you come from. How did you know?"

I shook my head. If I ever made it home, mom and dad would never believe my story. "Just a… good guess… I guess." I pointed at the hearth, where we'd placed my things. "Would you hand me my tuning fork, please?"

Revna picked up my tuning fork and frowned. "Where are your sticks," she asked.

Torsten reached into his pocket. "Oh, damn! I almost forgot." He handed me my drumsticks, now connected by a ten-inch-long, crimson chain. "I improved them," he said, "but I'll say, boring into that metal was akin to laboring in the pits of the

Horned One. Harder than anything I've worked with that hadn't

been forged with dragon's blood."

"They're titanium," I said, letting one drop loosely and

realizing that I now owned a set of lethal looking nunchucks...

er... drumchucks?

"Oh, what I could do with titanium and dragon's blood,"

Torsten marveled.

I placed my drumchucks into my inside jacket pocket and

put Max's strap over my neck and right shoulder. Then I held out

my hand for my tuning fork, which Revna passed along with a

smile.

I struck the tuning fork on the edge of the large table and

set the base against the table's surface. Revna reached in and

steadied the fork for me while I plucked the thinnest string... *and*

opened a new wormhole.

The portal pulled me in like a feather into a vacuum cleaner. It churned me around a bit in what I can only describe as *the black void*, a place of absolute darkness, and a bipolar gravitational system that pushes and pulls at the same time. Every time I pass through one, I come out feeling like human silly putty. Then I puke like I've just been spinning in a hypersonic gyroscope.

That particular wormhole deposited me in the middle of what appeared to be a barren desert wasteland. Max was sticking out of the sand next to me, and my tuning fork was conspicuously glowing that chroma-key tone of green again.

As I reached for Max, I suddenly heard more retching. Unless Max was now prone to inner ear issues, I wasn't alone.

I rolled back, feeling my stomach lurch again. I closed my eyes and counted to ten before finally trying to speak. "Hello," I asked weakly. "Who's there?"

"Revna," a weak voice responded from the other side of the closest dune. "Is that you, Bo?"

"Yeah, it's me," I muttered, wishing I had something to rinse my mouth out with. "Is your da or Torsten here?"

She didn't respond, but neither did anyone else.

I heard her shuffling in the sand. She was clearly having the same issues as I was. "Da? Torsten? Are you there?"

Crickets. Only we were in the desert, so no, not even crickets. Hell, I didn't even see a vulture or a scorpion. We were alone.

"We're the only ones here," Max said finally. "Regrettably, Sir Darbinyan and Master Torsten are not with us."

"I think they're the lucky ones," I muttered as Revna retched again.

~

It took a few minutes to get our bearings, but once we did, we could see that we were not nearly as alone as I'd first assumed. About a hundred yards away, several creatures that looked like bear-sized scorpions were erupting from the sand. As they pushed out into the heat, they all turned in our direction and began to advance. They were slower than sand sloths, but looking around the desert, it was clear that Revna and I had no place to run. As long as the creatures could outlast us in the sand, slow and steady was a winning strategy.

Revna nodded at Max. "Then we fight?"

I pulled on the tremolo bar and the blades snapped out and locked into place. "It looks like it."

"If I may make a suggestion," Max asked.

"Please," I replied.

"As much as I'd love to fight, I don't see this ending well for either of you," he said. "The tuning fork may be a better option."

I held up the fork, which had just stopped glowing. "You mean, we run?"

"And live to fight another day," Max said.

I looked at Revna, who nodded fervently.

I tapped the fork on Max's headstock, then placed the base of the fork on my knee. "Grab the fork," I said. As soon as she did, I plucked the same string as I had in her home. We were on our way to a new universe and a whole lot of puking.

Welcome to my life.

12
Shit's About to Get Real

When I opened my eyes again, freshly shaken by another vivid in-game memory, I saw we were on a dirt road. The new coliseum was being assembled less than a quarter mile away.

I sat up straight and looked at our surroundings in a post-nap fog. We were driving along the water's edge, with the Bay to our right and a row of poorly maintained trees and shrubs to our left. The path ahead veered to the right slightly and narrowed to little more than a mountain bike trail. KM straddled the narrow pathway like a champ and slowed when we came into view of Hunter's Point Expressway on our left. A three-foot-tall concrete barrier ran along the road, preventing us from merging.

KM stopped about ten feet from the low wall. She idled quietly for a moment before asking, "Packard, would you like me to crash through the barrier?"

I scanned the area and saw that we hadn't attracted any attention, at least that I was aware of. I looked back at a row of tall, gnarled trees we'd just driven past. "No. Let's back up and take cover by those trees. There are police and news helicopters flying over the stadium site. We should do our best to keep out of sight."

"A sound plan," KM replied, dropping into reverse and pulling up under the massive old trees.

The road to the left of the barrier curved east and looped back, following the peninsula around what was once a thriving stadium. A chain link fence ran the entire length of the far side of the road, preventing tourists from taking a stroll onto the property to relive the good old days.

Becky put her hand on my forearm. She looked concerned. "Are you okay, Pack? You've been scratching your forearms since you woke up."

"No, I'm fine." I held out my arms to show her that I was okay, but her expression said otherwise.

"You're not fine," she gasped, her breath hitching in her chest. "What the heck is wrong with your arms?"

I looked down and saw what looked like a row of sores running up each of my arms from wrist to elbow. As we watched them, they all simultaneously erupted in a bloodless pop, revealing — uh, don't think I'm crazy here — but they were the plasma nodes from *Tournament of Warlords*. I held my hands open, afraid of what might happen if I clenched them.

Clem, Cool, and Kyle leaned forward, all equally horrified and intrigued by what they were seeing.

"I know what's happening," I said finally, "in here, and out there at the stadium site."

Then, without any warning, my Legion of Evil Geniuses t-shirt vanished, and a scabbard holding a black-handled sword with a large silver pommel materialized, leaning on the seat between Becky and me. I felt something moving at my feet. When I looked down, I saw my white tennis shoes turn into black leather knee-high boots. I glanced at my right thigh, and as if on cue, a thigh dagger holster holding a silver-handled dagger materialized out of thin air.

"Alright, Matthew McConaughey," Becky said, sounding more nervous than usual. "What just happened to your shirt, and what the hell are those things on your arms?" She motioned at the sword and dagger. "And why is there a sword and knife in here with us?"

"The nodes on my arms, the weapons, the boots, the bare, uh, bare chest thing..." I looked back at the guys in the back seat as I spoke as well. "These are all a part of my gladiator persona from the *Multiversal Tournament of Warlords*. I think I'm becoming my in-game character."

Kyle looked scared. "Why would that be happening now?"

Knightmare replied without hesitating. "Because we are now in proximity to the coliseum where the tournament is held. I believe the Quantum Nanops expect Packard to compete."

I wasn't exactly happy to hear KM's assessment but considering everything that had happened over the last couple of days, I wasn't surprised either. "And what if I don't? What if I just stay right here, or we drive away?"

"There is a high probability that whatever is waiting for you inside the coliseum walls will simply come out and seek you for whatever conflict they're anticipating," KM offered. "Then again, it's possible there's nothing inside and nothing would happen either way."

Becky sighed. "And what are the odds of that?"

"Quite low, I'm afraid," KM said softly, her voice resonating eerily through her speakers.

Suddenly, Kyle shrieked and began to fumble with his clothes. "What's happening to me?"

We all turned our attention to Kyle, whose clothes had also disappeared, leaving him wearing a simple tunic and a loincloth. Flat, unadorned leather sandals laced up past his calves, completing the ensemble. A bow and quiver of arrows materialized between Kyle and Clem, making them both jump.

Becky abruptly opened her door and hopped out of Knightmare, batting at her clothes like she was on fire. I got out and ran around to where she was standing, only to find her clothing replaced by an impressive assortment of armored pieces. Her armor appeared to have been fashioned out of leather and iron, accented with flowing sections of dark red fabric and gold piping. A small shield with a diameter slightly larger than a Frisbee appeared on her forearm and a short sword, no longer than a machete, hung at her waist. She wore sandals similar in style to Kyle's but made of woven gold.

Kyle tilted Becky's seat forward and climbed out behind her. I wouldn't ever tell him so, but while Becky looked pretty badass, Kyle just looked silly. He looked like the guy who cleaned out the stables at the annual Renaissance Festival down in San Jose.

Cool, still in Clem-form, exited the car from Kyle's side, gripping the bow and quiver of arrows. He handed the weapons to Kyle, who accepted them, but looked positively terrified of them at the same time.

Clem departed Knightmare from the driver's side as his beloved Western garb changed into something more coliseum appropriate. From what I'd seen in the *Multiversal Tournament of Warlords* game, Clem wore the armor of a retiarius. Arm and shoulder guards, called manica and galerus, protected his left arm. Like Kyle, Clem's pants had been replaced with a slightly more substantial loincloth, known as a subligaculum, held in place by a wide leather belt. Clem's battle gear came with no head protection, and while armor plates held in place by thick leather straps protected his lower legs, his feet were conspicuously bare. I won't share the gory details, but he needed a pedicure almost as badly as the old warlock Aconitum did.

The last things to appear on ol' Clem were a leather bandana, wrapped around his forehead just beneath his hairline, a large fishing net, and a huge, lethal-looking trident. The net draped over Clem's shoulders like a cape. The trident, which sported a long wooden handle and three iron spikes that would have made Neptune jealous, appeared in his left hand. If my time in the game taught me anything, it's that Clem's weapons were symbols of death. The Quantum Nanops saw Clem as a viable threat and clothed him in such a way that his opponents would recognize that fact as well.

Cool looked down at his clothes, his typically happy-go-lucky expression looking a little more disappointed-go-sadly. Okay, that wasn't one of my better ones, but you get the picture. He reverted from his Clem-itation to his own lanky form, and looked even more dejected when his clothing didn't adapt for the impending tournament. "Why did all of your clothes change, but mine didn't," he asked sullenly.

Knightmare beat the rest of us to a response. "I believe it's the same reason I didn't turn into a war chariot," she said. "You and I are already versatile and capable of manipulating our appearances. Our offensive and defensive capabilities exceed our human counterparts. It's likely the Quantum Nanops do not deem our adaptation necessary."

Cool frowned. "In English, please, bruh."

I saw what KM was getting at. "Knightmare means you already make your own clothes and weapons, so why bother? Am I right, KM?"

"Right as rain," she replied.

Cool's grin returned as he morphed his signature purple board shorts into a wicked-looking, purple, spiked gladiators skirt, which we in the arena called a tunica. His metal shoes wound up around his lower legs like vines to create the illusion of metallic sandals that resembled Kyle's and Becky's. Finally, as if he couldn't get any more intimidating, he morphed his forefeet into twin morningstars, which he clanged together loudly. "When in Rome, right?"

I shook my head. "Technically, this isn't Rome… uh, never mind."

Cool shrugged and nodded at Kyle's feet. "Our sandals match, broski!"

Kyle smiled, forgetting how ridiculous he looked. "Huh, yeah! They do." Kyle turned to me and pointed at Cool with the end of his bow. "I nominate Cool to scout ahead and check things out."

I was about to agree when Becky put her free hand up and waved it back and forth, signaling a disagreement was at hand. See what I did there? *At hand?* Come on, I know you laughed.

Anyway, what Becky said next made sense. "While I can't deny that Cool looks awesome and pretty scary, Pack's the only one here who has any experience in that, uh, game... arena..." She sighed, barely holding it together. "We need him in the lead."

Kyle looked at the rest of us, panicked. "We? Who said anything about *'we'*? I'm no warrior... even though I do look pretty tough."

Clem held up his trident, looking like he was ready to defend Sparta. "Now look, while I ain't too keen on my duds bein' re-placed with this here costume, I'll be damned if I'd send the Marshal, Cool, or any y'all into that there structure on yer own. We go together or we don't go at all."

Kyle's face dropped. He looked ashamed.

Clem spotted Kyle's expression immediately. "You jest stick with me, young gunslinger. I'll have yer back."

Kyle nodded, still frightened, but he managed a half-smile that said he was grateful for the gesture.

Becky took a deep breath and looked us over. She shook her head and smiled. "I don't know what we're doing here, but we look like a Halloween party." She walked closer to me and patted my shoulder. She looked at the others, telling them, "Pack's in the lead then, alright?"

The three of them answered in succession.

"Alright."

"Alright."

"Alright."

KM, who was probably feeling a little left out, spoke up, saying, "shall I crash the barrier now?"

I shook my head. "We don't know what's waiting for us in there, girl. We may need an escape plan... a Hail Mary play. Can you be that for us?"

KM was less than thrilled. "You want me to wait here and miss out on all the fun?"

Kyle held up his bow. "She can go with you, and I'll be the backup plan."

KM grunted. "If I had a head, I'd be shaking it. Go on, have fun storming the castle," she sighed.

I patted her hood. "Something tells me we're gonna need you, KM." Then I thought of something. "Hey, girl, would you pop your trunk, please?" KM did as I asked, and I retrieved an old, duct tape covered ice chest from the trunk. I used my dagger to cut the tape and removed Clem's revolver. "I know there are only five live bullets chambered, but I think she'll be useful."

Clem accepted his pistol, looking like he wanted to cry. "Oh, how I've missed you, Jackson." He tucked the gun carefully into the front of the heavy leather belt that held up his loincloth and grinned at me. "Now I ain't nekkid no more. Whatever comes our way, I'll be ready fer it."

13

Bold of You to Enter the Melee Range

A few moments later, after I'd retrieved my sword from KM's front seat, the five of us hopped over the graffitied concrete barrier. Well, Cool just stepped over it, but the rest of us hopped. I'm sure I wasn't the only one who was relieved to find that the Quantum Nanops had left Kyle and Clem's underwear intact when they'd replaced their pants with loincloths.

We crossed Hunter's Point Expressway, which was actually just a poorly maintained two lane road, and Cool lifted us carefully over the six-foot-tall chain link fence separating us from our destination. Once on the other side, Cool flattened out his body and formed a makeshift tent, complete with legs. We knew the helicopters hovering overhead would easily spot us, but if all they could see was a yellow and brown blob moving across the parking lot, they'd be less likely to investigate. Given the fact that there was a coliseum growing just a few feet away, we were fairly certain we'd be less than a blip on their radar.

Under cover of Cool, we crossed a dirt road that had, once upon a time, been the other half of the expressway, and hopped down a small embankment into the old Candlestick Park parking lot. Stacks of I-beams, concrete drainage pipes, overhead highway sign supports, and several rows of powder blue shipping containers filled the lot. Massive piles of bags of sand, and what was presumably concrete lay on wooden pallets, covered by heavy, weighted down tarps.

To our left was a steep, man-made, weed-covered hill that stood about twenty feet tall. Atop the hill, was the coliseum.

We couldn't have seen it from where Knightmare parked, but once we were standing at the base of the hill, we saw something that took our collective breath away. The piles of construction materials, shipping containers, and even the blacktop and concrete from the parking lot itself, were breaking down into a fine dust and flying up, as if caught in a whirlwind. A row of old eucalyptus trees was being broken down to their roots, leaving gaping holes in the sandy loam where they once presided over the parking lot. The dust was flying up the hill and directly into the coliseum. More accurately, the dust was *becoming* the coliseum.

~

As we climbed the hill before us, we became aware of a distinct hum coming from the coliseum walls. It was as if the structure was alive. I suppose, given the nature of the Quantum Nanops, it was. When we crested the hill and stood alongside the massive, curved wall of the coliseum, we could feel the hum as clearly as we could hear it.

Clem placed a calloused hand against the wall and narrowed his eyes. "It's real. And the dang thang's buzzin' like a forest full of cicadas." He turned to me. "Any idear why, Marshal?"

I shrugged. "It's most likely the Quantum Nanops, but the only one who'd know for sure is Irene."

Clem looked at Kyle and sighed. "It's almost like she should be a part of this," he said, his frustration equally clear in his voice and his expression. "Yet here we are, walkin' into the unknowable, like a bunch of damned fools."

"Nobody forced anybody to leave," Kyle replied defensively.

Clem bristled. He was less comfortable with our situation than he wanted to let on. "I'd still be sittin' at that big wooden table, in my own damned clothes, if I wasn't yer friend, young man. Try an' show a little gratitude."

Kyle looked like he was about to respond when Becky reminded us who the grown-up in the room was. "Right or wrong, we all made a choice to leave. Smart or stupid, we all left Knightmare behind and walked up to this wall. Whatever we do next, we have to be united." She looked from Clem to Kyle, then made eye contact with Cool, his face stretched out disconcertingly overhead, and finally, me. "If we're harboring bad feelings, anger, resentment, fear... whatever you're feeling, if we don't have each other's backs in there, then we could get hurt. Or die." She touched the tip of one of the spikes on Clem's trident. One tiny prick from the razor-sharp point drew blood. "These aren't toys, and regardless of what the Nanops think, this isn't a game!"

We all looked at the thin line of blood running down Becky's finger, and we knew her words were true.

Kyle reached out and patted Clem's shoulder softly. "Thank you for being here. And thank you for being my friend."

Clem nodded knowingly. "Where I come from, them're hard to come by, and even harder to keep alive." He extended the hand that had just been on the wall. "I 'preciate yer bravery, young, uh... arrow-slinger?"

Kyle held out his bow, looking more confident than he had in years. His expression matched one he might've worn when he was about to head into a first-person shooter tournament. He'd slung his quiver so that the arrows stuck up just over his right shoulder. He was a lefty, so he held the bow with his right hand. Assuming he fired any arrows, he would retrieve and nock them with his left. "I'll stick with you, Clem," he said boldly. "I'll have your back, Pack."

"We all will," Cool agreed.

"I know you will," I told them. "But if anybody wants to back out, I wouldn't blame you for heading back to Knightmare right now."

Clem spit on the ground, making me glad he'd dialed back on that bad habit since showing up in our world. "Shoot, Marshal, you know me better than that. Wherever you go, I go. Even if that destination happens to be the Devil's own basement."

Cool's grin widened conspicuously overhead. "Bruh, we've fought dragons, ogres, witches, Eleventacles, ice giants…" He paused, suddenly looking pensive. "Huh… we never did rescue that prince." His grin vanished, and a glimpse of serious Cool, which was as rare as brave Kyle, suddenly shined through. "Whatever comes, we face it together, dude."

Becky patted the hilt of her sword. "I'm so scared, I just might pee myself, but we've faced scarier things together, too. Haven't we?"

I smiled and nodded. "Yeah, we sure have."

"And I'm still the fish out of water," Kyle muttered. "But like Cool said, we face it together. Just like we always have."

"Only *together* means a whole lot more than it used to," Clem added. "I do have one question, though."

"What do you want to know," I asked.

Clem held out the trident. "Is someone s'pectin' me to bale some hay? Because other than the Devil, I don't know many fellers who have much need fer a pitchfork."

I tried to make the laugh that followed a *laughing with* laugh, instead of a *laughing at* laugh, but I think I failed. "That's not a pitchfork, ol' buddy. That's a trident. It's the chosen weapon of Neptune, the Roman god of the sea, rivers, and springs."

"He was also the god of earthquakes," Becky offered. "Legend says he caused the eruption of Mount Etna. Neptune was a powerful and important god."

"That net you've got draped over your shoulder is a weapon, too," I said. "The gladiators used it like a lasso, taking down their opponents by snaring them."

Cool giggled. "If you were a superhero, you'd be Fisher Man."

Kyle laughed at Cool's quip. "That's actually really funny, dude."

I punched Kyle in the shoulder lightly. "Cool's always got jokes, man." I looked at the wall again. It was still growing taller. "We'd better find a way in if we're gonna figure out what's going on in there."

"Maybe there's nothing," Kyle wondered aloud. "KM said there might be nothing, right?"

Becky patted her sword again. "I don't think we'd have these if we were walking into an empty coliseum."

Kyle nodded, frowning slightly. "Yeah, you're probably right."

Clem started walking east, along the wall. "Let's get movin' then. Last one there is a one-eyed meerkat."

The others looked at me curiously. "Don't ask me, I just work here." I shrugged and followed Clem to search for an entrance.

~

We walked more than a hundred yards, following the lower wall of what was turning out to be a massive structure. The ground around the coliseum was still mostly the native San Franciscan soil that had been there since the days of the old stadium, and probably long before that. Cobblestones, though, kept appearing in the ground at our feet, connecting and sealing gaps like a strange game of Tetris. Walking on the soil was quiet, but the cobblestoned sections were noisy and made our little band of... What were we? Adventurers? Heroes? Dumbasses? All of the above, I imagine. But the sound of our footfalls echoing off the densely packed cobblestones had us all feeling a little jumpy. We were definitely not operating in stealth mode. In fact, my old *Animehem* friend, Dirk Claymore, probably would have shushed us at that point. That made me smile. Dirk was an odd duck but knowing he was actually lumbering around somewhere in the multiverse, arguing with Angus or fighting rogue ninja gnomes, was somehow comforting.

We looked back and realized we'd lost sight of the spot where we'd ascended the hill. Knightmare's tree-covered hiding spot was well out of visual range as well. The view from where we stood was breathtaking. Off to the east, the San Francisco Bay was in full view. Ships loaded with shipping containers, sailboats, and even a garbage scow passed closely enough that they might be able to see us from where they were in the water. A fleet of police and Coast Guard boats were playing sheepdog, herding them to what they hoped would be a safe distance from whatever was happening. A trio of Black Hawk helicopters flew overhead, causing Cool's body to flap wildly.

Cool tightened up a bit, forcing us to group in more closely. "We need to find an entrance soon, bros," he hollered over the sound of the helicopters. "The military dudes're getting curious!"

The entire coliseum consisted of massive, thirty-foot-tall by ten-foot-wide archways built side by side at five foot intervals. The incredible rows of archways were stacked three high, with an approximately ten foot section of clean flat concrete layered in between each level like a cake. In total, if my eyeballing was correct, the structure was about a hundred and ten feet tall, not including decorative pillars, and flags. The arches were decorative only, though, and surrounded perfectly flat concrete walls. We continued forward, looking for the one that would allow us entry into the belly of the beast.

Another thirty feet or so, and we found an archway that would have rivaled the famous Arc de Triomphe. Okay, I don't know that for sure, since I've never actually been to Paris, but it was bigger than the others. On each side of the massive arch, stood enormous statues that looked like they'd been carved out of flawless marble. Each of the statues portrayed one of the more famous combatants the coliseum had hosted. I was shocked to see one of myself positioned conspicuously close to the entrance, my arms raised in my signature defensive move.

Cool's head stretched away from his body, staring at the statues, awestruck. "Bruh, look up there."

I craned my neck a bit to see what he was looking at. Behind my statue, and amidst several of my fellow warriors, stood perfectly carved renditions of Pharaoh and El Scalar. I shuddered, suddenly remembering the tournament's rules. There was always at least one death. Pharaoh and Scalar were my allies in *Animehem*, but they were somehow different in the coliseum. I can't tell you how many times I'd killed both of them in combat... or been killed by them. I will say, when they faced each other, the coliseum's foundations shook like no other battle I can recall.

Cool looked down at me, his eyes wide. "Are the brawl bros inside, dude?"

I looked at Clem, Becky, and Kyle, realizing I'd made a terrible mistake in bringing them along. While Cool had faced many monsters in his time, there was no way any of the other three could stand up to the living horrors that competed in the *Multiversal Tournament of Warlords*. Pharaoh alone could pulverize any of them with a single punch, and Scalar was a born warrior. Use your imagination. Oh, and they were relatively tame when compared to some of the other gladiators.

I had to go in alone. "Hey, guys-"

"Only one way to find out," Kyle declared as he strolled boldly under the archway. As he did, a crowd roared somewhere in the interior. The roar echoed down the corridor ahead of Kyle. As he advanced, torches sprung to life, lighting the way to certain doom.

Kyle had triggered the game. It had begun.

~

I called out to Kyle, begging him to turn around, but the roar of the crowd had him in its sway.

"Ain't got no choice now, Marshal," Clem said, shaking his head. "I'm a'feared that boy'll die without us." And with that, Clem followed Kyle's lead, running under the archway.

Cool, who didn't seem to realize how serious things had just gotten, hooted like a kid running into a candy store and returned to his gladiator form. "Tally ho, dudes," he grinned, and strode through the archway like the champion he knew himself to be. With two stretched strides, Cool easily caught up with Clem.

Becky and I stood at the archway, staring at each other dumbly as the others advanced towards the arena.

"You stay here," I told her. "This could be so much worse than I remember."

Becky shook her head. "You don't get to do that, Pack."

I was confused, but in a hurry to catch up with Kyle and the others. "Do what?"

She scowled at me. "Bring me here like I'm a part of this and then dismiss me like a child. We go into this like we started it, like we did in Laboratory 311. Together. I may not be a warrior, but you should know by now that I'm loyal, and I won't let you face whatever's in there alone." She looked down the corridor, where the others were walking away. "We'd better catch up with our friends, yeah?"

I was stunned. Impressed, frightened, and conflicted, too, but mostly stunned.

I must have looked like an idiot because Becky suddenly snapped her gloved fingers in front of my face. "Earth to Packard! You here with me? Kyle and the others need us! Are you coming?"

I glanced at our friends. Their retreating shadows grew steadily smaller in the depths of the corridor. A doorway of light appeared just ahead of Kyle. I knew what lay just beyond that light. I'd been there many times. A bloodstained battlefield, littered with bones, teeth, and chunks of charred flesh.

"Yeah," I said finally, realizing I'd just be insulting Becky if I continued to protest. "Together."

And that's exactly how we went in. Becky took my hand, and we stepped over the threshold in perfect unison. The moment we cleared the archway, a massive wrought iron gate slammed down behind us, preventing any retreat. There was truly no turning back.

Becky released my hand, and we ran to catch up with the others. The roar of the crowd was intoxicating. The closer we got to the battlefield, the more I looked forward to unsheathing my sword, and the less I feared, well… anything.

"Is it just me," Becky shouted over the roar, "or is that a stadium full of mythical sirens? The closer we get…"

"I know," I hollered back. "I think it's how they get us to fight each other, I just never realized it before!"

Kyle crossed the threshold first, stepping into the blinding sunlight. The crowd lost its collective mind when he appeared, and he held his arms out in the air like a rock star greeting a stadium full of adoring fans. His bow hand waved, like he'd made the same dramatic entrance a million times. I wondered if maybe he had in some other universe.

Clem passed through next, and if I hadn't seen what happened next with my own eyes, I wouldn't have believed it. He held his trident over his head and twirled it like a cheerleader's seven-foot baton. And then he dropped it. The crowd went silent as he picked up his weapon. They finally passed judgment on Clem's mishap with a sudden, unforgiving boo.

Cool ambled into the arena with his usual heightened level of enthusiasm, but surprised both Becky and me when he roughly shoved Clem and Kyle off to each side, drawing all the attention to himself. He held his makeshift morningstars over his head and clanged them together dramatically, the sound resonating across the battlefield like Big Ben.

The crowd resumed its roar, louder than ever.

Finally, Becky and I stepped through the archway and onto the arena. Becky waved nervously, but nobody seemed to notice her. All eyes were on me.

A booming announcer's voice suddenly rang out across the battlefield, whipping the spectators into a frenzy. I looked around as the voice introduced Kyle – the cosmic assassin, Clem – the most dangerous hombre west of the Milky Way, Cool – the shapeshifting wildcard, Becky – the unfair maiden, and an *extra special* guest. I never knew where the voice actually came from, and I didn't expect I'd find out then either. The stands were packed full of fans from every corner of the multiverse imaginable. Ultrarich fans, of course, because who else would fund such a thing. This particular subset of the frighteningly wealthy had grown well beyond political aspirations and corporate takeovers, and had moved on to betting their fortunes on multiversal death battles. Occasionally, one of the wealthy would take their betting too far, and wind up tossed into the arena as a combatant to pay off their debt. One final wager, I suppose.

The announcer suddenly hollered out my name. "Packard Campbell, ladies and gentlemen! Do you remember that name?" The voice's pause for effect paid off, and the crowd went into a vocal frenzy, indicating that they *did indeed* remember my name. "Good! Then let's welcome Packard and his fellow warriors to the battlefield, *Multiversal Tournament of Warlords* style, shall we?!"

Finally, just in case any of us got any funny ideas, another gate slammed shut behind us, preventing our return to the possible safety of the corridor behind us.

Game on.

14

Wince and Repeat

I can't believe I never noticed it before, but the pure adrenaline coursing through my veins and the unnatural level of aggression I was suddenly feeling were undeniable. I wasn't exactly feeling like a berserker. It was more like I was riding a wave of liquid euphoria… like I was invincible, and nothing I did would have consequences. The sights, sounds, and smells assaulting my senses were intoxicating to say the least. The worst thing about that was, the sensory input was horrifying and should have repulsed us, not whipped us into a homicidal frenzy.

Becky grabbed my arm. "Something is very wrong, Packard!" She gritted her teeth, studying the spectator-filled stands that surrounded us on all sides. The cheering turned into chanting. They were chanting our names. Becky turned her head, making eye contact with me. She looked like someone fighting off

a migraine. "I feel so angry," she yelled. "I just want to fight...
somebody... anybody!"

As the chanting continued, a series of massive iron gates on
the inner walls of the coliseum's perimeter began to lift. The
visceral sounds of grinding gears and clanking chains added to the
unending cacophony. It only took a few moments for the gates to
open completely, and when they did with a metallic thud, the
crowd began cheering again, our names as good as forgotten. That
part of the game always made me angry. Was that feeling even
real, or just another manipulation?

Shadows darkened each of the previously gated archways,
all lit from behind by torchlight. I knew all the combatants, as well
as their moves and weaknesses. But that knowledge didn't change
how aggressive I was feeling, or help me to protect Becky, Kyle,
Clem, or Cool. Cool stepped forward defiantly. Kyle and Clem
stepped up as well, not having an inkling of the trouble they were
in, nor caring about it.

Becky's nails dug into my arm. I appreciated the pain, actually, as it seemed to clear my head a little.

The announcer's voice boomed throughout the arena like we were sitting in the middle of a bass speaker. "It's the time you've all been waiting for, friends! Your former champion, Packard Campbell, and his companions will face ten of our deadliest champions in an all-out free for all! A battle royale that will end with one man..." He paused for a moment, using his flair for the dramatic to his benefit. *"Or woman..."* The crowd began chanting Becky's name again, and I felt her nails dig in deeper. "...standing as the one true Multiversal Warlord!"

The cheers continued, and I saw Kyle, Clem, and Cool standing defiantly, awaiting the battle to come. My head ached like I'd already taken a beating, and Becky dragged her nails up my arm.

The announcer was silent for a moment, and the crowd followed his cue, their chanting and cheering dropping to a low rumble.

"Are you ready for today's lineup of brutes, bludgeoners, and bastards," the announcer shouted.

The crowd loudly confirmed that it was indeed *ready*.

~

"Beginning at the northwestern curve," the announcer began, "please give it up for Ah Puch!"

The crowd cheered as a skeletal figure, standing roughly six-foot-six, emerged from the formerly gated enclosure. Ah Puch wore a cloak that appeared to be as black as the depths of space, and yet, at the same time looked transparent. On his head, he wore a ceremonial headdress made of his victims' bones, while a gruesome necklace that looked like a string of pearls hung loosely around his neck. At a second glance, one would notice the large beads adorning the necklace weren't pearls at all. They were eyeballs, also presumably taken from his victims. The eyes all faced forward. Once an opponent noticed them, they were impossible to ignore, becoming an incredibly effective intimidation tool. Ah Puch's long, bony fingers curled around the curved handle of a long, sinister-looking scythe. The scythe's blade was ancient, yet sharp enough to cut atoms. Legend said that when Ah Puch killed an opponent, the death wasn't merely physical. He set fire to his victim's soul, killing them in the afterlife as well.

"Stay away from his blade," I hollered at the others, though only Becky seemed to register what I said.

The announcer sounded like he was coming down from a case of Lightning Rod Energy Drinks. He was in hype mode, and the audience was all about the promise of impending death and destruction. "Ah Puch stands six-foot-six, weighs in at twenty-four pounds, and hails from the depths of Hell itself. In the ultimate version of the double-tap, this god of death can burn your soul to a crisp once he's done with your body!"

The audience roared in approval, and Ah Puch stepped into the arena, waving his scythe with the flourish Clem had attempted with his pitchfo- uh, trident, only the death god did it way better. Let's be real. Anything short of dropping it would have been better.

The announcer continued on. "Next in line is a warrior who requires no introduction! From the war dimension of Tatk, standing seven feet tall and weighing an impressive 398 pounds, let's hear it for aicraG drahciR yendoR... doR, for short!" Again, the announcer's words had the desired effect, and the crowd's roar increased appropriately.

doR stepped forward boldly, clenching a deadly light-blade, known as a chuknuryss, in each hand. The weapons were leather-wrapped handles housing a small hard-light projector on each end. The projectors generated a large, curved blade of pure light that arced out in front of his fists in a half-moon shape. I'd always imagined the chuknuryss to be the weird, angry offspring of brass knuckles and an oversized holographic meat cleaver.

doR scraped the blades against each other, creating an impressive spray of sparks. Then, to the delight of the spectators, he drew the blades across his chest in a crisscross pattern, leaving twin lacerations that dripped a viscous, purple fluid on the ground at his feet. doR was a fierce warrior, and I'd had the displeasure of fighting him to the death many times. He was some flavor of humanoid, deep blue-skinned and covered from head to toe in wicked, black, tribal tattoos. His face was like an old boxer's; beaten, but defiant. He was a killing machine, and his close-combat weapons were proof of his confidence in the arena. He threw back his head and let loose with a deep, throaty battle cry that sounded like a terrifying cross between a tuba and an air raid siren.

The announcer continued his introductions as the crowd roared its continued approval. Next up was Chok, a decapoid from the distant Brachyuras galaxy. If the rumors were true, Chok began her life as a warlord, serving as a surrogate for her brother, Malacos. Her brother was supposed to have been their generational warrior, bringing glory to the family line. When he died under suspicious circumstances, the family sent Chok to compete in the tournament against her wishes. It turned out to be a better fit than anyone could have ever predicted. Chok was born to be a fighter. Given her natural armor-plating and ten appendages, four of which served as arms while she used the other six for maneuvering around the arena, she was versatile, agile, and hard to kill. Each of the two forward most appendages bore a massive claw, which made Chok look like a huge hermit crab. The next two appendages bore three-fingered hands, complete with opposable thumbs. Aside from her deadly claws, Chok always started her matches weapon-free. She preferred to acquire her weapons from her opponents in the arena. She relished the idea of disgracing another combatant by killing them with their own tools of death and mayhem. It was also rumored that Chok had a wall dedicated to displaying her collection of liberated weapons.

After Chok came the dreaded ChuChuLo. Nobody actually knew where ChuChuLo came from, what its species was, or how it came to participate in the tournaments. Some believed the creature was actually responsible for the whole thing, playing it out like some twisted undercover boss routine. Most of us believed ChuChuLo to be one of the Ancients, a powerful race of god-like creatures who toyed with lesser beings like a cat would toy with a mouse. Actually, we would probably be more like a cockroach to it, considering how the warrior looked down on us. ChuChuLo stood almost nine feet tall, was covered in eyes and tentacles, and had rows of gnarled teeth set into its body at distressing angles. The teeth suggested that perhaps a mouth might exist somewhere in their vicinity, but none of us had ever seen one. The creature seemed to be able to master any weapon, and had been known to enter battles with axes, swords, laser cannons, and even molecular disruptors. This time, however, ChuChuLo, just like Chok, had come empty-handed. That was worrisome. Unlike Chok's proclivity to steal her opponent's weapons, ChuChuLo had an alternative weapon that it only used on special occasions. Those occasions always began weapon-free. ChuChuLo is a master of dark magic, wielding powerful spells that can make short work of most traditional weapons, and their wielders. Try fighting with no arms or legs… or a mouth… Yeah, I've died that way before at the hands… uh, tentacles of ChuChuLo.

The next combatant to emerge from underneath an archway was Gipak. I know a Mayan death god and an ancient cosmic horror should be two of the most terrifying things imaginable, but Gipak gave me the willies more than any of the other combatants. See, the neighbor's dog that spent a month with us when I was a kid didn't just make my bed smell bad. It brought fleas into our house. That was my one and only experience with the tiny, high-jumping nightmares until I faced Gipak in the arena. Gipak was a reddish-brown, five-foot-tall meta-flea. The giant bloodsucker was the fastest competitor to ever enter the arena, not to mention, it could easily clear a hundred-foot wall in a single bound. Fighting the beast was like fighting a spray of ricocheting bullets. Nobody knew much about Gipak's history. All we really knew was to stay away from the razor-sharp talons at the end of each of its fingers, and to avoid the three massive proboscises protruding from its grotesque maw. If it stabbed you with one of those things, it would pump you full of anticoagulant saliva. Even if you escaped the next horrifying step, where Gipak drained you of all your blood, the anticoagulant ensured the first cut you received would be a death sentence. As you can imagine, cuts and lacerations in the arena were more common than not.

The overseers of the tournament denied Gipak any blood between battles, and the creature skittered anxiously around its platform, driven insane by hunger.

The next combatant to appear was an older humanoid who resembled a Norse god. His name was Mentor Zephyrlynden, and he was as cunning and brutal a warrior as had ever set foot in the coliseum. His armor was constructed from some sort of living stone. He could create zombie minions from dirt, sand, and even rocks to fight on his behalf. I'd say he fights dirty, but that's too obvious a joke. Carrying himself with the same confidence you might expect from a Viking god, he held an old, battle-worn, stone war hammer over his head. He didn't have a battle cry like doR. He didn't need one. His rage-filled stare reminded the audience that one day, if they made an unwise wager, they might be the ones facing his hammer and zombie warriors.

The audience grew silent under his homicidal gaze, but quickly resumed their cheering when the announcer called out the name of their next champion, a cybernetically enhanced, metallic-furred silverback gorilla named Alpha Male.

Once upon a time, Alpha Male had been an interdimensional traveler on an assault team known as The Urban Gorillas. His team would hop from dimension to dimension, looting, pillaging, and plundering as they went. Their ultimate goal was galactic conquest, but they were ironic victims of a quantum-based event that left them unable to remain in the same dimension for more than a couple of weeks. Alpha Male and his companions slingshotted between worlds like a cosmic pinball machine. One day, however, when the rest of his team was sucked through their bi-weekly wormhole, the silverback was in a Faraday prison cell, and got left behind. The prison sold the beast to the proprietor of the tournament to serve as a gladiator, and he never looked back. Killing for glory suited Alpha Male just fine. His cellular structure, consisting of one part organic cell, and one part nanobot, made him incredibly dense and gave him an insane healing ability. Not to mention, he could grow complex weapons from his cells and create projectiles from whatever he was standing on. The sand he stepped into as he entered the arena would make deadly silicon bullets. The rocks, dirt, and trace minerals in the soil just added fuel to the fire. Alpha Male beat his chest and screamed wildly at the other gladiators in a display that was meant to intimidate them. While his act of aggression was plenty intimidating to the thousands of spectators watching from the stands, the other warriors might as well have yawned. In fact, I think Ah Puch might have actually gotten bored and dozed off.

The next warrior called forth made my heart skip a beat. It was one of my friends from the *Animehem* game. El Scalar was raised to be a warrior from birth. An evil shaman cursed him to live out his life as a hybrid man-beast with the body of an Aztec warrior and the head of a bison. Thankfully, the brain inside the head was still his own, but man, there were times I wondered. Interestingly, Scalar was still carrying the massive axe and set of hatchets given to him by Sir Scabiosa Atropurpurea, another friend from the world of *Animehem*. Scalar snorted angrily and dug his boots into the soil at his feet. He waved the axe overhead menacingly before lowering it and swinging it back and forth, daring the other fighters to break tradition and face him first. His muscles rippled underneath the Yeti-hide he wore as a cape, and I could see traces of blood on the tips of his horns. He really *had* started early, and the spectators loved him for it.

My stomach lurched when I saw the next combatant. As I watched another of my friends stalk out of his enclosure, the announcer called out his name. "Let's make some noise for the mighty Pharaoh!"

The crowd literally went wild. If they'd been wearing hats, they would have thrown them into the air. Of all the combatants to ever call the arena home, Pharaoh was the only one to have bona fide fans. There were spectators who had actually grown out dreadlocks just so they could look like him. Others affected a Jamaican accent, so they could cheer for him appropriately. Pharaoh raised his fists over his head boldly before spreading his arms out before him, claws extended like so many daggers, declaring victory before the contest had even begun. He was as lost in the moment as Kyle, Clem, and Cool, seemingly drunk with power, and ready to prove his superiority to the unwashed masses.

Suddenly, Pharaoh looked in my direction. For a fleeting second, hope sprung forth like spring flowers. I could swear he recognized me. Then, with a soul crushing sneer, he spat on the ground at his feet.

He'd recognized me, but *not* as his friend.

The final combatant to be called forth was not nearly as popular as Pharaoh. Heck, *I* was higher on the likability scale. But Xirokirud had more kills than any other combatant in the entire history of the tournament. Much of the carnage that littered the arena floor was there courtesy of Xirokirud.

"Please welcome back to the ring, our undefeated, undisputed, but never underrated all-time champion, Xirokirud!"

Xiro, as most of the other challengers called him, myself included, had to duck under his archway when he exited his enclosure. He was perhaps the finest specimen of a silver dragon I'd ever seen, and you know how many games I've played… a lot, in case you've somehow forgotten.

Xiro emerged from the archway and stretched his limbs and massive wings out to their fullest extent. The two hundred-year-old, fifteen-foot-tall nightmare's joints popped as he was finally able to move about freely after several days of being confined in a cage barely larger than himself. The enclosures where the combatants lived were more than a hundred feet below the coliseum. Antigravity lifts brought them to the surface, cage and all.

Someone, or something, hurled Xiro's sword and scabbard out from the enclave behind him, and the dragon picked it up like it was a child's toy. The sword, which Xiro had affectionately named Rujar, was a ten-foot-long, thirteen-inch-wide blade fixed at the end of a three-foot-long carved slab of solid blightwood. The blade had a slightly angled, flat end that most closely resembled a giant tanto knife. Xiro slung his scabbard over his shoulder like a purse, and carefully flung an additional strap around his neck, attaching it with a set of large metal grommets.

Once he was satisfied the strap was secure, he took a deep breath and spewed an impressive stream of fire over the arena floor before him. Talk about going all scorched-earth.

The crowd stood and roared as Xiro flapped his wings and flew up ten, then fifteen, and finally stopped at twenty feet over the charred soil beneath him.

The announcer, knowing he could only push the unruly crowd so far and still maintain a reasonably orderly battle, raised his voice one last time. "Are you ready?!"

The crowd screamed, cried, and howled.

The announcer wasn't ready to let them off the hook just yet. "I said, ARE YOU READY!?"

The crowd finally lost their shit.

It was time.

15

Aggro

The Multiversal Coliseum was a carnival of violence and bloodlust. Electricity charged the air, and the roar of the crowd was a constant, thrumming pulse that beat at the very heart of the arena like war drums. Death and decay clung to the walls of the complex like a living thing. The air reeked of desperation and greed, of power and corruption, of the worst civilization had to offer.

The combined scents of sweat, blood, urine, and feces from the gladiators and the animals used to hunt them were overwhelming. Black, acrid smoke wafted across the arena, adding to the pungent, yet strangely alluring blend of visceral odors.

Becky squeezed my arm so tightly, I was afraid she might seriously injure one of us. Her nails had definitely broken the skin. I could feel a warm trickle of blood pooling on the underside of my arm before falling away in thick droplets, adding new color to the already blood-soaked soil at our feet.

"Packard," she groaned. "I'm barely keeping it together..." Becky pulled away and thrust her hands over her ears. She gritted her teeth and squinted her eyes. Tears streamed down her cheeks. She looked like her head was about to explode. "Plug my nose," she hollered as the announcer introduced the final gladiator to join the fray, the giant silver-scaled dragon named Xiro.

I couldn't have heard that right. *"What?"*

She looked me square in the eye and growled, "I said plug my nose! *Now!"*

I did as she asked, careful that she didn't bite me or something. The moment my fingers pinched off her nostrils, she opened her eyes slowly and began taking shallow, cautious breaths.

"It's the smell and the sound," she said, the word 'smell' coming out nasally, sounding like 'sbell', but neither of us was in the mood to laugh. Her voice was almost too quiet to hear. She must have known I was confused. "That's what they're using to control us. It's called psychosensory manipulation. We read about it in Mr. Heath's psychology class."

Becky winced again, and I felt a burst of pain just behind my eyes. It felt like my brain was trying to escape by digging its way out through my eye sockets with a rusty spork.

"It hurts to resist," Becky shouted at the same time as the announcer asked the audience and gladiators alike if they were ready. "But we have to try!"

I nodded weakly.

She took her hands from her ears and took my face between them. "Cover your ears as much as you can and try to breathe only through your mouth."

I nodded again, removing my hand from her nose, and covering my ears. Even with my hands firmly cupped in place, I could still hear the announcer holler, "Then it's time, gladiators! Tear each other to shreds!"

~

From that moment forward, time seemed to lose all meaning. Some events happened too fast for me to register, while others played out like a video shown in super-slow-mo.

Clem, Kyle, and Cool had all but forgotten we existed, and ran towards the center of the arena. Exactly the spot I knew they shouldn't want to be.

The arena was laid out like a circular maze carved into the ground. A twenty-foot-wide staging area ran around the entire inner perimeter of the massive walls surrounding us. That was where my friends and I entered. It was also where the ten gladiators who'd just been turned loose upon us now stood at varying intervals. Slightly closer to the center of the arena, and just beyond the staging area, was a ten-foot-wide, eight-foot-deep trench that ran in a full circle around the perimeter. The trench separated the staging area from another raised ring of dirt and stone that was narrower than the one where we stood, probably about fifteen feet wide. Small but sturdy stone bridges had been erected at strategic spots over the trench, allowing us to move closer to the center-most part of the arena, affectionately nicknamed the killing grounds. Only one more trench stood between the second ring and the killing grounds.

The trenches were inaccessible to the larger gladiators. There were tunnels running between them, allowing smaller combatants like Becky and me the opportunity to hide and strike from below. The trenches often seemed like a lifesaver in the beginning, especially to newcomers. However, it was a little-known fact that the sewage system ran directly into the trenches, creating a muddy, foul-smelling mess I only considered as a last resort. Many of the gamblers sentenced to fight for their debts died down there, cowering in the tunnels like groundhogs hiding from their own shadows until a firebreather like Xiro was called into battle to finish the job.

Clem, Kyle, and Cool ran over the first bridge, advancing to the middle ring. Without missing a step, Cool morphed into a bridge, allowing Clem and Kyle to run over him, crossing over the next trench, and advancing directly to the blood-stained killing grounds.

As Cool's body advanced, catching up with the others, he did something decidedly *uncool*. He morphed his hooves back into his favored morningstars and swung them wildly at Kyle and Clem. Kyle stumbled backwards, pinwheeling his arms, but didn't notice the trench behind him. A moment later, he toppled over the edge, tumbling down into the depths of the fetid trench.

When Clem saw the massive morningstar-shaped hoof bearing down on him, he rolled to the side and parried with his trident, stopping Cool's attack just a few feet above his head. Cool raised his weapon again, stretching his arm backward to achieve a guaranteed killshot on his unwitting friend. He circled around Clem, effectively blocking the only bridge leading off the killing grounds, but he didn't notice the massive tentacle reaching out to meet his approach.

ChuChuLo wrapped one moist, terrifying tentacle around Cool's wrist and yanked, hurling him from the center island, all the way back to the starting point of the outer ring, like a pawn in a sadistic game of Chutes and Ladders. Cool's head and neck twisted in midair to face his attacker, and he stretched out his body to envelop ChuChuLo's bulk like a massive tarp.

Ah Puch moved towards Becky and me slowly. He wasn't in any hurry, and he held his scythe out in front of him casually, swishing it gently, like it was a parasol, and he was merely out on a Sunday stroll. His skull, frozen in the same perpetual grin that all skulls bear, glinted in the sunlight, flawless and white. Becky reflexively held her shielded arm up in front of her and drew her short sword. The blade, essentially being an extension of her arm, wavered nervously. If Ah Puch could have actually smiled, the sight of us would have done the trick.

Chok and doR, both seeing Clem standing on the island alone, ran across their respective bridges and prepared to leap over the trench that separated the second ring from the killing grounds. Chok's massive claws opened and snapped shut repeatedly, clicking loudly, only rivaled by doR's battle cry. doR left a thin trail of blood droplets, as his chest wouldn't heal for quite some time. He held his arms out like wings as he approached the trench, his chuknuryss extended outward, ready to strike when he landed.

Pharaoh lunged at El Scalar, who swung his massive axe at the lion in a defensive move that might have connected had he been the attacker. Pharaoh, however, took advantage of El Scalar's forward momentum, and went in low, picking the cursed warrior up over his head and hurling him backward at Xiro.

Xiro, who was still almost twenty feet in the air, tried to dodge the flying El Scalar, but my old friend managed to grab one of Xiro's wings and pull the dragon off-balance. The two tumbled to the ground in a pile of limbs and wings as Pharaoh moved on to Alpha Male like a lion on a mission. According to my *Evolutants* books, he had a dark history with the cybernetic gorilla, and I imagined there was an old grudge fueling his rage. Pharaoh was all about finishing unfinished business.

Pharaoh ran headlong into the beast and drove him directly into Mentor Zephyrlynden. The three of them, like Xiro and El Scalar, hit the ground violently and rolled into the massive stone wall of the coliseum itself. As they rolled, the dirt and stones around them rose into the air and began to whip wildly, like an Arizona dust storm on steroids. The dirt coalesced in several places within a few feet of the trio's skirmish, quickly taking shape as Zephyrlynden's dreaded zombie army.

As the surrounding madness ensued, the three Black Hawk helicopters we'd seen on our way into the coliseum flew overhead and hovered menacingly just above the upper rim of the coliseum's outermost wall. More choppers, presumably from local police precincts and competing news organizations, flew at a much higher and safer level.

It was clear the Black Hawks were mostly present to investigate, as two of them carried no weapons. The third, however, was armed to the teeth, sporting rockets under one wing and missiles under the other. I didn't know what the protocol would be for a situation like ours. My only military experience came from the game *War is Hell*. I suspected the rules of engagement in the real world would be drastically different.

As Chok and doR cleared the trench in very impressive leaps, Gipak, driven into a frenzy by the smell of doR's blood, launched itself across the arena like a guided missile. The meta-flea crashed into the warrior with incredible force, and the pair tumbled down into the trench to their right.

Chok scrambled towards Clem like a juggernaut, snapping her claws hungrily, ready to tear my friend apart and eat his head. Oh, yeah, Chok was into the head eating thing, too, which made the possibility of being decapitated that much more horrifying.

Once again, Clem bravely defended his ground with his trident. He was getting used to its range and usefulness. Devoid of any fear or reservation, he adapted to using it incredibly fast. He pulled the net away from his shoulders and swung it towards Chok, ensnaring one of her claws in it, leveling the playing field for the cowboy-turned-gladiator.

Becky shrieked in my ear, snapping me back to our current predicament. Ah Puch was practically on top of us. He swung his scythe at us in a downward arc that might have killed us both if I hadn't raised my arms and activated my plasma shield in time. The shield's coloration shifted from blue to a soft violet when the weapon struck it. I noticed that Becky had also raised her shield, but hers extended outward, just over my head. She was protecting me.

Ah Puch raised his scythe over his head once again, his skull tilting slightly. I'd fought him enough times to know that tilt. He was annoyed.

I turned to Becky. I'm ashamed to admit that whatever psychomental crap they were pulling on us was working, and I had to remind myself that she was not my enemy. "Follow me," I shouted, and dove under Ah Puch's legs. Becky was right behind me, and as sure of himself as our attacker was, he couldn't have possibly foreseen what I did next.

If you recall, my shield is a highly effective defensive weapon. When used creatively, however, it can also serve as a devastating offensive tool. As I dove under Ah Puch's lithe frame,

I kept my shield activated just long enough to cut through his lower legs with the front edge, dropping him like an old bag of, uh… well, bones. He clattered down onto Becky, who pulled herself out from under him, reminding me of my fight with the warrior known as L'OthruC'ant. Only he was about twenty times heavier. The scythe cut into the ground before Ah Puch rolled and swiped at us one last time. He aimed his weapon perfectly. If it wasn't for Becky's quick use of her shield, she'd be dead for sure, and I might've been too. The impact of the scythe against her small shield knocked her off-balance and into the trench where I knew more enemies, including Kyle, awaited her.

Disregarding the putrid, ankle-deep bio-soup that made up the floor of the trenches, I dove in after Becky, rolling through the mess and rising to my feet just in front of her. I extended a hand, which she took warily, clearly fighting the urge to initiate a battle as much as I was. Once she was on her feet, we sloughed through the muck towards a tunnel system that would take us to a small chamber underneath the killing grounds. Yeah, we'd suddenly become the vermin who took cover, but I couldn't risk them getting to Becky. I needed her safe, so I could focus on getting to Kyle, Clem, and Cool, and hopefully even Pharaoh and Scalar. If Becky and I could resist the mind control, then maybe they could, too.

~

With the individual battles raging on the divided sections of the arena overhead, I pulled Becky into a narrow tunnel that led underground to the second trench. The entrance to the catacombs underneath the killing grounds was directly across the trench from us. I peeked out of the tunnel, careful to stay out of the line of fire or anything else that might mean us harm. The trench was clear to our right, but just a few feet to our left, Gipak and doR were engaged in fierce, life or death combat. Gipak's proboscis was mere inches from doR's chest. The beast repeatedly thrust forward, already leaking its anticoagulant onto doR's exposed flesh, but as far as I could tell, it hadn't achieved penetration.

Screaming like a madman on fire, doR grasped Gipak's proboscis and twisted it roughly. The mouthpiece snapped off like a dried twig, and a grisly mixture of the anticoagulant saliva and blood flowed from the wound like a garden hose. The massive flea fought back savagely, its razor-sharp talons slicing doR's arms and chest like cheese on a charcuterie board. Signaling that I was ready to move, I squeezed Becky's hand, but instead of moving forward with me, she pulled back.

I swiveled on my heels, almost slipping in the filth at our feet. I was half-expecting to see Becky's short sword plunging towards my back, since that's what every fiber of my body told me I should be doing to her. But instead of a blade to the back, she hit me in the face with a handful of crap. Okay, so maybe I'm exaggerating a little bit, but it's pretty accurate. As I turned to find out why we weren't moving forward, she shoved a handful of the mixture of blood, urine, and feces into my nose. She let go of my hand and treated me to two earfuls of the stuff as well.

I couldn't believe what she'd just done. In all my years in the arena, I'd never gotten that stuff inside my ears or nose. "Shit!" I went to wipe it away, but Becky shook her head, indicating that I should leave it where it was. Then she looked at me quizzically, as if asking me a question that I couldn't hear. I got it. That was her plan. I could barely hear anything. In fact, outside the raw shock of having the vile mixture shoved up my nose, and that awful moist sensation in my ears, I'd started breathing through my mouth and couldn't smell anything. I nodded. She was a freaking genius.

She responded to my nod with a cute little half-smirk that I'll remember until the day I die. Then, ruining the moment completely, she shoved handfuls of the fecal blend into her own face. I vowed to forever let her believe it was mud.

Then, covered in excrement and God knew what else, Becky took my hand and nodded towards the entrance to the tunnel across the trench.

I took one last look in both directions and found the situation unchanged. Then we ran.

~

We made it across the trench in a half a dozen long strides. doR and Gipak were still locked in battle, so they either didn't see us, or didn't care that we were there. As we entered the next tunnel, doR grunted loudly in the trench behind us, sounding both enraged and in pain. We turned back to see an arm fly into the tunnel mouth. It was one of doR's, and it still gripped a deactivated chuknuryss loosely. Becky looked at her short sword for a moment before sheathing it and relieving doR's hand of its weapon.

I must have looked impressed, surprised, or something because when Becky turned back to me, she stopped and gave me the *'really?'* look.

"He wasn't using it," she said, shrugging her shoulders. "Besides, I get the feeling my little sword isn't going to cut it in here."

I saw what she did there, but before I could comment, she ran past me and into the dim light of the tunnel.

Now when I say tunnel, it's not like a labyrinth or anything. Four tunnels run under the killing grounds, leading from one side to the other, perfectly bisecting the raised battlefield. They all intersect in the middle, creating a chamber about ten feet in diameter. If you could look straight down at the tunnel system, it would resemble the spokes on a wheel. Charred bones and weapons littered the ground of the central chamber, though the floor was slightly raised, so it wasn't as thick with foulness as the trenches.

From the central chamber, I spotted Kyle in the trench just at the end of another one of the tunnels. He stood with his back against the wall that faced us, but he was looking up, presumably at the battle between Clem and Chok. He had an arrow nocked, and his bowstring drawn back tightly. Before I could say anything, he let his arrow fly. A moment later, Chok fell into the trench right next to Kyle, who scrambled into the tunnel before nocking another arrow and spinning expertly to meet his foe. I'd never seen Kyle like that before. He was like... fearless and badass.

Chok's head came into view. An arrow protruded from one of her eyestalks. Kyle had shot out her eye! Before she could withdraw, Kyle let the second arrow loose, taking her remaining eye out with it. Even through the horrid crap in my ears, Chok's shriek sounded like a police whistle. But blindness and excruciating pain wasn't going to stop her from destroying her adversary. Chok thrust one of her claws deep into the tunnel, snapping and reaching for Kyle.

Kyle was backing up cautiously, preparing to fire a third arrow, when he saw Clem's net wrapped loosely around Chok's claw. He reached out and snatched the net from the claw and stepped back out of his foe's reach. He stretched the net out before him, clearly intending to entangle the snapping appendage, but Becky, surprising even me, dropped the chuknuryss and lunged forward. As if giving him a bear hug, Becky reached around Kyle, grabbing the net and pulling backward with all her might.

My two friends hit the soft ground with a splosh. Becky looked up at me, screaming, "mud, now!"

I dropped to my knees and took two handfuls of the, uh… yeah, we're going with mud, here, and shoved the devil's pudding up Kyle's nose and into his ears. Kyle struggled for a moment before his eyes widened. At first, I thought it was fear I saw, but after a couple of seconds staring back, I realized it was morbid recognition. Yeah, there was a little fear, too. Not bogeyman fear, but the type of fear one experiences when they realize they might have hurt someone they care about.

"Pack?" Kyle looked so confused. The animal instincts that the smells and sounds of the arena elicited had completely taken him over. He normally wasn't one to give in to the more primal emotions like rage, so I'm guessing it felt good to just let go. Thankfully, the arrows hit Chok, not Clem, so remorse didn't have to accompany the other emotions for too long. "Pack, what's happening? And what the hell did you put all over my face?!" He went to wipe off the gooey mess, but Becky held his arms back roughly.

I shook my head slowly, pointing at my ears and nose. Then I held my hands out in front of me, signaling 'stop'. I pointed back at my nose and ears again before wagging my finger back and forth in the universal 'no-no-no' motion.

Kyle, who had gotten a mouthful of the stuff, spit and wrinkled his face like he'd just eaten some — oh, come on, there's not much worse than what he was tasting, so we'll just let that one go, ok?

Kyle finally nodded, showing that he understood, and Becky let him go. Once on his feet, he extended a hand to Becky and pulled her up. We all stepped back another foot, distancing ourselves from the blindly snapping claw behind us. He looked at both of us, deeply concerned. "Did I hurt you?"

Becky shook her head. "No, but you might have if we didn't get the drop on you." She looked at the bow that lay on the ground between them. "You're really good with that thing. Like Robin Hood, good."

Kyle looked shocked. "Legolas good?"

"Maybe even Artemis good," I replied, "but don't go getting a big head."

Becky stepped away from us and picked up the fallen chuknuryss. She played with the handle for a moment before it sparked to life, causing her to jump slightly. She waved it in front of herself, testing the weight and feel before turning to the giant snapping claw and cutting it off cleanly. "You can go eff yourself," she told the twitching stump.

She turned back to find us pretending not to be impressed. "Grab a handful of mud. We've got friends to save."

~

As much as we felt safer and less exposed in the tunnels, we had to get topside to help our friends. Before we could escape the tunnel system, though, we had to figure out which exit would be safest. Mostly using our charades skills, we decided the one-armed doR and frenzied Gipak were far more dangerous than a giant, blind crab with only one claw.

Kyle, though decidedly less aggressive than before the doo-doo in his ears and nose, still seemed different. He was carrying himself taller. He looked... confident. I'd never seen that side of him in the *Assassin's Inc.* game. Yeah, he was always a little cocky when he was sporting one of the guns from the Montana compound, but in a clumsy, comical way. Now he was self-assured, and carrying the compound bow in a way that made him appear genuinely dangerous. He stepped towards the tunnel exit and regarded Chok's wildly waving stump with a withering look. He said something neither Becky nor I could hear and pushed at the bleeding tip of the stump with the end of his bow. Whether out of pain or confusion, or maybe a bit of both, the stump pulled back warily.

I clenched my fist and waved it back and forth in front of me, mimicking the use of a chuknuryss, and Becky nodded. I then placed a hand on Kyle's shoulder, gently pulling him back from the twitching stump. Kyle turned quickly and looked at me, thinly veiled surprise skittered across his eyes before vanishing once again behind the newly hung curtain of bravado. I held my arms up, allowing my plasma shield to spark up briefly before unclenching my fists. Then I motioned forward, showing that I'd take the lead. Finally, I pointed at Kyle and pantomimed drawing back a bow and releasing the string. Kyle nodded that he understood, looking to Becky to make sure she was also ready to move.

Becky, who appeared to have been born ready, winked at Kyle and held up her chuknuryss and shield menacingly.

Then they both turned to me.

I guess I was in charge. *Oh boy.*

~

I stepped in front of Becky and Kyle and brought my plasma shield back to life. The bare spots between the nodes on my arms tingled, just like in the game. The blue haze of the shield made me feel even more calm, and I held out my arms, allowing the plasma to touch Chok's damaged limb. The limb pulled back again, and I positioned my shield in a way that allowed me to push the stump out of our way like a battering ram. I pushed forward aggressively, keeping the limb from reaching over or under my shield. When I exited the tunnel, I pushed the limb against the opposing wall, pinning it there with my shield. Becky and Kyle ran out of the tunnel behind me. Becky was planning to rush forward with the chuknuryss, and lop off Chok's other claw, while Kyle was going to fall back and provide cover.

Chok, however, had other plans.

Before Becky could take a step forward, Chok thrust her remaining claw forward and clamped it around my waist. I should have considered the fact that, even though she was blind, she still could feel me pushing on her injured limb. She lifted me off the ground roughly and slammed me against the dirt wall, knocking Becky backward into Kyle. My friends tumbled to the ground, and I got another unwanted look at Kyle's tighty-whities. I groaned loudly as she squeezed. The only thing keeping her from cutting me in two were my dragonhide pants, which were as cut resistant as most heavy armor, but considerably lighter. I unclenched my fists, realizing that if I slammed into the wall with my shield activated, I could end up cutting off the top of my own head. *That* would be a problem.

I reached for my sword, but before I could draw it, a shadow from above descended upon Chok's head. It was Clem!

Clem dropped onto Chok like a, well… a cowboy dropping onto a bucking bull. Chok did not disappoint. She bucked in all directions, swinging me around like a rag doll. I slammed into the dirt wall of the trench three or four more times. I honestly couldn't say how many times for sure, as my head was spinning like a goldfish in a garbage disposal. Then, Clem raised his trident into the air, shouting what sounded like, "I am NOT entertained," and plunged it into Chok's head as far as it would go.

Chok dropped me then, and I tumbled to the ground in front of her, rolling back like a trained martial artist. My head was still spinning. Becky grabbed me and pulled me away from the fracas before Chok fell to the ground in front of us, dead.

Clem pulled the trident out of Chok's head and grinned at us maniacally. He hadn't killed Chok to save me. I was his next target. He pulled Jackson from his waistband and took aim.

A second later, there was an arrow embedded in Clem's throat, and he fell backward onto Chok, his feet twitching.

Kyle cried out. His cool demeanor finally shattered. "I'm sorry! I'm sorry! Oh God, I'M SO SORRY!"

I looked back at him, shocked, but alive. Becky looked as horrified as Kyle sounded.

I turned back to Clem, only to find doR and Gipak barreling towards us, locked in a final confrontation that would likely leave both of them dead. doR white-knuckled his remaining chuknuryss in a death grip that spoke volumes about his mindset. The two combatants didn't see Clem and Chok in their path and tripped over their corpses, taking the power struggle to the ground with a thud that we could feel in our bones.

I turned back to Becky and Kyle and frantically pointed behind us. "Go that way," I shouted, though I'm fairly certain they couldn't hear me.

Becky nodded. We turned to run, but Kyle was rooted in place. He kept mumbling what I'm pretty sure was still, "I'm sorry." With tears in his eyes, he nocked another arrow, drew the bowstring back as far as it could go, and released. The projectile moved faster than any of us could possibly track and ended up sticking out of what remained of Gipak's proboscis. The meta-flea whipped around furiously for a moment, giving death throes a whole new meaning. doR punched Gipak several times with the remaining stump of his arm, an act which made me fear the barbarian that much more. Suddenly, doR's attention fell upon us and stayed there. He stared at the three of us with a frightening level of laser focus. Then it dawned on me what he was staring at.

Becky had his missing chuknuryss.

~

I slapped Kyle across the face, snapping him back to reality, or maybe it was surreality? Either way, he needed to be on the same page as Becky and me.

I motioned away from doR with my head before realizing there was a stone bridge just overhead, the rough-hewn supports were set deep into the dirt, allowing the perfect opportunity to get topside. Kyle was already looking at me, so I grabbed Becky's shoulder and pointed at the potential hand and footholds.

Kyle put his bow over his shoulder and started to climb before looking back at Becky. He suddenly looked guilty and began to come back down. Becky punched him in the butt, as if to say, *'ladies first doesn't apply in the arena, weirdo'*, and he resumed his ascent enthusiastically, scaling the wall in record time. Becky followed, though a little more slowly, as she didn't have a place to stow her chuknuryss while she climbed.

I faced doR as he advanced, climbing over the three bodies in his path. I wasn't going to make it. He was too close. I put up my shield and moved towards him bravely.

In a blind rage, doR began to rain down blow after blow on my poor shield. The plasma color was darkening with each strike, meaning my shield was about as effective as thoughts and prayers against his weapon. I'd have to keep that in mind if Becky ever got angry with me.

Suddenly, doR flew up and out of my sight, leaving me standing with my shield raised awkwardly, the plasma easing back to a nice, cool blue. I looked up, confused, and saw doR fly over the trench sideways, his arms and legs flailing in a rare moment of panic. As he flew back out of sight, I finally understood what happened. Someone had reached down and grabbed doR by his considerable head of hair and swung him in a circle, like a living

bolo.

When the hand released him, doR went sailing off into the

distance in what felt like a moment straight out of a Popeye

cartoon.

And then the hand reached down for me, but not to grab

me by my hair. It was offering help. I'd recognize that massive

paw of a hand anywhere.

It belonged to Pharaoh.

16

The Mane Man

I'd known Pharaoh for as long as I'd known Cool, Becky, Kyle, and… (sigh) Clem. I'd trusted each of them with my life on various occasions, but of all of them, Pharaoh was a born protector. If he were a D&D character, he'd be straight-up lawful good. If he went to Hogwarts, he'd be a Gryffindor. The fact is, lawful goods and Gryffindors aspired to be as honest and honorable as Pharaoh. He was like King Kong with Mr. Rogers' moral code.

When he extended his hand to lift me from the trench, I took one look into his big, kind, almond-shaped eyes, and immediately knew I could trust him again. He was more than my friend; he'd been a big brother to me in the *Animehem* games since I first jacked in. He was literally the strongest ally I had, and aside from Sir Scabby, who could have inspired his own religion, I knew of no one more noble.

Pharaoh's massive hand wrapped around mine like a parent clutching a child's, enveloping it well beyond the wrist. He tugged me out like I was made of crêpe paper and gently set me beside Becky and Kyle. As the battle raged on around us, Pharaoh pointed at his ears, shaking his head. Somehow, he had figured out what Becky had, but unlike Kyle, Becky, and me, he was not covered in blood and excrement.

Without any warning, Pharaoh shoved the three of us aside and stepped around us. We looked around him and saw that Ah Puch had managed to reattach his severed legs, and was quietly approaching us, his perma-grin telling us all we needed to know about his intentions.

Ah Puch, as always, was in no hurry. He was like that big dude in the horror movies with the hockey mask. He moved slowly, but never stopped, and when he caught you, you were very likely going to die. His scythe glinted in the sunlight. As he advanced, I chanced a look around the coliseum to see how Cool and El Scalar were faring.

Aside from the color differences, Cool and ChuChuLo were difficult to distinguish from one another as they grappled, slithered… uh, whatever it was they were doing. It was a bizarre display of elasticity and pliability. One moment they were trying to escape the other's embrace, like excess toothpaste squeezed out of a tube, the next they were winding around each other, fighting for the high ground, coiling and writhing like a bowlful of earthworms. I knew what Cool was doing. As powerful as ChuChuLo's dark magic was, the monster couldn't cast spells while in contact with its opponent. Cool's ability to stretch and reshape his entire body, made him the ultimate close-combat grappler. Pharaoh was no slouch, but Cool's pliability made him more dangerous than his happy-go-lucky demeanor would lead most people to believe.

Directly across the coliseum from Cool and ChuChuLo, and significantly closer to us, El Scalar and Xiro were getting dangerously close to the spectators in the stands. Xiro darted around at sharp angles, trying to unseat Scalar, who had decided the massive silver dragon would make a fine steed. Scalar grabbed onto the base of each of Xiro's wings and was pinching and pulling at them to control the direction of Xiro's flight. It looked like he was trying to make Xiro land. As the two flew about haphazardly, slamming into the pillars that supported the upper box seats where the wealthiest patrons luxuriated, Xiro spewed fire in uncontrolled bursts. It was clear that whatever El Scalar was doing to Xiro's wings was effective.

Roughly halfway between the two other contests, Alpha Male and Mentor were trading blows in a very different way. Mentor's minions were impossible to kill with force, as they just kept returning to their bastardized forms after taking any significant damage. They could be contained, but as long as there was more dirt, sand, rocks, and such, Mentor could easily make more of his grunge-brigade. It was never-ending.

Alpha Male, it seemed, had discovered a way to use Mentor's scuzz-squad against him. The cybernetic silverback was absorbing the materials the troops were made of as they attacked and firing them back at Mentor as deadly projectiles. Mentor resorted to calling some of his troops back to use as a dirt-shield. As far as I could tell, their battle was going into extra innings.

I looked back at Ah Puch, who had already halved the distance between us, but was still moving like a snail in a drag race. Pharaoh stepped forward and cracked his knuckles loudly. He wasn't going to let the death god get any closer to us.

Kyle, Becky, and I stepped forward to join him. I raised my plasma shield, which had returned to a steady, cool shade of blue. Becky sparked up her chuknuryss and Kyle nocked another arrow.

This was our fight, too.

Bring it on, death god.

~

Pharaoh looked down at me and raised a bushy eyebrow quizzically, as if to say, *'Yuh know, Packard, me can manage dis on me own, right?'*

I shook my head defiantly. I was happy to see Pharaoh, and even happier to have him back on our side, but there was no way in hell I was going to let the big palooka fight Ah Puch alone.

Becky and Kyle clearly felt the same way. Kyle's eyes were wet with tears, but that was the only thing about him that didn't look every bit as ready as Becky and I did. His jaw was set forward, and he was gritting his teeth so tightly that spittle flew from them as he breathed. Becky was also processing the shock of losing Clem, but she wasn't the one who'd put the arrow through his throat. I felt like Kyle might just be whispering 'I'm sorry' until the day he died, which given the circumstances, might have been sooner than any of us expected.

If we waited for Ah Puch to make it to us on his own, we would have been bored out of our minds. He was giving us Batman level prep time, so we made the first move.

I poked at Pharaoh's side because I couldn't reach his shoulder, and he met my eyes. I motioned with my hands in a flying gesture. He frowned before offering an uneasy, but affirmative nod. Then, before I could change my mind, he picked me up. I curled into my best semblance of a ball — Cool could have done much better — and he hurled me at the terrifying Mesoamerican death god.

When I was practically on top of Ah Puch, I straightened out and brought my shield to life. I struck the blade of his scythe with the front edge of my shield and used the kinetic energy to launch myself over his head in a very impressive somersault. A second later, I was standing behind old Boney Moroney, dropping my shield and reaching for my sword.

Imagine how I felt when I drew it and there was no blade attached to the hilt.

I was freaking ecstatic! Okay, so I was a little jarred for a split second, but when I recognized the hilt I'd drawn hundreds of times — you know, the one with the flaming sunflower in the Freemason-looking eye on the quillon block — I knew I'd just been reunited with another old friend.

The mighty Sword of Helianthus!

That phrase always deserves its own line.

~

Surprisingly, Ah Puch turned much faster than he walked. In a single sweeping motion, he pivoted and brought the blade of his scythe down. Of course, my head was his target.

Lacking enough time to spark up my shield and strike an effective defensive pose, I extended my arm and put the sword's crosspiece directly in the path of the rapidly descending blade. When the blade struck the hardened steel of the crosspiece, I invoked the name of Helianthus. A blade of pure sunlight sprung to life. The unstoppable sword consumed the hell-forged scythe's blade, enveloping it in the equivalent of a self-contained solar flare. The flare overlapped onto the old, gnarled wooden handle, leaving Ah Puch holding little more than a slightly curved, impotent-looking bo staff. The blade of his scythe clattered to the ground and came to rest in a pile of dust and blood-encrusted rocks.

I swear, just for a moment, I saw his eye sockets widen.

Suddenly, feeling the effects of the Quantum Nanops surging throughout my entire body, I came to the terrifying yet comforting realization that I had actually become the living embodiment of my in-game persona. I was a warlord.

I leapt forward, springing into the air like a tiger, and swung my flaming sword in a deadly arc. Ah Puch took one step backward and raised the handle of his ruined scythe in a lame attempt to block my attack. My sword's hand guard had only succeeded in blocking his scythe's blade because it, too, was the weapon of a god. The handle he still clutched like a child's security blanket, however, was not divine in any way. It was extremely hard, insanely durable wood, but that was all. Against my divine blade, it might as well have been a balsa wood toothpick.

When my blade connected with the scythe's handle, the wood instantly turned to ash and blew from my foe's hands like dust in the wind. My sword and I weren't finished, though, and the superheated blade continued on its deadly arc until it had separated Ah Puch's head from his shoulders. His skull bounced away, finally coming to a stop next to the enormous gate that had served as our initial entry point, grinning like he'd just told the world's funniest dad joke. His body suddenly lost cohesion, the bones dropping in a melodic series of thunks that sounded like a bone xylophone. Come on, you've never seen the old cartoon? It's a classic. The skeleton banging away on the... Uh... sorry... you know I squirrel sometimes. Anyway, Ah Puch was down for the count, his weapon utterly destroyed.

As I resheathed my weapon, Pharaoh, Becky, and Kyle joined me at the pile of bones that had once been a formidable enemy. They all looked appropriately impressed.

Suddenly, a boom we could all hear through the crap in our ears rang out overhead.

We all looked up in unison to see what had happened, and when I say *we all*, I mean *ALL*. Every combatant still standing and every spectator in the seats above joined Pharaoh, Becky, Kyle, and I in a collective glance skyward. I was half-expecting to see Scalar and Xiro duking it out in the upper echelons of the coliseum, but instead saw that one of the Black Hawk helicopters had just exploded.

But that wasn't exactly right.

The helicopter looked like it was exploding in slow motion.

But that *still* wasn't right.

The other two choppers quickly veered away from their dying comrade, but as they tried to flee the coliseum's airspace, they appeared to fall victim to the same explosive fate before they could escape the perimeter.

The three remaining battles quickly drew our attention back to the arena. El Scalar and Xiro were still in the upper seating, circling each other like sharks in a feeding frenzy. They were too high up for us to get to easily, so I set my sights on the wars being waged at ground level. Mentor and Alpha Male weren't our allies, so their conflict was none of our concern, so long as they continued to focus on each other. The battle between Cool and ChuChuLo, however, was an entirely different story. Cool was holding his own, but if the monstrous tentacled spell-weaver could shake our friend, then it could wreak all kinds of havoc that neither Cool nor the rest of us were equipped to counter. We'd be helpless.

I pointed towards Cool and ChuChuLo, and pantomimed separating them, before exaggeratedly plugging my nose and covering my ears. I put my hands out, palms up, and twisted my face a bit, wondering if they understood my instructions.

Becky and Kyle, free of the mind warping effects of the invasive sensory input, nodded apprehensively. Pharaoh, however, shot me a thumbs up that would have made The Fonz proud.

We ran forward, curving to the left around the second ring of the arena. We stopped a few feet away from the melee, hoping to stay out of range of any stray tentacles or flying hooves that might whip in our direction, and I turned Becky's face to meet mine. I pointed at Cool, then touched my ears, pulling them forward, as if I was going to seal them shut. Becky's eyes widened, and she nodded that she understood. I turned to Kyle and waved my arms around wildly — hey, I was mimicking tentacles, not losing my mind. Then I pointed at my eyes, and mimicked drawing back a bow and firing an arrow. I was getting pretty good at that one. Kyle nodded. He was also on board.

I finally turned to Pharaoh and put out my arms, signaling that I wanted him to hold Cool and ChuChuLo in place while we did our collective thing. Pharaoh, who was equal parts lover and fighter, thought I was giving him an oddly timed hug and reciprocated warmly. If you've never gotten a hug from Pharaoh, then you won't understand why my first instinct was to hug back. He was like a father, brother, and best friend all rolled into a big cozy kitty cat. Granted, he was a kitty cat that probably knew more ways to kill you than the Devil himself, but he was *still* a kitty cat.

I pulled away from the hug, hoping my face displayed my sincerest apology for doing so, and shook my head no. Then I pointed at the writhing mess of wriggling limbs that was Cool and

ChuChuLo and made the hugging gesture again. Pharaoh opened his mouth and nodded in a gesture that perfectly conveyed *'Aha!'*, then he winked and punched me in the shoulder affectionately. I'm a little ashamed to admit, that love tap hurt enough to warrant a tube of Ben Gay.

Then, without any further ado, we snapped into action.

Pharaoh stepped forward first, spreading his Herculean arms wide as he carefully approached the strange wrestling pair. Then, with a tilt of his head, and a moment of what I assumed was calculation, the Prince of Beasts took the Elastic Giraffe and his foe into his arms and squeezed. He lifted the writhing mass and pivoted 180°, so the pair was in between him and us, then he set his feet and anchored them in place.

Next, Kyle stepped back and nocked another arrow, which he leveled at Cool and ChuChuLo. His aim was true and his stare resolute. How I'd missed that side of Kyle in the games was beyond me, but I knew at that moment, he was every bit the warrior I was.

Finally, Becky and I stepped forward. She knew what we were looking for, and it would only be a matter of time before it resurfaced. We were looking for Cool's head.

Nearly thirty seconds later — yes, I counted — our patience was rewarded when Cool's face erupted from the wildly thrashing mass. Honestly, that was the first time I ever thought of him as scary. Seeing him with his teeth gritted, nostrils flared, and eyes narrowed like an enraged beast, made me want to step back and rethink my next move. I could see that Becky was unsure as well, but seeing as she didn't give an inch, I couldn't either.

We both sprung forward.

Becky climbed onto the horrifying mass, scaling the whipping, pulsing pair like a skilled mountaineer. When she reached the top of Cool's head, she grabbed onto his ears and pulled forward, shoving his earflaps down into his ear canals. At that very same moment, I shoved both hands — being careful not to make fists, for fear I might activate my plasma shield — deep into Cool's nostrils.

Cool's eyes widened, a mixture of confusion and rage contorting his face. Then, as the external stimuli faded, his expression changed. The confusion remained, but something resembling fear replaced the rage. Cool doesn't generally do fear.

After allowing a moment for his head to clear, Cool looked at me through a very different lens. He nodded as best he could with Becky grasping his ears and my hands shoved up his nose. And then he sneezed.

The pressure of the sneeze forced my hands out in an awful spray of what looked and felt like homemade slime. Cool's head jerked so abruptly that Becky lost her grip and fell. Thankfully, the drop was less than ten feet, and I was able to catch her and set her down beside me. Without acknowledging each other, or the fact that I'd just gotten elastic snot all over her armor, we both looked back at Cool, afraid he'd already be falling back under the spell of the smells and sounds of the arena.

He had not. I was happy, and not the slightest bit surprised, to find he'd used his morphing abilities to completely seal off his ears and nose. Cool was a bit of a creative genius.

My elastic friend grinned at me, though there was a tinge of something else hidden behind his eyes.

Regret?

Remorse?

No... it was shame. I smiled back warmly, hoping he'd understand there were no hard feelings, and caught Becky doing the same out of the corner of my eye. Cool's eyes shone brightly, sparkling with the relief that is a wonderful little byproduct of unconditional forgiveness.

Oh, by the way, did I forget to tell you about the next part of the plan? Probably, because I also forgot to tell Becky and

Kyle. Well… at least Pharaoh and I were on the same page. He and Cool had a very specialized, well-practiced move, and I might have dropped a signal suggesting using said move after our poorly timed hug.

Let me tell you, when Pharaoh ripped Cool free of ChuChuLo and hurled our stretchy compadre towards Scalar and Xiro like a javelin, none of us were particularly happy to see the tentacled terror in its birthday suit!

Without skipping a beat, Pharaoh grabbed one of ChuChuLo's tentacles in each hand and swung it overhead, slamming the monster into the ground on each side of him like a big, squishy sledgehammer. On the third swing, Pharaoh released the tentacles and hurled the furiously flailing creature at an altogether unsuspecting Mentor and Alpha Male. The three of them tumbled, head over tentacles, more than twenty feet before slamming into the coliseum wall and pulling away from each other in the most severe defensive postures.

I took that opportunity to look up at Cool and found that he'd completely enveloped El Scalar in another yellow tarp-form, complete with brown spots of course, much the same way he'd done with ChuChuLo.

While the spectators in the area where Xiro and our bison-headed amigo had been trading blows were screaming and scattering out of terror, the rest of the fans cheered like they'd never cheered before. None of them had ever seen a battle quite as chaotic as the one we were fighting at that moment.

From somewhere within Cool's protective sheath that was covering El Scalar, it was clear ol' Tatanka Head was trying to fight his way out. Fist sized lumps erupted one after another, snapping back into place as soon as the fists withdrew. After several of his strongest punches failed, Scalar began hacking at Cool's hide with his battleaxe. We could see the sharp-edged blade push forth, but it was incapable of penetrating Cool's elastic skin. We had no idea what Cool's skin was made of. I'm fairly certain even Cool didn't know. Whatever it was, it was durable. The only thing I'd ever seen hurt him was my divine sun blade.

The mighty Sword of Helianthus!

And that was purely an accident. He was goofing around once while I was practicing parrying against a pile of rocks, and I inadvertently nicked his nose. It healed fine, but as I said, it was the one and only time I'd ever seen him injured.

Scalar's axes were of no consequence.

After taking a faceful of fire from Xiro, Cool dropped to the arena floor, still grinning from ear to ear... at least, where his ears should have been. Once he was back on solid ground, Cool tightened his grip around El Scalar like a spacesuit. I knew what he was doing. I'd seen him do it before. He was cutting off Scalar's air. Once Scalar passed out, he'd release him, and we'd be back in business. In theory anyway.

As Scalar continued to struggle against his airtight straitjacket, we ran towards Cool, returning the way we came. Skirting the killing grounds on our left, we were almost back to the area where we'd first entered when we heard a roar and a ruckus coming from the tunnel beyond the massive gate's iron bars.

Pharaoh put up a protective hand and once again placed himself at the front of the pack. Seconds later, the gates exploded inward, and my dear old friend Knightmare burst through, grinding to a halt in the dirt. Torrents of dust and rocks stirred up by her tires flew forward, the dust being caught up in the ever present breeze that whipped through the arena in whirling eddies. A pair of nasty-looking, three-foot long plasma cannons erupted from her front fenders, and rotated, aiming directly at ChuChuLo, Mentor, and Alpha Male.

I couldn't hear much with the load of number two in my ears, but I swear I heard the song "Dragula" playing at full blast, only with an acoustic guitar and an odd country twang.

The moment she cleared the gate, her roof, which she kept conspicuously shut, suddenly raised just enough for a lone occupant to spring forth from the passenger seat and soar through the air, using KM's forward momentum as propulsion.

The man moved like something straight out of a superhero movie, planting the back of his long-handled weapon against the ground in front of him like a pole vault, and launching forward to intercept Pharaoh, Kyle, Becky, and me. Our jaws dropped in unison as he landed in the dirt with a thud, and brought the business end of his weapon forward, shoving it directly against Pharaoh's throat!

I scooted under Pharaoh's legs and popped up between the man and his supposed enemy, my hands waving wildly in the air. "No, he's with us! Oh god, it's great to see you, Clem!"

17

Stranger Thangs

Did you forget about respawning? Because Kyle, Becky, and I had.

Seeing Clem fly into battle to save us from what he thought was a nine-foot-tall, musclebound threat nearly brought tears to my eyes. Kyle *did* cry. He stumbled forward and hugged Clem tightly, babbling about something I could only assume was, "I'm sorry", on repeat.

The touching reunion was cut short when Knightmare began firing concentrated plasma bursts at our three enemies across the arena. She managed to drive Mentor and Alpha Male back into the curved stone wall of the coliseum, but ChuChuLo, no longer bound by Cool, was free to work its magic! Tentacles waved in every direction, reminding me a lot of my true to life pantomime

I'd performed for Kyle only minutes earlier. I really *was* good at charades!

With each wave of its tentacles, ChuChuLo redirected plasma bursts back at Knightmare. She easily deflected them, but realized they could be deadly to us.

Clem removed the sobbing Kyle from his person like one might peel a static-charged sock from a blanket and patted him on the head awkwardly. He then pointed back towards the tunnel and the ruined gates. We all nodded and ran towards the mouth of the tunnel.

I watched Becky stop and pick something up from the dirt as we made our way forward. A moment later, she was back by my side, wrapping her find in a piece of cloth she'd torn from her warrior's get-up.

Knightmare waited for us to get to the tunnel mouth before backing up. Before we could enter, Xiro flew down, flattened his wings against his body, and soared into the tunnel, blasting it with fire as he went. We could hear what sounded like a sonic boom come from the tunnel as he exited the other side.

Cool deposited El Scalar and his battleaxe into KM's back seat and flattened himself out into a massive shield, allowing the rest of us to get into the tunnel safely.

Have you ever heard the term 'out of the frying pan and into the fire'? I feel like I understand what that saying means after entering the long tunnel we all hoped would lead to freedom. As soon as we stepped across the threshold, we felt the effects of Xiro's superheated breath. The heavy masonry that made up the tunnel walls was bordering on molten. Just walking into the opening felt like walking into a blast furnace, *in Hell*.

Becky froze, and I recognized the same look I'd seen when I asked her to put on an envirosuit in Laboratory 311. She was a severe claustrophobe. She shook her head, indicating that out of all the things she'd faced so far that day, the molten tunnel was the one thing that might finally beat her. Going in had been fine, as the tunnel was as tall and wide as an average bedroom. But with the walls on fire, the mortar dripping from between brick and stone menacingly, and the oppressive heat that radiated inward, the exit might as well have been the diameter of a tube in a McDonald's Play Place.

I picked Becky up, not caring that she'd be furious with me later, and plopped her into KM's back seat, right on top of Scalar. Kyle hopped over the door and wound up in the driver's seat. I slapped KM's fender and shouted, "GO!" And *GO* she did! The plasma cannons on her front fenders rotated 180° and blasted falling chunks of brick and rock as she sped backwards. I nodded at Clem, tilting my head towards the tunnel. With one final suspicious glance at Pharaoh, he returned the nod and ran into the tunnel, gripping his trident like he'd been born with it.

As Pharaoh and I backed towards the tunnel and Cool ran interference, ChuChuLo extended one of its tentacles and wrapped it around Alpha Male's barrel of a head. The colossal silverback reached up and gripped the offending tentacle in both hands, trying to rip it free. Before Alpha Male could free himself, though, ChuChuLo lifted him high over its head, and heaved him at us like a big, butt-ugly hand grenade. Cool could have easily deflected the cybernetic monstrosity, but before the roaring beast made contact, ChuChuLo shot a bolt of hexed lightning through the air and did something none of us could have anticipated. It shattered Alpha Male into dozens of screaming cyborg monkeys that rained down on us in a living wave of anger and confusion. Each of the monkeys had a pair of brass cymbals strapped to their hands and wore the unhinged grins of those sinister-looking windup toys — you know, those monkeys that sit and cackle and bang their cymbals together? Yeah... we were suddenly facing an army of them!

Cool snapped back to his original form and batted wildly at the screaming, clanging, metallic monkeys. Pharaoh grabbed as many as he could and hurled them back at Mentor and ChuChuLo. I drew my divine blade and began chopping them down like weeds. Once the monkeys realized the three of us weren't going down that easily, they scattered and disappeared into the searing depths of the tunnel behind Clem.

Pharaoh, Cool, and I ran in behind them, into what felt like Satan's butthole! The heat was incredible, and I suddenly developed even more respect for Cool's durability, considering he'd taken a direct blast of Xiro's rock melting fire and come away unscathed. Once the three of us were about ten feet in, Pharaoh lumbered back to the mouth of the tunnel and began slamming his ginormous fists into the stone arch that marked the threshold like a punching bag. It only took a few of his deathblows to break the archway apart, and he quickly returned to us as the entrance to the tunnel collapsed. As the bricks and stone cascaded down, I caught a brief glimpse of ChuChuLo and Mentor locked in mortal combat. Then the rest of the tunnel destabilized and started to crumble!

Seeing that Clem was already halfway to the sunlit arch that represented freedom, I waved my arms, and pointed at the exit. I didn't really have to do that, as Pharaoh and Cool were already on the move. Pharaoh caught up with me quickly and snatched me up like a firefighter tossing a child over his shoulder, and he and Cool barreled forward like the superheroes they were.

As we moved swiftly past Clem, Pharaoh picked him up as well and slung him over his other shoulder, his trident scraping the crumbling tunnel ceiling as we moved. Clem's eyes narrowed when we made eye contact across Pharaoh's broad back, and he shook his head at me, as if to say, '*we ain't never speakin' of this, Marshal. Not ever.*'

And that was when Pharaoh and Cool really poured on the speed! A few moments later, we exited the tunnel at the other side and Pharaoh and Cool skidded to a stop in the dirt, joining KM and the others.

Pharaoh set the two of us down gently, but seemed distracted by whatever he was looking at outside the coliseum. I looked up and saw that Cool looked equally perplexed. I turned to see what they were looking at and almost crapped my pants.

~

In retrospect, nothing should have surprised me at that point, but when we exited the coliseum and saw an honest-to-goodness steam train roaring past less than fifty feet ahead of us, I shook my head in disbelief.

KM had stopped about twenty feet away from the coliseum entrance. The soil where we all stood was nothing like the bulldozed parcel that had been underfoot when we'd arrived a half hour earlier. The new dirt was fresh, barely touched. It was as if we'd gone back in time and were walking on virgin land, previously only trod on by animals. Speaking of animals, the metallic musical monkeys — *that totally sounds like a band* — that escaped through the tunnel were hanging all over the steam train as it sped south along what appeared to be freshly laid tracks. The rails leading south disappeared into the brush along the waterfront pathway we'd driven in on. About a hundred yards to the north, something else was happening that took our collective breath away.

The tracks were building themselves.

Not only the tracks, but the train that ran along them, was being assembled out of thin air while it moved full steam ahead. If I were to take a guess as to how many cars the locomotive was pulling, I'd have guessed at least a hundred, but new cars kept growing at the back like they were coming out of an invisible tunnel. I could only assume it would eventually end in a caboose.

Speeding away from us, I could see flat cars, cattle cars, and even some tankers, but the bulk of the cars passing by the time we'd caught up with KM and the others were passenger and luggage cars. I glanced over at Clem. His slack-jawed expression validated my gut instinct about the steam-powered blast from the past. The beautifully crafted train was the Imperial 221, and it was headed straight for Rotgut, Arizona, leaving a trail of dissipating black smoke in its wake.

~

My attention returned to the point where the Quantum Nanops seemed to be the most active, the spot where they were knitting the train together like an army of grandmothers in a quilting competition.

As one cloud of my tiny benefactors seemingly willed the train into existence, yet another cloud was busy building a massive tunnel, completing the illusion that the train was actually coming from somewhere. I found myself wondering where the tunnel might lead once the train was no longer barreling forth from its dark, mysterious depths.

Kyle pulled himself out of Knightmare's driver's seat, and

Becky, looking a little embarrassed and a lot pissed off, climbed

over the back, and slid down the trunk. Her armor squealed as it

dragged along KM's flawless black paint job, peeling away a ribbon

of paint suitable for a goth's birthday present, and leaving an

unsightly groove that exposed a layer of gray primer and bare

metal.

Becky's expression crumbled when she realized what she'd

just done, and she stepped back and sighed. "I'm sorry,

Knightmare. I didn't mean to-"

"Think nothing of it," Knightmare said, cutting Becky off

before she could ingratiate herself any further. Her voice carried a

hint of empathy. "With my highly advanced nanotechnology, it

takes a lot more than an armor scrape to damage me."

Becky's defeated grimace actually softened as she watched

the scratch that many insurance companies would total a car over,

vanish like acne scars under laser surgery.

I wanted to run to her, hug her, and apologize for tossing her onto El Scalar, but I also realized that particular action would serve zero purpose. She and the others needed a leader more than anything else, and Becky had already said it earlier. *I was the only one who'd been in every world the Quantum Nanops could cook up.*

El Scalar was still slumped in KM's back seat. The big fella was unconscious but breathing. *What the hell,* I thought, *let him have a nap.* I had a sneaking suspicion that things were only going to get worse.

Glancing around at the others, I asked, "is everyone okay?"

Clem grunted. "Less'n you count me dyin' at the hands of young Kyle, here, and findin' myself wedged inta' Knightmare's backside alongside yer pa's 'lectric printin' press, I ain't no worse for wear." Before Kyle could resume his incessant apologizing, Clem turned to him and grinned. "And please allow me to say, that was one helluva shot! Ace high!"

Kyle's mouth dropped open even further before it curved up into an awkward, self-conscious smile. "Uh, thanks! But I really am sorr-"

Clem's hand shot up, silencing his would-be protégé. "Not another word about it."

The rest of us breathed a sigh of relief when Kyle closed his mouth and nodded reluctantly. A moment later, he spoke again, thankfully without the apology shtick. "I'm okay," he said finally. "And I can hear again. That's a plus."

Becky touched her ears and blew a puff of air out through her nose. "The heat in the Devil's tunnel of love dried out all the mud. It should just flake away now."

Pharaoh looked confused. "Dat was no mu-"

"Well, beats digging it out with a stick, right?" I cut into the conversation before Pharaoh could get Becky and Kyle more upset than they already were.

Cool looked at us, clearly confused. When he spoke, it was bordering on a shout. "Can any of you dudes hear me? Because I can't hear any of you!"

Becky pointed at his ears and nose before making fists and reopening her hands, like she was mimicking a flower opening. Cool stretched his neck down to her, and she touched where his nose and ears should be, raising her eyebrows quizzically.

Cool laughed as his nose and ears popped back into place. "Heh, thanks, Becky! I forgot I did that!"

Pharaoh rolled his eyes and shrugged, which reminded me of something I'd forgotten to ask. "Say, Pharaoh, how did you resist the sounds and smells? You didn't have any of the poo-uh, mud in your ears and nose."

Pharaoh's expression darkened as he considered my question. "Me nuh undastand anyting about sound an' smells. Me can't smell nuttin', mon. Di last ting me rememba, before me wakin' up in a cell, was me divin' into Hemlock Swamp t'save yuh from di Eleventacles. When me wake up in di cell, dis cold me been fightin' was worse, an' me ears filled up wit swamp water an' moss. Den, me see El Scalar in anotha' cell. Him was ragin' an' bangin' hims axe against di cell bars. Dat made me feel some rage inside. Before me know it, me was in dat arena wit all dem crazy fightahs."

Clem squinted suspiciously at Cool, who was nodding thoughtfully. "You mean t'tell me that you un'nerstood even a lick of what he just done said?"

Cool returned the incredulous look. "He was speaking plain English, dude."

Pharaoh shrugged. "Me know me accent hard tuh undastand, mon."

Clem nodded. "I ain't too clear on all you just said, friend, but I'll trust the Marshal to keep me up to speed with whatever's important." Then Clem looked at me and said, "his accent calls to mind the way folks in the bayou speak, and I ain't never been able to un'nerstand them either."

I sighed. "It's okay, Clem. We'll get there." I looked at Becky, Pharaoh, Cool, and KM. "What about you guys? Are you all okay?"

Cool grinned. "You know me. I'm always good, bro!"

Becky looked at the others, waiting to see if anyone else would answer. When no one did, she finally spoke. "What just happened in there, Packard?" She looked at the train, which the Nanops had finally completed. The caboose rolled away, clickity-clacking noisily along the freshly laid tracks that crossed Hunter's Point Expressway and disappeared into the dense foliage that ran along the water's edge. The train's whistle cried out as it headed towards Highway 101 and parts beyond. She shook her head. "I mean, I know what's happening, but… this is just… it's escalating in ways I never could have imagined."

I locked gazes with her, trying to stay strong and confident for her and the others. Truth be told, I wasn't sure of anything. We just fought a battle in an arena that shouldn't exist in the real world, against enemies that would shatter most average people's grasp on sanity, or at least grease the rope a bit. "You're right. It's bad. It's really bad. But as much as I was upset with Kyle's need to leave Arete, I'm glad we came here. Otherwise, Pharaoh and El Scalar might still be fighting in there, or worse." I looked up at Pharaoh, who was gazing pensively at our bison-headed friend in KM's back seat. They were both tough, but neither was completely invincible. Now that they were in my world, their safety was my responsibility. "I know one thing for sure. We need to follow that train. If it's going where I think it is, we might be needed there as much as we were needed in the arena."

Becky gazed at the tracks absently. "Where do you think it's going?"

Clem spoke up. "I believe that train's headin' di-rectly to my hometown of Rotgut, Arizona."

I nodded. "That's my suspicion, too. I saw the number on the side of the engine before it vanished into the brush. It was the Imperial 221. It connects with the Regal 831 in Flagstaff, then it passes through Payson, Phoenix, Tucson, and finally Rotgut, before heading out to New Mexico and Texas."

Kyle scratched his head. "All those cities are in Arizona. Why would the Nanops recreate part of Arizona in California? Bro, you have an Arizona... right?"

"Yeah," I said. "We have an Arizona, but not a Rotgut." I looked at Clem, wondering how my admission would affect him. "Rotgut never existed in this world. It's fictional here."

Clem sucked at his teeth, looking like he was uncomfortable with the idea, but still capable of accepting the unbelievable set of circumstances he'd been thrust into. "I s'pose them Nanops, as you call 'em, needed a Rotgut to carry out the next stage of their plan, whatever that may be. Would that be an accurate assessment, Marshal?"

Everyone looked at Clem like he'd just announced he'd received a doctorate from MIT.

"Uh, yeah," I said finally. "That pretty much sums it up."

Clem nodded, clearly glad to have a grasp on an otherwise mind-bending situation. He looked at Becky curiously. "You never did say if you was alright, Miss Becky. Are you okay to mosey on down the tracks?"

Becky sighed. "Yeah. I'm still just trying to wrap my mind around all this."

"Me too," I said softly. I waited another moment before turning to Pharaoh. "Are you okay, big guy?"

"Me nevah bettah," he replied. "Me just happy t'see yuh good, bredren. Me am grateful tuh yuh an' yuh friends, rescuin' Scalar an' me outta dat place before tings got outta hand."

I smiled at his upbeat response. He wasn't perpetually happy like Cool, but he was generally a very positive guy to be around. Interestingly, many people would have taken the latter part of his response, the part about things getting out of hand, to mean he was afraid he and Scalar might have gotten hurt. While injury was a possibility, what he actually meant was that he was glad they didn't have to kill anyone. Under the influence of the coliseum, all of us were capable of some horrible things, but under normal conditions, Pharaoh wasn't that guy. As scary as he looked, and as powerful as he was, he was still just a big kitten. I mentioned it before because it's true. He was a gentle giant... for as long as he was allowed to be, anyway. Even the mighty

Pharaoh's limits had boundaries, and his big red button was his family. A big game hunter named Jungle James murdered the big guy's parents right in front of him when he was just a cub, so anyone Pharaoh called family was part of his pride. I was his family, Cool and Scalar were his family, and if our current little band of misfit toys remained together long enough, I knew he'd consider each of them family as well.

Pharaoh would do anything for his pride.

I smiled and turned to KM. "How's about you, girl? Hangin' in there?"

"I ran a complete diagnostic. All systems check out fine," Knightmare chirped. "Or as Clem might say, I am rooty, tooty, fresh, and fruity."

Clem looked a little confused but chose to let the inaccuracy slide. "Darn tootin'," he said, nodding amicably, causing Cool to giggle. Apparently, our elastic friend got the reference.

I glanced at all of my friends, remembering that not all of them knew each other. I introduced them individually, and they all said their obligatory hellos and howdys. When I introduced Clem, Kyle, and Becky to Pharaoh, Becky put out her hand and said in a very solid Clem voice, "I'd be Becky."

Clem, who was just opening his mouth to ensure nobody mistook him for anyone but Clem, looked at her sideways. "Now, nobody is goin' to mistake you for anyone but Bec- oh, I see what y'all did there. Hardy har har."

Becky punched Clem lightly in the shoulder before turning back to Pharaoh and saying, "and he's Clem." She pointed at Kyle. "And he's Kyle. And Knightmare is the beautiful black Pontiac, and Cool-"

"Me already know Cool. Him an' me been bredren a long time now," Pharaoh said with a smile.

"Okay then," I announced. "I guess that's it for the introductions until El Scalar wakes up. Unless anyone has any objections, let's follow those tracks and see if Clem and I are right about Rotgut. Pharaoh, the rest of us can fill you in on where you are and why while we're walking."

No one voiced any objections, so KM drove up onto the tracks and used her nanotech abilities to reshape her tires enough to resemble bogie wheels. That's just a fancy name for the wheels on the cars pulled by a train.

Once she was securely on the tracks, we began our trek westward.

~

Aside from Scalar, who didn't wake up until we were almost at our destination, we all chose to walk.

I was happy to stretch my legs a bit, and it was clear nobody else wanted to be cooped up in KM. El Scalar smelled pretty ripe, and the afternoon heat wasn't helping at all.

Even though the train had a massive head start on us, we really weren't that concerned. If Rotgut was indeed being constructed somewhere ahead, the Quantum Nanops seemed to be mostly anticipating *my* participation. After going through the trouble of planning a surprise party, no good host would start without the guest of honor, right?

According to KM, who had access to most of the global satellite feeds, the distance from the stadium to our next destination was roughly two miles. The freshly laid tracks replaced Harney Way, and the Nanops had erased everything on either side to match the narrative of the game. Prime land, once populated with condominium complexes, single family homes, and bustling business parks, was suddenly nothing more than a bona fide set of arid foothills dotted with stunted patches of sagebrush.

The tracks continued under Highway 101 by way of a perfectly crafted tunnel that vaguely resembled the other one the Nanops were building back by the coliseum.

We passed under the highway, uneven gravel crunching noisily underfoot. I looked back at the overpass, wondering if anyone was still driving up there. I suppose either answer would have come with its own level of surprise but seeing a few cars speeding past made me feel a little less apprehensive about what was going on in the rest of the world. As far as I could tell, whatever was happening to us was mostly isolated. What surprised me, though, was the lack of spectators. People, like many species of animal, are pretty curious, especially when there's some sort of danger or unexplained phenomena going on. But where I would have expected an audience of news vans, helicopters, police, military, and other first responders, as well as the throng of dumbasses who couldn't help but gawk at the strange group of warriors, there was nothing. Nobody was watching. There was zero air traffic, and like I said before, the few cars that actually passed over the overpass, were clearly not interested in slowing down to participate in the great American sport of rubbernecking.

On the other side of the short tunnel, we found more of the same virginal landscape. I'd played *Marshal Blood* so many times that I honestly wasn't surprised to see a herd of more than a hundred buffalo grazing atop one of the newly formed hills. It took a few moments to reconcile what I was seeing, but the lack of homes and other structures suddenly registered, and I stopped dead in my tracks. I walked away from the parallel rails and stood on a patch of parched, cracked earth, staring at the newly formed hills to the north. The area within close visual proximity of the tracks was now a perfect recreation of southern Arizona. We were in San Francisco, less than a mile from the Bay, but the air where I stood felt so dry, the bushes would probably follow the dogs around.

Becky joined me and took in the view. Not being familiar with my version of San Francisco, she had no context to serve as a basis for a conversation about it, yet she genuinely wanted to know what I was seeing. "What's the matter?"

I had a very bad feeling about what I was seeing. "There are supposed to be homes here," I replied. "Homes, businesses, condos, apartments..." I trailed off as I looked around. "I think there's supposed to be a building supply store right about where we're standing."

Becky looked at the freeway curiously, then back at me. "Where did it all go?"

I pursed my lips and sighed. "Let's go find out."

~

As we walked back towards the rest of the group, who were all were eyeing us like two kids in the back seat of a car, an older man, probably in his sixties, burst out of the bushes ahead. He wore a pair of khaki pants and a dark blue polo shirt stretched uncomfortably around a respectable beer gut. Completing the ensemble was a pair of tan work boots and a ball cap that bore the familiar H-shaped logo for 'Handydude Builder's Supply'. When he saw us, he began running in our direction, but slowed dramatically when he saw Pharaoh.

"You're with them, aren't you," he shouted, though his voice sounded hoarse, like he'd been screaming. "More of those damned monsters!" He looked around, his eyes wild with panic.

I put up my hand and shouted back, hoping to draw his attention away from Pharaoh. Cool, too, since I didn't think he'd seen him yet. "We're not monsters! We're lost, just like you."

The man stared at Becky and me, clearly suspicious of our clothing and unsure of what to make of Pharaoh. But he was frightened and alone, needing desperately to be seen and heard. "What the hell happened to everything," he wondered aloud. "Where are the buildings? A-and the people? My-my friends… where are they?" He pointed back into the scrub brush he'd just come from. "Mrs. Lewis wanted one of the five gallon maple trees. I went to the back lot to get one, but everything is gone… everything." He turned back to face us, pale, like he'd just seen a ghost. "Where did everything go?" I tried to respond, but before I could say anything to comfort him, he pointed back the way we'd just come from. "What in the HELL is that?!"

We turned to see what he was referring to and saw the coliseum towering less than a half a mile away.

I turned back to the man, hoping to calm him a bit and maybe find out what else he'd seen, but he'd begun batting at his clothes and arms frantically.

"Oh no," he cried. "No! No! Please, God! Not like them!" As he batted at his clothes, they flaked away like they were made of ash. Unlike ash, they dissipated before they could touch the ground… like they'd never existed. His hat flaked away, leaving a mostly balding head and a half-hearted attempt at a comb-over exposed.

And then the unthinkable happened.

Starting with his Homer Simpson-like strands of hair, and continuing downwards like a cold chill, his body began to fly apart. The man, whose name tag identified him as Mike, screamed like he was being tortured. In retrospect, I believe he was. We all ran to him. None of us was sure what we were going to do, but we were also unable to simply stand around and do nothing. It took a few moments before I could really process what I was seeing, but the man was being disassembled right before our eyes... part by part, atom by atom.

Even as fast as Pharaoh was, Mike had broken down to nothing more than a fine mist and the echo of a gurgling scream before we could reach him.

We all stopped a few feet short of where he'd been when he dissipated, our expressions reflecting various levels of disbelief and revulsion.

Becky, of course, was the first one to react out loud, and despite the strength and courage she'd exuded since leaving Arete, she finally broke. "Somebody, please tell me what just happened," she said through short, uneven breaths. Her tone bordered on hysterical. "Because any explanation my mind can offer is just too awful to be true."

Becky's eyes welled up with tears. She was on the verge of hyperventilating.

Knightmare's answer didn't help. "The man who ran from the bushes was native to this world. The Quantum Nanops broke down his body, and everything that used to be here, to use as material."

Becky's tears quickly became sobs when she heard the answer, but ever-inquisitive Kyle had to press on. "Material for what," he asked.

KM's answer was so casually clinical, you'd forget she possessed empathy and an understanding of the human psyche. "Material for other organic lifeforms; including, but not limited to, people."

Kyle looked at his hands and asked the million-dollar question. "Am I... uh... are we... made of other people?"

KM continued on, not realizing the distress her words were causing. I didn't stop her, though, because the others needed to know the truth. I suppose I was being selfish, letting her be the bearer of bad news, even though I was fairly sure I understood what was happening, too.

Every one of my friends suddenly looked like Luke Skywalker after finding out Darth Vader was his father. Even Cool and Pharaoh looked unnerved by the revelation.

Clem put a hand on Kyle's shoulder. "As awful as the thought of what they're doin' is, son, we cain't lose our focus." He stepped to the middle of the group, still gripping his trident like a batter stepping up to home plate. He spoke to all of us, but I felt like his words were mostly meant for me. "Now y'all know me..." He looked at Pharaoh and raised his eyebrows thoughtfully. "C'eptin maybe you and Buffalo Bill sleepin' over yonder. But y'all know this, some folks talk 'cause they got somethin' to say, while others jaw on 'cause they got to say somethin'. I'm a straight shooter. This nonsense about them Nanops chewin' up folks to play God 'n make other folks has got me mad enough to swallow a horn-toad backwards. Now I'll tell y'all, bein' a cowboy ain't just the fancy duds you dress in. Nor is it what you breed on the ranch or ride on the trail. It's more than that. It's the fire deep in yer guts. It's knowing how to treat folks, 'n doin' more fer yer neighbor than you do fer yerself without 'spectin the same in return. It's bein' brave enough to face fearsome thangs and not turn tail 'n run when you know standin' yer ground is the right thang t 'do. But mostly, I s'pose bein' a cowboy is about integrity, 'n doin' right when other folks ain't lookin' on. I ain't survived long enough t' become an old cowpoke 'cause I do cowboy thangs. I do cowboy thangs 'cause I'm an old cowpoke. The words I speak are as honest as the gun in my waistband, and my life is as plain as the ground I walk on. I ain't seen none of my breed around these here parts since I showed up in yer world, but I'm from a long line of gettin' shit done folk." He turned to Becky. "Pardon my French. But whatever's hapnin' up ahead, make no mistake, as much as I want it to be Rotgut, I know it ain't. It's jest a glorified flea circus, complete with smoke, mirrors, and illusions. C'eptin' this time 'round, the fleas are in control." Clem turned and looked at each of us, meeting our eyes with a steel gaze that said he meant business. "If we don't continue on, then who's to say what'll happen next? More folks and their homes gone? I'd say that's likely. Mayhaps we're the only thang standin' between the Nanops and whatever they're after. I ain't never run from a fight before, and I ain't about to change that today." Clem walked over and ruffled Becky's hair in a touching, fatherly manner. "Listen here, Becky, I've learned a lot of thangs in my years as a lawman: don't go in if you don't know the way out, don't mess with somethin' that ain't bothering you, never drive black cattle in the dark, and a pair of six-shooters always beats a pair of aces. But the most important thangs I've taken to heart are the thangs I need y'all to hear right here and now. Sometimes the best cowboys ain't cowboys at all. Now I know that aside from the Marshal an' me, y'all ain't cowfolk, but I can sense that one lives in each of yer hearts." He looked pensive for a moment before adding, "oh, and life is short and full of blisters."

And then he stepped back, clearly having nothing more to say.

Becky sniffled and wiped her eyes. She took a deep breath and looked like she was still fighting back tears. "Yee effing haw."

While Pharaoh and Kyle both appeared impressed by Clem's speech, they remained impassive. Cool, however, was looking fired up again, the horror of being composed of Soylent Green all but forgotten. He was in, hook, line, and sinker. "Cowboy up, dudes!"

Clem looked at me sideways. Cool's exclamation had left him confused and amused. "Well then, cowboy up, y'all."

18

Dust, Wind, Dude

The mood as we walked was somber, to say the least. I stayed close to Becky since she was still processing. As much as I could tell she was listening to the surrounding conversation, she wasn't ready to talk yet.

The sheer level of accuracy the Nanops had put into recreating the area surrounding Rotgut astounded Clem. From the tracks to the gravel underneath, and on to the mostly featureless foothills that prevented us from seeing the town that presumably lay in the distance, everything looked authentic. Clem and I even recognized an old tree where we'd once intervened in a lynching. The rope burns were still present on one of the thicker branches, as well as the bullet scars we'd left in the bark after our lethal exchange with some very bad men in long white robes.

Clem scowled as we approached a familiar landmark. "Jest around yon bend ahead, and past a line of scraggly ol' pinion pines, we should see the entrance to the ol' Kincaid ranch."

Clem's distaste for the ranch was written all over his face, with good reason. C. Randall Kinkaid was the wealthiest, most corrupt man in the entire county, maybe the whole state. Hell, possibly the entire southwest. Clem and I had survived so many shootouts on Kincaid's ranch, we'd nicknamed it 'The Gunfight Corral'.

The timbers at the entrance to a ranch were appropriately called ranch entrance posts. They were almost always made of wood and supported the ranch gate. Metalwork, antlers, or something that uniquely identified the ranch and its founder's values usually decorated the posts. They also marked the boundaries of the ranch and gave a sense of security and welcome. In Kincaid's case, however, he used his posts and crosspiece as an opportunity to instill dread in any passerby or would-be caller. Bloodstained parts of destroyed firearms that had once belonged to Kinkaid's enemies covered the entire archway. It was a weird flex, and there were times I'd fully expected to find the fences that ran off from the timbers in either direction lined with heads on pikes.

Pharaoh, feeling much better after clearing the fluid from his ears and congestion from his sinuses, sensed Clem's unease as we came within visual range of the ranch. "Is dere sumtin' we should know 'bout dis Kinkaid, mon? Yuh body language change soon as yuh mention him. Me sense, from di change in yuh pheromones, him probably a bad person."

Clem grunted. He was beginning to understand Pharaoh's less-than-common accent fairly well. "Kinkaid's so crooked, he could swallow nails and drop corkscrews out of his rear end. He's done hornswoggled more folk outta their hard-earned savin's than an en-tire army of snake oil salesmen."

Pharaoh nodded. "Me know men like dat, except di ability tuh make corkscrews wit him rectum. Is dat a superpower?"

I smiled at the innocence of the question and caught Becky grinning as well. "No, Pharaoh, that's just a figure of speech. It means he's untrustworthy. That would be a pretty awful superpower, though, if you ask me."

"Mine come out like springs, sometimes," Cool said matter-of-factly. He was sauntering casually behind Clem, Becky, and me.

The three of us looked back at him, wide-eyed, not even trying to hide our disgust. Kyle, who was walking next to him, turned his head and stared, promptly tripping over one of the railroad ties and landing in the gravel with a painful sounding thud. He righted himself quickly but winced when he dusted himself off. He'd skinned his palms pretty badly.

Even KM had to question what she'd just heard. "If I may, would you mind clarifying what you mean by that?"

"I mean my number twos," Cool replied, unaware of the spectacle he'd suddenly become.

I was about to put a stop to the conversation when Clem suddenly exclaimed, "now *this* is more like it!"

I looked at Clem and saw his original clothing was replacing his gladiator's gear, right down to his boots, hat, and gun belt. He took Jackson from his waistband and holstered the six-shooter lovingly. "Right back where you belong, ol' friend."

I turned to face Becky and saw that her armor was morphing into an outfit that would have made Calamity Jane blush. When the process was complete, she was wearing a saloon girl style dress that accented... uh... showed... well... let's just say it didn't leave much to the imagination. The top was basically a corset. It laced up in the back, but left Becky's shoulders and arms bare. The skirt was about mid-calf in the back, but mid-thigh in the front, and sported frills along the front hem. Three bows added to the aesthetic, one on each hip, and the third was between her...

uh… on her top. The dress itself was black, as were her high heels,

fishnet stockings, and choker, but all the frills and delicate accents,

including a huge gaudy feather that appeared in her hair, were hot

pink.

I might have been staring a bit too intently, as she took my

chin in her hand and brought my eyes up to meet hers. "I'm going

to kill your dad," she said just a little too convincingly.

I know I blushed because she smirked and released my face,

looking around at the others.

Maybe I should have told her why I was about to ask her

what I did, but I wasn't exactly running on all eight cylinders at

that moment. "Pull up your skirt," I said, not thinking about how

she and the others might take that.

Becky glared at me like I'd just asked her to pull up her

skirt or something. "Excuse me?"

Clem echoed her sentiment. "Shame on you, Marshal."

"I didn't mean it like that," I said, realizing how my request must have sounded. "I know it sounded bad," I added. "But I know that costume from the game. I just wanted you to see if you were wearing garters." I put up my hands. "Okay, that sounded bad, too. Listen, if you *are* wearing garters, they should be all stocked up with guns and knives."

Becky and the others eyed me suspiciously, but while everyone was busy looking at me, she lifted her skirt just enough to see the frilly superhero utility belts strapped to her upper thighs. "You're right," she said. "Sorry, I made an incorrect assumption."

"It happens," I replied, shrugging. "You should have a small pistol there, along with several bullets, and a half a dozen throwing knives." Then, before any further uncomfortable conversation could start, I turned my attention to Kyle.

Brown laced shoes, tan slacks, and a dress shirt were the foundation for Kyle's outfit. He wore a long, Colonel Sanders style bow tie and a black bowler hat. Topping off the ensemble was a herringbone-patterned vest and a black waistcoat. At his hip, a single pistol was slung low, gunfighter style, though he looked more like a banker than a lawman. His bow and quiver of arrows were nowhere to be seen. Come to think of it, Clem's trident and net were gone, as were Becky's weapons, including her newly acquired chuknuryss.

He looked down at his fancy new duds and wrinkled his forehead. "Just when I was rockin' the loincloth," he said, sounding disheartened.

Becky grimaced at me before saying, "you're definitely more suited to the cowboy look. Trust me."

Kyle turned, giving us a full view of his new attire. "Are you sure?"

Becky nodded. "Oh yeah. Very sure."

Kyle smiled, suddenly quite pleased with his new clothes.

Clem, looking much like the cat that got the canary, nodded approvingly. "Yer what folks in Rotgut would refer to as a dude."

Cool, whose costuming didn't seem affected by location like the rest of us, suddenly stretched his head between Clem and Kyle. "Dude? Ha ha! Then I should wear that too!"

Cool quickly morphed his body to appear like he was wearing clothing identical to Kyle's, right down to the fancy shoes and bowler hat. Bonus points if you can guess what color it all was. Honestly, it was a good look on both of them.

Cool grinned at Kyle, reaching out and high-fiving him with a massive, polished giraffe-shoe. "Now we're both dudes, dude!"

Kyle smiled. "Hell yeah, bruh!"

Pharaoh stepped towards us hesitantly, clearly confused by his new attire. He wore a one piece leopard-print slingshot bathing suit that had only one strap, which was draped tightly over his left shoulder, with knee-high lace-up black canvas high top shoes. He had a gold manica on each wrist and a matching gold belt strapped tightly around his waist.

Looking down, he realized how revealing the outfit actually was. Pharaoh placed his hands over his crotch self-consciously. "Wah me wearin', Packard? Dis here make me feel some shame."

"Oh, boy," I replied, unsure of what to say. "I uh…"

Clem stepped forward and clapped Pharaoh on the back, or at least as high up on his back as he could reach. "Well now big feller, it seems them Nanops have a sense of irony about them. You're dressed in the costume of a circus strongman. I was fortunate enough to see The Ringling Bros. and Barnum & Bailey Circus when they done come to Phoenix. I was trackin' a right wily varmint up in them parts and had occasion to stop in and see what them ol' boys was up to there."

Pharaoh scowled. "Me nuh like di circus. Me have bad memories 'bout one."

I nodded. "In Pharaoh's world, he was sold to a circus and, uh..." I sighed. "I don't blame him for not liking this, to be honest."

Pharaoh looked at me sideways. "Is yuh fadda responsible fi dis too, bredren?"

I shrugged. "I suppose, in a roundabout way, he is," I replied glumly.

Suddenly, a rustling came from KM's back seat.

"Your smelly friend is waking up," Knightmare announced.

"Who are you calling smelly," a voice with a distinctly Mesoamerican Spanish accent replied from the back seat.

Pharaoh, forgetting his unwelcome costume change, rushed to KM's side, and peered into her back seat. "Good t'see yuh, bredren! Me did worry 'bout yuh!"

El Scalar sat up slowly and stared at his dreadlocked companion warily. "What in the holy name of Quetzalcoatl are you wearing, compadre? Forgive me for saying, but it looks quite silly. You should stick with the coveralls."

Pharaoh looked back at me and frowned. My dad had some heartfelt apologies to make. "It a long story. Me promise t' tell yuh soon. But first, yuh have tuh meet some new bredren, and Packard have a story t' tell."

El Scalar's face brightened when he turned and saw the rest of us standing a few feet away. "Packard! Amigo! Where are we? The last thing I remember is fighting a dragon..." He turned to Pharaoh. "And fighting *you*?" He looked puzzled. "That can't be right."

Pharaoh nodded. "Whoever take we from di swamp, dey put we in di arena and control we mind, makin' we fight."

Pharaoh didn't mention he'd been fortunate enough to avoid the mind control, but humble might as well have been his middle name.

Scalar frowned. "Mind control? How?"

Becky cleared her throat. "It wasn't mind control per se. More like a manipulation of our fight or flight responses. The smells and sounds inside the arena manipulated our testosterone, dopamine, cortisol, and norepinephrine levels. It's quite diabolical when you get down to it-"

El Scalar waved a dismissive hand in Becky's direction. He looked back at Pharaoh for an answer. "Who is the woman?"

Pharaoh began to respond when Clem interrupted. "I'll have you know, *sir*, her name is Becky, and I'd ask that you show her the same re-spect you'd show a man. She's more than earned it by now. Not to mention, it's the law of this here land… and we abide by the law." Clem narrowed his eyes, trying to look intimidating. "Also, seein' as we ain't been properly introduced, I'd be Clem." He pointed at Kyle and me. "This here's the Marshal, and young Kyle here's a gunslinger, just like me."

Kyle beamed at the admonition.

Clem pointed at Cool. "And this here's Cool, the eee-lastic jee-raff." He shook his head. *"Durndest thang."*

Cool spoke up. "Uh, actually, me and him are dudes, dude."

Scalar stood up and hopped out of the back seat with a single bound. As he made his jump, the warrior's garb he'd worn in *Animehem* as well as in the arena fluidly changed into an old fur trapper's outfit, complete with a coonskin hat. His twin hatchets thunked against his hips when he landed, and he stopped, looking down at his clothing. He wasn't used to wearing a jacket, and the rough-stitched rawhide leather clothing seemed to shock him into a quiet stupor. "What is this devilry," he asked after a moment's hesitation.

"Dat's wah me did plan tuh tell yuh 'bout, bredren," Pharaoh replied softly. "Dis world nuh follow di same law as our own. Both we seen other worlds beside our own. Dis one new to we both, an' very dangerous."

El Scalar looked at me and the others. "And this is why you are all dressed like that?"

I looked down at my clothes and realized that while we were all talking, my costume from the *Marshal Blood* game had replaced my gladiator get-up. "Yeah, buddy... it is. And we have a lot to share with you. There are some parts even Pharaoh doesn't know. We waited to share the story with you, too." I nodded at his new clothes. "Nice fur trapper outfit."

"Why me couldn't get di fur trapper outfit," Pharaoh lamented quietly.

El Scalar tilted his head, clearly confused by something else. I looked around at the others, everyone except Clem was looking at me funny.

"There he is," Clem exclaimed. "The Marshal I know and love!"

Becky finally said what everyone else was thinking. "What's wrong with your voice, Pack? Why do you suddenly sound like George W. Bush? And why does Scalar have *socks* on his horns?"

~

As it turned out, I'd never actually realized my voice was different when I was playing as Marshal Blood. According to Clem, however, the voice that confused everyone else so much, the voice that belonged to the famous actor and country singer, George W.

Bush, was the voice he'd always heard when I spoke. Our clothing and weapons of choice weren't the only things that changed when we passed from one of the Quantum Nanops' simulated worlds into another.

"At least Bush was a decent president," Becky shrugged. "You could sound like irritating orange."

"President?" I wasn't sure I heard that right. "He was *president* in your world?"

Becky eyed me for a moment, clearly unsure if I was joking. "Yeah. President. Why? What is he in this world?"

I couldn't believe we were even having the conversation. "Um, an actor and a country singer. Academy Awards, Grammys, you name it. He's bigger than Elvis."

Becky looked even more confused than when we'd started. "Who?"

Kyle responded next, though his answer left me confused as well. "President Presley, right? The greatest president since Fred Rogers in the '70s!"

I felt like we were doing a bad reimagining of 'Who's on First'.

"Kyle's the president in my world," Cool interjected, causing us all to turn and face him abruptly.

Kyle was more shocked than any of us. "Really?"

"Naw, dude," Cool replied with a giggle. "I was just playin'. I don't even know who the president is."

Kyle looked around at us, embarrassed for getting so excited. "I'm the president somewhere," he grumbled.

Scalar raised a hand tentatively, trying to be polite. In his other hand, he was holding a dirty pair of socks. If we were confused, he had to be losing his poor little mind. "Can somebody please tell me what's going on here," he asked. "Please?"

~

After properly reintroducing Scalar to the others, I walked

Pharaoh and Scalar through our checkpoint ritual on the Lanier,

graciously powered by KM. Then, we told our collective story

while we walked.

Once we passed the Kincaid ranch, Clem loosened up quite

a bit, though I feel like being back in his normal clothes, with

Jackson strapped securely to his hip, made a difference, too.

Surrounded by what appeared to be several miles of arid,

featureless desert, with the top battlements of the massive coliseum

looming on the eastern horizon, the walk was surreal to say the

least. Aside from our voices, the only discernible sounds were the

crunch of pea-gravel underfoot, KM's tires rolling slowly along the

train tracks, creating a gritty, staticky sound like on an old record

player, and confused-looking songbirds that only Clem recognized.

Like Pharaoh and Cool, El Scalar had been in situations similar to ours on more than one occasion. He'd travelled through time, fought battles in pocket universes, and still had surprisingly little opinion on alternate worlds and the ramifications of interdimensional doppelgängers.

He and all the others travelling with me would adapt to our circumstances in their own way, and their own time. You can't blame me for hoping for sooner, rather than later.

As we crunched along, Clem leaned in and whispered, "yer bison-headed com-padre smells like a mildewed saddle blanket after it's been rid on a sore back horse three hundred miles in August."

El Scalar, for better or worse, had incredible hearing. "If you cannot say something nice, then it's best to say nothing at all." He sighed. "A shower would be nice. Wet dogs smell better than me right now."

I shot Clem a look, making sure he didn't plan to answer. I wanted to say something when I saw his mouth open, but it wasn't the response I was expecting, so, yay for Clem.

"I'll tell ye Bill, the Marshal an' me have been pinned down by desperadoes in rock-gaps tighter than Phay-row's grip fer days on end. I've smelled worse than a Louisiana pigpen in the summertime, friend. If'n my town is as I 'spect it to be, I'll find ye a bath." He looked around at the rest of us. "I'll go last if'n y'all need one, too. It takes a while t' boil the water, so we might not all... aw, hell, let's jest see what we find."

What we found was almost what Clem was expecting... but not quite.

As KM had informed us, Rotgut was a little more than two miles from the coliseum. We made it to the outskirts of town well before the sun was due to set. The first landmark we came across was the Rotgut train station. As we rounded a slow, gradual curve in the tracks, we spotted a brown picket fence stretching off to the right and perpendicular to the rails. Just beyond the fence was a water column, which supplied water for the steam engine's boiler tank, and several large wooden barrels. Just beyond them stood the station itself.

Though the train was nowhere to be seen, I could still smell the distinct odor of the coal that would have been burning in the firebox. The air, though normally dryer than Pharaoh's wit, carried the slightest hint of moisture. As if to congratulate me on my observations, a train's whistle sounded in the distance. I looked up, but aside from knowing instinctually that the train was probably already a few miles south, I couldn't see anything else.

Not only was the train already gone, but even more noticeable, and damned unnerving, was the utter absence of any people.

The station itself, from the water tower to the station agent's quarters, was about eighty feet wide and twenty feet deep from front to back. Just beyond the water column was the ticketing office and baggage claim. At the far end, was a tiny two-story living structure that was about two hundred square feet. A low roof, maybe eight feet high, ran between the two buildings, creating a covered waiting area that housed two dozen benches, which had been painted to match the fence.

All in all, hiding places were extremely limited, if someone were so inclined. My friends and I might have looked scary to most onlookers, but the station looked sterile, as if nobody had ever set foot on it, like the dirt we'd just walked in on.

"Where is everybody, dude," Cool asked.

"I don't think they've built the people yet," Becky replied. She turned to me, thinking. "Do you think they'll recycle us," she asked.

"What do you mean by *recycle*," I asked.

"Recycle," she replied. "You know, use our parts for other people once they don't need us anymore? Like the spectators at the coliseum. Are they really even needed once we've left battle-

town, USA?"

I thought for a moment. "I don't think they would. Since

they went to the trouble of uploading a quantum-entangled

consciousness, they'd definitely want to keep it intact. Does that

make sense?"

Becky nodded. "Yeah. I'm just having a hard time

wrapping my head around being made of someone else's atoms."

"Isn't that what we all are," I half-asked, half-reminded

her. "Matter is neither created nor destroyed, only

rearranged. The Nanops are just doing it more efficiently than

nature ever has." I sighed. "To me, you're Becky." I looked

around. "And Kyle, Clem, Cool, Pharaoh, Knightmare, and El

Scalar. You're all the real deal to me, not something the Nanops

built. You're my friends... my family." To Becky, I added, "but

not like my sister or daughter. That's just wrong."

We searched the station and found evidence of occupation there. Our proof, however, felt more like props meant to reinforce the illusion that Rotgut Station was the honest-to-god gateway to the 1890s boomtown of Rotgut. Nothing felt natural or even touched by human hands.

In the ticketing office, just inside the window where travelers could purchase their little paper passports to freedom and points beyond, we found some familiar items. Familiar to Clem and me, anyway. On the counter, next to the station agent's arrival and departure bell, we found a quill pen, scrap paper, a bottle of ink, a half-used book of tickets bearing the name ROTGUT RAILROAD CO., and a handful of rubber stamps. Along the back wall, but still noticeable from the little arched ticket window, was a chalkboard with detailed information about the train schedules and fares written in neat script. On the far side of the counter, and out of physical and visible reach of the window, was the telegraph the station agent used to communicate with other stations. Also out of view of the window, was a black safe roughly the size of a modern mini fridge. It had a pristine white border around the door and proudly displayed the name MOSLER SAFE CO. across the top.

Behind the ticketing office, we found a surprisingly smelly outhouse. Apparently, the little quantum menaces weren't going to spare any details, no matter how small or disagreeable.

Leaving the others waiting at the office, Clem and I crossed the deserted station, passing the rows of benches in the covered waiting area, and made our way to the station agent's living quarters. The tiny home, which would have made most walk-in closets look like a palace, was also empty. A modest stack of freshly cut firewood was piled neatly next to the front door. I tried the latch and found it unlocked. The interior smelled like body odor and pipe tobacco, like someone had been living in the sweltering little sweat box for years. Downstairs was a small wood burning stove, a high back leather chair, a small table, and a water basin. A cabinet on the wall held a single set of dishes, a can of coffee, and a few dozen cans of assorted peaches, beans, and condensed milk. Upstairs, we found a small featherbed, a seaman's chest, and a mirror. On a small shelf next to the bed, was a shoebox containing some photographs, a few books, and an ancient looking pipe. A leather pouch with a few days' worth of tobacco sat on the shelf, leaning against the box.

Clem looked at a few of the pictures. "These here photographs are of ol' Bob Miller. I'm fairly certain you've met him. He's a kindly feller, a bit on the portly side, and has an affinity fer baked goods, though not the kind Kyle partakes in, if'n you catch my meanin'. Ol' Bob's got a white mustache that many have mistaken for a dead ferret, so he'd be right hard to miss." Clem glanced over at me. "Where do you think he is, Marshal?"

I sighed. "I'm pretty sure Becky's right about them not being built yet. I guess we'll find out when we get to town."

Clem nodded. "It looks like home, but it sure don't feel right." He returned the pictures to the shoebox, and we went back downstairs. "Them peaches sure do sound good right about now," he commented as we stepped back out into the dry Arizona heat.

Only it wasn't Arizona... I had to keep reminding myself that we were still in San Francisco, and only about three miles from my home in Noe Valley, *as the crow flies anyway.*

An old smoker's voice suddenly shouted angrily at us as we headed back to the others, surprising both of us. "What are you doin' in my home?"

We heard a shotgun being racked back by the outhouse and turned to face our assailant.

"Marshal? Sheriff?" It was Bob Miller and his face-ferret. He looked about as confused as one might have expected. "I almost shot ya'. He looked at the others for a moment before returning his gaze to us. "These friends of yers?"

I put both hands in the air and signaled for Clem to do the same. "Now, why don't you put down that peashooter, and we'll talk about it, Bob."

Bob looked around warily but didn't lower the gun. "The hell's goin' on around here, Marshal? I kin' smell the train... but I ain't seen one fer days. Yer the first people I've seen in a long time." Bob sniffed the air again. "Coal 'n steam, fer sher." He shook his head, clearly frightened and frustrated. "Why the hell cain't I remember?" Then Bob spotted KM. "Good lord, what in *THE HELL* kinda train is *that?*"

I ignored his question. "We didn't see you when we arrived here. Where were you hidin'?"

Bob wrinkled his nose angrily. "I was most certainly not hidin'! I was in the outhouse, though I cain't remember why I took my shotgun in thar." He finally lowered his firearm and sighed.

We knew Bob hadn't been in the outhouse, but he wasn't lying either. The poor bastard had *appeared* in the outhouse.

Bob began walking towards his living quarters. The butt of his gun dropped to the dirt at his feet, and he dragged it by the barrel, leaving a thin, unsteady trail in the dust. "I think I need to lie down, Marshal, Sheriff... pleasant regards to you 'n yer friends."

It was time to get to Rotgut and investigate.

19

Back on Track

Once ol' Bob disappeared into his little home, the door and floorboards creaking noisily behind him, Clem gathered the others around to deputize them. It was an oddly game-accurate moment. Clem didn't seem to recognize the absurdity of it, but through the power of Quantum Nanops and in-game logic, he just happened to have six deputy badges in his vest pocket.

He started with Kyle, who appeared to be holding back tears as the symbol of peace and justice was pinned to his vest. Next, he moved on to Becky. She insisted she pin the badge to her own costume, as anyplace on her body that was actually covered by clothing was not a place she wanted Clem, or anyone else for that matter, pinning *anything*. In a moment of what could have been interpreted as mild body-horror, Cool took the badge from Clem and absorbed it into his chest with an odd sucking sound. A second later, it emerged in the right place, the polished silver star looking like a new, permanent part of his character.

Cool grinned widely. "Deputy Cool at yer service, bruh!"

The sheriff just tipped his hat respectfully and moved on to Pharaoh. The pinning was relatively easy, as Pharaoh only had one strap available to him. Clem tiptoed to reach the spot on the Prince of Beast's chest. Pharaoh actually seemed pleased with the addition, understanding its meaning and valuing the symbolism at a profoundly deep level. He even seemed less self-conscious about his poorly chosen clothing.

El Scalar seemed confused by the ritual, as badges were never an important part of his cultural background, but since the others had graciously accepted their little silver symbols of solidarity, he solemnly accepted his badge of honor. When Clem finished, Scalar nodded his big old bison head, and Clem returned the gesture with a wink.

Clem finally moved on to KM, who was patiently, and surprisingly quietly, waiting on the tracks. Clem held up the final badge, unsure as to where he should place it.

KM could sense his uncertainty. "If you're wondering where you should place the badge, Sheriff, may I recommend an open spot on my passenger-side grill, opposite my GTO badge? It should balance quite nicely, aesthetically speaking."

I walked over to Clem and pointed out the spot on her grill, just above her right turn signal.

He placed the badge against the spot I'd pointed out. Much like Cool had done, KM allowed the star to integrate with the shiny black grill, the silver contrasting pleasantly.

"As Cool can attest, shapeshifting has its advantages," KM quipped.

"No doubt," Cool agreed heartily.

The formalities done with, I pointed down a dirt trail pocked with hoof prints and creased with stagecoach wheel scars. It was the only road into town from the train station, and it was as poorly maintained as one might imagine.

After Knightmare drove off the tracks and morphed her tires into something better suited to an off-road trek, we began the last leg of our journey into Rotgut.

~

The proper town of Rotgut was another half mile to the southwest. Which wasn't bad, actually, considering many train stations of that era were about a mile away, and sometimes as much as two. The cost of land was a key factor in that decision, as the prime land was ordinarily left open to homes and businesses. Not to mention, if a town grew enough, the industrial parts of it typically expanded in the direction of the station anyway. Planners also considered noise, air quality, public safety, and navigable terrain when plotting a town versus a train station.

We casually sauntered towards town, knowing that nothing of consequence was likely to happen in our absence. I thought about dubbing us 'The Crazy Eights Gang', as there were too many of us to be 'The Magnificent Seven'. I kept the name to myself, though, as I was fairly sure not everyone else would be thrilled with the idea, and Cool and Kyle might just like it so much, they'd be inclined to overuse it.

The walk, while not overly long, was hot, dry, and dusty... *so* dusty. Dust covered everyone's shoes with an ever-thickening coat of powder-fine dirt. KM had even put up her top and windows to defend her interior against the stuff.

I looked over at Clem and saw that he had the back of his hand against his mouth and nose as he breathed. Suddenly I remembered the old, red bandanna that always hung around my neck in the games. I was about to pull it up when I thought about the others.

I glanced at Becky. Knightmare had offered to let us hop in, but there wasn't enough room for all of us, so everyone opted out. Nobody wanted to be that person. But Becky was in heels, and though she wasn't complaining, I couldn't begin to imagine how rough the walk was for her.

She caught me looking and screwed up her face. "What? Do I have socks on my head, too?"

I looked away. "No. I uh, was just wondering if you wanted my bandanna?"

Her confusion pressed in the clutch and power-shifted into disdain. "You didn't offer it to anyone else," she replied sharply.

"Nobody else is wearing high heels," I told her. "Besides, Cool's got himself covered, Clem's used to this, and I know Kyle, Pharaoh, and Scalar would say the same thing."

Becky looked back to see what I meant about Cool and saw that his face had morphed into a gas mask, the kind Preppa Pig had in their logo. "Please don't pull the 'chivalry's not dead' line on me," she groaned.

"No," I replied. "But I do recall you saying once that you had asthma. And I don't see an inhaler on you, so I wanted to make sure you'd be okay."

Becky was about to answer when Cool interrupted. "Hey dudes, what do you call a happy cowboy?"

Clem looked at the giraffe and pondered the question before answering. "Is this one of them youngin's riddles? 'Cause I ain't never been good at 'em."

Cool nodded, grinning. "Yeah, it is. Anybody know the answer?"

Everyone except Becky offered a collective shrug. She rolled her eyes halfway to Boston.

"We give up," I replied. "Even the *real* cowboy doesn't know."

"A Jolly Rancher," Cool giggled.

Kyle joined the giggling before adding, "watermelon is the best, bruh."

Cool shook his head. "Nah! Sour apple, dude."

"Cinnamon," Becky muttered, though only slightly interested.

Pharaoh and Scalar looked at each other and shrugged again.

"I know the reference, but I do not have taste buds," KM lamented.

"Tequila," Clem finally added.

I was shocked. "They make tequila flavored Jolly Ranchers?"

Clem looked at me funny. "I don't know what y'all're talkin' 'bout, but tequila does make ranchers jolly."

Before anyone could respond to Clem's comment, the familiar sounds of Rotgut hitched a ride on an errant breeze and greeted our ears like an old friend's voice.

~

Unless you've ever played *Marshal Blood*, you've probably never been to Rotgut. I'd bet that, barring a visit to Disneyland's Frontierland, you've never been to the Old West, either.

The sounds were the first thing we noticed as we got close. Horses whinnying, men shouting, the lowing of cattle — no, it's not actually called mooing — and the frequent discharge of a firearm. As we got closer to town, we could make out the distinct sounds of the two local saloons, upbeat piano music and heated debates mixed with the clink of glasses and the occasional outburst of profanity.

A little further along, and we could hear the steady clink of the blacksmith's hammer, which immediately made me think of

Darbinyan, the blacksmith in *Max Axe*, and the creator of my enchanted weapon in that game.

On the surface, it appeared to be a good day in Rotgut. Clem and I both knew, the rowdier things were, the more normal the day was bound to be. It was the quiet days that raised the hackles on your neck, and made you click your gun's safety off.

The next thing we noticed was the smells. The air was thick with the pungent scents of sweat, whiskey, and gunpowder. An occasional whiff of tobacco and horse manure joined the united assault on our senses.

All in all, Rotgut was a dusty, ramshackle collection of buildings, with a poorly maintained main road, rough, splinter-laden, wooden sidewalks, and swinging saloon doors. Ironically, Rotgut's boomtown status was responsible for its haphazard layout.

In 1878, a transient miner named Levi Skinner discovered gold in the area. A year later, Skinner filed paperwork establishing Rotgut as a mining settlement. In 1881, in addition to the gold mining that was already underway, a surprisingly large vein of silver was discovered, and the town, suddenly a dual-mineral producer, became a mecca for all manner of dreamer and schemer.

Incredibly, by 1893, the year Clem became sheriff of the growing community, miners discovered lead and zinc deposits. Rotgut was heralded as the most mineral-rich settlement since Lead, South Dakota, or Mullan, Idaho. Over the course of a few short years, the town grew from a few hundred to nearly three thousand residents. Without a proper city planner, the town grew in all directions without any sort of blueprint.

Becky swatted at her dress. She was supremely displeased with the costume itself but seemed even less pleased with the amount of dust that clung to all of us like an Italian mother saying goodbye to her kids. "So much dust," she grumbled.

Clem nodded. "A'yup, if there's anything in Rotgut more plentiful than big dreams 'n strong whiskey, it's the dust." He looked over at me and smirked. "I re-call a conversation with the Marshal here, 'bout findin' a way to sell the dust. If'n we could do that, we'd a-been rich men! 'Course if'n I warn't a lawman, I coulda' made one helluva livin' as a miner. But without Estella and Maggie..." Clem trailed off. There would be no more words from him for a while to come.

Cool began to ask who Clem was talking about, when Becky stopped and called out to everyone but Clem and me, requesting assistance with the lacing on the back of her top.

"I'm afraid it's gotten too loose," she said, feigning concern. "Can one of you check it for me?"

Naturally, everyone rushed to her aid, leaving Clem, KM, and me to continue in relative silence.

"Are you okay, old friend," I asked once the others were out of earshot. El Scalar looked up at the question. His hearing was better than most dogs. He nodded at me, clearly understanding what was happening, and stepped into a position that would afford Clem a bit of privacy.

Clem's voice wavered as he tried to answer, so he just sighed and nodded. "Yeah," he whispered. "Thank ye."

"Don't mention it," I replied, patting him on the back.

Clem cleared his throat, trying to remove the lump that had suddenly grown there. "Seems I was jest here yesterday. But so much has changed in that short time." He looked back to see Cool and Kyle fussing over the lace that secured Becky's top in place. A small sideways smile cracked through the emotion like a sliver of sunlight peeking through storm clouds. "Am I even the same person I was when I was here last," he asked.

KM, always wanting to be helpful, offered her perspective before I could respond. "Your consciousness is the same. Your body, however, while a perfect duplicate, is not the same body your mind occupied when you last strolled through your beloved town. Then again, Rotgut isn't the same tow-"

"He was talking more figuratively than literally," I told her. "But thank you. Your input is always valuable, girl." I felt a bit rude cutting her off like that, since she was genuinely trying to help, but I knew Becky couldn't hold the others off for long.

KM was quiet for a moment before her computer chirped ominously.

The noise immediately raised my hackles, as it was expressly reserved for emergencies. "KM? What's going on? Why the alarm?"

More silence, then, as the others wrapped up their impromptu mission, she finally replied. "I set an internal alert to notify me if the Quantum Nanops became active in other parts of the city. They have."

"The city," I wondered out loud. "Rotgut?"

KM's sensors beeped again in a new, even more distressing sequence. "No, Packard. San Francisco. The Nanop activity in Rotgut is tremendous… off the charts, as you might say. However, there are several pockets of Quantum Nanop activity ranging from the Tiburon area in the North Bay, all the way south to Santa Cruz. The area of projected activity is roughly 1,207 square miles."

"That's a whole lotta' miles," Clem whispered. "I'm gonna assume it ain't all Rotgut and coliseum. Would that be right?"

"While it's impossible to tell exactly what's happening at all the locations, I can confirm that each pocket of activity appears to be unique in composition, density, and availability of resources."

"You mean the people," I said. My mouth went completely dry.

"Among other things," KM replied. "I am sorry to share such distressing news."

Something suddenly occurred to me, and some of those implications dad had alluded to hit me like a runaway dump truck. "KM, can you tell me if there's any activity at my home, or at Individual Gaming?"

"Or Arete," Clem added urgently.

"Yes, there is increased activity at all three locations," KM said, sounding as worried as Clem and I were feeling.

Cool and Kyle rejoined us, grinning like they'd just received hero's medals. "Crisis averted, dude," Cool said triumphantly.

Becky, Pharaoh, and Scalar returned a moment later.

Becky immediately read the concern in my expression. "Is everything okay, Pack?"

I shook my head. "No. I don't think it is, Becky."

~

Clem's personal crisis all but forgotten, the eight of us discussed Knightmare's dark revelation. It was easy to make assumptions about what the Quantum Nanops were up to. My best guess, which the others agreed with, was that the Nanops were busy creating the worlds from some of the other games I'd played, if not all of them. That idea worried me to no end, as so many of the games were dangerous on levels humanity couldn't possibly comprehend.

Never mind the warlords we'd faced, or the gunslingers and savages of the Old West. If I was right, then our world was on the brink of being overrun by aliens, vampires, giant robots, evil wizards, zombies, and so much more. The thought scared me half to death. Also terrifying was the idea that dad, Irene, Gunner, and poor Jasmine were in places where the Nanops were already digging in their heels.

We had no way of knowing if any of them were still alive, and that made me want to throw up.

I felt dizzy.

My first and strongest instinct was to stuff the others into Knightmare and head back to Arete. But I wasn't even sure if dad had stayed there or gone out looking for us. We had taken an ill-advised course of action, and I knew beyond a shadow of a doubt, we had to see it through. "We have to do this," I said finally. My voice shook like Clem's had a few minutes earlier. Honestly, I was unsure of what we were even there to do, but I was sure the Nanops were expecting us to find out.

The train had been an open invitation. It might as well have shouted 'follow me' as it roared past us earlier.

As in the gaming world, I suspected we had to follow a set of rules or parameters to advance... to win. But with the Nanops using humans and other life forms as fodder for their manic machinations, the stakes were impossibly high.

What even *was* the game anymore? Was there any point to it? What did winning even look like at that point? I was afraid that if I kept considering the possibilities, I might not be able to move. I looked ahead at Rotgut and realized I wasn't excited to go there... not one bit.

Becky took a few deep breaths. Seeing how desperately I was trying to keep my shit together, *and* inside, she took point on the conversation.

She looked at all of us, her expression switching to investigator mode. "So, what do we know so far?" The question was clearly rhetorical, as she began listing facts and raising her fingers one at a time to keep track of said facts. "One: The Quantum Nanops are using anything available to bring worlds that

Packard has only seen in games, *our worlds*, and the people in them, to life. Two: The amount of detail they put into everything says they'll go to incredible lengths to achieve perfection, which means they're going to need a ton of materials, organic and non. That means nothing is safe... *nobody* is safe."

"Except us," Kyle said softly. "I mean, we can die, but we respawn. That guy that we saw back by the coliseum, Mike? I don't think he respawned."

Becky nodded. "Then that's three," she sighed. "What else do we know?"

"This don't seem to be about any of us, ceptin' the Marshal," Clem offered. "I'd wager that if any of us walked straight into town right now, ev'rythang would re-main business as usual. The Marshal is the one they want. That's four."

Becky looked from face to face. It felt like pop quiz time at Nanop University. "Okay, then *why* is it that way? Why do they want to interact with Packard?"

"Cause dem see him as dem god," Pharaoh said, seeming surprised at his own words. "Him give dem life, an' dem waan please him."

"Like a cult," Scalar said, nodding.

Cool suddenly looked more than a bit concerned, finally grasping the enormity of the situation. "Then how do we tell them that isn't what Pack Man wants, Beck?" He turned back to me. "It isn't, is it, dude?"

"Jesus, no," I moaned. "I mean, you being here is *incredible*, but..." I didn't know how to say what I was thinking.

"But not if it mean dem have tuh sacrifice otha people tuh make it happen," Pharaoh said. His big, lawful-awesome heart knew exactly what I was thinking.

"Yeah," I sighed.

Becky grabbed my shoulder and squeezed it tightly. "Then we need to find a way to shut them down. All of them. And before you say anything, yes, that includes the ones holding us together." She looked away from me, knowing what my eyes would be doing at that moment. "You all understand what that means, right?"

Everyone nodded, and KM offered a quick, reassuring chirp. Kyle's nod seemed less than enthusiastic, but who could blame him?

Scalar cleared his throat before speaking. "I still do not understand what is going on completely, but I get the impression none of you really do. What I do know is that Pharaoh, Cool, Packard, and all of our friends, present or not, fight against precisely what this threat represents, every day. Whatever lies ahead, whatever we have to do to triumph, then we will face it together. Packard is my family. If you are his family, then you are also mine."

Clem raised an eyebrow. "I'll be damned if I warn't thinkin' the same thing, Bill."

KM interrupted before Scalar could ask the question written all over his big ol' bison face, '*why do you keep calling me Bill?*' "Packard, all Nanop activity at and around your familial home has ceased. It's on the move."

Nothing could surprise me at that point. "Any idea where it's going?"

"Activity levels are erratic. I'm sorry, but there is no rhyme or reason to their movements," KM replied.

"Well then," I said, taking a deep, reassuring breath. "We can't do anything about what's happening over there, but we can investigate what's happening here." I straightened my hat and checked my guns before facing the others once again. I needed to do something to take my mind off dad and the others. Forcing a half-baked smile, I asked, "does anybody have a hankerin' to see where Clem hangs his hat when he's not arresting bad guys?"

"Uh, I do arrest bad guys *there*, too," Clem added.

"Yes... yes, you do. And you're damned good at it," I conceded.

The others agreed that, despite the frightening goings-on in the rest of the world, seeing Clem's stomping ground might just be the pick-me-up we all needed. Besides, where else were we gonna go?

"Keep an eye out for familiar faces," I reminded them. "Pharaoh and Scalar spawned in the coliseum, so we might find other friends popping up here in Rotgut." Then I looked at Clem and motioned ahead, bidding him to lead the way. "Any more words of wisdom while we stroll, Sheriff Pickett?"

He thought for a moment before brightening up. "Well, if'n yer gonna drive cattle through town, it's best to do so on a Sunday. There's less traffic and people are more prayerful and less disposed to cuss at ya'."

Kyle, looking as confused as ever, leaned towards Cool and whispered, "does he just make this stuff up as he goes? He could start a greeting card company."

20
C. Randall Kincaid

Rotgut, from a short distance, looked exactly the way I remembered it from the games. Vern Findley's General Store was the first building on the left, followed by Long & Waggoner's Hardware and Mining Tools, The Rotgut Gazette, and finally, Rose's Eatery. On the right was Doc Weatherholt's office, The Moose Lodge, The Hundred Grand Bar, and The Painted Lady, which was an upscale cathouse owned by the town's very own C. Randall Kincaid.

A little further ahead, and facing each other like angry, sneering rivals, were two of the town's most profitable casinos, The Old Almaden, and The Scarlet Huckleberry. On any given night, or day for that matter, both casinos and their integrated bars were as busy as human beehives. Their patrons came and went at varying stages of inebriation. Some whooped and hollered about their winnings, while others pissed and moaned about their losses. Occasionally, and by that, I mean 'pretty much every night', some poor bastard would end up on the wrong end of a gun barrel after a bad hand left them desperate and angry. As Marshal Blood, I'd dealt with the games, the gunfights, and the bloodshed that followed more times than I could remember. Clem, I suddenly realized, had dealt with it all as well, but in a reality that I'd never quite grasp. Clem was the real deal. I was just some punk who'd been unwittingly hijacking his world's history for a bit of entertainment.

Many more thriving businesses populated the streets ahead, surrounded by several residential outcroppings, and large, fenced-in homesteads. At the end of the main street, facing us like a giant gargoyle watching over the heart of the town, was a large, whitewashed church. A forty-foot-tall bell tower cast a long, ominous shadow to the east as the sun began to flirt with the western sky.

The errant sounds of life we'd heard grew louder as we made our approach. It wasn't until we stepped over the invisible line that designated the town limits, however, that the townsfolk began to materialize, as if out of thin air.

Hundreds of people faded into view around us like they were lazily emerging from a thick fog, talking, laughing, and going on with their lives like they'd been there all along. I suppose to them, they had been. It occurred to me that the deception was as important to them as it was to us. Maybe even more so. We knew Rotgut wasn't real, but *they* didn't. For the game to play out properly, they *couldn't* know. The meticulous attention to detail kept them doing what they were supposed to be doing, and acting the way they were supposed to be acting. Compliance and blissful ignorance were the only way to maintain the elaborate illusion the Nanops had created from my memories.

We were meant to fit right into their narrative, blending in like happy little trees in a Bob Ross painting. The only trouble with that plan was, nobody in the town of Rotgut had ever seen anything like Pharaoh, El Scalar, or Knightmare. KM was from the future, but Pharaoh and Scalar were from other realities altogether. They all stood out like sore thumbs wearing name tags reading 'Hi, My Name is Sore Thumb'. Surprisingly, Cool garnered very little attention, as color aside, he was dressed the part.

As we walked, heads simultaneously materialized and turned, following our progress with morbid curiosity. Not a single person screamed, fainted, or ran, though. They just watched.

Pharaoh looked suspicious. "Why dem nuh run away? Me feel like dem should be frightened of we."

"They prob'ly take yer strange appearance fer costumes," Clem replied. "Either they think yer circus folk, or mayhaps they take y'all fer Injuns. Either way, they're curious, but they ain't a-feared." He looked around at us, his demeanor remaining calm and cool. "Just act natural and follow my lead. Y'all are in the comp'ny of the Sheriff and the Marshal."

Despite my usual feelings about Rotgut, being a U.S. Marshal and all, and taking the safety in numbers factor into consideration, I felt a palpable sense of danger and unease as we made our way up the dusty thoroughfare.

As if on cue, a tumbleweed rolled drunkenly across the street in front of us, coming to rest against a hitching post outside Rose's place. Jimmy Hankins, a fourteen-year-old kid I'd rescued from amateur bank robbers a hundred times over, sat in the shade near the hardware store and played a jaunty tune on his juice harp. If I didn't know that this world existed somewhere else in the multiverse, and not just in dad's imagination, I would've thought the scene a bit too cliché. But you know the old saying, *truth is stranger than fiction.*

Clem walked with a purpose-filled stride, marching directly past The Old Almaden and on towards his home away from home, Rotgut's modest jailhouse. My coattails billowed out behind me like a superhero's cape as I hurried to keep up with him. We were almost to the entrance when a metallic thud drew our attention back toward Knightmare. One of the smaller children, a dirty mutt of a kid whose name I couldn't recall, had thrown a sizeable rock at KM's fender. The rock bounced off harmlessly, but the act of hostility was uncalled-for, and Clem had a few words for the child.

He turned and narrowed his eyes to slits, staring the youngster down like a hawk studying a field mouse before snatching it up for a light lunch. When he spoke to the child, it was slow, deliberate, and intimidating. "You do know that was rude, dontcha?"

The kid nodded sheepishly and pointed at KM. "What is it," he asked.

Clem thought for a moment before patting Knightmare's fender. "She's one o' them newfangled horseless carriages. She come straight outta Japan. I hear tell they make the best horseless carriages West of the Pecos."

"Konnichiwa," KM added, causing the boy to finally run away, shrieking in terror. "I apologize. I didn't intend to frighten the child, I mean, youngin'," she said as the kid disappeared around a corner, screaming all the way.

"It's okay," I said. "That kid's always been a juvenile delinquent."

Clem shook his head and sighed heavily. "That boy's August Colcoy's son, Luke. He's a bit of a hellion, but his ma's been in the grave nearin' a year now, and his pa's a mean drunk. That boy's seen more by six years old than most people see in a lifetime."

Pharaoh pointed towards the alleyway young Luke had run into. "Yuh waan me go get him and bring him back?"

"No," I said immediately. "Whatever's coming for us, this is no place for a child."

A cold, damp voice — yes, a voice can be damp... *because I just said so* — with a slow, distinctly Texan drawl spoke up behind us, startling most of us with its casual yet calculating tone. "Do you want to know what's coming for you?"

Clem and I went on high alert right away. That voice was as dark and foreboding as any demon spawned from the pits of Hell, but as smooth as a politician on a baby kissing tour.

We turned and found ourselves standing within spitting distance of C. Randall Kincaid. Whenever he stood that close to anyone, you could be certain there were more than a dozen hired guns close at hand, prepared to open fire at the first sign of trouble. Kincaid had more gunmen in his employ than the Presidential Secret Service detail.

Kincaid, who never dressed in anything but the very best, adjusted a low-bodied top hat before lighting a cigar that might have come straight out of Winston Churchill's private stash.

"Afternoon, Sheriff," he said, his tone as aloof and disinterested as if he were greeting a mule pulling a dung wagon. His tone was only slightly less dismissive when he nodded at me. "Marshal." He glanced over at the others, glazing over Kyle like he was the dung wagon. He slowed down creepily as he looked over Becky, and finally registered a mild level of curiosity when his eyes found Pharaoh, Scalar, and Cool. His legendary poker face wasn't infallible after all.

Kincaid rolled his eyes ever so slightly, making sure we understood just how unimpressed he was with our growing posse. He turned to a dapper-looking man in a bowler hat that might have come from the same haberdashery as Kyle's and made eye contact briefly. The man took a half step forward from the shadow-darkened alleyway that ran next to the Sheriff's office. He bore a scar that rivaled Bly's, only his continued down his jaw, and took a sharp turn across his throat. A jagged stitch-job that even Frankenstein would be embarrassed by moved him out of the dapper column and placed him squarely in the sinister category. "Regis," Kincaid said, after drawing heavily on his stogie. "You failed to notify me the circus would be in town today." He blew half a dozen smoke rings before continuing. "Tonight, you dine at the trough with the pigs." The businessman watched his henchman closely for a reaction. Seemingly satisfied by the lack of response, he finally asked, "how does that suit you, Regis?"

Without showing an ounce of disagreement, Regis took a pen knife he was holding and casually scraped under a well-manicured thumbnail. "It suits me just fine, sir," he replied.

"Yes," Kincaid agreed. "Yes, it does. And you will come a runnin' when Bosco hollers *sooie*... won't you?"

"Yes sir, I will," Regis replied without hesitation.

Kincaid turned to face Clem and me, treating us both to a faceful of thick cigar smoke. He didn't even bother with the smoke rings. The theatrics were over. "Yes sir. He will." He let the thought hang in the air between us for a moment like an angry piñata, just daring us to whack it with a stick. "Now that's control, gentlemen," he stated, poker face back in effect. "Who in the hell needs the law when you've got control like that?"

"Fear a bad foundation tuh build anyting on," Pharaoh said, clearly no more impressed with Kincaid than the millionaire was with us.

Kincaid smirked for the first time since we'd encountered him. "I didn't expect the freak to speak." He looked at Scalar. "And Tatanka Head? Does it speak, too?"

Man... I really liked that nickname for Scalar. It took me years to come up with it. Leave it to an Old West douchebag like Kincaid to spoil it for me.

Clem and I studied Kincaid, and he studied us.

Without having to turn my head, I spotted at least eight of Kincaid's henchmen. They lurked in the shadows with pistols, lay on balconies with rifles, and hid behind the curtains of a handful of the homes and businesses that surrounded us on both sides. Those were the hired guns I *could* locate. What concerned me, were the ones I *couldn't* spot. Those smart, patient, self-aware gunslingers were the dangerous ones.

Clem, knowing what I was doing, as we'd done it countless times in the game, turned his back to Kincaid, his face an exaggerated mask of disgust. "I've heard enough," he said, and spat in the dirt behind me.

"You'll each count no more than eight," Kincaid said without a hint of bravado or pride. "Those are the men I wanted you to see. They're a nice distraction, wouldn't you say?"

Clem spat again but didn't answer. I didn't answer either, but spitting wasn't really my thing.

I just stared.

Our little group was noticeably on edge. Everyone looked between Clem and me for any hint of a next move. We were busy watching everyone else. The first move rarely won. The second move generally took the fight once the first move had been made. It was tricky, though. The second move had to be faster.

Cool reached over and touched my elbow, causing me to recoil slightly. I was wound up tighter than a clock spring. "Dude, uh, *Marshal...*" He giggled at his usage of the word 'Marshal'. "What do we do?"

I finally looked away from Kinkaid and his men. I'd spotted all the hired guns I was going to find. The rest would have to play out on its own. It comforted me a little bit to know that at least we would respawn if we died. Then it hit me, I wasn't sure I would actually respawn. The Lanier recognized me, but I wasn't an NPC, and I sure as hell wasn't thrilled about the idea of putting my potential immortality to the test. Kyle and Clem had done it, yeah, but the idea of dying just to find out if I was the same was pretty terrifying, to be honest.

I looked at Cool, whose grin had loosened into a comical sneer. His eyes narrowed to match Clem's, and his slouch was slightly more pronounced than usual. Though he carried no weapons, his stance absolutely screamed gunfighter.

While Clem and Cool squinted menacingly, Kyle's eyes had grown. He did the deer in headlights look better than anyone I knew. His right hand, however, was hovering dangerously over the butt of his gun. Rattled as he looked, he was mentally prepared for a fight. A closer look at his hands told me the injuries he'd sustained on his palms in the coliseum had disappeared, likely a result of moving between the Quantum Nanops' fictional worlds. Just like in the games, injuries would be shed as casually as our odd costume changes. Another win for Team Packard.

Becky, while brave in the coliseum, made a conspicuous effort to casually slip between Clem and me. I'm fairly certain her move was a direct response to the creepy leer from Kincaid, but I could also see her eying the guns that Kyle, Clem, and I carried. Lifting her skirt to fish out a pistol in front of the good folks of Rotgut was probably an uncomfortable proposition. I could understand why.

Pharaoh stood with his massive arms crossed, the exact opposite of Cool's relaxed slouch. Instead, he rose to his full height of nine feet and took a deep breath, allowing his chest to expand like a pair of steel oil drums. He rarely went out of his way to intimidate anyone, but I could see he was on full alert. God help the person who decided to test his mettle.

El Scalar, who was still steaming over the tatanka head comment, stood closest to Knightmare. He was grasping the handles of his hatchets tightly. I hadn't even seen him pull them from their slings. His nose was wrinkled, and he looked ready to charge, but as in *Animehem*, he knew to take his cues from me. He was nobody's puppet, but he tended to trust my judgement.

KM, as always, was impossible to read. Her engine idled quietly, and she spoke not a word. I looked a little more closely at her fenders and saw the paint shimmering right where her nanotech plasma cannons lived beneath the surface. Good girl.

Then all hell broke loose.

~

It's occurred to me that when all hell breaks loose, by definition, it happens without any warning. Like a dam suddenly shattering and unleashing millions of gallons of water onto an unsuspecting village without so much as a leak first. Truth be told, we had a skosh of a warning… but it was confusing, so I don't think it really counted.

The first indicator that something was wrong was the sound of the train returning.

The Imperial 221 wasn't due to pass back through Rotgut for another eight days. Naturally, the scream of the train's whistle and the sound of the locomotive thundering back up the tracks towards town attracted everyone's attention. The train's return was particularly unnerving because there was no place, barring a huge teardrop-shaped loop, for the train to turn around in the short amount of time it had. It was too damned long, and there were no switching yards within a hundred miles of Rotgut.

I had to imagine it was the Quantum Nanops working their modern-day alchemy.

The next red flag was the monkeys.

Several dozen of ChuChuLo's cybernetic simians burst onto the scene like children turned loose on an Easter egg hunt. They seemed to be everywhere, all at once, screeching and clanging their damned cymbals together like a robot's pulse. The townspeople screamed and shouted as the metallic pests invaded the casinos and other businesses, wreaking absolute havoc as they advanced. Scores of poker chips of all colors sailed out through the batwing doors of The Old Almaden, clinking against each other as they landed in the dusty street not far from where we stood. Patrons from both casinos made their exodus as alcohol bottles began to crash against the inside walls. One of the bottles struck a window, shattering the thin pane of glass before slamming into a hitching post and breaking into a minefield of dangerous shards.

Amidst the ruckus, Clayton Claypool, one of the town's more successful miners, galloped into town from the south. "Runaway train," he shouted. "The 221's covered in monkeys, and it's headed back towards the station!"

I turned to Pharaoh and Cool, who were busy swatting monkeys away left and right. "Take Knightmare and stop that train, guys!"

Cool started to say something, but Pharaoh grabbed his shoulder and literally yanked him off his feet, tossing the disoriented giraffe into KM's front seat. Then, Pharaoh leaped into the back. "We gonna stop dat train!"

KM accelerated away, leaving a violent wake of dust and rocks that swept past us like a dirt tsunami. Pebbles peppered everything within thirty feet, thudding against the building's walls, water troughs, hitching posts, and even cracking a few more panes of glass.

Pharaoh's dreadlocks blew around his face wildly as they tore back up the trail. A combination of the roar of KM's engine and Cool hollering *'yee haw'* echoed down the main street as they disappeared from site.

Clem, Kyle, and I drew our sidearms and began firing at the monkeys, and El Scalar was finally able to put his hatchets to use.

The monkeys were like a noisy, irritating, and highly destructive plague. We fired, punched, and hacked at them until Kyle stopped and slapped my shoulder. I turned to see what he needed and found his eyes even wider than before.

He pointed back at where we'd met Kincaid and the ever-obedient Regis.

They were gone.

I quickly scanned the spots where our enemy's gunmen had been perched and found nothing. When the monkeys attacked, Kincaid and his men had all taken the opportunity to slink away like the yellow-bellied varmints they were.

I turned to update Clem, Scalar, and Becky, but Becky was gone too, her Remington Double Derringer laying in the dirt where she'd been standing just minutes earlier.

Kincaid and his men had taken her.

21

K.O. at the Gunfight Corral

I suddenly felt like I understood a little of what dad probably experienced when he realized we'd flown the coop earlier. Only I hadn't been taken by a creepy Old West villain who'd just looked me up and down like a meat lover finding the last slab of bacon on Earth. Seriously, I don't think vegans ever look at any food that way.

Okay, all joking aside, I was worried. Like so worried, my stomach felt like it might just fall out of my... uh, you know. I was *that* worried.

Kyle stared at me, helplessly, while Clem and Scalar continued to stave off the horde of living annoyance. He held his pistol loosely in his right hand, and cradled half a dozen or so bullets in his left palm. Without even thinking about it, he rolled them between his fingers deftly, like a magician might roll a coin in and out of sight. The bullets dipped and rose like a tiny, armored platoon, marching unquestioningly into battle. Kyle, in his world, had the coordination of a beached jellyfish, but in my world, he'd become something new, something incredibly dangerous. It was as if the Nanops interpreted him as he saw himself when he played video games… the ultimate marksman.

I nodded at his hand. "Where'd you learn to do that?"

He glanced at the repeating wave of dancing bullets and promptly dropped them. They clattered off the wooden sidewalk noisily. A monkey ran past, picked one up, and tossed it impotently at Scalar.

Kyle retrieved the remaining bullets and reloaded his six-shooter. He looked me in the eye while he did it. "I don't know," he replied. "But it seems to work better when I just let my hands do it. Thinking about it makes me mess things up." He spun the barrel noisily before slapping it shut and holstering his gun as smoothly as a seasoned gunfighter. The remaining two bullets began doing a little cha-cha across his fingertips, an observation I kept to myself. Kyle looked like he was carrying the weight of the entire world on his shoulders. "What do we do, Pack-uh, Marshal? Do I really have to call you that?"

"No man, I don't think it matters," I shrugged. "We're going after Kincaid, and we're going to rescue Becky from that son of a bitch."

Scalar turned and stared at me. His eyes had also widened, though not comically, like Kyle's. His eyes looked like Whisper's when she got spooked. "You're saying the señorita has been taken?"

I nodded. "Yes, but we're going to get her back!"

"Damned right we are!" Clem fired off three more shots before reloading Jackson and turning to face the rest of us.

More of the monkeys scrambled forward, but Scalar was very over their hijinks. His nostrils flared, and he hurled his coonskin cap at our assailants before roaring at them viciously. The little legion of ne'er-do-wells stopped dead in their tracks. They actually looked frightened for a change. Scalar snorted loudly and roared a second time. It was a guttural, primal roar that he might have learned from some lost species of carnivorous dinosaur. Spittle flew from his lips as he leaned into the roar. It looked like he might just take a few bites out of the little troublemakers if they got any closer.

The second roar did the trick. The monkeys took one last look at their fallen brethren and scampered off into the foothills surrounding Rotgut without so much as a single glance backward. The last I saw of them was Scalar's coonskin cap disappearing stealthily over a ridge to the west of town.

Scalar turned back to us, wiping spittle carefully from his facial hair, uh, fur, with his sleeve. "I've had enough of their monkeyshines," he said dryly.

I stared at him blankly for a moment, waiting for him to smile at a joke I don't think he even realized he'd made.

"Let's go get Becky back," I said after a moment of uncomfortable silence.

"Now would be a right good time to have Knightmare on our side," Clem lamented before starting to walk back the way we'd come. "Kincaid and his hired guns are likely on horseback. By the time we get there, we'll be ridin' straight into an ambush."

I couldn't agree more, but KM, Pharaoh, and Cool were off saving a train, and any potential passengers on board, from almost certain doom. "Then this time, maybe we don't knock at the front door?"

~

The walk, though a brisk one, took almost thirty minutes. Before you go judging us, keep in mind, we were all wearing cowboy boots, except for Scalar, who wore thin, flat moccasins. The terrain was uneven, making running virtually impossible, and as we got closer, we had to proceed with caution to avoid falling victim to any potential traps or ambushes along the way.

Kyle, who wasn't exactly the outdoors type, spent a good bit of time learning about life from his video games and the internet. As we hurriedly made our way along the trail and back to the train tracks, he informed us that there was a proper form for walking long distances. "I remember finding some tips for walking at a brisk pace on the web," he started. "Keep your back straight and your shoulders relaxed. Swing your arms naturally at your sides. Take long, even strides. Breathe deeply and evenly. And, uh..."

I had no idea where he was going with his fun facts, but they were an okay distraction from the walk and the task ahead of us. "And what? Did you forget the last one?"

"No," he said, sounding a bit embarrassed. "It just sounds silly."

"Ye might as well spit it out, deputy," Clem said, huffing as we crested the last rise before reaching the tracks. "If'n you climb into the saddle, be ready to ride."

Kyle nodded, silently mouthing the words 'deputy Kyle'. He smiled, clearly liking how it felt to say it. "Smile and enjoy the scenery," he finally blurted out.

Despite Becky's predicament, I joined Kyle in a momentary smile. His facts, while practical under normal circumstances, sounded so trite when applied to our current mission. But that last one was true in all things. "I like the last one," I told him. "Thanks, bro."

"Oh, uh, you're welcome," Kyle replied. He was sadly unaccustomed to compliments, and I made a mental note to give him more.

As we crested the rise, I could hear the roar of the Imperial 221 continuing along the tracks, heading back towards the coliseum like a two and a half-mile-long bat out of hell. Her whistle shrieked like a banshee, and I imagined my three friends were doing everything in their power to get her back under control.

Clem huffed again as we began down a lazy grade towards Rotgut Station. "My walkin' advice is to put one foot in front t'other. That'll always get 'cha where yer goin'."

"Here, here," Scalar agreed. "Though Kyle's advice about enjoying the scenery is sound as well. We don't take nearly enough time to appreciate what's around us. Take Señorita Becky for example. We may never see her again, so-"

"We're coming up on the train station, guys," I said, not wanting to hear another word of Scalar's floundering motivational speech. "We need to be extra quiet from this point forward."

The others nodded, though I could see Scalar felt slighted. He could finish *after* we rescued Becky if he wanted to.

We approached the station cautiously. Clem and Kyle had their pistols out and cocked, and Scalar had his hatchets back in hand. I'd removed my shotgun from its scabbard and loaded it for bear.

We were ready for anything.

Which was too bad because nothing happened.

Unless you count hearing ol' Bob singing "Oh Susannah" while taking a dump in the outhouse to be something. He actually sang 'Old Susannah', messing up the lyrics something awful. It was good to know that people have probably been messing up lyrics since the first songs were penned. Ol' Bob was in good company.

Once we passed the station, we left the tracks and continued towards the Kincaid ranch off the beaten path. His men would be watching for us for sure, but it was unlikely they knew that Cool, Pharaoh, and Knightmare weren't with us. They'd be on the lookout for a larger, less stealthy party.

Another ten minutes and we came to a jackleg fence that ran towards the train tracks and off as far as we could see in the other direction. Kincaid's land was huge. Once we were on it, we were fair game. If they shot us, they could make up any story about who they thought we were or what they thought we were doing there. It wasn't ideal, but Becky was worth the risk.

Clem leaned in closely after we'd climbed over the fence. "Remember ol' Marshal Mathers? He was doin' 'bout the same thang when Kincaid's men killed him dead. Only he went up the front entryway with a warrant, so's no one would mistake him for a trespasser. We've already done overstepped any semblance of legality, here, Marshal. That said, I'm with ye, all the way. We'll get Becky outta there or die tryin'."

~

I always hated crawling, especially over rocks, grit, and the prickly things that grew in southern Arizona. Not to mention snakes, scorpions, spiders, and ants the size of ponies. It was a tedious and often painful task, but there weren't any land features or significant foliage to hide behind along the way, so crawling was our best option. The main ranch house was about a hundred yards ahead, and the bunkhouse where the hired hands lived, was about half that distance. There were barns filled with bales of hay and stables for the horses, but they were beyond the main house, and not options for hiding or laying down an offensive plan. The sun was beginning to blur on the horizon, meaning we had an hour of daylight left, maybe less.

We succeeded in making it as far as the bunkhouse without being seen, but that was where our luck ended.

The bunkhouse was almost as big as the main house, though furnished far less lavishly. It housed thirty men comfortably, though forty could fit with extra bedrolls and cots if necessary. There was plenty of room in the main house, but Kincaid liked his privacy, and the men assigned to protect him while he slept were employees, not guests, *and most certainly not family.* Their place was, and always would be, in the bunkhouse.

On that evening, for obvious reasons, the majority of Kincaid's men were posted in and around the main house. It was just dumb luck, I suppose, that one of his lackeys was in the bunkhouse, grabbing candles and a few oil-burning hurricane lanterns when we forced our way in through the back door. The gunman, whose hands were full when we entered the building, thought for a moment before dropping the box he was carrying. He probably wanted to see who was coming in before risking breaking the glass and becoming the next esteemed dinner guest to join Bosco at the pig trough. His hesitation was all we needed to get the drop on him.

Before he could drop the box, the young man, whose name I recalled being Enos Joseph, found two pistols and a mean looking shotgun aimed directly at his face.

A second later, Scalar's massive frame darkened the doorway, causing Enos to finally drop the box and reach for his sidearm.

I made sure he could see the shotgun aimed at his head before ratcheting it loudly. "Nope! Bad idea, Enos! Do you really think you can rail that smoke wagon before I can squeeze my trigger?" I nodded at Clem and Kyle, who stood on either side of me. "I count three guns, Enos. And the big guy behind us has a pair of hatchets he can throw with deadly accuracy."

To illustrate my point, El Scalar hurled one of the hatchets at the unsuspecting man. The weapon knocked Enos's hat off and wound up embedded in the wall just above his head.

"One hatchet," I said. "One remaining hatchet that he can use to split your face in two. Do you like those odds, Enos? Because I wouldn't bet on 'em. Not a penny."

Enos looked at us nervously. "Yer gonna kill me, ain't cha?"

I shook my head. "That's completely up to you, Enos. If you're useful to us, and the information I know you're dying to give us turns out to be accurate, then you might live to see another day. If we *wanted* you dead, then that hatchet behind you would be buried six inches into your skull." I stared at him, unblinking. "Nobody in this room has to die tonight," I said reassuringly. "Am I making myself clear, Enos?"

Enos nodded. "Yessir, Marshal sir."

"Okay," I began. "This first question could mean sudden death or overtime, depending on the answer you give me."

Enos nodded and looked at the floor, clearly terrified of what we were about to ask him.

"Where is the girl you brought in this afternoon?"

"In Kincaid's bedroom," he volunteered immediately. "He ain't touched her, though… n-n-not yet."

I wasn't a fan of cryptic conversations. "What's stopping him?"

"Y'all are," he replied. "He wants you dead before he makes the woman his own. And he is mighty curious 'bout that horseless carriage of yers, too."

Clem extended his arm forward, putting the barrel of his gun to Enos's forehead. "How many men are inside, and how many on patrol on the outside," he growled.

Enos swallowed hard, his eyes crossing as he tried to focus on the gun barrel pressed against his head an inch or so up. "Uh, evenly split, I'd say. Maybe twenty inside, and twenty out,

Sheriff." He was beginning to sweat. "I was on the outside. If'n I don't come back with the candles and lamps soon, they'll come looking for me."

I knew he was telling the truth. Funny, but in the *Marshal Blood* game, I always had a built-in bullshit detector, and as much as I knew all systems were 'go', Enos wasn't setting off any alarms. I glanced at Clem and saw that he was looking thoughtful as well. "Well, Sheriff, what do you think?"

Clem nodded. "I think he's bein' forthcomin' with us, Marshal." He looked past me and met Kyle's eyes, his gaze as cold as liquid nitrogen. He then looked back at Scalar and raised a thinning eyebrow. "What say you, deputies? Do y'all concur? Should we believe this thievin' polecat?"

"I think he knows we'll kill him if we find out he's lying," Kyle said flatly.

Enos, in a moment of defiance, replied, "if you shoot me, the rest of Kincaid's men'll surround this place and fill y'all full of lead. Y'all are in some deep shit."

Scalar finally stepped forward, pressing between Kyle and me in a move so passive-aggressive, we hardly noticed. He towered over all of us by almost a foot and was as wide as Clem and me combined. He held up his remaining hatchet and twirled it menacingly. "Who said anything about shooting?" His nostrils flared, and his eyes burned with deadly intensity. "I can kill you very quietly, and just as dead, with this, amigo."

Enos squirmed in his seat like we'd filled his pants with cockroaches. "Oh, Jesus… what are you?"

Scalar was used to the question. Depending on his level of respect for the person asking, he sometimes graced them with an answer. Enos, however, had not, and would likely never earn Scalar's respect. Instead, Scalar just stared.

Clem offered an answer. "Bill here is one o' them kachina dolls them Injuns…" He glanced over at me briefly, processing the correct word. "…uh, native 'mericans favor, brought to life by a powr'ful spirit. So, ya' got three choices, my unfortunate friend. You kin cooperate, Bill here kin kill ya', or he kin jest call on a kindred spirit, n' force' ye to spend the rest o' yer life with the head of yer spirit animal, which judgin' by yer nature, would be a prairie dog, or some other cowardly varmint as such."

Enos looked as terrified as Scalar looked confused, but thankfully the cowardly henchman spoke first.

"Look, I'm terrible sorry, Sheriff. I know my mouth gets me in'ta trouble now and then. I'll be helpful. Consider me on team Bill… mu-minus the animal head, please." Enos looked from Clem, to me, and then to Kyle. He wouldn't look at Scalar, though. He finally nodded at Kyle. "Yer deputy's 'bout my size. If he wears my coat 'n hat, and carries that box, h-he kin walk straight in'ta the main house. Kincaid's bedroom is the last room on the left. The one with the bi-big, oak double doors."

Considering how helpful Enos had been, I almost felt bad for clocking him across the skull with the butt of my shotgun. I tied a gag around his head, effectively silencing him if he regained consciousness before the inevitable shooting started. After I took his coat and disarmed him, Clem tied him to a chair, his knots as precise as a Boy Scout's.

Kyle slipped the coat on and replaced his fancy bowler hat with Enos's old, dusty cowboy hat. He went to pick up the box, but I stopped him.

"I have a better plan," I announced.

~

About two minutes later, Scalar and I marched out through the front door of the bunkhouse, with Kyle at our backs, carrying Enos's handgun. My weapons were loaded and hidden underneath my coat, while Scalar's hatchets hung at his waist, but slightly further back than normal, making them invisible to the casual onlooker. We proceeded slowly, with our hands raised, directly towards the dozen or so men guarding the main house and the bad man inside.

Kyle moved, so the others could see him better in the waning sunlight. He waved to them with his free hand, which clutched a sack that presumably contained our confiscated weapons. "Lookit what I found sneakin' round the bunkhouse, fellas!" Kyle acted like he was pushing us forward, poking us in the backs repeatedly with Enos's revolver. "The Marshal and one of his deputies!"

The men all drew their weapons when we'd exited the bunkhouse, but relaxed when they saw Enos herding us forward like a loyal sheepdog trotting home with his charge. "Sheeit," one of them proclaimed with a whistle in his voice. "Enos captured the gol-durned Bloodhound!"

The group of men erupted in unified praise for the otherwise inept Enos. Comments about how they 'never would have expected it to be him', or 'dumb luck following Enos wherever he went', seemed to be the common denominator. Ironically, Kyle and Enos probably had more in common than anybody would ever know. Anyway, their juvenile level of conversation kept any of them from looking at us too closely. Until Kyle's ego took over, that is. All caught up in the grandeur of the moment, Kyle took a bow, removing his hat and swishing it in the air in front of him.

"That ain't Enos!" The sentiment echoed across the courtyard before us, and all those drawn weapons raised once again.

The first shot rang out before any of them could take aim, and a big, balding man with salt and pepper mutton chops danced backwards clumsily. When he tried to right himself, he staggered forward, showing off the shiny new hole in his head, courtesy of Clem Pickett, duly elected sheriff of Rotgut, Arizona.

Leaving Clem in the bunkhouse with the rifle had been my idea, and I was sure patting myself on the back at that moment.

The other gunmen scattered, taking defensive positions behind wooden planters, hitching posts, and balcony supports. One of the dumbasses even tried to hide behind one of his fellow gunmen, an act which got him cursed at, and shoved back out into the open. Clem ventilated his skull next, making sure his gray matter would be able to enjoy the nice, cool breeze that had kicked up with the setting of the sun.

Kyle tossed the bag he was carrying, which only held Enos's boots and socks, at the man standing closest to him. The man fumbled with the bag for a second before Kyle shot him square in the forehead, at almost point-blank range. Kyle apologized to the already dead man and dove for the safety of a large barrel used to collect rainwater. Kyle's was the messiest of the kills up to that point, as the back of his unwitting victim's head exploded all over the men behind him. I say *'was'* the messiest, because El Scalar, the prince born to be a Mesoamerican warrior king, had just unsheathed his hatchets. *He* was out for blood.

While Clem laid down cover fire from the bunkhouse, and Kyle showed everyone close enough to target with a revolver just what an ultimate sharpshooter could do, El Scalar went to work on the rest of the gunmen.

That left me to head inside to rescue Becky.

~

I reached the doorway, running past several men who were trying to hide from Scalar, and carefully entered the great room. A second later, Kyle was at my back, covering me from the rear.

"Those guys don't know what to do with Clem and Scalar," he said, his breath heavy from the exertion.

I ducked back into the doorway with him. "Are you okay, man? Are you okay to do this?"

"Yeah," he replied solemnly, "but I don't think I like killing as much as I thought I did." He cleared his throat and took a deep breath. "I don't have to like it to do it, though. I've got your back."

I nodded, seeing movement on all sides of the room. "Then let's go save Becky, bro."

Together, moving as close to perfect unison as I'd ever experienced in a game, let alone real life, Kyle and I stood and fired at everything that moved. Kyle unloaded his revolver three times as we advanced through the living room and down the arched hallway, reloading it with a series of precise clicks and spins that sounded more like techno music than a deadly weapon.

I had my shotgun in my left hand and my pistol in my right. Each time the pistol ran dry, I fired two cover blasts from my boomstick and reloaded them both almost as smoothly as Kyle.

When we reached the end of the hall, we found the double doors locked. I tried shooting out the locks, but oak isn't exactly plywood, and the hinges were on the inside.

Kyle's eyes were characteristically wide. "Any ideas?"

I shook my head. "So close, and yet so far."

A voice behind us startled us both. "I might have an idea." We turned to find El Scalar standing in the hallway behind us, his twin hatchets covered in blood and gore. "Step aside, compadres," he said calmly. "I think it would be polite to knock first."

Kyle and I did as he suggested, turning to see if anyone had followed. I was fairly certain the bloodbath that was once the hallway would be a sufficient deterrent to anyone who thought they might be brave enough to ambush us in the narrow passageway. What I really hadn't considered was the ambush coming from the other side of the door.

Scalar lifted a foot that would make most snowshoes jealous and kicked in the double doors with one solid kick to the lock. "Knock, kno-"

A series of shotgun blasts rang out as the doors swung open, and Scalar took all of them directly to the chest. A moment later, he vanished, leaving Kyle and me facing a roomful of well-armed desperadoes. Unlike Pharaoh and Cool, Scalar was not bulletproof.

We each backed off into the hallway, straddling a corner behind the door frame and using the edges of the partially opened doors as protection.

We traded several volleys with the men inside before hearing Becky shout. "Kincaid's getting away! He escaped through the window and headed for the stables! Shoot me! I'll go back to the Lanier, and you go after him."

I considered two things at that moment. One, I couldn't shoot a friend, even if it meant sending her back to Knightmare's trunk. The second thing was even more disconcerting than being asked to shoot her. If Scalar had materialized in KM's trunk, was he even okay? Even if I was okay with shooting Becky, I couldn't risk her getting crushed in the trunk with Tatanka Hea- you know... Scalar. Man, I needed a new nickname for him.

I shouted back to her, hoping she'd hear me. "KM's trunk is gonna be awfully crowded!"

Gunshots continued to ricochet off the oak doors and tear up the walls behind us.

"Don't shoot me," Becky finally called out. "That was a bad idea!"

"Don't shoot me either," Kyle said nervously from across the hall.

"Come in with yer hands up," another voice called out from the inside. "Or else the hooker gets it!"

"Hooker?" Becky sounded like he'd just insulted her entire family line. "Watch who you call a hooker, Hop Along!"

I nodded at Kyle, hoping Scalar had already gotten out of KM's trunk, or Clem would be bringing up the rear. Either option would be preferable to the predicament we were in. But you probably already know what I'm thinkin'.

I've survived worse.

Kyle and I tossed our guns into the room. They clattered across the floor noisily. We put up our hands and followed our weapons into the room, fully expecting to be shot on sight. We were only half right.

Shots rang out immediately, and as Becky shrieked in surprise, Kyle and I shrieked in pain. One of Kincaid's men had just shot each of us in the kneecaps. Okay, so it was only one kneecap apiece, but good god, the pain was excruciating!

"Someone get the boss," one of the men said as we dropped to the floor in utter agony. "We're eatin' steak at the dining table with Mr. Kincaid tonight." I recognized the voice. It was Regis, and he was bucking for a seat at the grownup's table.

Both Becky and Kyle had begun to cry, and I was damned close. The only thing keeping me from blubbering like the world's oldest toddler was the sound of hoofbeats outside the house. I tried to focus on them, wondering if Kincaid was coming or going.

The hoofbeats sounded like they were getting closer.

Kincaid was coming back.

There was something about the approaching horse's stride that made me listen more closely. A misstep, like a bad lifter in a finely tuned engine that only the owner could hear. The approaching horse had the equine equivalent of a limp, but only a limp the horse and its rider would ever notice. A limp caused by an unfortunate tumble resulting from an unseen gopher hole and a sprain that never quite healed correctly.

Closing my eyes, I listened. I listened to Becky and Kyle's cries of pain and fear. I listened to Regis and the man Becky had called Hop Along, laughing at their good fortune. But most of all, I listened to the approaching hoofbeats. The closer they got, the more I found myself trying to recall how we got there. Kyle and I were losing a lot of blood. His cries had become pitiful whimpers, and my heart thundered in my ears like bass drums.

I rolled, hoping to see Clem striding up the hall, guns in hand and eyes narrowed like a scary cross between Popeye and Clint Eastwood. What I saw instead made me wonder if I was dying… or already dead.

Galloping up the hall towards me like a four-legged angel was my faithful horse, Whisper. In her saddle, riding like he was born there, was Gunner.

~

Unlike the rest of us, Gunner was not in western gear, which I suppose made sense, since he was neither an NPC nor me. In his hand, instead of our Old West revolvers, was his .45 semiautomatic. He ducked as he and Whisper burst into the room, and Whisper slid to a stop next to a massive four-poster bed. Hop Along pointed his revolver at Gunner, but the FBI trainee turned chief of security was quicker on the draw by far. The stunned cowboy was flung backward by the impact of the armor piercing slugs that Gunner kept loaded in his emergency-only clip.

Out of the corner of my eye, I could see Regis taking aim at Gunner's head. Gunner was fast, but there was no way he could dodge that bullet.

Before I could say anything, a shot rang through the room and Regis slumped to the floor, a trickle of blood leaking from his temple.

I looked over at Kyle as he dropped Becky's Derringer to the Spanish tile floor.

Then everything went dark.

22
Rebel Without a Claus

When I finally came to, I was laid out on Kincaid's kitchen floor, a tourniquet tied tightly just above my left knee. Kyle lay next to me, still unconscious, a matching tourniquet expertly tied just above his left knee. His breathing was labored, and his complexion was pale. I was still light-headed, but glad to be alive.

Then I moved.

How is it we can go between 'joie de vivre' and 'please let me die' so quickly? The pain in my knee was excruciating, and I suddenly became jealous of Kyle, lying there so peacefully, blissfully unaware of his injury, or the pain that went with it.

Becky knelt beside me, dabbing at my face with a damp cloth. "Welcome back. You've had a fever," she told me quietly. "A bad one. Kyle's just broke a little while ago. You say funny things when you're delirious, you know that?"

"What was I saying?" I imagined myself crying over my secret desire to have an automail arm or ranting about secret wars between Atlantis and space. "Anything super embarrassing?"

Becky smiled. "No, I think you were remembering another game. Maybe several." Seeing my clear confusion, she rattled off a laundry list of things I'd said in my fever-induced delirium. "Let's see, there was something about a lint trap, someone named McBain, four leaf clovers, leprechauns-"

"LepreKong," I corrected her.

"LepreKong," she said, only slightly confused. "Oh, and you've *really* got a thing for dysentery, did you know?"

"Yeah, I was aware of that," I said unironically. "Honestly, you can blame my dad for that one, too."

I heard a cough and looked past Becky. Clem was sleeping in an old wooden chair, a blood-soaked bandage wrapped around his right bicep.

"What happened to Clem," I asked.

"Flesh wound. The bullet just grazed him. He'll be fine. If it had been a few centimeters to the right, he would've been respawning in the trunk with Scalar." She looked away, searching for someone or something. "Gunner's the one who patched you all up. He wanted to know when you woke up." She smiled sweetly. "Everyone wanted to know."

I looked around the room, finally grasping where we were. I tried to move again, but that wasn't going to be happening right away. Not without a level of pain and effort my body wasn't prepared for, anyway. "Why are we still in Kincaid's house?"

Becky shrugged. "Kincaid's gone. All his men are dead. Except for some goober you had tied up in the bunkhouse." She wrinkled her nose in distaste. "When I took off his gag, he tried to flirt with me, so I put it back. I think he's peed himself since then."

I shook my head, finding even that simple action to be painful. If Becky hadn't been in very real danger of some really awful circumstances if we hadn't rescued her, then Enos flirting with her might have been humorous. Instead, it was just infuriating. "I might just shoot him after all," I grunted.

Becky's expression went grim. "I think enough people have died here today. Don't you?"

My stomach tightened. These were real people. I hadn't realized that before all this began. Maybe the cavalier, shoot-em-up mentality wasn't our best option. I knew it would be our only option sometimes, but I vowed at that moment to be a little more discerning when it came to taking lives. *They were real people*, I thought again.

Becky touched my shoulder softly. "Thank you for coming for me," she whispered. "Kincaid was, um... he was going to..." Becky trailed off, her eyes welling up with tears.

I touched her hand, the warmth of her flesh reminding me that she and the others were flesh and blood. "I know," I whispered back. "But you're safe now."

She nodded, the terror still fresh in her mind. She took a deep, shuddering breath. "My dad…"

"Did he hurt you," I asked after a moment's silence.

She shook her head and sniffled. "Not like Kincaid wanted to, no. But he was rough." She sighed. "He was rougher with my mom." She looked at me, and for just a moment, she allowed me a glimpse of her soul. Not in some weird, supernatural way, but in a moment of vulnerability and trust, which frankly, means so much more. Her eyes, her expression, the little crease between her eyebrows that only showed up when she was closest to the edge… or maybe when the real Becky was closest to the surface… she let me see it all.

I squeezed her hand gently, and she used the other one to wipe away her tears. Her mouth moved. Though no sound came out, I didn't have to be a lip-reader to recognize 'thank you'.

~

Kyle woke up a few minutes later, asking for a juice box and a fruit roll-up. When he realized that Becky was not his mom, and that everyone else sitting around him looked happy to see him, he blushed and asked what was going on.

"You're a hero," Becky told him. "A regular old Lyle Swann."

Another name I'd never heard. "Who?"

"Lyle Swann," she repeated. "He was a legendary cowboy where I come from. Invented the first motorcycle, or something crazy like that. He was supposed to have made his way from New Mexico to Los Angeles in 1877, but never got there. His story's in tons of history books."

Clem nodded. I thought he was sleeping, but he was just practicing a bit of his cowboy Zen. "I've heard tell of Swann," he said casually. "Becky's right about that one. Craziest durned story I'd ever heard… until our own story, here and now."

"Well, she's right about you being a hero," I told Kyle. "Gunner'd be dead if you hadn't shot Regis."

Kyle looked surprised. "I hit him?"

"Son, you hit everything you fire at," Clem said, sounding more jealous than impressed.

"What's this I hear about me being dead?" Gunner's voice was unmistakable.

"If he hadn't shot Regis with Becky's Derringer, Regis would have shot you," I replied.

"If you kids…" Gunner turned to face Clem, "and a grown-ass man, hadn't snuck out and worried the bejeezus out of all of us, there would have been no shooting in the first place!"

"But then we wouldn't have rescued Pharaoh and Scalar from the coliseum," I told him. "But thank you for coming to save us."

"Hell, Clem was already on his way in when Whisper and I showed up." Gunner shrugged. He wasn't in the mood to argue. "That darned horse of yours sure loves you, by the way. I was taking her back to Arete. Right around where that crazy coliseum popped up, she started losing her mind in the horse trailer. I was afraid she was going to hurt herself, so I pulled off the road and tried to calm her down. That was when she broke loose and knelt in front of me, like she wanted me to get on. Obviously, I did. She wouldn't stop running until we were in Kincaid's bedroom, and you were safe."

"I owe you one," I told the big man, smiling. "And I owe Whisper a hug."

Scalar entered the home through the front entrance, now riddled with bullet holes. Congealing blood was spattered and smeared all over the walls extending from the door frame on either side. Somewhere in the neighborhood of forty men had died there that night, and if it weren't for the magic of checkpoints, we would have lost Scalar, too.

"Hey, buddy," I said, already feeling better than when I woke up. "How're you feeling?"

"I'd say it would take more than a shotgun blast to the chest to take me down," he said pensively. "But now I know that's not true." He knelt by my side and whispered, "perhaps we can tell Pharaoh it was a magic shotgun that killed me? Just to maintain respect, you see."

"It was several magic shotguns, from what I saw," I replied matter-of-factly. "Becky? Kyle?"

"Several," Becky said.

"Too many to count," Kyle added.

"Let's just stick with several," I told him.

Speaking of Pharaoh, when he and Cool joined us, they had quite the story to tell, *and* they brought a couple of guests with them.

~

When Pharaoh, Cool, and Knightmare finally caught up with the runaway train, it was barreling down on the coliseum area at a frightening pace. According to Pharaoh, it had been going so fast, it looked like it was going to tip whenever it hit a bend, no matter how slight, in the tracks.

KM tracked the train using live satellite feeds and was able to determine its location and rate of travel. With Pharaoh in the back seat and Cool up front, the trio sped up the tracks in a race against time and a speeding locomotive.

They caught up to the behemoth in record time, and KM jumped from the tracks and began passing the mighty iron beast. As she passed the caboose, Cool reached out and grabbed hold of the upper railings. A second later, he was sailing from KM's front seat and trailing alongside the dangerously careening train. He reeled himself in, an impressive feat of strength and agility, and waved to KM and Pharaoh once he was in place atop the caboose.

KM accelerated, her shocks taking an incredible amount of punishment as her tires bounded over terrain barely meant for horses, let alone a car. Pharaoh stood in the back seat, looking a lot like the American car-surfers of the '70s and '80s. Precious seconds passed as the train finally came to the coliseum and what the team thought was the end of the line.

Much to their surprise, the tracks extended well into the distance. The extra miles of track gave them more time to stop the train, but it also meant the city of San Francisco and her citizens lay directly in its path. Hundreds, if not thousands, of lives could be in peril if the monster derailed in the city at the speed it was moving.

Pharaoh was pleasantly surprised when his clothing returned to his warrior's garb. He silently thanked the coliseum for its contribution to his dignity.

Her hope restored, KM poured on the speed. While it took several minutes, she eventually overtook and passed the Imperial 221.

Just before KM passed the monstrosity, Pharaoh dove from the back seat and took hold of a side rail on the coal car. He pulled himself up and onto the half full coal car and watched Knightmare speed forward. She hopped back onto the tracks, putting herself directly into the oncoming titan's path.

Pharaoh scrambled forward, his sights set on the cramped little cab of the steam engine. A few more seconds passed, and he dove into the cab, almost crushing Steve and a handful of chittering monkeys in the process.

Steve, Pharaoh's friend and teammate from his adventures in Capitula, was desperately trying to fight off the maddening little monsters while pulling on the engine's brake. He was far too small, though, to gain any real leverage, as the brake lever was taller than he was. What he did have a lot of, however, was attitude. "Watch where you're jumping, ya' big galoot!" The E.L.V.E. grunted and pointed at the brake. "Why don't you make yourself useful and kill some monkeys? Maybe yank this lever while yer at it?"

Pharaoh stared at Steve for a moment, utterly slack-jawed, taking in the tiny gladiator's costume he was dressed in. "Wah yuh doin' here? Me tink dem arachnodactyls did eat yuh all up, mon!" Pharaoh backhanded one of the chimps that thought it would try to sucker punch him, tossing it directly into the coal-burning oven underneath the boiler.

Steve put up his metal-gloved hands questioningly, in a WTF gesture. "Really? That's all you got? Nice to see you, too, dreadhead!"

Pharaoh reached down and patted Steve on his helmeted head affectionately. A three-inch red plume stuck up from the helmet, making Steve appear taller than usual.

Steve batted the lion's huge hand away. He hated the patronizing feel of it. "Less patting, more slowing, bub! I'll kill the monkeys!"

While Steve went to work on the clanging, yowling monkeys with a pair of short swords, Pharaoh leaned in and squeezed the lever at the end of the stick, pulling back on the brake slowly. He knew better than to pull hard and fast. That was just a way to break off the handle and create a whole new set of problems.

Steve watched the brake slide back with ease. "Showoff," he muttered.

The moment the train began to slow, Cool morphed his front and rear feet into enormous hands and, resembling a giant yellow gorilla — with brown spots of course — grasped the front edges of the caboose tightly. Then he let his body get caught up in the wind and pull away.

Cool had become a very stylish parachute.

The train began to slow even more, but even the parachute and fully engaged brake wouldn't be enough to stop the mechanical beast before it hit town... literally.

As Cool watched the train ahead of him barrel forward like a rail gun, he felt something slip. It wasn't until it was already too late that he realized the caboose had broken free and was slingshotting back into his face like a catapult.

Cool and the caboose tumbled backwards, head over hooves, until he was finally able to untangle himself from the wreckage. Then he did the only thing he could. He stretched.

He stretched, and he stretched, and he stretched some more, until he had a firm grasp on the *new* rear car of the train. Then, as if in a rinse and repeat cycle, he let his body catch up, grabbed on with his foot-hands, and released his body to the mercy of the wind.

Ahead of the train, Knightmare sped along dangerously, waiting for the train to slow. She was aware of the plan to slow it down, as she was the one who'd come up with it.

Pharaoh caused the first decrease in speed. She knew that because the second one, which Cool was supposed to initiate, couldn't happen unless the first one had already occurred. The actions had to be in order and well-timed.

The second drop was her cue to start phase three of her plan.

A pair of wide-spectrum laser beams that were typically meant to be a defensive countermeasure, extended from the rear bumper and rotated down, pointing at the tracks behind her.

The weapons lit up like tiny twin suns. Their beams focused on the center-most part of each of the rails, heating the tracks until they glowed bright red, like perfect trails of molten steel behind her. The train barreled onto the heated tracks like they were of no consequence, the momentum of unbridled kinetic energy bearing it forward like an unstoppable meteor.

Then the train bucked forward, gaining speed again, and KM knew that one of her team had failed. She sped up again, increasing the intensity of the lasers. If she made them too hot, she feared the tracks would warp, causing the train to derail immediately.

Then, just like it had once before, the train began to slow. Her teammates had regained the upper hand.

It was that extra bit of slowing, and the increased intensity of KM's laser beams, that finally brought the train to a slow, grinding, bone-jarring halt.

When all was said and done, the train wouldn't be going anywhere for a very long time, as its wheels were now welded to the tracks.

Cool fluttered to the ground and let his body slowly pull back into its own shape. That was when he spotted the monkey sitting on top of the last car; the monkey holding the pin it had pulled from the coupler between the car it sat atop and the caboose.

Cool's hoof shot out like an elastic pugilist, connecting with the sneering little imp, turning its mocking expression into one of surprise. The monkey flew so far, that by the time it plopped into the San Francisco Bay, Cool had lost sight of it.

The pin dropped to the ground next to Cool with a thunk.

"Surprise, mother chuckler," Cool said with a grin.

~

So, when I mentioned guests, I pluralized the word intentionally. You see, Steve wasn't alone on the train when

Pharaoh hopped onboard. He and Angus had been unlucky enough to materialize in the cab of the train together. Apparently, the only reason Angus wasn't carrying on when Pharaoh had arrived, is because Steve had immediately tossed him into a corner and threatened him with incineration if he didn't shut up.

Needless to say, Angus kept his alicorns as quiet as possible on the train, but once he was in Kincaid's ranch house, and safe from Steve's wrath, he was right back to his old self. He complained so much you might forget that Kyle and I were the ones who'd had our knees shot out, or that a maniacal masochistic misogynist had kidnapped Becky. Even Clem, with his flesh wound, had more to complain about. But Angus refused to be outdone. First, he complained about the humidity of the swamp, then he complained about the dryness of the desert. One moment, he was mad at Dirk for losing him, and the next, he was crying about missing the brash Scottish ninja. He was like Goldilocks, without the Goldilocks zone.

Steve's armor had turned into a child's sparkly red and white cowboy costume. It was pretty damned cute, if you ask me. He'd clearly had enough of the gibbering magic bagpipes. "Anus has been like this since we got snatched up in the swamp."

"It'sh Angush, ya' wee cree-tin!"

I was going to send Steve and Anus — I mean Angus — to separate bedrooms if they didn't both shut up.

Before Steve could respond, Becky stepped in and pointed a finger at each of them. "Has it occurred to either of you that Packard and Kyle have both been shot, and your petty, selfish arguing is only making things worse?"

"Packard can take care of hisself," Steve spat back before nodding at Kyle. "I don't know this guy from Blitzen." He looked back at Becky, his eyes blazing. "And I sure as hell don't know you either, toots!"

I had just opened my mouth to say something, but when Steve called Becky 'toots', I knew there was nothing I could say that would stop what was coming next.

"TOOTS?" Becky looked like she was about to explode. "Just who the fu-" She stopped herself short. "Just who do you think you are? Coming in here with zero clue as to what's been going on and treating everyone like garbage? Walking around here like Little Lord Fauntleroy! Well, I'll tell you what, buster-"

"Spare me the high and mighty crap! You're one of those entitled kids who has Santa wrapped around her finger every year! I work my fingers to the bone in a friggin' sweatshop so's you could have yer stuffed Mohinder the Royal Punjabi Elephant Doll," Steve yelled, cutting in like a drunk on the dance floor.

Becky's jaw officially hit the floor at that. "How did you...?"

"*Know?* You wanna know how I knew?" Steve laughed, but there was no humor in it whatsoever.

"He's one of Santa's top E.L.V.E.S.," Cool said, like Becky should have already known.

Becky's jaw remained dropped. Her eyes went wide enough to give Kyle competition. "You mean, *Santa's real?*"

"In some universes," I was finally able to get in. "Yes."

Steve was beside himself. He was confused, angry, and probably scared, too. He put his hand up to his forehead at a ninety-degree angle, like he was saluting. "I've had it up to here with entitled kids!" He looked at his hand and frowned before raising it as high as he could, even tiptoeing to get maximum lift.

Cool, who had just graced us with a good bit of the story of the takedown of the Imperial 221, extended one of his legs and lifted Steve, so his hand was just over Becky's head.

"That's not helping Cool," I said with a sigh.

Cool immediately set Steve back down.

Becky knelt next to the E.L.V.E., her expression sad. "I had no idea." She made sure he was looking at her and said, "I'm sorry. If it helps, I still have the Mohinder doll in my bedroom back home. He's always been my favorite. He's got the perfect amount of squish."

That made Cool laugh. "Heh heh! Just like the real Mohinder!"

Pharaoh nodded, smirking at the thought. "Him be soft and squishy."

Steve ignored the others and stared at Becky. "You're serious, aren't you? You might be one of the decent ones." He looked at her a moment longer, his eyes beginning to look sad. Then he laughed. "You're gonna have to do a lot better than appeal to my emotions, little girl," he grunted. "My default settings are anger, rage, and hostility. If you can deal with that, then maybe we'll be okay. Don't expect any miracles, tooooots." He drew out the last word dramatically, probably hoping to drag the f-word out of Becky.

She didn't bite.

She shrugged. "If I could make progress with Clem, then I'll break through your nasty little shell, too."

Clem started to say something, but stopped when he realized what a compliment she'd just paid him. A small, sentimental smile graced his lips. A moment later, it faded into a gentle blush like an Arizona sunset. He looked at her the way a proud father would look at his daughter, and his eyes twinkled with the slightest sheen of tears. That expression was the final nail in what I'd been feeling about my friends and their existence. They were every bit as real as I was, and I would protect them with everything I had... everything I was.

I'd known most of them for more than a decade. I'd been on adventures with them, laughed and cried with them, and been scared out of my wits with them. It occurred to me at that moment how much I loved them all.

They were my family.

"Where's KM," I asked. "I know she can't exactly waltz in and out of here like the rest of you, but she just went toe to toe with a ten ton behemoth. Is she okay?"

Gunner nodded, kneeling beside me, taking Becky's spot. He looked haggard, but more alive than I'd ever seen. He was in protector mode and was fulfilling his life's purpose. Although it probably wasn't the way he would've ever expected, he was living a dream. "Knightmare's out patrolling the grounds. She's the best suited to the sentry job, and the rest of us actually get tired." He looked at my knee and winced before looking at Kyle's bandage. "You boys doing okay? I wish I had some Tylenol or something. I found some whisky, but Becky and I used it to clean all your wounds."

"It's okay," I shrugged. "I'm coming up on eighteen years sober. I'm not about to fall off the wagon now."

"Speak for yourself, bro," Kyle groaned. "I think I'd take liquid courage if it was available."

"Naughty list," Steve mumbled to Becky. They both grinned like they belonged on the very same list themselves.

Gunner smiled. "Anyway, Knightmare's been asking about you. You sure do share a bond with her, don't you?"

I nodded, wondering what I would've done if she hadn't come back from her David vs. Goliath matchup. Things were so different in the game. Here in the real world...

Gunner patted my shoulder gently. "Speaking of bonds..." He tried to whistle, but either his mouth was too dry, or he'd just never learned how to whistle. His attempt sounded like a broken teakettle crying out for mercy.

Clem sat up straight and licked his lips. "I gotcha, friend," he told Gunner. He placed his fingers to his lips and let loose with a high-pitched sound that made almost everyone in the room jump. It was a requisite skill for cowboyin'.

About ten seconds later, Whisper came galloping through the door and slid to a halt by my side, almost trampling Becky and Steve in the process. She looked back at them and snorted apologetically before dropping her head and nuzzling me like a lost puppy. "Hi girl," I told her, hugging her as best I could with one arm. "I missed you, too."

"So," Gunner finally said. He was back in business mode. "Your dad's worried about you." He looked around the room. "All of you. Irene and I were, too."

"It was my fault, sir." Kyle looked like he had one foot in the grave, but he made an impressive effort to shift himself so he could look Gunner in the eye. "I was scared of what you and the others wanted to do with us."

"That's nonsense," Clem interrupted. "I take full responsibility."

"No," I said, before Becky could try to take any of the blame. "This is my world. I'm responsible."

Gunner nodded. "You're all responsible," he conceded. "But as Kyle said, you were scared. Hell, I might've done the same thing if I was in your shoes." He looked at me sternly. "Maybe."

"Look, Gunner," I sighed. "I really am sorry for running. But we've found more of my friends because we did. Bottom line, we're in a dangerous place right now. Like super dangerous. We'll probably be safer staying here for the night." I looked at Kyle. "We shouldn't move Kyle at night. We don't know what else is out there."

I really need to learn to just keep my mouth shut, you know?

The second I mentioned being safer inside, something thumped against the roof of Kincaid's home. Then another thump came… followed by yet another. In less than a minute, it sounded like it was raining actual cats and dogs.

Then the screeching started.

Cool, who rarely looked anything but happy, suddenly looked like he'd seen a ghost. His eyes widened as he shouted, "arachnodactyls!"

LEVEL SIX
LET'S PLAY

23
Quick Time Event

When Packard and the others left Arete, leaving Irene, Gunner, and me with our thumbs up our bums, I'll admit, I was a little angry. Mostly worried, but a little angry, too.

I felt like I'd failed at everything. Everything important, anyway. It was no secret that Individual Gaming was a multi-trillion dollar company. Only the third ever, competing solely with a Saudi oil company and another American tech firm. As a corporate founder, I was a success story for the ages. The man who everyone wanted to be. Or at least have my financial resources.

Who in their right mind would envy my personal life? As a husband and a father, I was the punchline of a bad dad joke. Victoria died young, leaving me with a nine-year-old son to raise on my own. A son who was destined to inherit the same disease that took the love of my life away from me. One of the loves of my life, anyway. The other had just vanished into the wind with an army of Nanops swimming in his bloodstream.

I was a curse to everyone I loved.

After verifying they'd indeed left the parking lot, the three of us reconvened in our regular meeting room and discussed our next moves. I say moves because we all knew, as worried as we were, we couldn't stick together and expect to be effective. We all had jobs to do. We all had roles to play.

Game pun unintended.

We agreed to head in separate directions and work on individual tasks necessary to either get the Quantum Nanops under control or shut them down.

We hoped we were prepared to do whatever it would take to get the job done.

Irene stayed at Arete. Once Gunner and I left, she was planning to head into a tech-free zone. No cell phones, laptops, wireless mp3 players, or anything else that could interfere with the scads of sensitive electronic equipment Arete developed could pass beyond the military level security checkpoints. Even employees who had pacemakers with wireless capabilities could only pass if their physician disabled all wireless functions first. There were no exceptions under any circumstances, even for Irene.

I was heading up to San Francisco, to vanish into an equally tech-free zone in the Individual Gaming headquarters.

Gunner would be going to my house to retrieve Whisper before returning to Arete to establish new security protocols. He'd moved an older, more seasoned guard to the front gate and delegated the task of setting up NPC living quarters to Jasmine. She was already aware of Packard's friends' existence, so bringing her into the loop, even marginally, ensured fewer questions from the team at large. We all agreed that, to ensure damage control, as well as the safety and freedom of everyone involved, everything happening would be on a need to know basis.

As for our need to disappear to our respective tech-free zones, we knew that dynamic would place us firmly out of each other's reach. Each of our roles was critical if we were going to find a solution. The zones were essentially giant Faraday cages, where we could work with our proprietary systems without any possibility of outside interference or corruption.

For our plan to work, Irene needed access to Packard's quantum database, which is why I needed to get to my Batcave at Individual Gaming Corporation. We'd shared data once before, when we'd linked the quantum database to the Nanops' subroutines. I set up an SFTP connection and allowed her system unfettered access to my son's hopes, dreams, and memories.

Gunner had taken one of the company trucks and made a stop in Los Altos to rent a horse trailer before continuing on to San Francisco.

I'll admit, driving through south San Francisco to get to my office was terrifying, and I plunged deeper into my guilt-ridden conscience by the minute. Entire neighborhoods and business parks seemed to be vanishing from the surrounding cityscape. I couldn't even imagine what was happening to the people. Frankly, had I known, I might have just pulled off to the side of the road and let the Nanops take me.

I knew Packard had been upset by the appearance of the coliseum. On a whim, I exited on Harney Way and drove towards the coliseum, hoping to spot Knightmare. At the t-intersection where Harney Way and Hunter's Point Expressway met, I encountered a police roadblock.

A tired-looking officer approached my car and pointed to a dirt patch, motioning for me to turn around. "You'll have to head back towards the freeway, sir," she called out.

I nodded, indicating that my intention was to comply. I waved her closer, hoping to ask her a question first. The officer, whose name tag read A. FRASSICA, obliged me by stepping up to the window, her eyes telling me that whatever I wanted better be good.

"I'm looking for my son and his friends," I told her. "He's seventeen, dark blonde hair, and driving a black convertible, a 1965 Pontiac GTO. One of his friends is a girl with short brow-"

The officer put up her hand to stop me before I described everyone in the car. "I've been manning this roadblock for more than an hour and I haven't seen anyone matching that description. I'd remember a car like that." She looked at me with restrained concern. She knew something was up. Deep down, she was probably just as scared as I was. "You sure they came this way, sir?"

I shook my head. I really wasn't. "No, officer. I'm not... I was just hoping."

She offered the sincerest smile she could muster. "I'm sure they'll turn up, sir. But if I can offer a word of caution, it would be best if you and your family stayed clear of the stadium land, and its vicinity. Okay?"

"Okay." I nodded and thanked her before pulling Arete's electric loaner onto the dirt patch and going back the way I came. Turning on the radio and tuning it to 92.2, I pulled onto the freeway on ramp. I glanced back absently in the direction of the roadblock. I can't say with any real certainty, but I could swear Officer Frassica and her police cruiser were gone.

As I joined the surprisingly light flow of traffic, a trio of heavily armed Blackhawks flew overhead, heading directly for Candlestick Park.

~

"You're listening to 92.2 FM, the EpiphanyMill News Network. The Assistant to the President for Science and Technology, Doctor Neil deGrasse Tyson, has made an official statement about the unexplained occurrences in San Francisco County and adjacent areas."

"Ladies and gentlemen, members of the press, esteemed colleagues. What we are witnessing in the San Francisco Bay Area is utterly without precedent. At this stage, it would be easy to speculate about the cause. We caution against that, however, as speculation leads to conjecture, and without a properly coordinated scientific investigation, we run the risk of spreading disinformation. We have our top scientists en route as I speak, as well as a joint military taskforce, to ensure the safety of everyone involved. If the evacuation of the surrounding areas becomes necessary, we ask that everyone cooperate implicitly with any instruction from law enforcement or military personnel. At the request of President Cena, Vice President Walken and I will be rendezvousing with scientists at the California Academy of Sciences before the end of the day. I will personally update the press as we learn more about any potential threat. Thank you."

Considering the news reports and the ominous warnings from government officials, I expected traffic in and out of San Francisco to be a nightmare. It wasn't until I pulled off the freeway near the Embarcadero Center, though, that traffic became noticeably thick.

When I finally arrived at Individual Gaming, I parked in the lower level parking garage and used my key card to access the uppermost level via a private elevator.

Then I went to work.

24
Night Terrors

If you recall, arachnodactyls are essentially wolf-sized spiders with wings. You know, the ones that'll eat anything with a soft, chewy center. Aside from KM being metal, and Cool and Pharaoh being virtually impossible to get a bite out of, we were all fair game.

As is always the case when the shit hits the fan, several things happened all at once.

Steve, suffering from a brief flash of PTSS, scrambled underneath a billiard table and pulled his little cowboy hat down tightly before remembering who he was.

He crawled back out and stood up, reaching for his trusty blades. Instead, what he found hanging at his hips were twin toy guns. He cursed as he stared at them and hurled the one in his right hand squarely into the face of an arachnodactyl pressing its way through one of the broken-out windows. The second of the toy pistols, which were polished aluminum with white plastic handles, probably meant to look like ivory, struck the angry beast in one of its many onyx colored eyes before Steve sprinted into the kitchen. Despite having been pulled down so tightly, his little cowboy hat fell backwards and hung against his back, held by a length of colorfully braided lanyard.

He looked like a fifty-year-old toddler in a Halloween costume.

I'm pretty sure Kyle was going to need clean underwear after the eight-legged, leather-winged nightmares began swarming the ranch house. It had never come up in the past, but he apparently suffered from severe arachnophobia. He dragged himself awkwardly, like a three-legged hermit crab, eagerly taking Steve's place under the pool table, where he whimpered a few times like a kicked dog before breaking into audible sobs.

Becky, who'd faced the wingless, but still terrifying spiderlings with me in Laboratory 311, dropped to her knees at my side and clutched the Derringer bravely. She nodded to my other side. My guns had been brought out of Kincaid's room and set close at hand.

I smiled at her. You know, to say thank you, but she was already aiming her tiny pistol at the windows, waiting for the right opportunity to shoot. "Don't forget you have bullets in your garter," I told her loudly. Then I looked at where Kyle had been laying and saw his gun, abandoned when he'd taken cover under the heavy oak pool table. I reached out with the butt of my shotgun. Using it like a hockey stick, I slid Kyle's pistol across the tile floor.

The gun clattered up against Kyle's injured leg, and he almost batted it away in a panic. When he saw what it was, though, he grabbed it and held it tightly to his chest, where it would be of no use to anyone.

Cool, though virtually invincible against things like the arachnodactyls, shuddered as the ravenous beasts pushed through broken windows and skittered hungrily over the rooftop and outside walls, searching for entry points. It's not like I could blame him. They were the stuff of nightmares — of *night terrors* — and they'd found their way into my unsuspecting world. Cool stretched his limbs towards the windows in a valiant attempt to block their entry, but there were just too many of them, and they'd broken through windows in more than just the room we all occupied. As fast, flexible, and creative as he was, he still couldn't be everywhere at once.

The arachnodactyls shrieked with malicious glee as they made their way into the lamp-lit great room. Their shadows distorted in the flickering light, stretching across the walls like ghastly, opaque versions of Cool. We could hear more of them entering through broken windows down the hall, their screeches resonating through the sprawling building like a lunatic chorus of demons.

Scalar disappeared down the hall, his hatchets raised over his head, and Pharaoh followed closely behind, dodging the bodies of recently fallen gunslingers as they went. The sounds of slamming doors and dactyls yelping in pain echoed back towards us. Pharaoh and Scalar shouted to each other, though it was impossible to make out their words over the piercing cries of the invading monstrosities.

In three quick bounds, Whisper leapt over Becky and me, effectively shielding us with her body.

Clem had begun firing at the things as they pushed past Cool. He was a freaking rock. He had to have been at least a little frightened of the creatures, but if he was, he didn't show it. His expression was a grim mask of determination, and his fingers moved more like a pianist's than a warrior's. His hand and Jackson were one, and reloading bullets was as natural to him as using a TV remote was to most modern people. Clem Pickett was every bit the warrior El Scalar, Pharaoh, or even Cool was. But as fast and competent as he was, the monsters continued to push past our defenses.

Gunner ran to Clem's side and began firing at any of the monsters that made it past Cool with him. He was careful with his shots, aware that once we were out of ammo, there would be no more coming. Gunner released a clip, allowing it to drop to the floor noisily, and slammed another into the base of his .45. I had no idea how many of those clips might have been in his jacket pocket, but when in Rotgut, I typically assumed the worst.

From underneath Whisper, Becky and I began firing at the legion of winged terrors, though from my position on the ground, I wasn't much use. Becky stood, blocking Whisper, and extended a hand. Without so much as a second thought, I handed her my freshly loaded shotgun. She clearly remembered what Stan had told her about firing a rifle or shotgun; brace it against your shoulder, find your center of gravity, and squeeze the trigger gently. She fired off a shot, blowing an approaching dactyl into a bloody, twitching pulp that landed with a splat on the pool table.

Becky tried firing at another, but the trigger jammed and the arachnodactyl flew directly at her face.

Without realizing what I was doing, and without any regard for my knee, I sprang to my feet, and caught the arachnodactyl by its front legs. I held it at bay, though without a gun in my hand it was going to be a very short-lived wrestling match. Becky stepped back instinctively as the thing thrashed and lunged, wings and legs fighting me for a bite of raw Packard-steak. The thing was mere inches from my face, and all I could see were black, bulbous eyes and huge, gnashing teeth. Its breath reeked like the swamp water of Artemisia and whatever it had been feasting on before being brought into our world. I marveled in silent terror once again at the artisanal level of detail the Quantum Nanops had put into their creations. My mind reeled with the thought. I imagined I must be going insane... about to die in that thing's jaws yet focusing on the stench of its breath.

And then it exploded all over my face. One second, I was fighting it and the next, I was retching up its blood and teeth. I peered between the twitching, disembodied legs that I still clutched in a death grip, and saw Kyle, propped against the pool table, grimacing in pain. A smoking revolver dangled loosely from his hand.

Once again, he'd come through at just the right moment.

~

Becky and I lunged forward and caught Kyle before he toppled to the floor.

Kyle looked at me, dazed and clearly confused. "How are you standing, bro?" He and Becky stared at me, both surprised that I was suddenly mobile.

Before they could question me any further, Steve rushed past us. The E.L.V.E. had requisitioned two large meat cleavers from the kitchen, and immediately went to work dismembering any of the dactyls that had fallen but were still moving. He shouted at the creatures as he hacked off legs, wings, and even heads, in a berserker-like frenzy that would have made Dirk proud. "Merry Christmas, ya' filthy animals!"

Angus, who we'd propped up in a corner, so he'd be less likely to antagonize Steve, cried out for help. Steve turned and saw one of the downed monsters cocooning the irritating magical bagpipes in thick, viscous webbing. Both of its wings had been severely damaged, but that didn't stop it from hunting for its next victim. The arachnodactyls were voracious, single-minded hunters, intent upon feeding and storing more food. Angus must have still smelled like a meal to them.

Steve ran at the dactyl, bloody cleavers poised and ready to strike. He shouted at the monster as he approached it, distracting it long enough to stop chewing. "Oh no you don't! I'm the only one allowed to hurt him!"

The dactyl screeched and turned towards Steve, leaving Angus covered in a half-assed mass of what looked like snot and silly string.

"Shombody get this crap off me," Angus yelled as Steve swung his cleaver downward, splitting the dactyl's head in two, right down to what might have been its shoulders. Eyes and a mass of nerves that probably served as a central nervous system of sorts spilled from the split head like a handful of seeds scooped out of a jack-o-lantern.

Without looking at Angus, Steve shouted back. "I'm a little busy right now, ya' old windbag! Show some gratitude for a change! For Christmas' sake, you're worse than the kids!"

Angus began to say something but decided against it. His horns drooped and he went silent.

"That's what I thought," Steve grunted.

Two more of the screeching terrors breached the perimeter simultaneously, but Gunner and Clem dropped them in what sounded like one resounding gunshot before they could cause any more mayhem.

In true form, Steve was on the angry, writhing beasties in record time. He'd gotten quite handy with the cleavers. Before you could say Quantum Nanops, he'd disassembled them as expertly as a butcher in a meat market.

El Scalar came running up the hall, hot on the tail of two more of the soaring invaders. All at once, several guns pointed at the approaching things, but nobody had a clean shot without risking shooting Scalar. He hauled back with his hatchets, ready to eviscerate them, but before he got the chance, an ear-splitting wail cut through the building like railroad spikes on a chalkboard.

Everyone covered their ears, but the dactyls didn't have that option. The creepy beasties flew in circles, appearing confused and panicked. Some slammed clumsily into the walls, while others began beating their wings against the ceiling, frantically trying anything to find a way out.

One of the dactyls turned and flew over Scalar's head, screaming as it soared back up the hall. The other, in a desperate act of self-preservation, veered directly at Kyle, Becky, and me. Its jaws snapped dangerously and its eyes, though searching for an escape from the piercing whine assaulting its ears, settled upon us. The monster's instinct to feed was just too great, and it dove at us like a kamikaze pilot attempting a pass at a drive-through.

Every available gun in the room pointed at the thing, but before anyone could fire, I heard a familiar chittering sound that was surprisingly louder than the awful sound echoing through the house. The new sound wasn't painful, just loud. Like a primordial bat's battle cry. A second later, a small mass of fur and tentacles, no larger than an average house cat, slammed into the dactyl at an opposing angle, knocking it completely off course.

The new arrival wrapped eight glorious tentacles around the struggling dactyl and squeezed tightly. The pair slammed into a wall hard enough to dent the wood paneling, but the little bat-winged creature with the rabbit's body, octopus tentacles and eyes, and nasty-looking fangs on either side of her adorable bunny buck teeth, refused to let go.

Gunner and Clem immediately took aim at the creatures, but I dove between them and their targets.

I knew they wouldn't be able to hear me clearly over all the noise, so I waved my arms wildly like a ChuChuLo charade, and shook my head back and forth, mouthing NO!

I turned and watched as the little winged furball, whose name just happened to be Moreau, tore the throat out of the dactyl with her savage fangs. She slipped her tentacles free and let it fall in a broken heap. Then she turned and blinked at me innocently, her octopus eyes focusing on the surrounding room. Moreau chittered happily at the sight of me and looped in the air, her wings propelling her right into my arms. Her tentacles wrapped around my neck and head, and she nuzzled me with her gore-covered face. I didn't mind the blood. I'd already taken a mouthful of the awfulness when Kyle killed the last one.

Moreau was a chimera from the *Hiromon* game. She was my partner in the tournaments, and as dear and trusted a friend as anyone else in the room. She settled onto her favorite place on my right shoulder and draped her tentacles loosely over my arm, chest, and back.

As the awful shrill sound faded, and the last of the arachnodactyls escaped through the broken windows, I turned and faced the rest of my friends. "Everyone, this is Moreau," I said. Then to my fuzzy friend, "Moreau, this is everyone."

~

Reactions to my little companion were varied. Cool and Kyle, predictably, gushed over her and how adorable she was. Gunner, and even Pharaoh, who'd just returned from the hall, covered in blood and spider guts, seemed genuinely taken by her cuteness, but were less of the gushing type than my nerdy friends. Clem, Scalar, and Steve looked her over suspiciously, each of them silently reserving the right to judge her based on whatever happened next.

Becky, though, looked horrified.

"Are you okay," I asked, genuinely concerned that something was amiss.

"T-tentacles…" Becky stammered before shivering like she had a case of the willies. "I'm uh… not real fond of them." She took a tentative step backward, awkwardly bumping into Kyle. She looked at Moreau apologetically. "Laboratory 311… you know… I was already afraid of tentacles, but-"

"It's okay," I said. "You'll have plenty of chances to get to know her."

She swallowed hard at the thought, but when Moreau raised one of her tentacles and waved at her, chittering sweetly, Becky sniffled and cracked a little smile. "The rest of her is cute," she conceded nervously.

Moreau tweeted happily.

Kyle reached out and touched one of her tentacles, allowing it to coil gently around his finger. "Does she understand us?"

I nodded. "Every word. Right, Moreau?"

She chirped again, indicating that she was already up to speed with the conversation.

Becky shuffled uncomfortably. "So, she knows what I said?"

Moreau chirped again. The noise was a little less cheerful, but the tone was still upbeat.

"She says it's okay," I told Becky. "Most people react that way the first time they see her."

"I know how that feels," Scalar muttered.

Becky sniffled, holding back a sob. She reached out and touched the tentacle that had coiled around Kyle's finger. She shivered again but was clearly determined to make peace with my little friend. The tip of the tentacle extended to meet Becky's finger, and a single suction cup caressed her fingertip like a kiss.

Moreau blinked, but otherwise remained silent.

Becky suddenly laughed. It was an awkward, uncomfortable sound that was as much a sob as a laugh, but it marked her acceptance of Moreau as one of our growing family.

Becky wasn't the one I really needed to worry about, though.

As Becky and Moreau made friends, movement in the kitchen caught my eye.

Whisper was watching us, and by the look she was giving me, I realized she was feeling very left out.

~

As soon as I saw her face, I excused myself and coaxed Moreau's tentacle away from Kyle and Becky's fingers. I turned and approached my other constant, ever-loyal companion. "Whisper! I saved the best introduction for last, girl!"

I heard Cool questioning my statement as I closed the gap between Whisper and me. My horse looked at us like a wife who'd just found out about a mistress, her dark eyes darting between Moreau and me accusingly. "She's a friend from another game, girl. I want her to be your friend too."

Whisper took a step back, snorting defiantly. She shook her head, her mane snapping to and fro.

"Come on, girl," I pleaded. "It would mean so much to me if you-"

Whisper snorted again, not giving up any ground. She stomped her foot in a rare assertive gesture. She stomped so hard she cracked one of the pristine Spanish tiles.

Suddenly, Moreau's tentacles lifted, and she flew off my shoulder, leaving Whisper and me facing each other in an uncomfortable moment of silence.

I watched Moreau fly into the kitchen before looking back into Whisper's eyes. "You don't really want to hurt her feelings, do you, girl? She's new here, too. She could use a friend."

Whisper glared at everyone else, causing them to look away awkwardly. Her look clearly said, *she has PLENTY of friends.*

"Okay," I agreed. "I see your point." I shrugged, not sure what else to say. "I just hope that-"

Moreau, who had found an undamaged bowl of apples on the kitchen counter, interrupted me in the best way. She flew between us and, hovering there, held out a carefully chosen apple in one trembling tentacle.

A bright, shiny, red olive branch.

Whisper looked at me, as if to say, *'you're lucky I'm so forgiving'*, and took the apple from Moreau.

That was the tenuous beginning of a beautiful friendship.

~

While Moreau and Whisper whinnied and chirped back and forth, happily gossiping about me like a couple of little old ladies, I had to field a barrage of questions from the rest of the group. Actually, it was just one question, asked by everybody.

"How are you walking?"

Okay, so Gunner's question was why I was talking like George W. Bush, but *everyone else* asked how I was walking.

I reached down and touched my knee, expecting to find a bloody mess, but instead found shredded Levis over completely intact flesh. There was dried blood on the fabric surrounding the hole, and drip stains that extended almost all the way down to the bottom of my pant leg. There was no denying I'd been shot, but my knee itself was as good as new.

Gunner and Becky beat me to an answer. "The Nanops," they said in unison.

Kyle was still struggling to remain upright. He looked down at his knee. "Then why haven't they healed me?"

Clem, who had been paying a lot more attention to everything than anyone first thought, offered an answer. "'Cause we ain't him. As much as the Marshal says we ain't none of them enpeesees, he's still the one whose noggin's fuelin' the fire behind this here mess."

Gunner raised an eyebrow at the comment. "That makes sense, Clem."

The others nodded, though enthusiasm in any form was in short supply.

Kyle frowned. "So, what? We just have to live with our injuries?"

"No," I replied. "Remember when your current clothes replaced that tunic you were wearing?"

It was fresh in his mind, so I continued. "You skinned the palms of both your hands in the coliseum, but when we crossed over into Rotgut your injuries vanished. It was like the Nanops reset you or something. You got a clean bill of health."

Becky wrinkled her nose. I think she was trying to visualize the bigger picture but could only see scattered puzzle pieces… most of which were upside down. "It keeps coming back to *you*, doesn't it, Pack?"

"Yeah," I sighed. "It seems that way, doesn't it?"

Pharaoh cleared his throat. "Me sorry fi ask dis, but Irene and yuh fadda… dem bad people? It look like dem do bad tings."

I shrugged. "They did the wrong thing, for what they believed was the right reason." I looked up and met his eyes. "They're not bad people." I looked at Gunner, who was silently mulling over the question as well. "But they made a terrible decision without thinking it through. I think a lot of people are going to pay the price for me being alive."

"The boatman always demands his toll," Clem muttered. All eyes were suddenly on him. He looked around at us, embarrassed. "That ain't my sayin'," he offered, his tone humble. "My wife was an educated woman. Knew how to read and write and cooked a mean possum pie. She was partial to a book she packed in our trunk on Greek stories. Gods, monsters, demons..." He trailed off, probably thinking about his family. "There was a boatman who'd ferry folks inta the afterlife, but he always needed his payment first. She said that's where coins on the eyes of dead folk came from... like some sorta' bribe to the boatman to git 'em thar safely. I did that fer my wife n' daughter... the coins." He looked at me, ignoring everyone else. "The boatman *always* demands his toll."

I looked around at the bodies on the floor. Dead gunslingers and arachnodactyls littered the place, and blood covered the walls like a madman's mural. I knew the same was true outside as well. "Yeah, Clem... and something tells me the toll is going to keep going up."

~

While Becky, Gunner, and I got Kyle situated on the least bloodied up couch we could find, the others went from room to room, making sure there were no more living arachnodactyls left hunting for a meal.

Once I was sure Kyle was comfortable, I went outside, telling the others I wanted to check on KM. Gunner insisted on joining me, even though I had my guns, and Knightmare was a veritable weapon of mass destruction.

We found KM circling the house slowly. Her tires had tamped down the soil into a solid set of perfectly spaced dirt trails.

She stopped as we approached. "I'm pleased to see you're well," she said. "Both of you." She paused for a moment before continuing. "Heat signatures indicate nine living beings inside the home. That's one more than expected. Is there a winged spider still alive, or has another of your many friends joined us?"

"You don't miss a thing, do you," I asked.

"I do not," she replied.

"Speaking of the winged spiders," Gunner cut in. "Are they all dead?"

"Unfortunately, no," KM replied. "When they first flew onto the property, they approached from all directions, making them difficult to track. I apologize. I mistook them for Nanop generated bats. By the time they were close enough to scan properly, they were too close to the house to fire upon without risking killing any of you. Especially you, Gunner."

Gunner shrugged. "Why me?"

"You don't heal... or respawn," I replied.

"Precisely," KM agreed. "I was able to dispatch a few of the creatures with my flamethrowers, but-"

"You're saying you have flamethrowers," Gunner interrupted. "Actual functional flamethrowers?"

I couldn't hide my surprise. "Flying spiders, a chimera, and one of Santa's E.L.V.E.S., and you're surprised by flamethrowers?"

"Not really *surprised*," Gunner shrugged. "More like... *impressed.*"

"Understandable," KM allowed. "They are accurate and quite effective up to one hundred yard-"

"KM," I interrupted. "The arachnodactyls?"

"Oh, yes. Perhaps your tendency to squirrel has rubbed off on me?" She paused a moment, but when I didn't take the bait, she continued. "Once the creatures were in the house, I had few options available to assist. Thankfully, I was able to produce a self-modulating frequency that was highly distressing to them. Once I began emitting the frequency, the arachnodactyls rapidly dispersed. Between thirty and forty fled."

That was a lot. I scanned the night sky, expecting movement, but aside from some fireflies that I knew didn't belong in San Francisco, all was quiet on the western front.

Gunner looked worried. "Where did they go?"

"That would be the bad news," Knightmare told us. "They've flown towards the city."

I glanced at the low foothills on the not too distant horizon. "Towards Rotgut?"

"No," she said, sounding as troubled as Gunner. "San Francisco."

25

Hiromon

I'm not sure anybody but Kyle got any sleep that night. Well, Steve was perfectly okay sleeping on Kincaid's bed. He even let Angus sit on one of the chairs in the room. If you've never heard bagpipes snore, consider yourself lucky. It's anything but musical.

By morning, the sky was still free of arachnodactyls, but thin tendrils of black smoke rose lazily on the horizon, winding towards a thin layer of clouds like so many vines sprouted from Jack's magic beans. The muted wail of what sounded like sirens echoed from somewhere in the distance, dulled, like a scream heard through a thick wall.

Things were already so bad out there, but I knew in my heart they were only going to get worse.

Seriously. I had my mobility back, Nanops that healed any injuries I got, crazy weapons, and most importantly, *friends*... but the price was just too high. All those lives... lost... because of me. Because dad couldn't let me go.

The more I thought about it, the more frustrated I felt. I wanted so badly to be able to enjoy what was happening to me. Like, what teenager wouldn't want to play their favorite games for real? But instead of joy, elation, exuberance, or any of the good feelings I should have been experiencing, all I felt was guilt and a lingering hint of anger towards my dad and Irene... which made me feel even *more* guilty.

Becky found me standing outside the front door, contemplating our next move. Clem had whipped up a cowboy breakfast in the kitchen, complete with a big pot of authentic dirt-water coffee. She was trying to get coffee grounds out of her teeth when she stepped through the door. "What I wouldn't give for my toothbrush right now," she said, blowing air through her teeth. She looked at the bodies of men and flying beasts strewn across the courtyard and winced. "Oh my god... it's so much worse than I thought."

"Not any better inside," I muttered.

Becky sighed heavily before answering. "No, it isn't... but I'd gotten used to it." She looked distressed by the thought. "What does that say about me, Pack? That I can become desensitized to something this awful so quickly."

"That you're a survivor," I said, turning my head to face her. "You've always been a survivor. Every time I've visited your world, you're one of the few people I can count on to be strong enough to have my back, every time. I'd bet my life on you, without hesitation."

Becky's cheeks flushed and she shook her head. "You've got more faith in me than I do in myself." Then something registered, and she looked confused. "Why can you remember many times in Laboratory 311 with me, but I can only recall one with you?"

I thought about it, but I really had no answer. "I don't know... because it's how the game works?"

Becky shook her head. "So, what is it? I'm an NPC, or I'm not an NPC? Because if I am, then I'll just reset and be whatever the gameplay makes me for each playthrough of the game. If I'm not, then I only experienced the rip in space once."

I was confused. "Then why can I remember hundreds of playthroughs?"

Becky looked away before answering me. "I think each time, you interacted with a different me... in a different universe."

"How is that possible," I asked, dumbfounded.

"How is *ANY* of this possible," she snapped back. She closed her eyes and took a few deep breaths. "Sorry. I'm just on edge... you know, after Kincaid and his goons. And I *HATE* this dress."

I wasn't really sure what to say. "It looks nic-"

"Nope... please don't. Just allow me to hate it." Becky thrust her palm forward in an open invitation to *talk to the hand.*

"That's fair." I nodded, wishing I could say anything that would help.

Becky beat me to it. "Not to be a broken record, but I really miss my mom. I'm worried about our friends back at the particle accelerator. Even that guy who worked there. What was his name? Sussudio?"

"Shishido," I said, not really feeling like joking around.

"Shishido," she said, sadly. "They're probably all dead, you know. My mom probably thinks I died there. And your parents over there... you *did* die." She swallowed back a sob. "I don't know how long ago that field trip feels for you, but for me, it was just a few days ago." She looked at me sideways. "Do you even have any attachment to your parents there?"

I'd never thought about that before. Until Becky showed up, I'd never really thought about any of the characters, uh… *people* who populated the games outside my closest friends and allies. "You probably think I'm a monster," I muttered, feeling like the world's biggest turd. "… but n-no. I thought about you, Brad, Jamal, Stan, even Mr. Pan, but not the Mr. and Mrs. Campbell from your world." I looked into her eyes, dreading the judgement I'd convinced myself was coming. Instead, I saw compassion tinged with a touch of pity, which might have been worse than judgement. "I have a dad. What I didn't have were friends, or an extended family. You and the others… you're my family."

"That's a nice sentiment, Pack, but you have to remember, the Campbells in my world, and people in so many other worlds, they thought about *you*. Good and bad, Pack. They all thought about you." Becky pointed at the distant spires that marked the location of the coliseum on the eastern horizon. "There was an entire stadium full of people who thought *a lot* about you. Did you hear them cheer when the announcer introduced you? They were real, Packard... not some game programmed to give you the touchy-feelies. I'll bet there are people you've interacted with in other worlds who think about you more than you'd feel comfortable knowing. *Good and bad.*"

I found myself at that rare crossroads where speechless and dumbfounded intersected.

Becky shook her head. "I'm sorry, Pack. I didn't come out here to beat you up or make things harder for you. I'm frustrated, frightened, and a little angry. But not at you."

I really didn't have to ask, but I think she needed to say it out loud. "At my dad?"

"Yeah," she shrugged. "And Irene, too, I guess. I really didn't mean to take it out on you."

"It's okay." I put on the best smile I could muster. "I'm a little angry at them, too, so you're not alone." I thought of something that made my smile go from forced to mostly genuine. "Pharaoh's pretty upset with dad, too. I'd say we're in good company."

KM's voice suddenly echoed from the south side of Kincaid's home. "Though I do not share in your anger for Hal, would it be acceptable to join you? I wouldn't want to intrude if anger is a prerequisite to participate in this conversation."

~

After everyone finished breakfast, we all agreed that given the circumstances, we couldn't just hide out in Kincaid's place indefinitely. Angus was the only one who voted against leaving. Oh yeah, as always, Pharaoh called it to a vote. I mean, come on, would you have expected it any other way?

Following a spirited discussion, which Steve laced with f-bombs and other colorful metaphors that would keep him on the naughty list for the foreseeable future, we agreed the train tracks were as good a place as any to begin. KM had been scanning for Nanop activity and made an exceptionally distressing discovery. The Nanops had become increasingly busy in a location just about a mile south of us, at the base of Serbian Ravine. It was distressing because, aside from a golfer's driving range, a large cluster of cemeteries, graveyards, and memorial parks dominated the area. I wasn't afraid of graveyards or anything, but I will admit, my imagination began to question what the Nanops would want with several thousand square feet of two century old burial plots. According to KM, the train tracks, though blocked by the Imperial 221 to the north, seemed to extend south for almost a hundred miles. They'd already reached well beyond Campbell and seemed to end somewhere south of Santa Cruz.

Though he'd become quite accustomed to his dapper, western-themed clothing, Kyle was literally aching to escape the world of *Marshal Blood*. He just wanted his knee to heal. Considering the fact that I'd briefly shared in his pain, and found it to be excruciating and debilitating, I wanted him healed, too.

I looked around at our growing group and realized there was no longer enough room in KM for everyone. "Guys, if we're gonna do this, we're going to have to get creative. There's only so much room in Knightmare."

"Angus can sit in the trunk," Steve offered.

Angus was happy to return the verbal fire. "Ash can ye, ye wee troll!"

I cut in before Steve could fling another insult. "You can both sit in the trunk if you want to act like a couple of tool bags. Or you can shut up and treat each other like friends!" Steve scowled at Angus, but I wasn't going to give him the satisfaction. "If you hadn't noticed, all that bullshit out there is dangerous! If we're busy fighting each other, we're making ourselves easier targets for our enemies." I locked gazes with Steve, matching his scowl. "Are we clear?"

Steve grunted and scoffed. Then, as if I'd just told him a joke, he smirked at me. He looked at Angus and laughed. "Since when did the bard grow a pair?"

Angus tooted in mock celebration. "Well, the drinksh are on me tonight. A few weeks ago, I bet Dirk that he'd never shtand up to ye. Of coursh, I'll need to borrow the money for the drinksh. I'm not made of money, ye know."

"Okay," I relented. "That was pretty funny. Ha, ha, ha, the joke's on Packard." I sighed. "I'm serious, guys. We need to be united, or we're going to get ourselves, each other, or some poor innocent bystanders killed. Do any of you want that on your consciences?" In a move I'd learned from Becky, I showed Steve my palm, offering it up for conversation. "I know, I know. You don't have a conscience, right, Steve?"

Steve grunted indignantly. "Damn. I was just about to agree with you, kid. Don't push your luck."

Clem cleared his throat. He did that when he thought he might be interrupting. "I say we let the Marshal finish." He glanced at Steve, then at Pharaoh and Scalar. "I unnerstan' some of y'all don't know me from Adam, but he's been my friend fer a right long time, and I trust him with my life. Mayhaps y'all feel the same about him. I'm here to tell ya', if'n he's the tie that binds us, then we should trust his judgement, both in what we're to do next, and 'bout trustin' one another."

Nods rolled through the group like a wave at a ballgame, and I was back in the limelight.

"There's only so much room in Knightmare," I continued from where Steve had interrupted me. "And Kyle is going to need the back seat."

"Leave Kyle to me, dude," Cool said. He reached over and fist bumped Kyle with his hoof.

Kyle winced at the movement but returned the gesture with a gusto that I'd never seen in him before. He was alive in ways I'd never imagined.

I looked at Whisper. I'd neglected her since she'd shown up. That was about to change. "I'll be riding Whisper. Moreau can take my shoulder. Is that alright with you, Whisper?"

My faithful steed nickered softly. Her eyes shone with love and gratitude.

I smiled at her before continuing. "There are several horses in the stables. I plan to cut Enos loose before we leave, so he can tend to them. That said, I know Clem and Gunner are both comfortable in the saddle. Anyone else wanna ride?"

KM chirped unexpectedly. "Yes, please. I'd like to."

We all turned to stare at her, a collective look of confusion spreading across our faces like wildfire. A silly, perplexed wildfire.

Knightmare was silent for a moment, probably hoping to be let off the hook. "Was this not a good time for a joke?"

As you might have expected, Cool and Kyle giggled. Everyone else breathed a sigh of relief. Nobody wanted to be the one to tell the four thousand pound death machine that she couldn't ride a horse.

El Scalar, smiling at KM's quip, raised a hand politely. "I am quite good on horseback, compadre," he offered.

I nodded and looked at Steve. "What about you," I asked. "You ride reindeer, right?"

Steve blanched at the suggestion. "Horses are huge compared to reindeer, bub. Unless you've got a pony in those stables that can keep up, I should be in the car."

"If I take the driver's seat, Steve can sit up front with me, and Pharaoh can share the back seat with the bagpipes," Becky said.

Angus despised being referred to as 'the bagpipes' and was not shy about making it known. "For God's shake, woman, it'sh Angush! Get it right!"

I sighed at Angus's outburst and began counting heads. I calculated riders but counted Cool and Kyle as a separate package. "Well," I said, cracking a genuine smile. "Becky is officially better at math than me."

"I ain't never been too keen on cypherin' neither," Clem agreed quietly, garnering a few puzzled looks.

"Okay, then," I said, ignoring Clem's comment. "Clem, why don't you take Gunner and Scalar and pick out the three best horses. Pharaoh and I will go deal with Enos. The rest of you, see if you can gather a few supplies for the road. Dried meat and fruits, but not too much. We're only going about a mile, but the terrain's rough and we don't know what we're going to run into along the way." I thought about the arachnodactyls and the awful monkeys that had once been Alpha Male. "Gunner, while Clem's getting the horses saddled up, why don't you look for some useable firearms and ammo?"

Gunner nodded and grinned. "Way to take the bull by the horns, kiddo."

Scalar frowned at the statement, and Gunner wrinkled his nose. "Sorry, friend. It's a figure of speech." He looked at Clem and sighed. "Now I know how *you* feel."

Scalar winked at Gunner. "It's okay. I actually kind of like it."

Gunner pursed his lips and nodded, still uncomfortable with the idea that he'd just found common ground with Clem's regular faux pas. He finally smiled, unable to avoid the weird irony, and left to find the guns and ammo.

Clem and Scalar turned towards the stables, but Kyle called out before they began walking. "Hey, Clem? Can I share something with you?"

Clem told Scalar, whom he still insisted upon calling Bill, to go on ahead, and that he'd catch up momentarily.

Clem stepped over to Kyle's side, careful not to bump him, or jostle his knee. "What's on yer mind, son?"

Kyle looked flustered. "Can I tell you something?"

"Anything," Clem nodded.

Kyle blushed, his cheeks going deep crimson. "I uh... you see... I was a gunslinger in my world, but I wasn't a lawman, Clem. I was a killer. A hired gun. An assassin."

Clem looked away from Kyle for a moment, processing the words and considering his reply. He finally looked back at Kyle. "Was they bad people," he asked. "The ones ye killed?"

Kyle nodded, looking pained and relieved all at once. Kind of like my dad's expression when he'd passed that kidney stone. Please keep that between you and me... will you?

"Yeah," Kyle confirmed. "I only took contracts on bad people."

Clem sighed. "Whilst I don't agree with operatin' outside the law, I sincerely appreciate ye tellin' me." He placed a calloused hand on Kyle's shoulder. "I ain't gonna judge ye. All's I'll say is that it's never too late to change, son. Take yer life, and yer freedom, and make somethin' better of 'em. When my wife and daughter died, I was a mosquito's stinger's width away from becomin' a lifelong drunk." Clem nodded in my direction. "But the Marshal, well, he gave me friendship and purpose. Then I found my true calling. He helped me find my spark, and then the law lit my way. Does that make sense?"

Kyle's expression softened, like Clem had single-handedly lifted the weight of the world off his shoulders. He nodded. "So much sense." Then, for just a moment, he looked troubled again. "Hey, Clem? Am I a real deputy?"

Clem's face became stone stern. He took the law, and his responsibility as a lawman, deathly serious. "Well, I'm a real sheriff, and I done deputized ye. So yes. You, son, are a real deputy. Ain't no one can take that from you. Not now... not ever."

Kyle looked at Clem like I'd never seen him look at any other grownup. He'd been treated with respect, and whether Clem knew it or not, he'd just forged a bond that would last the rest of his life. "Thank you, Clem," Kyle said. He took a deep breath and looked... noble.

He looked like he belonged.

I couldn't have been prouder. Of him, or Clem for that matter.

"Well," Clem said. "If'n that's all, I should be helping ol' Bill with them horses." He turned to me. "Three horses, then?"

"Yeah," I replied, feeling like we might actually be forging a real team... a real family. "Three horses'll do."

Clem tipped his hat and headed off to help Scalar.

"He's alright," Kyle told me once Clem was out of earshot. "Rough around the edges, but I think we need as much of that as we can get right now."

Becky sighed, but it wasn't a defeated sigh like earlier. There was something else there. More like an unexpected ah-ha moment. "I think we're going to be okay," she said finally.

Steve threw his hands in the air, obviously over all of it. "You had to say it, didn't you? We're gonna be okay? Haven't you ever watched a damn movie? It's like whenever Han Solo says he has a bad feeling about something." He shook his head at her. "You've just jinxed us. That's what you've done. You've jinxed us all!" Steve stomped away, leaving Becky looking perplexed.

Once again, he had officially ruined what had otherwise been a really nice moment.

~

About twenty minutes later, my friends and I reconvened in the courtyard.

True to my word, Pharaoh and I released Enos. After spending an entire night tied to a chair, and desperately needing a fresh change of underwear, he was indignant, but grateful to be free. Soiled and soaked pants, stiff joints, and a bruised ego were the worst of the indignities he'd suffered up to that point. All it took to ensure his compliance upon release, was for Pharaoh to pick him up and toss him into the air like an infant, and then catch him like he weighed no more than a bag of marshmallows. After taking in the absolute horror of all the dead cowboys and arachnodactyls, which probably made Enos crap himself again, he scurried off to the stables, tugging at the seat of his pants, too terrified to look back.

Clem and Scalar had saddled and prepped three strong-looking horses, while Gunner had returned with a large trunk full of guns and ammunition, as well as an assortment of bladed tools. Most of the tools were for use on the ranch, but they could be useful in a pinch. After moving the Lanier to the floor of the back seat, Gunner put the contents of the chest into KM's trunk and carefully laid the tools on top of them. It was likely we'd never need them, but safe was always preferable to sorry in dad's games.

Becky and Steve returned a few minutes later, carrying some dried food and a small pile of sheets and towels. Becky explained that the linens were for medical emergencies, or if we needed to redress Kyle's wound. Steve added that strips of it could also serve as *'excellent bum wipe'*, should the need arise. Becky looked disgusted but didn't argue his claim. He wasn't entirely wrong, after all.

While the others loaded their respective finds into Knightmare, Whisper and I performed one last patrol of the perimeter. Moreau flew around overhead, chirping happily as she scanned the distant horizon like a military-grade drone.

As we were finally getting ready to leave Kincaid's ranch behind, Clem excused himself and ambled back to the house. A few minutes later, he returned with a big tinplate bucket and a ladle. "Y'all are gonna need hydration fer the trip. Fact is, we don't know if there'll be water where we're headed."

Another round of nods and words of gratitude ran through the group. Even Steve, who'd been extra grumpy since Becky's innocent proclamation that all would be okay, took a ladle full of water and thanked Clem for his thoughtfulness.

Once everyone drank at least a ladle of water, we all took turns in the outhouse, then set out for parts unknown.

~

We left the ranch by late morning. If you recall, the train tracks ran almost directly past Kincaid's front gate, allowing us easy access to the rails. KM mounted the tracks, and we headed south.

Whisper and I took the lead, with Clem, Gunner, and El Scalar following about ten feet back on their chosen steeds.

Clem's horse was a young brown and white Paint. Enos told us Kincaid called him Barnaby. Barnaby was more spirited than the other two, but Clem, being one of the most experienced riders I'd ever met, was the perfect match for the young horse's temperament and energy level.

Gunner had selected a calm, almost sleepy Appaloosa named Churro. The mare was taller than Barnaby by almost a full hand and carried herself with aloof dignity. If it hadn't already been obvious when he and Whisper stormed the Kincaid compound, watching Gunner adapt to Churro's cadence with such ease, drove home the fact that he had more than a little cowboy in his blood.

El Scalar, being much heavier than either Clem or Gunner, needed a very special horse to partner with. It just so happened, that in addition to having a Texas-sized ego, Kincaid had expensive taste in horses. His personal steed, though far too big for the man, who couldn't have been more than six-foot-one, was Destrier, a massive Percheron, a French breed best known for its size, strength, and endurance.

The three riders looked like some odd, modern take on the tale of the three wise men.

Behind them was Cool and Kyle. Cool walked on all four legs, but he wasn't mimicking a horse. Instead, he'd become a kind of stagecoach with legs. Cool's body formed into a makeshift enclosure, which allowed Kyle to ride in a lounging position while remaining out of the direct sunlight. A peek inside revealed a surprisingly comfortable ride, though to be honest, I preferred being back in the saddle with my Whisper.

Knightmare brought up the rear. Just as she'd suggested, Becky sat up front with Steve. The two sat as far apart from each other as KM's doors would allow. Steve made faces at himself in the side mirror, while Becky ignored him and took in the scenery.

I can't say I blame her. For all the underlying horror behind the Nanops and their actions, it was still easy to get swept away by the sheer beauty in their work. I remember my 7th grade English teacher, Mr. Carlson, saying, "not all that is good is recognized by the eye as beautiful, nor does evil always present itself as ugly." Life isn't black and white, my friends. Heck, even shades of gray have a hard time capturing the reality of it all.

Pharaoh lounged in the back seat, though his expression said he would have rather been walking, or maybe running. The Prince of Beasts was not the type of guy to sit still for long. He liked being active, and I'm sure riding in the back of a vehicle moving slower than he could run felt inefficient. Angus complained about the dust, and how having Pharaoh in the back seat made it impossible to close the roof. Though one withering look from the mighty lion was enough to shut up the magical bagpipes, at least for a little while.

We made good time. There were no arachnodactyls or metallic monkeys to contend with, which honestly worried me. For every one of the escaped monstrosities we didn't see, there was some innocent person who was probably being terrorized by it... or worse.

I tried to keep that thought out of my head as we pressed forward.

And then everything changed again.

Okay, maybe not *everything*, but our clothes did, and that meant everything else would soon follow suit.

Speaking of suits, our western clothing, including Becky and Pharaoh's less than ideal garb, suddenly morphed into matching 1970s-style cobalt blue sweatsuits. A logo on the lapel depicted a pair of katanas crossed in front of a fractured rising sun. In addition to the sweatsuits, we each found ourselves wearing matching white tennis shoes and yellow protective glasses, the kind racquetball players would wear.

Kyle practically broke into a cheer when he realized his knee was healed. Before he could tell Cool otherwise, the Elastic Giraffe morphed himself into a yellow and brown Paint colt with a ridiculous grin and slightly oversized hooves. The pair galloped up to Gunner, Scalar, Clem, and me. Cool excitedly announced that Kyle was all healed, stealing our friend's thunder.

Kyle, who was unaccustomed to riding horseback, gripped the saddle horn like my dad gripped the oh shit handle when I drove. "Hey," he shouted to Cool. "I'd like to make it to wherever we're going without any new injuries, okay?"

Cool rotated his head back a hundred and eighty degrees, causing Whisper and the other three horses to do the horse equivalent of a double take. "Sorry, dude! I forgot you weren't a rootin' tootin' cowboy!"

"I beg to differ. I've heard him toot quite openly on more than one occasion," Knightmare offered.

Kyle sighed and dropped his head, the indignity hitting home more than he wanted to show.

I let KM's comment slide and reached out to give Kyle a high five. "Glad to have you back at full strength, man!"

Kyle reached back but had to steady himself a few times before actually making contact. He grinned, despite feeling so awkward. "Thanks, bruh! And it's good to have your voice back to normal, too." He laughed. "Who would've ever expected to see me on a horse? Heh… if my folks could see me now."

"I liked the Marshal's voice t'other way," Clem replied sadly. "As fer yer kin, I'm sure they'd be right proud."

Scalar and Gunner nodded in agreement.

Kyle shrugged. "Eh, probably not," he said softly, his smile fading.

"But *we* all are," I told him, glad I was no longer speaking with the involuntary Marshal Blood drawl. "And that sweatsuit looks great on you!"

Kyle looked down. "Really? Because it looks pretty outdated on you, bruh." He looked around at everyone. As with the previous games, everyone's clothing changed except

Cool's. Gunner and KM were also free of any changes that would otherwise indicate a new game.

I suppose it was to be expected. *Hiromon* was a multiplayer game, a team-based MMO of sorts, so all of us wore matching uniforms. Same colors, same logo, and same glasses and shoes. It would be abundantly clear to anyone who saw us coming that we were indeed a team.

Without any warning, the three horses we'd borrowed from Kincaid's place vanished from underneath Clem, Gunner, and El Scalar. My three friends fell to the hard ground next to the tracks with a painful thud.

Gunner was the first to react. "What the...?" He staggered back to his feet clumsily, clearly feeling the impact of the five-foot drop in his tailbone. He brushed off the seat of his pants self-consciously before extending a dusty hand to Clem, who'd landed flat on his back. The pair then turned and extended their hands to

El Scalar, who was sadly examining a small tear in the knee of his new sweatpants.

I quickly brought Whisper around to face them. "Are you guys okay?"

Cool about-faced as well, gently setting Kyle down as he morphed back into himself and joined in helping Scalar to his feet.

"What just happened," Gunner asked, turning to face me as he spoke. "Where'd the horses disappear to?"

I'm not gonna lie, there were times I liked being the authority on things, but that was when I actually knew the answers. I was less comfortable with the hypothetical. Science was dad and Irene's thing. Even Becky was far more sciencey than me. "Uh..." I looked around at the others, and then back to Gunner. I had no idea. As I was about to say so, it hit me. I looked right at Becky when I spoke. "*That's* the difference between NPCs and you guys. My best guess is that the horses have returned to the stables where you guys found them, safe and sound. Confused, but safe and sound. Like a world reset. Enos is probably wondering how the hell they got there."

"If I may ask a question," KM interjected.

"Of course," I said, nodding.

"The weapons and ammunition Gunner collected are still in my trunk. As are the food and bed sheets packed by Becky and Steve. Why have they not vanished?"

I shrugged. "I really don't have all the answers here, but it seems to come back to games. Most games have an inventory system for players to store items they might need later. Since the horses are alive, I'd guess they can't be considered possessions?"

Kyle, epic gamer that he was, got where I was going. "Yeah. Yeah, I see it, bro. They're true NPCs. The Nanops only want them to function in certain areas or something. Hmm. I wonder how those screechy monkey things from the coliseum got into Rotgut, though."

Becky nodded. "We're all figuring this out as we go, guys. We can't expect Packard to understand everything that's happening or to be able to interpret the Nanops' every move as they make them." She hopped out of KM and stepped over to help Clem and the others dust themselves off. "This may be Packard's world, but the Nanops have changed the rules for him as much as for us."

Pharaoh, who had also hopped out of KM, sighed deeply before speaking. "Me nuh undastand much of dis, so me gonna trust Packard's intuitions. Becky's too."

Becky shuffled her feet at the statement. "Don't look at me for answers. I'm along for the ride, just the same as you."

Clem, who was just getting used to having his traditional cowboy garb back, tugged at the polyester jacket that replaced his beloved blue chambray shirt. Remarkably, his hat had not been taken from him, leaving him with a strangely detached, renegade-like look that set him apart from the rest of us. "I unnerstan' what Phay-roh's sayin' Becky. He jest trusts yer assessment of the sitch-ee-ation better than his own." He motioned to his clothing. "Not to change the subject, but this here material sure does feel strange. *And* a tad bit itchy."

"It's called polyester," I told him. "Not one of the fashion world's prouder moments."

"Just be glad it's not acrylic," Gunner chimed in. "Or *rayon.*"

Clem nodded, not really understanding anything we were talking about, but trying to make sense out of it all, nonetheless. He motioned casually at Gunner and arched an eyebrow quizzically. "How come yer clothes ain't changed, pard?"

Gunner looked down and realized that his own filthy clothes hadn't changed. "I guess I'm not special enough to count," he replied, actually sounding a little disappointed.

"It's probably because you're not an *N.P.C.*," Becky said. She put a little extra emphasis on the last three letters.

"I suppose that could be it," he conceded. "But the ability to respawn sure would be nice right about now," he said with a sigh. "And like Packard and Kyle said, we really can't compare you to the other NPCs anymore, can we?"

Becky shook her head.

"Di grass always greena pon di odda side," Pharaoh mused.

"I like this outfit," Steve interjected, sounding more positive than usual. "Maybe Santa'll let us add these to the list of work-appropriate duds on the workshop floor."

"What's the lettering mean," Becky asked, abandoning the uncomfortable philosophical NPC discussion.

I wasn't sure what she meant. "Lettering?"

"On the backs of our jackets," she replied. "Is it kanji?"

Honestly, I'd forgotten the kanji were even there. I rarely looked at the back of my own jacket, and it'd been a while since I'd logged into a *Hiromon* tournament. "Oh, yeah," I replied, craning my neck around to see the lettering on the back of Scalar's jacket. Right there, stitched into the fabric like a giant tattoo, were two symbols, 浪人. "It is Kanji. They mean rōnin. It's the team I always play on. I've been a team captain for a long time."

Scalar looked genuinely interested. "What is a rōnin, compadre?"

KM chirped happily. "May I," she asked.

I shrugged. "Knock yourself out."

KM chirped again before continuing. "In feudal Japan, a rōnin was a samurai who had no lord or master. The term literally means 'wave man', so the connotation is that he is a drifter or a wanderer. Rōnin were often seen as dangerous and unpredictable, as they were no longer bound by the rules of the samurai code. However, they were highly skilled warriors. Some rōnin became famous for their exploits. Rōnin have been depicted in many works of Japanese fiction, including novels, movies, and anime. They are frequently portrayed as wanderers searching for purpose or redemption. Rōnin can also be seen as symbols of freedom and independence."

Clem cleared his throat thoughtfully. "Seems t'me, by Knightmare's definition of the word, that rōnin defines all of us quite nicely." He looked back at the others before continuing. "Less'n I misunnerstood what she meant, we're all wanderers of sorts, without any ties to where we come from. I see us searching fer purpose, more so than redemption. And if'n we're successful in this here mission, then we will indeed be symbols of freedom and independence."

"Leave it to the cowboy to find some bullshit nobility in everything," Steve yawned from the car.

"Me tink him right. An' me tink him words did beautiful, little mon," Pharaoh said, not hiding his distaste for Steve and his negativity. "Tanks fi share dat, Clem."

"Twarn't nothin'," Clem replied. His expression was unlike anything I'd ever seen on his weathered face. He looked at peace, even a bit content. It occurred to me, then, that I'd met him after his wife and daughter had died. I'd never known him when he had family other than me... when he'd actually been happy. I realized what I saw in his expression. *Clem felt included.*

I let my gaze drift to Kyle and realized that his expression was similar. The difference was, though, while Clem had been truly happy once upon a time, I don't think Kyle ever really had been.

Scalar broke my moment of melancholic reflection when he shouted out excitedly. "Is that where we're headed, amigos?"

Off in the distance, at the base of the hill we'd just crested, surrounded by the sparse remains of thousands of tombstones, was a giant, perfectly manicured sports field.

Bleachers surrounded the massive complex. It looked ready to host the next Olympics. Giant lighting structures towered over the bleachers, ready to illuminate events that were sure to last well into the night.

Moreau chirped excitedly on my shoulder, and Whisper, who seemed to understand my chimera's language perfectly, nickered loudly, a clear sign she was also excited.

"That's the place, gang," I announced. "The next game." I swept my hand in a grand gesture worthy of a circus ringmaster. "Welcome to Hiromon Field!"

26
MMOMG

As we approached the massive field like the victims of circumstance I suspected we were, I wondered how much of our collective destiny we controlled. In retrospect, it was probably more than I gave us credit for, but I still couldn't help imagining us as a bunch of toddlers in highchairs, being spoon-fed our fates like puréed turkey and beets. *Here comes the airplane, open the hangar wide!*

I dismounted Whisper and together we trudged, trotted, and rolled forth. The open-air bleachers, flagpoles, and giant lighting arrays loomed large like the coliseum we'd left behind only a day before. A spectators' entrance lay ahead, inviting loyal fans to buy tickets and cheer on their favorite *Hiromon* team. Like the backs of our jackets, the overhead signage and all the posters touting the teams due to participate in the games were written in kanji. Some signs included English translations, but they were clearly translated by folks who could not claim English as their first language.

Clem looked confused when I didn't immediately head for the main entrance, where hundreds of what I presumed to be Nanop generated people milled about excitedly, speaking Japanese far more rapidly than I could follow. Oh, yeah, I can speak Japanese when I'm in the *Hiromon* games. It's uploaded as a part of the overall experience. At least, I think it was uploaded. The whole multiversal aspect of the interactions was making my head hurt.

"Are we not goin' inside," Clem asked, pointing back at the archway.

"Nope," I replied, shaking my head. "We'll be going in through the competitors' entrance." I pointed off to the left side of the field, where a neat, angled row of gaudily painted buses was parked. It looked like one of those huge music festivals of the '80s and '90s, where all the popular bands of the day would roll up in their rock and roll tour buses and play all weekend long. My dad used to tell me about the legendary 'Day on the Green' concert he'd attended in 1985. He was just a kid, but it was a memory that, at least in part, inspired aspects of the *Max Axe* game.

As we approached the competitors' entrance, we passed one of the rows of team posters. Cool stopped dead in his tracks.

"Dude," he said, pointing at the poster. "That's us!"

We all stopped and gawked at the poster, hardly able to believe our eyes. It was us, alright. Well, most of us, anyway.

Moreau and I were front and center. She sat comfortably on my shoulder, and I stared off into the distance pensively. My hair was hot pink, and raised in several severe looking spikes that I only wore in the *Hiromon* game. It was a dashing look, if I do say so myself. At my sides, and slightly behind me, were Becky, whose hair in the poster was blue and considerably longer than normal, Kyle, Clem, Pharaoh, Cool, Scalar, and Steve. Each of them wore identical tracksuits, had brightly colored, wildly styled hair, and had a dog or cat-sized chimera perched on their shoulder or standing at their feet. Steve's poster persona sat atop a fierce looking beast that fit his personality perfectly.

Becky squinted at the picture before quickly glancing at her shoulder, as if expecting what she saw on the poster to already be there. I couldn't exactly blame her, none of us was certain how the rules of this new world would apply to us.

Nothing was there, of course. Not yet anyway.

She touched the poster, tracing her finger over a small animal that looked like a fluffy, white pig, but with tiny, pink hands that bore opposable thumbs, and gripped her jacket like it had always been there. "What is it?"

"Beats me." I shrugged. "Normally, the chimera chooses the player when they enter the field for the first time. Then it's your partner for life."

"Like one of them pre-arranged weddins I hear tell of in other countries," Clem commented.

"Only no cool dowry," Becky retorted, eliciting another confused glance from Clem.

We stared at the poster for another moment before I turned to Gunner, who was visibly disappointed he wasn't on it. Whisper looked like she was feeling left out again as well.

I felt so bad for them. Not to mention KM and crotchety old Angus. "I'm sorry, guys. I really wish I knew how the game worked... like *really knew*... you know?"

They knew.

"If I had feelings," KM offered flatly, "they might very well be wounded." Then, her tone changed, sounding very much like she did have feelings, and they were badly hurt. "However, I do *not* have feelings. None whatsoever. And I do not give one flying tuck and roll whether the Nanops choose to include me in their nonsense or not."

I glanced at Gunner again, and he caught me looking. "Don't look at me," he said, looking both guilty and hurt. "I clearly don't even belong here. Besides, I'm a grown man. Why would I care about some stupid game?"

"A grown-ass man," Clem muttered to himself absently.

Whisper grunted at the comments, making it clear she did care about a stupid game. She cared *a lot* about that stupid game, thank you very much.

Angus tooted from the back seat. It was easy to forget he was there when he wasn't yammering on about how he was uncomfortable or being inconvenienced by 'shlumming about with the lower life formsh'. Without Pharaoh back there to stare him down, he was back to his emboldened, narcissistic self. "Well, I do care!" He was quiet for a moment, probably waiting for someone to argue with him, before asking sheepishly, "what ish it I'm shupposhed to be caring about?"

Steve climbed back into KM and propped himself up so he could see Angus in the back. "Some of us are on a lousy poster that shows us with a weird little creature," he explained. "And some of us ain't."

"I shee," Angus replied, sounding interested. "Sho, yer shaying they're all on a poshter with you?"

"Eff you," Steve hissed before hopping back down to the grass, a middle finger waved over his head, like the many colored flags flapping in the breeze high above.

"Look," I said. "Whisper, Gunner, KM, and Angus. I... I'm sorry about how all this is happening." I looked from one to the other, pausing briefly on all of them. "I don't care what the Nanops think of you. You're here for a reason, and I'm glad we're all together. I value all of you."

Gunner tousled my hair, almost knocking my glasses off. "We'll be fine, kid. We're all in this together, whether the Nanops like it or not. Game or no game, I have your back."

"Hear, hear," Angus said from the back seat, tooting softly.

Steve was unmoved by Angus's rare moment of positivity. *"Ass kisser."*

~

We entered the field through the participants' entrance a few minutes later. Gunner, Knightmare, Whisper, and Angus were all given spectator badges on blue lanyards. When the woman checking team credentials questioned Cool's identity, a tracksuit and glasses conveniently materialized on him. Satisfied, and surprisingly unsurprised by the sudden appearance of Cool's uniform, the woman nodded, and the Elastic Giraffe's grin widened even more than usual.

Four other teams, each dressed in matching tracksuits, watched as we entered. Some waved or nodded, while others scoffed and scowled venomously. We were the last team to arrive, though I was fairly certain the others had just materialized there without realizing it.

There were always five teams on the field, as four was considered bad luck. One year, because of a scheduling conflict, the competition went forward with only four teams, and that was the year tragedy struck. A legendary team, Team Haraguro, lost their team captain, The Elven Mistress B'lar, in a freak accident that shook the *Hiromon* community to its core. Since that fateful day, the commission would rather cancel a tournament than move forward with only four teams. In fact, superstition so strictly governs the rules, that the first round of battle is designed to eliminate two teams, leaving three to duke it out for the title of Hiromon Supreme.

I hadn't played in a *Hiromon* tournament in a few years, but I could tell by the activity and positioning of the teams that we were mere minutes from the first competition.

We were guided to an area that somewhat resembled a dugout on a baseball field and told to wait for further instructions. Several banners, all the color of our uniforms, celebrated our arrival by snapping loudly in the breeze like tiny bullwhips.

The four other teams were ceremoniously led to similarly appointed dugouts, their banners greeting them with excited snaps and flutters.

Underneath a set of red banners was Team Tsubaki. Their logo was a red camellia, which in hanakotoba — that's the Japanese language of flowers — means 'a noble death'. The members of Team Tsubaki were some of the most fair-minded *Hiromon* warriors I'd ever faced. As far as I was aware, they'd never had a penalty brought against them.

Beyond Team Tsubaki, a set of bright orange banners rustled noisily. Beneath those gaudy banners was one of the teams whose reputation was not always considered good. The members of Team Kitsune, whose logo was a fox with a long, swirling tail ending in a puff of smoke, were known to be mischievous and highly intelligent. I'd learned the hard way that trusting them to be anything but unpredictable was a dire mistake.

Under a set of silver banners was Team Mizuchi. Their logo was a beautiful but dangerous-looking water dragon, representing the virtues of wisdom and strength. They, like Team Tsubaki, were exceedingly noble, though they were less apt to let virtues, just for the sake of being virtuous, get in the way of a win.

The last set of banners were as black as the mythical void and represented Team Haraguro. The word haraguro means 'black stomach'. It's a play on an old Japanese metaphor. A person with a black stomach is known to be evil or mean-spirited. If you recall, it was Haraguro's team captain that was lost in the ill-fated 'Battle of the Four'. Considering they were the first team to petition for postponement of the event until a fifth team could be added, they've never forgiven the events commission for the loss. In fact, it's rumored that their late captain, The Elven Mistress B'lar, and her chimera, Tardagon, an absolutely evil mix of tardigrade and dragon, haunt the events, appearing like wild wraiths to the losing teams.

Since I'd never actually lost a tournament since the time of her accident, I could neither confirm nor deny the rumor... but it always sounded ridiculous to me.

Clem suddenly jumped back from the rest of the group, recoiling like he'd found a snake in his boot. "What in THE hell?!"

The rest of us turned to find what appeared to be a sea turtle nuzzling Clem's lower leg affectionately. Upon closer inspection, I saw the turtle had a razor-sharp dorsal fin protruding from its armor plated back. The turtle's elongated face bore eyes blacker than Team Haraguro's banners and a mouth filled with multiple rows of deadly-looking teeth. The creature looked up at Clem sadly and tried to bond with him again, resting its head on Clem's shoe in an act of submission.

Clem looked shaken, but over the past few days, he'd proven to be more adaptable than I'd ever given him credit for. "Is this my Moreau? My, uh... life pard'ner?"

I smiled at the simple innocence behind his question. "Yeah, Clem. It sure looks like it." I glanced up at a digital roster on the wall behind us and almost laughed out loud. In a Herculean show of restraint, I held back the laughter, not wanting to spoil the moment for Clem or the others. "Its name isn't Moreau, though."

Clem turned to see what I was looking at and raised an eyebrow at the roster. "If'n you re-call, readin' ain't one of my God-given skills, Marshal."

Kyle and Cool, not possessing my Zen master level of wisdom, did laugh. Very loudly.

Cool snorted before I could quiet either of them. "Shartle!? *Its name is Shartle!?"*

Clem frowned and shook his head. "I don't see what's so durned funny about its name."

Pharaoh and Scalar shrugged, the context having flown completely over their considerable heads.

"Perhaps you call it Shartnado," Scalar suggested.

Clem nodded thoughtfully. "It does sound more intimidatin'," he mused.

KM chirped, which, if you've noticed, always preceded one of her *insightful offerings* the same way a clearing of the throat heralded one of Clem's uh... *Clemisms.* "According to the online Urban Dictionary, a shart is a small, unintended defeca-"

Becky interrupted poor KM, who was probably beginning to wonder if she was somehow related to Rodney Dangerfield, who, in case you didn't know, was the undisputed king of getting disrespected. While Becky explained to Clem that his chimera was named Shartle because it was clearly a shark and turtle hybrid, I quietly thanked Knightmare for her help. I told her that Clem, being from a more sheltered culture, might be offended by the definition.

KM chirped knowingly and thanked me for the explanation. "I would hate to say anything that would make any of my friends sad," she whispered in a tone that reinforced my suspicion that she had feelings as real and as valid as any of the rest of us. I might never understand the complexity of her thoughts and emotions.

"You're incredible, girl," I whispered back.

KM was silent. Not so much as a chirp, a buzz, or a whir. Then, even more quietly than before, she said, "thank you, Packard. Is it appropriate to tell you that I love you?"

"I think you just did," I replied, my voice breaking unexpectedly. "I love you too, KM."

And then she really was silent… for a very long time.

Even Angus, who was often cranky and bullish, kept whatever he was thinking to himself.

~

In the minutes that followed, I explained the basic rules, and some of the more necessary details of *Hiromon* tournaments. Granted, they'd have a lot to figure out on the fly, but there were many things that could get a team disqualified, or even dead.

As Clem had just discovered, you don't pick your chimera, it picks *you* when you enter the field for the first time. From there, it's up to you to figure out what your new life pard'ner's skill sets are and how to meld with them symbiotically.

The roster board behind us lit up as our names popped up one letter at a time. My name was already at the top of the roster, listed as team captain, and followed by Moreau's name. Underneath Moreau and me was Clem and Shartle. A moment later, Becky's name popped up with Pigmoset listed as her chimera.

Becky let out a genuine squee when she finally saw her new friend. It was a shy hybrid pig and pygmy marmoset, no bigger than a chihuahua. The little creature clung to her shoulder nervously with tiny, white-knuckled hands. "Well, hi there little one," she cooed. "It's so very nice to meet you."

Pigmoset blinked slowly, sizing Becky up, before yawning and stretching its fingers out, one hand at a time. Then, as if it had known and trusted Becky its entire life, it put its head down and went to sleep. Becky's eyes widened enough to give Cool or Kyle a run for their money, and she stared at me with absolute adoration in her eyes. "OMG! It's precious! What does it do?"

I shrugged. "Beats me," I replied. "You'll find out after you bond."

Becky frowned at the answer. She looked like she was going to say something, but Clem suddenly knelt down and patted his new friend timidly. He was probably afraid it might bite, but instead it nuzzled his hand with all the ferocity of a baby panda bear. Becky smiled at the sight and petted Pigmoset gently. The tiny creature mewled approvingly and stretched out, making full use of the real estate that was Becky's shoulder.

The next name to appear was Ferradillo, showing up just after Cool's name. The cute, but squirmy little thing was a weird combination of a ferret and an armadillo, and it wound itself around Cool playfully like a snake exploring a jungle gym. It squeaked and chittered excitedly, and Cool giggled with unbridled glee. They were a match made in heaven.

A moment later, BatManta's name popped in just under Kyle's. I'm sure you guessed it, too. Kyle's new friend was part bat and part manta ray. The chimera had an impressive wingspan, probably around ten feet wide, which was evidenced when it settled in on Kyle's back and relaxed its wings over his shoulders like a huge leather shawl. Kyle crossed his arms and patted his new friend's wings gently, eliciting a joyous squeak from the newcomer.

The board continued to light up, and as the excited buzz in the bleachers reached critical mass, Pharaoh and Chamelion, a two-foot-long hybrid chameleon and lion, were united. Then, Steve was introduced to Elephant, a terrifying sheepdog-sized hybrid between an elephant and an ant that had a functional trunk, and bone-white pincers for tusks. Hey, don't shoot the messenger, Sparta, *I didn't name 'em.*

I looked towards Scalar and saw that he was still standing alone. I glanced back at the roster and spotted the name Quacken directly after his.

Scalar looked confused. Honestly, I was, too.

"I see a name on the board," he said, eyes narrowed suspiciously. "But nothing seems to be appearing or looking for me."

Clem pointed at a decorative hedge near the registration tables, a few feet away. "Could that be it?"

I stepped beside him. "What do you see, Clem?"

Clem pointed. "Right there. That chicken, duck, woman-thang… waitin' in yonder bushes."

Scalar stepped out in front of us and extended a hand to our shy little stalker. "Quacken?" The word came out like 'huaken'. Leave it to a Mesoamerican prince to invent 'dropping the Q'. Hex would be impressed.

The thing that scuttled forward was one of the strangest combos I'd ever seen, and I'd seen *a lot.* There was clearly duck in the mix, and definitely squid, too, but I suspected there might have been something more. Not a chicken or woman, as Clem had suggested, but undoubtedly more than just duck and squid. The more I looked at it, the more it looked oddly feminine.

A quick glance back at the board showed me that, like my little buddy Moreau, El Scalar's new friend was a bona fide Gen-1 Hiromon. Gen-1s were no longer legal, *to make,* anyway. They were too unpredictable and had health problems, like certain dog breeds that shouldn't mix. Moreau, Quacken, and a few other chimeras I'd seen over the years, were what the Hiromon commission referred to as tribrids. Any chimera with DNA traceable to three or more species, were tribrids; otherwise, I think Moreau would be considered a hexabrid, or something crazy like that.

Quacken pulled itself from the bushes with tentacles that weren't quite as dexterous as Moreau's, but I had no doubt they could be just as effective in their own way. The thing's head bobbed curiously as it approached, and its beak opened and closed rapidly, though it made no sound. Black, beady eyes darted frantically, making Quacken look like its emotional state was unstable as hell, the gauge landing somewhere between ravenous and longing. Scalar simply knelt and held out his hand like he was coaxing a kitten out of hiding.

Quacken finally got close enough to sniff Scalar's hand, but when the little creature decided that taking a nibble of his new friend's index finger might be appropriate, Scalar pulled back. The abrupt action caused Quacken to spray him with a large puff of sticky, black ink. Scalar watched the creature scurry back behind the shrubs and sighed as he turned to face us. His right hand, face, and chest looked like he'd taken a dip in the La Brea tar pits. His eyes stood out like twin moons in a starless night sky.

He shook his head and shrugged before standing, walking over to the bushes, and kneeling again. He extended his hand again in an act of pure trust and repeated the little chimera's name gently. "Quacken… amigo. Come on out, my little friend. Unlike you, I do not bite." He smiled through the tar, his teeth shining as brightly as his eyes.

And then, very slowly, and as tentatively as Clem embracing equal rights for women, Quacken reached a tiny tentacle out of the bushes, and curled it tightly around Scalar's finger. Always a sucker for a tender moment, Cool grinned widely. Finally, before any of us could say or do anything to help, Quacken roughly yanked Scalar into the bushes.

The bushes shook violently, and Cool's jaw dropped comically.

"Well, it looks like they're bonding…" Kyle commented, his voice cracking a little more than usual.

"Seems we might have'ta name that thar hedge, 'the bushes o' love'," Clem replied.

Becky grimaced at the comment. "Ew... come on! You guys are gross! He might be in trouble."

Before Becky could continue, Scalar emerged from behind the hedge, ink free. Quacken, like many of our other chimeras, found a safe place to perch on its new companion. It was already making a nest of sorts on the top of Scalar's head, in his huge 1970s bush of hair.

The crowd cheered when El Scalar and Quacken appeared, clearly ready to function as a team.

Scalar waved a hand in the air like a matador, both thanking the crowd, and reminding them that 'it was truly nothing'. He patted one of the purplish-gray tentacles as it brushed past his forehead. "My little amigo found it necessary to remove the ink from my person before allowing me to be seen again in public,

Clem." He turned to Becky. "And you're right, señorita. They are gross."

~

The two-minute warning came as Clem and Kyle were pretending to not know what Becky or El Scalar were talking about. The words, of course, were in Japanese, though much to my surprise, everyone present seemed to understand them, including Clem.

The only one who didn't follow the announcement was poor Gunner. He probably felt about as useful as a moral compass on a politician. "Anybody want to fill me in on what's being said?"

"They're speaking eye-talian," Clem told him casually. "Like that singer the Marshal's pa likes listening to. Lunchbox Panini, I seem to re-call."

Gunner looked at me curiously.

"You're close, Clem," I replied. "What we're hearing is Japanese, and the singer you're thinking of is Luciano Pavarotti."

Clem shook his head. "Nope, Marshal, pretty sure yer wrong. If'n thars anything I've got an ear fer, it's music. Hell, I can sing 'Camptown Races' like a gol-durned canary. Would ya like me to sing it fer ya?"

I smiled, knowing that arguing with Clem was almost as pointless as a debate with Angus. "I'd like that, Clem," I said, feigning interest. "But that was the two-minute warning, and we need to be ready for our first competition, ol' buddy."

Clem nodded, and the others gathered in tightly.

Becky was the first to ask the burning question. "What are we supposed to do?" Her expression could have accompanied the definition of 'confused' in the dictionary. "Seriously, Pack. At least in Rotgut, and even in the coliseum, we could wing it. This doesn't seem like a wing it kind of game."

Pharaoh, who'd been marveling at Chamelion's uncanny ability to blend in with its immediate surroundings, spoke up next. "Yuh say we gotta learn tuh meld wit dees creatures... symbiotically. Dat sounds complicated, mon. How we supposed tuh do dat?"

Kyle, without knowing he was doing so, answered Pharaoh's question with a resounding, "holy shit!"

We turned to see BatManta's huge cobalt-colored wings spreading out behind Kyle like theater curtains on opening night. Only they weren't BatManta's wings anymore, not entirely anyway. They were Kyle's, too. It didn't matter how many times I'd seen it happen, the merging of a chimera and their Hiromon host into one shared body was exciting, terrifying, and sometimes a little gross. Kyle's transformation was less invasive than some that I'd seen, and given the positive tone behind his reaction, I'd say it was less dramatic as well. A closer look at Kyle and BatManta revealed black, beady eyes, and a series of step-like ridges that ran from the bridge of their nose up into their hairline.

Their tracksuit, per its ingenious design, adapted itself to appropriately fit their new hybridized form.

Kyle and BatManta looked around the field slowly, taking in everything and everyone like they were seeing it all for the first time. "Dudes, we see sounds... Like... wow."

"It sounds like you have echolocation," Becky and Pigmoset said, though their voice had changed as much as Kyle's looks. It had become a squeak that reminded me of an animated chipmunk. We all turned to see Becky's medium length, auburn hair change into a white, fuzzy mop of fur. Their eyes were huge, like an anime character, and their nose turned up ever so slightly. She'd always been athletic, but their hybrid body was leaner than before, and their fingers had become elongated like a doctor's forceps. The knuckles bulged dramatically at each joint. Becky and Pigmoset looked at their hands, then down at their body. The tracksuit snugged up to fit them appropriately, making the transformation that much more apparent. "What the...?" They turned their hands over and stared at them in disbelief. "Pigmoset says I'm fast... *we're* fast. I mean... him and me. He's a him. We're melded somehow, aren't we? Not just physically, but mentally, too."

"Bingo-des," I replied, with slightly more Moreau, and a little less Packard in my voice than before. I held out my hands to see the tentacles that had sprouted from my arms. I knew that meant I would also have the suction-cupped appendages forming on my legs as well. Hopefully, Becky was too busy with her transformation to really notice mine, seeing how much she disliked tentacles. As the tentacles sprang forth, I watched the world change. Well, the world wasn't changing as much as my perception of it was. All the cool traits Moreau came with were suddenly becoming mine, including big, brown, leathery wings, bat-ass hearing — *bat-ass...* come on, that was great, admit it —

echolocation, and the ability to see colors not normally visible to the human eye. I could see anything on the infrared or ultraviolet spectrums, and some I'm not sure science had even identified yet.

As Kyle and BatManta and Becky and Pigmoset began testing out their newfound abilities, the others were just beginning to come into them.

Clem and Shartle turned into something straight out of my favorite anime, *Adolescent Mutated Shogun Armadillos*. The 'Sisterhood' version was better, but that's just my humble opinion. Their exposed flesh had become scaly and rough, but most of their body was covered in something that reminded me of L'OthruC'ant's bioresponsive armor. They looked like a tank with saw blades for teeth. Like Kyle, Clem's eyes had sunken in and glinted like black pearls hiding in the folds of an oyster's taut flesh. Suddenly, Clem and Shartle looked like they might stand a chance against someone like Scalar.

Speaking of ol' bison breath — *there it was...* my new nickname! Bison Breath. It'll never be as good as Tatanka Head, but honestly now, what could be? Anyway, he and Quacken were becoming something that Franz Kafka and H.P. Lovecraft couldn't have created during their best writing team ups. Tentacles flailed around the crown of their enormous head like a Gorgonite Minotaur and downy, white feathers ran down the length of their arms, which were no longer arms, by the way. They were suddenly the horrifying forefeet of a praying mantis! Well, it was safe to say I could finally identify what the other DNA in Quacken's chimeric fusion was... freaking *mantis*. If the other transformations weren't bad enough, they'd also grown an additional set of rear legs, which sprouted right out of their new and improved, extra-long butt. The little ducktail that topped off their butt might have been humorous if it weren't for the rest of them.

Cool, as always, was Cool. It was hard to tell the difference between the normal version of our squirmy, wormy, stretchy friend, and what he'd become after merging with Ferradillo. The funny thing was, after watching him shapeshift for so long, any differences, no matter how bizarre, just felt like another day on the funny farm with the lovable Elastic Giraffe. Don't get me wrong, there were changes, but I had to actually look for them. Their face, while still dominated by huge, friendly eyes, and a massive, dentist's dream of a grin, had become more streamlined, and, uh… ferret-like. The biggest difference was the armor plating they sported. It wasn't everywhere, like Clem and Shartle's, but almost everywhere. The best way I can describe what I was seeing, is that their skin was fluid, like lava, and the armor was akin to the cooling chunks of hardening tectonic plates floating along the magma's surface. It was positively captivating to look at, and Cool, in his own blissfully ignorant way, seemed unaware of his incredible metamorphosis with Ferradillo.

Okay. I take back what I said about Scalar and Quacken being horrifying. Because when I laid eyes on Steve and Elephant, I just about shat myself.

Our E.L.V.E. assassin and his chimera still only stood about three feet tall, but like Scalar and Quacken, they'd grown a rear segmented body and several rear legs. The body, while segmented like an insect's, was bloated, saggy, and leathery, like a baby elephant. Their mouth was unbelievably large and massive ivory pincers protruded from their cheeks like deadly, curved rapiers. The elephant trunk was also a part of the mix, though it didn't grow from the middle of their face, as one might have expected. Oh, no... because that would be too normal. Instead, the appendage grew from the top of Steve and Elephant's head and swayed around like some nightmarish combination of a radar dish, and a palm tree in a hurricane.

Steve and Elephant scuttled about on their newly formed legs and grinned around their new tusks. "We like this," they said, not caring one bit about the scads of slobber that accompanied their words.

Suddenly, the buzzer announcing the beginning of the first round rang.

I looked at the others, hoping they were actually ready to face two teams of more experienced, and in some cases, more ruthless players. About a minute too late to do anything about it, I realized Pharaoh and Chamelion were gone.

27

Adapt and Overcome

Like I said, I realized Pharaoh and Chamelion were missing just as our team and two others were called to the three circles of the Triad of Destiny.

There was us — Team Ronin, in case you'd forgotten — Team Tsubaki, and Team Haraguro. Leaving Gunner, KM, Whisper, and Angus at the dugout, we followed our guide to a large blue outline of a circle precisely seven meters in diameter near the center of the field. The other two teams went to identical, though different color-outlined circles. The three outlined areas, drawn in chalk like lines on a baseball field and called team zones, were all spaced exactly sixteen meters apart, and surrounded a bright white circle that was sixteen meters in diameter.

Three very stern-looking referees stood at the center of the white circle, observing us closely.

Together, they scrutinized the teams like my grandma used to look at cantaloupes at the grocery store. They stared at us, frowning, for more than a couple of minutes before moving on to Team Tsubaki. Their team had been corralled into a red-ringed circle, and looked about as comfortable as we did under the soul-piercing gaze of the Judgy Three. That wasn't the referees' official name, of course. I just liked calling them that... privately.

Team Tsubaki was a great group of players. Fair, honest, and rules oriented, Tsubaki would rather lose a game honorably, than bring shame upon their fans through underhanded tactics.

The team captain, a bruiser named Lars Steelhart, was already an imposing guy. Standing six-foot-four and carrying the bulk of a professional linebacker, not too many people would be foolish enough to face him in a physical competition. Once he fused with his chimera, though, a hippopotamus and scorpion hybrid named Heavy Metal, their hybrid form was downright terrifying. His natural bulk suddenly became inconsequential when compared to their merged persona. At least 7 feet tall, with a gaping maw filled with teeth the size of soda cans, snapping claws for hands, and a massive, segmented tail ending in a spike the size of a pineapple, they were not the guy you wanted to cheat at Black Eyed Susan.

Nayeli Blackfoot and her chimera, Beagle, were a force of freaking nature. To be clear, Beagle was not a snoopy dog. A hybrid bear and eagle, the chimera was another blend that would send most people running for the hills. The bear in the mix was a black bear. As a result, Beagle stood slightly less than five feet tall. The beast was still bigger than any of *our* chimeras, and it didn't have to be grizzly or polar bear sized to be intimidating. When they merged, Nayeli and Beagle possessed the strength, stamina, and durability of the bear, and sported huge wings, deadly talons on their fingertips, and a strip of feathers that followed their spine from skull to tail.

I always considered myself fortunate that Liam Logan and his chimera, Apex, a Canadian timber wolf and box jellyfish hybrid, were on Team Tsubaki and not Team Haraguro. Their combination was as dangerous as the resulting metamorphosis was horrifying. While not as tall as the Lars and Heavy Metal hybrid, Liam and Apex stood erect on two curved rear haunches and hunched forward menacingly. Their body and head, while severe and wolflike in their form, were translucent, and displayed their inner workings — you know, their organs — in full, disgusting detail. Long, almost invisible strands of flesh hung from their shoulders like a cape made of transparent bullwhips. If you ever find yourself facing Liam and Apex in battle, do yourself a favor and avoid their claws, teeth, and those awful, stinging strands of poisonous flesh. In fact, if you ever find yourself facing them, just run. Between their raw instincts as a hunter, and their offensive defense, Liam and Apex's merged form was the perfect predator.

Next in line to be scrutinized by the Judgy Three, was Lakshmi Meera and her partner, Spitter. Equal parts king cobra and horse, Spitter was fast, agile, and cunning. Plop Lakshmi's DNA into the mix, and the result was a four-legged powerhouse of a beast that was almost as flexible as our beloved Elastic Giraffe. Truth be told, their combination made them look more like a dragon than a horse or serpent. They could just as easily kick you into next week with their powerful legs as they could crush the life out of you within the coils of their body. A large, horse-inspired head bore the wicked fangs of a cobra, and a sail of a hood extended down both sides of their neck from their forehead to their middle back. They swayed defiantly as we waited, clearly more ready than we were to face the first round.

The resulting monstrosity of Abiy Enku and his chimera, Sandman's merge, stood quietly behind Lakshmi and Spitter. Abiy was already painfully shy. Adding a tsetse fly-ostrich chimera into the mix was not a cure for his already introverted nature. It did make them *super ugly* though. Come on, don't bust my chops over that. If you could see them, you'd agree. They were effing hideous! Flies are already some of nature's more disgusting creations, and when you make them big enough to see all their awfulness in perfect detail, they become total nightmare fuel. The ostrich in the mix didn't make them easier on the eyes... *then there was Abiy himself.* What we had to face on the playing field was a tall, lanky humanoid that could run like a cheetah, fly like an arachnodactyl, and put you to freakin' sleep if they touched you with their proboscis. Without an antidote, the effects of their sleep juice would escalate from an unplanned nap to a coma in 24 hours and cause full cardiac failure within 48. Jeff Goldblum had *nothing* on Abiy and Sandman.

If you're afraid of either velociraptors or narwhals, then Arnakuagsak Liuna and her chimera, Whaltor, is another combination you'd probably like to steer clear of. And Whaltor is such a chill sounding name, too, right? The only saving grace in the whole thing is that, as cool as the movies were, *Jurassic Park* got the raptors all wrong. They weren't nearly as big as they made them appear in the films. But what the chimeric team-up lacked in size, they more than made up for in intelligence, cunning, and speed. When combined, Arnakuagsak and Whaltor were like that lizard dude Captain Kirk fought in the original *Star Trek* series. But they were more flexible. And they had a badass horn sticking out of their forehead that made them look like they were ready to go out and join a jousting tournament. Needless to say, the North Pole native and her chimera were a deadly team.

Ziad Sayed and Bloodbag, the Amazonian mosquito and dromedary chimera, were another pairing I found incredibly hard to look at. Okay, honestly, I had a tough time with any of the pairings that included insect DNA. I'm not exactly afraid of bugs, but I find them to be pretty darned gross, especially when they're all big and in your face about it. Maybe I suffer a little PTSS from *Crawlspace*? Anyway, Bloodbag was bad enough without Ziad in the mix, but once you added in the human element, they became one of those things that could give the boogieman the willies. A misshapen human head with multi-lensed, insectoid eyes and several spikes protruding from where a mouth should have been, sat atop a long, curved neck, that in turn, connected to a compact and fatty, but powerful-looking body. Ten spindly but sturdy limbs extended in all directions. The six rear limbs were for walking, while the four front limbs served as arms, ending with clicking, claw-like hands. Oh, and then there were the wings. Those awful wings. They produced a high-pitched noise that was the more annoying little brother of all the nails, on all the chalkboards, all at once.

And who could forget everyone's favorite pukefest? Shania Tucker and her chimera, Frenemy, who was a hybrid tapeworm and basset hound — talk about a conflict of interests — were always near the top of my 'stay the eff away from' list. She was nice enough when she wasn't fused with Frenemy. I could even consider her a friend. But when she and that wormy, drooly, flop-eared mess of a creature became one, they would best be described as a sentient lump of toxic sludge. Alright, to be fair, they weren't really sludge, they were more like a lump of never-ending, hive-minded worms. But they *were* toxic. If those worms got into you, they'd wreak havoc with your ability to remain fused to your chimera. The effects of the secretions could last for days, destroying your chances of advancing in a tournament along with your team. Once they got it in their head that they wanted to remove you from the competition, they were second only to Liam and Apex in tracking abilities. It was like having a Terminator made of toxic worms coming after you. Worms that wanted to get into you by entering your eyes, ears, mouth, and *other* openings. A Worminator! Think that one over for a while and tell me how you sleep then.

Team Haraguro was the polar opposite of Team Tsubaki. Unfair, dishonest, and willing to do anything to win,

Haraguro cared nothing for honor or integrity. Their fans were like some of those toxic football fans we all know. They gloated when their team won and cried about how the win was 'stolen' when they lost. Like their fans or not, though, they were dedicated to a fault.

The Judgy Three stared the dark-hearted team down like they were the ones about to face them in combat. I had to hand it to them. They had nerves and huevos of steel.

The team captain, Rani Gunawardeni, and her chimera, Warca, were mean-spirited and ruthless, and enjoyed toying with their opponents before destroying them. Second only to Tardagon, Warca, a hybrid orca and Portuguese man o' war, was as cold-blooded a chimera as I'd ever laid eyes on. When Rani and Warca fused, they were one of the deadliest, most powerful combatants on the field. When you added their complete and utter disregard for fair play, and their penchant for causing pain and suffering to the playbill, they shot directly to the top of the 'I'll take *eff around and find out* for a thousand' category. Their combined killer instincts and bloodlust made them the perfect hunter, and their poison — okay, I'm going to sound like a disclaimer for a prescription drug here — but their poison can cause a variety of symptoms, including: pain, redness and swelling, itching, blisters, nausea and vomiting, chest pain, difficulty breathing, anaphylaxis, and the always dreaded diarrhea. Of course, the poison can kill you, too, but once you've experienced Warca levels of diarrhea, death might just be preferable. The Rani and Warca hybrid looks like nothing you've ever seen and would likely never care to see again. They're clearly humanoid, but that's where anything clear ends. They're a musclebound lump of black and white tissue covered in spaghetti-like tentacles that flow around them like a cat's whiskers, constantly seeking any potential victims to give a nasty case of the 'rhea to.

Krisna Wijaya and his chimera, Razorface, were a stellar example of starkly conflicting personalities. Krisna had a dark, quiet, brooding persona, while Razorface, a poorly planned combination of hyena and Indonesian needlefish, was anxious, jittery, and boisterous. When the fused pair was on the field, it was like watching Jekyll and Hyde occupy the same space without either giving any leeway to the other. As symbiotic relationships went, they were the worst by far. And if you want to talk about homely, the thing Krisna and Razorface became when they merged looked like Abiy and Sandman took the ugly stick to them! They didn't need any insect DNA to make them candidates for a bag over the head. Krisna was a pretty handsome guy when he wasn't sharing DNA with his chimera, but his chiseled jawline didn't translate over to the hybrid mix at all. Instead, he inherited all the crazy, mangy, and unhinged outward traits of Razorface's hyena DNA, and the scores of yellowing, needle-sharp teeth and mold-colored scales of the needlefish. The Krisna and Razorface hybrid was a cartoony-looking thing that desperately tried to assert Krisna's human need for dignity while prancing around with their tongue hanging out, sniffing for hints of blood and fear.

After years of playing *Hiromon*, I knew the hybrids that performed the best were the ones where the host and the chimera saw each other as equals... *actual partners*. The ones like Krisna and Razorface, however, that saw the other as a tool to take advantage of were poorly melded and reeked of internal conflict.

Aku-Onna Kageyami and her partner, Creeping Death, were not one of those conflicted units. Aku-Onna was calm, collected, and more Zen than an entire monastery. Her chimera, a flower urchin and Komodo dragon mix, was a cold, calculating hunter that ate patience for breakfast and pooped out Valiums. Okay, so that last bit wasn't true, but believe me when I say, they were the freaking ninjas of Team Haraguro. While not the fastest member of the team, their melded unit was powerfully built, stealthy, and covered in poison-filled barbs. Even the tiniest of scratches could cause the victim to lose touch with reality and wander around the field in a useless, hallucination-fueled stupor. Repeat after me, drugs are bad, m'kay?

If you hadn't quite latched on to the fact that some chimeric hybrids are nightmare inducing monstrosities, please allow me to introduce you to Gustavo Sousa and his chimera, a stonefish and Brazilian wandering spider hybrid called Rolling Stone. Bugs are bad enough, but when you introduce arachnophobia into the melting pot of terror, things just ratchet up to an entirely different level. A stonefish is deadly on its own, having some of the most toxic poison known to man, and the Brazilian wandering spider's venom is some of the deadliest spider venom in the world. *Do the math.* Two plus two equals *NOPE!* In their hybrid form, Gustavo and Rolling Stone's body resembles a rock pile with eight barb-covered legs that look like something a kid made out of giant pipe cleaners sticking out the sides. Their head was flat and their facial features, aside from dark, darting eyes, and needle-sharp teeth jutting forward from a lipless maw, were as nondescript as the living coral armor that covered their body and protected their leg joints. Thirteen spikes ran down what should have been their spine, and oozed thick, viscous venom more caustic than battery acid.

Becky and Pigmoset took a couple of steps to the side and planted themself firmly behind me and Moreau. Then Kyle and BatManta got behind them.

Irwin Stevens was a former teammate who'd destroyed his previous chimera, Lampraven, by pushing it beyond its safe meld time. The poor creature died of exhaustion after Irwin refused to release their merge in favor of a win. Well aware that his partner was very near death, Irwin sacrificed its life for a moment of glory. If it wasn't for the olive branch extended by Team Haraguro, Irwin would have been permanently expelled from the league. Haraguro offered him a clean slate, as well as a newly bred chimera, a bloodthirsty Sydney funnel spider and saw scale viper hybrid named Vortex. The only thing they asked of him was that he bring the same level of ruthless dedication to their team as he'd displayed during Lampraven's final game. And bring it, he did. Thankfully for his chimera, the funnel spider and viper mix created a hyper-resilient combination. As hard as Irwin pushed it on the field, the creature just kept taking it. Not that it made it right... you know? Speaking of 'not right', when Irwin and his unholy monstrosity were merged, they could give the devil himself a run for his money. With the head and body of a snake, and the face and thick, hairy legs of a large spider, they were one part arachnid, one part snake, and a hundred percent nightmare. Their venom was as caustic as hydrochloric acid, and their ability to produce thick, sticky webbing in mass quantities was unmatched by any of the other hybrids. They moved like a giant millipede on steroids and Lightning Rod energy drinks.

Bilawara Marrawinga and her chimera, Necrosis, were another snake and spider hybrid that made it clear Haraguro was a team that would haunt your nightmares well beyond any competition. An incredibly effective cross between inland taipan and brown recluse, Necrosis was fast, aggressive, and deadly. Bilawara complimented the chimera's physicality and aggressiveness with her observation skills and extreme levels of calm. Similar in appearance to Irwin and Vortex, but thinner and faster, and with bulbous eyes that brought praying mantises to mind, Bilawara and Necrosis were another combatant that ranked high on my nope scale. Oh, and the name Necrosis? It's accurate. One bite from them and your flesh will melt right off your bones like a slab of pulled pork. I've seen it happen to other players, and unfortunately, it's even happened to me. Let me tell you, death can't come quickly enough when your skin is falling away like hot fudge sliding off an ice cream sundae.

Not every chimera on Team Haraguro was half spider or snake. Kajari B'wanga and his partner, Black Death, brought none of the above to the party. Half Cape buffalo and half deathstalker, which is a shockingly big, uber poisonous scorpion, Black Death was a big, aggressive beast of a chimera that, when joined with a human, became something like a Minotaur and scorpion hybrid. The merged partners were another of the powerhouse couplings. Physically, they were big, muscular, and intimidating as hell. They walked upright on two hooved feet, and counter-balanced themselves with their five-foot-long spiked tail. The rear appendage was deadly enough when used as a defensive weapon, sweeping the legs out from underneath their opponents, and more often than not, breaking someone's ankles or legs in the process. But the railroad spike of a weapon at the end of their tail was sharp and filled with a neurotoxin that could reduce an enemy Pharaoh's size to a quivering, weeping mess in seconds flat. I knew that from experience, too. Oh, and if you enjoy night terrors, take a look at their face. While their body is deceptively humanoid, their head is flat and armored, looking something like an industrial-sized waffle iron with narrow, hate-filled eyes, and massive, black horns jutting out on each side.

Rounding out Team Haraguro's roster was Jingjing Lin and her partner, Sun Tzu. Jingjing and her golden poison dart frogcassowary hybrid had been the last combatant standing on more than one occasion, and with good reason. The chimera's name was clearly inspired by its impressive tactical senses. Without its host, Sun Tzu was already a master tactician, seemingly able to predict its opponent's moves several seconds before their foes even realized what they were going to do next. But when combined with Lin, who was one of China's highest ranked Sanda masters — Sanda is Chinese kickboxing — they became a veritable offensive and defensive unit built into one lightning fast, deadly creature. They could evade you just as easily as kicking your ass, and if they really wanted you out of the way, they could simply fire their Love Potion Number Nine barbs at you. Yeah, I made that name up too, but I think it fits. If those little suckers prick you, you fall in love with the first opponent you lay eyes on. Do you even realize how humiliating it is to die while you're trying to test out your best pick-up lines on Irwin Stevens and Vortex? Forget I mentioned that... I'd really rather forget it myself. Physically, Jingjing and Sun Tzu are mostly humanoid, though they move like a frog when evading enemies, and attack with deadly talons on their ankles when on the offensive. They seem to have the best of all worlds: climbing, fighting, hiding, and long and close range weapons. The only thing missing was flight. Their eyes were large, red, and bulbous. They missed nothing on the battlefield. A bony plate protruded from the top of their head like a horn, though to be honest, I'd never seen them use it to attack or defend. The flesh around their neck and face was bright blue, which contrasted against the black feathers that otherwise covered their body.

The Judgy Three waved to each of the teams. They were ready for the respective captains to step into the center ring.

~

Lars and Heavy Metal and Rani and Warca lumbered towards the judges like enemy tanks rolling onto a battlefield. Like those old war movie sound effects, I could hear echoes of squeaking, grinding treads in my head as they moved, though the sounds of bones being snapped and crushed, and blood-curdling cries for mercy were a far more likely future prospect. Compared to the two merged captains, I was a shrimp. Not even a big one, like a giant tiger prawn. No wait, more like one of those cool, boxing mantis shrimp. Hey, when I'm fused with Moreau, we're no slouch, seriously. I'm the team captain for a reason.

Rani and Warca, always looking for an opportunity to intimidate an opponent, made the mistake of glaring at the Judgy Three a few seconds too long. When they glared back, I could see the hybrid's resolve waver as they quickly looked away. *Pick your battles wisely*, my dad always says.

Lars and Heavy Metal and Moreau and I stood like soldiers in a bootcamp inspection lineup, and the judges finally nodded approvingly. There were no words spoken. None were needed. We knew their expectations, and we knew their intentions if their expectations, or those of the spectators, weren't met. We were fighters, similar to the warlords we'd faced the day before. Our sole purpose was to entertain the masses. Slice, dice, maim, eviscerate… whatever it took, we had carte blanche. Of course, humiliation was worth bonus points. A public case of the 'rhea was always good for that one. I'd hate to be the one who cleaned up the field after a game. Pro-tip, there's a bonus level in the *Hiromon* game that allows you to play as the janitor. There's even a trophy for it. It's pretty gross and not for the weak stomached. Just be sure to wear your hazmat suit and stay away from sharp objects that might still be coated in poison.

The trio of referees abruptly turned their backs on us. Each of them floated to one of three individually marked platforms on the field. The platforms supported what were known as observation orbs. The referees could watch us from the safety of the orbs without any danger of injury from our attacks. Notice that I said floated? I wasn't entirely convinced the referees were human. Not completely human, anyway. I'd long suspected that there was more to them than met the eye. If they were walking, then I was President Cena. Those guys were the unholy spawn of Ringwraiths and Dementors contained in the bodies of three middle-aged Japanese businessmen.

Once the referees were safe inside their observation orbs, Lars and Heavy Metal, Rani and Warca, and Moreau and I returned to our respective teams for a final huddle. Moreau and I flew back, so I could reacquaint myself with the wings we shared before having to use them in any sort of fight.

Everyone surrounded me and looked to me for answers. Even El Scalar and Quacken, who seemed to be adapting nicely to their new features, appeared uncharacteristically apprehensive. Tentacles floated around their head nervously, and they frowned like someone had just called them a Minotaur.

Clem spoke first, but only after clearing his throat, of course. His voice was more gravelly than usual, undoubtedly due to his meld with Shartle. "I have to agree with Becky, Marshal. I have no rightful idee'r what we should be doin' here."

I shrugged, not liking our lack of prep time or our odds. "Unfortunately, this is how *everyone's* first game goes. Doubly unfortunate, there's usually only one rookie on any given team at any given time. There are seven rookies on our team. We all know who we are."

Cool and Ferradillo looked around before laughing. "The Pack Man isn't a rookie, so I think he means all of *us*, dudes."

Becky sighed at Cool's comment. "There's a voice in my head. That's Pigmoset, right? He said to follow his lead. Should I trust him?"

"Absolutely," I replied. "If I can give you any advice before we break this huddle, it's to become one with your chimera. Don't resist. They're a part of you now, and they'll never betray you. It's an impossibility. Trust me on that."

"I still don't hear any voice, but we trust you, bruh," Kyle squeaked.

The rest of the team agreed in a variety of odd murmurs. Even Steve agreed, though not quite as enthusiastically as the others.

Then the countdown began. One of three gongs, which was struck by one of the three referees, pealed across the field, echoing like a war drum, or maybe a war gong?

"Uh, the voice… you know, Pigmoset? He says he has an idea," Becky said, with more than a hint of trepidation in her voice.

The second gong sounded from another referee's location on the field.

"Go with it," I replied boldly, mustering up the most confidence I could offer.

The third gong rang across the field and the fans began to cheer for their favorite teams with gusto. Moreau and I moved to the front of the pack, hovering between my friends and the other two teams.

Suddenly, Becky and Pigmoset were standing in front of me, holding an armful of yellow goggles.

I couldn't hide my surprise. "Where did those come from?"

They smiled, their huge, cartoony eyes crinkling at the sides, and nodded back at Team Tsubaki. The players looked at each other suspiciously, still not really understanding what had just happened. "Like Pigmoset said, I'm... I mean, *we're* crazy fast!"

Then, as if to accentuate their proclamation, they disappeared from their spot in front of me, the glasses they'd been holding clattering noisily to the ground. A moment later, they reappeared with an armload of red tracksuits.

I looked up and across the field to see every member of Team Tsubaki standing stark naked, with their hands, arms, tentacles, and claws covering their unmentionables as best they could. All of them, from Lars and Heavy Metal to Shania and Frenemy, were blushing brightly.

A living vending machine with short, stocky legs and an oddly clocklike face, was trundling across the field towards Team Tsubaki. The machine, whose name was Akasuki, 'Suki' for short, normally offered new sets of goggles to combatants who'd lost or broken theirs. When Suki saw that the team in question was going to need a lot more than just goggles, her digital face blushed a bright, neon red, and she ran back from whence she came.

Team Tsubaki huddled together and shuffled off the field, ending up in their dugout where they glumly separated from their chimeras and covered with towels.

Amazingly, Becky and Pigmoset eliminated them from the competition without so much as a punch thrown or a drop of blood spilled.

A scoreboard announced a flawless victory over Team Tsubaki and awarded us a boatload of bonus points for humiliating our opponents so badly.

The victory dance would have to come later, though, as the game was still afoot!

Rani and Warca barreled forth, followed by their doom team. They ran, leapt, and galloped behind their leader, like the cavalry of the damned.

Ready to prove that size didn't matter, Steve and Elephant bounded past Moreau and me and met Rani and Warca halfway. Seeing the two hybrids clash was like watching David throwing down with freaking Goliath… if Goliath mated with the whale that supposedly swallowed that Jonah dude. Unfortunately — yeah, a few unfortunate things happened on the field that day — Steve and Elephant underestimated the reach and sheer toxicity of Rani and Warca's tendrils. One moment, Steve and Elephant were climbing them like a honey badger attacking an elephant; their pincers snapped, and their head-trunk swayed and batted at Rani and Warca's face like a demented Three Stooges routine. The next moment, however, they were rolling on the ground at their feet, blisters and boils erupting all over their flesh. Elephant immediately separated and dragged Steve off the field before the rest of Team Haraguro could trample him into an oily patch in the grass. A trail of what might or might not have been the beginnings of a bout with the 'rhea followed behind Steve as Elephant hauled him into the dugout, where Gunner tended to him. Gunner's disgusted grimace confirmed my suspicion about Steve's gastric distress.

Becky and Pigmoset were the next to fall in — you guessed it — another *unfortunate* encounter. Taking advantage of Aku-Onna's slower reaction time when connected to Creeping Death, they tried to steal their clothes and glasses. Instead, Becky and Pigmoset took a poisoned barb directly to the neck.

Seconds later, they were prancing and twirling in the midst of the growing battle like a ballerina in combat boots, even stopping occasionally to bow and throw kisses to the audience. They, of course, ate it up in huge, hysterical bites.

Though we still held the advantage, we were losing precious ground in the humiliation point column with each fallen teammate.

A moment later, the tables turned unexpectedly.

Cool and Ferradillo, as flexible, wily, and creative as Bob Ross after binging on coffee and pixie sticks, stretched over Team Haraguro like a yellow rainbow with brown spots, and planted themself firmly behind them like a wall. They expanded the size of the wall until it was more than fifty feet wide, and thirty feet tall. The armadillo plating faced the enemy.

A few of Rani and Warca's teammates glanced back curiously, but when Cool and Ferradillo didn't advance upon them as they were expecting, they just shook their heads and continued forward like they weren't even there.

That was their fatal error.

A moment later, Rani and Warca flew backwards like Zeus himself finger-flicked them away. They struck the barrier like a wrecking ball, but instead of bouncing off like a trampoline, they found themself impossibly stuck. Cool and Ferradillo used their armor plating to ensnare Rani and Warca and hold them in place like a fish struggling against a fisherman's net. Their tendrils flailed desperately, seeking a soft spot on Cool and Ferradillo's hide, but between Cool's impermeable skin, and Ferradillo's armor plates, Rani and Warca were sorely out of luck. I mean, Cool was the guy who shrugged off a point-blank blast from Xiro without so much as a sunburn, but that didn't stop Rani and Warca from trying.

A second later, Krisna and Razorface and Aku-Onna and Creeping Death launched from the ground with a unified grunt and hurtled straight into Cool and Ferradillo's inescapable trap. The pair of hybrids struggled as valiantly as Rani and Warca, but still to no avail.

Completely confused by what was happening to their team, Jingjing and Sun Tzu, Bilawara and Necrosis, and Irwin and Vortex grouped together in what was normally a wise defensive move. This time, all they accomplished was giving their attacker a much appreciated advantage. Suddenly, and quite involuntarily, Irwin and Vortex's body wrapped tightly around both Jinjing and Sun Tzu and Bilawara and Necrosis, causing them to spray webbing all around in a blind panic.

The sticky, web-covered ball made up of the three Haraguro team members sailed into the Cool and Ferradillo wall like a home run hit into the stands. An errant strand of webbing stretching out behind them like a kite string was all it took to foil their assailant's plans. I followed the webbing back to where the trio had been standing only a second earlier and saw the mighty

Pharaoh and Chamelion tugging against the unbreakable strand of web like a contestant in a tug of war. And then they were gone again, the webbing whipping around like it had a mind of its own. I shook my head in disbelief. Pharaoh and Chamelion had been with us the entire time. They'd just been capitalizing on their new hybridized power. Invisibility.

Distracted by their other six teammates' unexpected takedown, Gustavo and Rolling Stone and Kajari and Black Death didn't see the loose strand of webbing veer in their direction until it was too late. Pharaoh and Chamelion ran around them like they were playing Ring Around the Rosy, effectively lassoing them in one of Team Haraguro's best defensive weapons. Then, flickering back into view for another brief moment, they picked them up and sprinted at Cool and Ferradillo's makeshift wall, hurling themself and their kicking, screaming payload at the awaiting plates of armor. At the same moment they hit the massive, elastic barrier, they shouted, "now, Cool!"

And just like that, Cool and Ferradillo went from flat to an orb, trapping all their enemies, and Cool's long-time friend inside.

"You can struggle all you like, dudes" Cool and Ferradillo shouted, so everyone inside the orb could hear. "You can't hurt us from in there, so you have two choices. Either your captain cries uncle, or we just pump out the oxygen and put you all to sleep. Either way, you lose, dudes. In chess, this is called a *check*, right?"

And that, my friends, is why Cool and Pharaoh are two of the greatest superheroes to ever live.

Incidentally, Rani and Warca refused to tap out, so Cool and Ferradillo made them all go night-night, including Pharaoh and Chamelion, but as sacrifice plays went, the big guy and his chimera would be going down in *Hiromon* history.

Then, Cool and Ferradillo relaxed and released their unconscious captives to the grass before returning to their own hybridized, but still lovable form.

Another solid win for Team Ronin!

28
The Final Three

It took a little while to clear the field of the unconscious players and move them to their respective dugouts. Pharaoh and Chamelion came around fairly quickly. Pharaoh took Becky by the hand, helping Pigmoset guide her back to our team's dugout, where she continued to skip around like a six-year-old at a dance recital.

Now, if you were paying attention, and I'm pretty sure you were, you'd know we were already down three players. That would send us into our next round against the always honorable, but also incredibly powerful, Team Mizuchi, with only five players on the field.

Takahiro Fujimoto and his chimera, O'gon were wisdom incarnate, and effing scary too, if you don't mind me saying. O'gon was an honest to goodness water dragon and owl hybrid. Yeah, a water dragon, from old world Japan. Apparently, Japanese scientists had been able to scrape together enough viable DNA to make the hybridization process possible. When combined, Takahiro and O'gon were more dragon than anything, though the human and owl traits accented their dragon-like appearance quite nicely. A dragon's head with deeply set, but very human eyes, sat atop a neck that rotated a hundred and eighty degrees with ease. Their body was long and flowed like a snake fused with a dancer. Heavily veined wings that could have belonged to a giant bat if not for the thin layer of perfect feathers that shimmered golden in the sunlight, hung loosely from their arms. Talons the size of small meat hooks protruded from the tips of their fingers and toes.

Just behind Takahiro, stood Imani Juma, who with Flipzee, her dolphin and chimpanzee hybrid, was a fast, dexterous, and incredibly smart combination. When merged, Imani and Flipzee looked a lot like what I imagined aliens might look like if they ever decided to introduce themselves. Gray skinned, but with the distinct features of a primate, they were sleek, athletic, and combined the hand-eye coordination of a chimpanzee with the sonar of a dolphin. They reminded me a lot of my friend and fellow time-warrior, Kaori Sato. I'd seen Imani and Flipzee fight in pure darkness without missing a beat. Their senses were well beyond any human, and probably beyond any dolphin, for that matter. In addition to their physical capabilities, their mental prowess was almost unheard of on the field. They could find a way to make almost any object function as a weapon. Like James Bond, killing people with ball point pens, paperclips, and wedding cake toppers. They were one to keep an eye on at all times.

Next to Imani was Ben Ngoy and his chimera, Cronobo. If it isn't obvious from the name, Cronobo is a hybrid crow and bonobo. With black, beady eyes, a troll-like stance, and a nose that looked like the business end of a wooden spoon, Ben and his partner were a far cry from the sleek, athletic-looking Imani and

Flipzee. But make no mistake, Ben and Cronobo's hybridized form was cunning, tricky, and a highly skilled fighter. They were strong as an ox and smart as a whip. Hmm… can whips actually be smart? Who really knows? Considering I knew a sentient vending machine that handed out goggles to players who needed them, and *she* was pretty smart, I wasn't willing to rule whips out of the intelligence race.

So, do you see a pattern here? Because if so, it would make you intelligent. Did you catch my clue? Because if you did, you're *smart*, like smart enough to join Team Mizuchi. Bingo! The team's selection process values intelligence above all else. Strong? *That's cool.* Fast? *Very nice.* Smart? *You're in!* Heck, if Becky hadn't been on my team by default, she would've been a prime candidate for Team Mizuchi.

It should come as no surprise that the remaining team members brought high levels of intelligence to the table.

Lestari Sumatra and her chimera, a hulking, orange and red feathered beast called Parrutan, stood almost shoulder to shoulder with Imani. Part parrot and part orangutan, when Lestari and her partner fused, they looked something like a beaked, feathered Winnie the Pooh. Imminent danger never looked so cute. Seriously, while they look like something I may or may not have suggested dad market as a stuffed animal, they're on Team Mizuchi for many good reasons. One of the primary reasons is their uncanny ability to mimic other people's voices, like that famous voice actor, Rod something, but so much better! And if you want to be embarrassed... like *really* embarrassed, try underestimating them before facing them in hand-to-hand combat. Not that *I'd* know anything about that, but with orangutan in the mix, they're as strong as they are smart. The takeaway here, cute doesn't necessarily mean weak... or defenseless.

If there was a weak link on the team, I suppose it would have to be Michael O'Shea and his chimera, Stubborn. Yes, both its name *and* demeanor were Stubborn. Michael was a great guy, fun at a party, always good to have your back in a fight, and hair almost as thick and luxurious as mine. Michael wasn't the issue, though. It was the goat-raven hybrid he fused with for the games that presented challenges. Okay, so goats and ravens are both hyper intelligent animals. They're problem solvers and tricksters at heart, but they're almost as stubborn and aloof as house cats, too. Michael wasn't the strongest guy on the team, so he couldn't lean into that. Nor was he the fastest, the best fighter, or the deadliest in some other way. What he had going for him was his innate ability to break down a complex situation and find the simplest answers in what seemed like no time at all. He was a genius, plain and simple, but when he merged with Stubborn, the hardwired goat and raven DNA caused them to occasionally root themself in place like a child throwing a silent tantrum. They could just as easily be the reason Team Mizuchi won or lost on any given day. Apparently, the wins were frequent enough to keep them on the roster. It certainly wasn't their looks… I can promise you that. They looked like a mythical satyr, but with beady, yellow eyes, and a mane of black feathers that made it look like they were wearing a nun's habit and robes. Oh, and when they weren't peacefully protesting something in the middle of the field, Michael and Stubborn could fly.

Moving right along. Karen Greene, while a really cool person outside of work, was another player I kept my distance from on the field. Her chimera, Nightmare Fuel — yeah, it's really named Nightmare Fuel — is pure, uh… well, nightmare fuel. The monster I'm referring to is a holy terror of a beast, fifty percent pink flamingo and fifty percent cockroach. Take a second to wrap your head around that terror inducing combination. Nightmare Fuel was already frightful to look at, but when fused with Karen, they became a bug-winged, long-legged, skittery thing with a wide, flat head, gigantic, rotating eyes, long, searching antennae, and an oddly out of place hooked beak that clacked hungrily at *just* the wrong times. Pink, wiry hairs covered their arms and legs, sensing vibrations in the air and allowing them to predict movements in advance. Karen and Nightmare Fuel also had an ability called stridulation, which enabled them to project sounds into otherwise empty places, causing mass confusion on the field.

Another bug-based merger that gave me the freaking willies was Baljit Singh and his chimera, Wonkey. Wonkey was a Rhesus monkey-paper wasp hybrid that was intelligent, agile, and flew better than most of the bird-based chimeras. Despite the extreme intelligence, and given the inclusion of paper wasp DNA, Wonkey was on the aggressive side, instilling a bit of a temper in the otherwise mild-mannered Baljit. Yellow and black skin covered with patches of soft, tan fur made Baljit and Wonkey really stand out on the field, and their long, narrow wings pointed straight back, like a compass with a needle that pointed perpetually south. Their arms and legs were almost completely simian, and a pair of bright red antennae poked out just over a set of deeply intelligent, brown eyes. Baljit and Wonkey had the unique ability to build weapons with only their spit and some plant-based material. Proteins in their spit allowed them to reshape the materials, which would then reharden into something that was as light as paper, but as hard as diamond.

Team Mizuchi's final member was an unassuming nerd girl who looked a lot like Velma from the old *Scooby-Doo* show. Instead of the orange cable-knit turtleneck sweater and red pleated miniskirt, she wore the team's customary metallic silver tracksuit. Ruby Goldberg and her chimera, Vermin, were exactly what you'd expect the combination of gamer girl, rat, and pigeon to be. Smart, curious, inventive, and as much a survivor as an explorer, Ruby and Vermin's merged form was a quick, twitchy creature that could crawl, climb, and fly. They were barely five feet tall, had oversized ears, a twitching nose, large orange eyes, and a long, pink, hairless tail. They were, like Becky and Pigmoset, a quick study, a loyal teammate, and a good friend.

The three-minute buzzer rang. Cool, Kyle, Clem, Scalar, and I moved forward, awaiting our imminent invitation to the middle of the field.

Behind us, Becky pranced around, singing about tulips and lightning bugs, while Steve moaned and projectile pooped in the corner of our dugout. I have to give it to Gunner, as disagreeable as Steve was, the big guy was right there with him, keeping him from falling into a pile of his own excrement. Steve would owe Gunner big time once his boogie with the 'rhea was over. Maybe Gunner had some childhood toy he'd never gotten over or something.

The two-minute buzzer rang.

Cool and Ferradillo were as hyped as ever. "We've got this, dudes!"

Kyle looked considerably less certain of our odds. Clem and Scalar didn't look optimistic either.

Scalar grunted. "That's easy for you to say, amigo. You're the only one who got to play in the last round."

"What Bill said," Clem agreed.

"Nah, dudes. Pharaoh, Steve, and Becky played, too." Cool stopped and thought about what he and Ferradillo had just said. "Oh... yeah." Their smile faded a shade. "Sorry, broskies. We didn't mean to steal your thunder."

"Steal away," Kyle croaked. "At least you know what the heck you're doing."

I flashed back to my brief conversation with Becky a few minutes earlier. "Have you guys even been *listening* to your chimeras?"

I was met with three blank stares. I found myself wishing Becky could explain to them what she'd experienced, and how she'd formed such a trusting bond with Pigmoset so quickly and so effortlessly. But unless she was doing interpretive dance, the world's worst cheerleader wasn't going to be imparting any wisdom on my three doubtful friends any time soon. "Reach out to your chimera... or inward... something like that."

Their stares went from blank to incredulous.

"Says the guy who played this game hundreds of times. I don't even *understand* this weird voice. It doesn't make sense," Kyle said, frowning. "What do you want from us, dude?"

"I want to win," I said without thinking.

"I thought ya' wanted to stop them Nanops and get us home," Clem replied.

Scalar studied me, watching my reactions like an FBI profiler. "Do you have a plan, Packard?"

The third bell rang, and the referees called the five of us to the center ring before I could be expected to answer El Scalar's question. *Saved by the bell.*

~

The Judgy Three remained in their orbs for the next part of the ritual. Team Mizuchi joined us at the center of the field and faced us, eight to five. Somewhere on the far side of the field, Team Kitsune was watching, waiting to see which team they'd be facing in the final showdown of the day. There was no way I would let my team down. We'd win this match at any cost.

The first gong rang, and I looked at my friends. None of them looked back at me. Even Cool's ever-present, blissfully innocent grin had faded into an expression that betrayed worry… and maybe even guilt.

"Good luck, guys," I said, hoping they'd rally behind me like the champions I knew them to be. Instead, though, they stepped into line with me and faced Team Mizuchi with expressions that belonged at a funeral.

"We're going to need it," Scalar said as the second gong sounded. "Look inward," he snorted.

Then it hit me. A plan. Scalar asked if I had a plan. Knowing I only had a few seconds to say what I should have said several minutes ago, I reached out and put my hands on Clem and Shartle's and Kyle and BatManta's shoulders, as they were standing closest to me. "Cool and Ferradillo, you run interference. Tangle and trip up as many of our opponents as you can. Clem and Shartle, you're armored, so do your best to stop Karen and Nightmare Fuel and Baljit and Wonkey. Scalar and Quacken, you get Imani and Flipzee and Ben and Cronobo. Kyle and BatManta, you take out Ruby and Vermin and Michael and Stubborn. I'll deal with Takahiro and O'gon and Lestari and Parrutan."

As the third gong rang, I heard Clem ask Scalar, "hey Bill, do you have any clue who Karen and Bal-jit are?"

Scalar shrugged. "I don't know who any of these cabrones are, so I'll just take the strongest looking ones and bash their heads together."

We were so screwed.

~

Without Becky and Pigmoset's speed, Pharaoh and Chamelion's strength, or Steve and Elephant's aggression, we were down some key team advantages. I mean, Scalar and Quacken were strong, but they really hadn't stepped up to the plate during the last encounter, so I wasn't sure what they were going to bring to the field, if anything. The same went for Kyle and BatManta and Clem and Shartle. I had nothing to gauge expectations by. Cool and Ferradillo's performance was spectacular, but given Takahiro's in-game experience with O'gon, and the combined intelligence levels of Team Mizuchi, I doubted they'd fall for the same trap twice. Besides, we needed Pharaoh and Chamelion for that strategy to succeed again, and they were out of the game. Pharaoh stood near the dugout, trying to keep Becky off the field. Chamelion and Pigmoset sat on a wooden bench a few feet away, watching them curiously.

Feeling Moreau's physiology added to mine, and hearing her voice in my head, I was ready to make Team Mizuchi wish they'd stayed home and watched reruns of *Gilligan's Island*. Oh, in case you're wondering, I really do hear Moreau's voice in my head when we're merged. It's adorable. She sounds like a higher pitched version of Becky.

I rose into the air, feeling my tentacles stretching out around me, testing the air currents like I was in a gently swirling pool of water. Then, with my wings spread out wide and my senses tuned to perfection, I dove in for the attack. The color spectrum ahead of me was unlike anything you've ever seen, courtesy of my incredible octopus and bat-inspired eyes. I could see thousands of colors, each one more remarkable than the last. Each of the opposing team members, given their unique body chemistry, glowed a different hue. Takahiro and O'gon glowed a shade of white so pure, you might imagine it to be the most perfect form of light ever created. Lestari and Parrutan, on the other hand, glowed a soft shade of what Moreau referred to as paluqe. I'd say it's like purple, but that's not accurate. It's a color *you* can't see, and probably never will. I was like a tetrachromat, but so much better.

My vision went way beyond seeing. I could track each of them in ways normal human eyes, or other senses for that matter, never could. With my tentacles swooping wildly around me, ready to block anything that came my way, I zeroed in on Takahiro and O'gon.

Before I could reach my target, I sensed movement in the peripheral part of my sonar and veered slightly to my right to avoid an ambush. Scalar and Quacken, putting their extra set of legs to work and swinging their claws before them, took Takahiro and O'gon by the head and began swinging them around like a banner. A big, angry, struggling banner. Before I could reach Lestari and Parrutan, ol' Bison Breath and Quacken grabbed them as well and began, as promised, banging their heads together like a kid making music with pots and pans.

I swerved once more, and against my better judgement, headed towards Karen and Nightmare Fuel. Before I could reach them, though, a sound to my right that hummed like an entire colony of angry bees captured my attention. When I veered off course to face whatever was flanking me, I found nothing. Karen and Nightmare Fuel duped me with their stridulation again. They *always* fooled me with that ability. You'd think I'd have learned by then, you know? I swooped back towards them, my senses lighting up from every direction, but that damned humming threw me completely out of my groove. I suppose that's why I didn't see

Michael and Stubborn dive-bombing me. To be honest, I think Moreau was trying to warn me, but I was too darned focused on trying to see what my teammates were doing. Imagine being taken down by the laziest, most unpredictable member of the opposition's team. Well, that's what happened to me. Michael and Stubborn swooped in out of nowhere and goat-kicked me like they were scoring a goal for the winning team on the soccer field. And if that wasn't bad enough, their kick sent me face-first into one of Ben and Cronobo's oversized fists.

Ben and Cronobo hit me like a sledgehammer, sending me sailing across the field like a kite. I hit the ground with a thud and tumbled the last few feet before slamming into one of the referee's orbs. As the referee looked down, I swear I saw him smirk when Moreau separated from me and fell to the ground, unconscious.

I shook my head, trying to regain my bearings, and picked up my little friend, cradling her against my chest. When I looked back up, the referee was back to judging the ongoing game. I frowned and sighed. I'd failed my team.

Before getting Moreau back to the dugout, I looked around. Pharaoh, in a desperate attempt to keep Becky off the field, had begun dancing with her. For a superhero, he had surprisingly bad rhythm, but kudos to the big guy for doing his part. My focus drifted to Gunner, who was still tending to Steve. The E.L.V.E.'s expression showed pure misery, like he was wishing for a swift death. Gunner's grimace, undoubtedly caused by the foul smell, looked like he'd probably welcome the Grim Reaper's cold embrace just to get away from the literal shit storm. And yet, like Pharaoh, he was doing his best to help.

I turned to face what I was sure would be an absolute slaughter. Instead, I found my four friends and their chimeras holding their own against an enemy that outnumbered them, two to one, and outclassed them in experience by a far greater percentage.

As I watched in stunned silence, El Scalar and Quacken succeeded in knocking out Lestari and Parrutan and Takahiro and O'gon. Unfortunately, before the latter duo lost consciousness, they wrapped their body around the lower half of Scalar and Quacken's huge head, covering their nose and mouth, completely cutting off their air supply. With both hands wrapped around their foes' heads, they had little choice but to hang on for dear life and hope they could outlast Takahiro and O'gon. With one final display of their warrior's spirit, El Scalar and Quacken hurled the battered, unconscious body of Lestari and Parrutan at Ben and Cronobo as they sprinted towards Kyle and BatManta, who were grappling with Michael and Stubborn. Ben and Cronobo never saw what hit them. Scalar and Quacken didn't last long enough to see if their effort actually bore fruit. They dropped to the ground with Takahiro and O'gon in a messy pile that looked like something spilled from a fisherman's net.

Several feet away, Lestari and Parrutan and Ben and Cronobo tumbled to the ground in a similar pile. Stunned, but still in the game, Ben and Cronobo began to get up, but one of Cool and Ferradillo's hooves snaked lazily across the field and cold-cocked them before they could even push back up to their knees. Incredibly, Ben and Cronobo had been KOed as well.

The match was suddenly three to five, still in favor of Team Mizuchi, but the odds had shifted enough that a Ronin victory looked possible.

Airborne, but clearly still getting acclimated to flying together, Kyle and BatManta wrestled with Michael and Stubborn, employing the aerobatic equivalent of sticks and jabs in their bid for a win. Michael and Stubborn, for all their intelligence and years of experience in the *Hiromon* arena, were visibly surprised by their relentless onslaught and sheer tenacity.

Clearly as surprised by the turn of events as Michael and Stubborn, Kyle and BatManta actually smiled when they realized they'd gained the upper hand. Confidence increasing by the second, their fist shot out in a pile driver of a punch that was worthy of a Rocky movie. They shouted at Michael and Stubborn as the young duo dropped from the air, landing next to Lestari and Parrutan. "Looks like somebody's been eating their Weakies!"

Okay, so I could have come up with something better. Like, *who's the GOAT now?* Or some play on the word raven... like raving, craving, you know, but Kyle wasn't normally the one who thought up insults or catchy catchphrases on the fly, so I'd call that one a win.

Still smiling like Kyle'd just gotten any kind of approval from his parents, he and BatManta flew down and joined Clem and Shartle as the armored duo battled against Imani and Flipzee and Ruby and Vermin.

Though Clem and Shartle were taking the beating of a lifetime, they really didn't appear any worse for wear. I wondered why they seemed to be defending instead of fighting. Then it dawned on me. Three of the four remaining combatants were girls. Clem had never hit a girl in his life, and I didn't expect he'd be trying for that particular demerit badge any time soon. Clem was a defender at heart, and he'd be hard-pressed to ever change that, especially for a game.

Kyle and BatManta raised their balled fists in a brave attempt to defend their friend and would-be mentor, but in a not-so-surprising move, Clem and Shartle placed their hands on Kyle and BatManta's fists and gently lowered them. The old cowboy said something I couldn't hear, but I imagined the words were something like, "never raise yer hand to a woman, young gunslinger."

I scanned the field, looking for Cool and Ferradillo. I was hoping they'd step in to end what was finally looking like a game we could win. They were a little busy, though, sitting in the middle of the field, taking a hell of a beating from Karen and Nightmare Fuel and Baljit and Wonkey. They looked sad but weren't fighting back at all. It was like Cool had fused with Stubborn instead of Ferradillo.

I watched, frustrated and horrified, as Baljit and Wonkey turned and hurled two spikes fashioned from their saliva and several blades of grass across the field at Clem and Shartle and Kyle and BatManta. The pair hunkered together, Kyle and BatManta seemingly in agreement with Clem and Shartle's refusal to fight back. When the diamond-hard projectiles struck them each in the throat, they went down as they'd chosen to end the game, without a fight.

Clem and Kyle both disappeared, eliciting a collective gasp from the spectators and anguished cries from their chimeras, who fell to the ground frightened and confused. It was then that Cool and Ferradillo realized they'd just let their friends be killed, and it was then that they decided to fight back. Only, by that time, it was too late.

As Cool and Ferradillo shrugged off their attackers and rose to take care of business, their knees buckled a bit. I'd never seen that happen to Cool in all my years of knowing him. I realized what was happening the moment before it did. Ferradillo was trying to unmerge.

It makes sense if you think about it. Young chimeras need to build up stamina to hold the merger longer. Inexperienced players tend to rely on their partner's abilities too much in the beginning. The combination of youth and inexperience ends up costing new teams valuable time on the field.

There was so much I should have told them in the beginning. From the moment I saw the tracksuits appear, I should have been preparing them for what was to come. But my damned ego had taken over. When they needed a leader, they got me.

Before Cool knew what was happening, he'd dropped to his knees and his chimera had unmerged, collapsing exhausted to the ground in front of him. Cool picked up his new friend like a parent with a sick child and exited the field with his head hung low.

I really had failed my team.

Worse than that, I'd failed my friends.

As Cool and I walked to our dugout in silence, the remaining four members of Team Mizuchi regrouped and returned to theirs. Those four would face Team Kitsune in the final match of the day. Five more teams would battle it out the next day. On the third day, the winners of days one and two would face off in a final match to determine the year's *Hiromon* champions.

One look at the scoreboard, however, made it abundantly clear that Team Ronin was out of the running.

29

Come Out to the Coast, We'll Have a Few Laughs

Have you ever felt so bad about something that you just wanted to vanish? To go somewhere nobody knew you or the garbage things you'd done? Someplace where you could feel like a piece of shit without being reminded that you were, in fact, a piece of shit? Wherever that safe, judgement-free, disappointed stare-free place was, I desperately wanted to be there. Of all the out-of-place places popping up in the world around me, I needed the one where I was blissfully alone, free to hate myself for as long as I needed to. If someone had put a mirror in front of me at that moment, I probably would have put my fist through it.

I mean, I'd disappointed my dad and Irene, put Gunner in danger, ignored Whisper, and treated my other friends like a group of expendable rubes. Clem and Kyle just died in front of me again. *Again...* as in *multiple times*, and I was just walking towards the

719

dugout like nothing happened because I knew they'd respawn. Who does that? I'd ask what the hell was wrong with me, but we don't need the rhetorical question. I know exactly what was wrong with me. So, why don't I just let you reach your own conclusions? Hopefully, by the time we're done with this story, you can see me in a better light.

I'll make a promise to you, a pact of sorts, okay? I promise to always be honest about who I was, who I am, what I was feeling, how I handled it... you know, the crucial details. And you? Promise not to judge me too harshly until you have the whole story. That's not too much to ask, right? I'm glad to finally be able to open up about all of this to someone who gets me. I feel like you do, or you've at least got an open heart and mind.

Holy cow... I haven't squirreled that badly in a while, have I? Feel free to stop me when I go off like that. I won't take offense. Keep me on track, you know? Pump the brakes on the detours, okay Pack?

Where was I? Piece of shit, crazy ego got my friends killed… oh yeah. Anyway, I made it back to the dugout at the same time as Cool, both of us carrying our unconscious little friends.

Cool approached me awkwardly as we rejoined the rest of the team. He nodded down at Ferradillo, cradling the little armored chimera gently against his chest. "Is he gonna be okay, dude?"

"Yeah." I nodded, barely making eye contact before looking down at Moreau. "I think so."

"But you don't know so," Cool asked softly.

"I know a lot less than I thought I did, Cool," I replied before continuing to the dugout where Clem and Kyle, looking dazed and confused, were climbing out of Knightmare's back seat.

Kyle looked genuinely shocked when he finally realized where he was. "You're kidding me. We died? *Again*?"

"I'd rather die than strike a woman," Clem replied. "Especially over a game."

"That's not the point, Clem," Kyle countered as BatManta and Shartle rushed towards Knightmare, baffled by their appearance, but thrilled to see their new pard'ners safe. "I mean, yeah, I guess it is, but… yeah… yeah it is. But that was a *game!* Hey, Pack! What the hell, bruh?"

I turned towards the pair and nodded. I knew I owed them an explanation. Heck, I owed everyone an explanation. I also owed them all an apology, and probably a public act of seppuku, but first, we needed to get Steve and Becky out of the *Hiromon* world. I didn't know what the Quantum Nanops had in store for us, but my friends were in distress, and I had to get them to safety. "I owe you an apology, and an explanation, guys. I'm still working on the explanation part of it, since I'm still trying to figure out what the hell is going on. Maybe we can all put our heads together and come up with some answers?"

"You do realize yer hemmin' 'n hawin' was enough time fer an apology, Marshal," Clem mused.

I sighed. "I just wanted to apologize to everyone and make it more meaningful."

"I unnerstan' what yer sayin'," Clem replied. "But any sincere apology is meanin'ful. If'n I've learned anythang as a lawman, it's that 'later' ain't guaranteed. Jest say what needs to be said. There's too many excuses to wait. Too little time, cain't find the right words-"

"I'm sorry," I interjected before he could continue.

Clem nodded. Shartle rubbed excitedly against his leg like a puppy and BatManta flew directly into Kyle's face, knocking him right onto his butt.

"I know y'are," Clem said, his voice stern, but kind.

He kneeled next to Shartle and scratched the chimera's chin gently. Shartle purred happily. I say purred, but it sounded more like a spoon in a running garbage disposal.

Clem sighed and looked up at me. "How's about we work on our communication skills t'gether?"

"I'd like that," I replied.

Clem stood and extended a hand in my direction. "Considerin' the nature of our relationship in my world, and how I come t'be here currently, we might not know each other as well as I once thought."

I opened my mouth to respond, but Clem put up a hand. "That said, I sense yer still that man at heart, the friend I've trusted with my life in the past. Please don't make me regret trustin' ye in the future."

"I won't," I replied, more than a little dumbstruck by his blunt words. Not like I should have expected any less from the man. Then, still cradling Moreau in my left arm, I shook his extended hand, feeling the seriousness in his grip.

"Then we're good," he replied, without a shade of doubt or concern on his weathered face. "What say you, Deputy Kyle? You an' the Marshal good?"

Kyle pushed BatManta's wing aside like a goth might push aside a curtain of hair, so we could see his face. "Yeah, bruh. We're good." Kyle's expression wasn't quite as convincing as Clem's, but I couldn't exactly expect them to be racing for the front of the line at the Packard Campbell fan club, now, could I?

"Thanks, Kyle," I said with a sigh. Then I turned to Cool, who, in my memories — *and I had a lot of memories* — had never looked as dejected as he did at that moment. I walked to him and placed my free hand on Ferradillo. "He's breathing," I told him after a moment. "He's going to be okay. He was just tired. Young chimeras get worn out easier than older ones. I should have told you guys that. I apologize."

Cool looked up at me, and what I saw brought tears to my eyes. Cool was crying. I'd never, in a decade of having him as a friend, seen him cry. And it had been my fault. "I thought I killed him," Cool whispered. "Like I got Clem and Kyle killed. I failed you guys."

"No, Cool," I said, wiping my eyes with my jacket sleeve. "I failed *all* of you. You needed a leader. You trusted me to guide you, to keep you safe in this world… and *I* failed *you.*" I reached out again and gave him a heartfelt one-armed hug.

Cool wrapped his free arm around me like a boa constrictor and hugged me back, squeezing the wind out of me.

"You're squishing Moreau and Ferradillo," I wheezed.

Cool immediately uncoiled his arm and stepped back. "I need to be more careful, dude. I'm a dad now."

"Uh, you're not really his dad," I said, but when I realized how much pride he'd just taken in his statement, I added, "but he knows how much you love him. Trust me on that."

Cool's smile crept back like a creeping laurentii, and he nodded. "He loves me, too, dude. I could feel it." His smile widened. "And from now on, no pointing fingers, dude. All we have to blame is blame itself."

~

I'd like to say the next few minutes were easy, but I'd be lying. Between getting poor Steve out of the dugout, wrangling all the chimeras together, and convincing Becky that she should take her dancing show on the road, we had our hands full. Needless to say, with his posterior still doing an impressive, and worrisome, impression of Old Faithful, nobody was thrilled about carrying Steve out of Hiromon Field.

In the end, no pun intended, Gunner fashioned a makeshift stretcher out of one of the sheets Becky and Steve brought from Kincaid ranch, and he and Pharaoh took on the carrying duties. Ironically, Steve had already used most of the sheets in exactly the way he'd imagined — as bum wipe.

As Gunner and Pharaoh carefully lifted the crotchety old E.L.V.E. between them, Elephant scuttled nervously about underneath, trumpeting occasionally to show his support for his ailing partner.

We exited the field with very little fanfare, through the same set of gates we'd entered through. The lady who checked us in gave us a wide berth as we left and complained that heads would roll if someone didn't clean the area immediately once she thought we were out of earshot.

Like I said, I wouldn't want to be the janitor.

~

Once we were back in the parking area, Steve asked if he could *please* use one of the porta potties. When Steve lowered himself to the use of the word 'please', we knew he was in serious distress. As soon as he spotted the bright sea foam green potties with the aggressively lilac-colored doors, he changed his mind. Powder blue placards, decorated with dignified-looking flowers and the kanji for 'restroom' graced each of the doors.

"Let's just get outta here," Steve groaned. "If I have to look at those hippy-dippy, day glow colors any longer, I'll start puking, too. I really don't wanna be draining the grease trap from both sides, ya know?"

Vile description aside, we did know. No one would have wanted to endure that, uh, crap. So, we made like a tree and left! Hmm, that really doesn't work in the past tense, does it?

Before we left, we asked KM where the majority of the Nanop activity was. You know, to get us a direction to head in.

According to KM, a coastal area about three miles due east, known as South San Francisco, was by far the biggest hotspot. She informed us that everything from the San Francisco International Airport up to the multiversal coliseum was lighting up her radars like a Christmas tree on Independence Day. She also told us that while we were playing games and getting diarrhea, *which she expressly forbade around the upholstery*, she'd been monitoring police scanners and emergency channels. All communications along the coast had abruptly ceased more than an hour earlier. Entire teams of emergency services officials that had gone into the area east of Highway 101 to investigate had joined the disconcerting radio silence. Perhaps the most distressing news, though, was that all IP addresses in that entire region — all the computers, smartphones, tablets, printers, and even smart TVs — had vanished from the network, as if they'd never existed. Our governor, Calvin Broadus Jr., declared a state of emergency and immediately hopped on the red phone with the feds, trying to figure out what in the wizzle was going on. But we knew. We'd seen what the Quantum Nanops could do firsthand.

I swallowed hard. My mouth had gone completely dry. As much as I needed to address my behavior, we had to get moving. "Guys, I really want to talk to you." I looked at Whisper. *"All of you.* But first, for Steve and Becky, we need to get out of the *Hiromon* world." I held Moreau close as I spoke. "We'll head east on Hillside Boulevard. The coastal area KM was talking about is a little more than three miles away. We can make it there by dark, but to be fair to Pharaoh and Gunner, we'll take at least the first part of this trek on foot. Once we cross the threshold to a new game world, reality, I don't even know what to call any of this anymore, everyone should go back to normal. That includes you, Steve."

"Well chop chop, then," Steve replied. "I'm afraid my liver's gonna fall out if we don't get outta this place soon!"

Becky danced past Steve and wrinkled her nose. Her jig became a bit of a troika after that, and she skipped over to Pharaoh, offering her hand extravagantly.

"Alright, Knightmare," I said. "You're in charge, girl. Lead on."

As she rolled towards Hillside Boulevard, KM chirped. "Me? In charge? You've never done that before."

I sighed. "I'm a slow learner, KM. But I get there eventually."

Cool walked up next to me, frowning. "Dude, if we leave the *Hiromon* world, will our, uh, kai- uh, what'd you call them?"

I knew where he was going with his question. "Chimeras?"

He nodded. "Yeah, our chimeras. Are they gonna disappear? Like the horses did when we got here?"

"I don't think so," I replied. "Remember, Moreau showed up all the way back in Rotgut."

"But our chimeras didn't appear until we were on the field. What if Moreau is like Whisper, and Ferradillo is like those horses we borrowed from Kincaid? What if only Moreau stays because she's the only one important to *you*?" Cool hugged his little friend tightly. "I don't want to lose him, dude."

"*You* are important to me, Cool. Your happiness... everything. You guys are my family. Seeing you happy makes me happy, and seeing you sad-"

"I'm *very* sad right now," Steve interrupted.

"Seeing *any* of you sad," I continued, "makes me sad." I sighed. "I've made a lot of my loved ones sad lately."

Whisper, who had been trotting close behind me, nuzzled my hair and nickered softly.

"Thank you for forgiving me, girl," I told her.

Scalar stepped up beside me and matched my stride. Quacken sat atop his head, burrowed happily into his thick mop of hair. "You've been under the false assumption that you have been playing mere video games for many years, compadre. In the games, you felt free to act as if there would be no consequences. However, it has become clear that the worlds you have been playing in are all too real. Whether they took place in my world, yours, Señorita Becky's, it makes no difference. The Nanops are here now, and they are in control. They make no distinction between what is supposed to be real or not real, fair or not fair, and they do not worry about the trivialities of life or death. All that seems to matter to them is that you play." He kicked the rocks in the path absently, sending them skittering across Hillside Boulevard. "You have some very grownup decisions to make as we take our next steps, hermano, and some important things to consider. I have fought in wars as a soldier, and I have led men to their deaths in battle. Victories are far less common than you might think, and many times, they come at a high price. As Señor Clem put it, the boatman always demands his toll. Be the compensation coin or blood, he will be paid. How will you pay? How will *we* pay? Because as much as you want to believe this is all about you — and to the Nanops, it may be — we are here, too. Our lives and our fates are all intertwined. Allowing Knightmare to lead was an excellent first step. But remember, some responsibilities must remain yours. Knowing when to take the lead and when to step back and delegate authority, that is the mark of a true warrior." Scalar placed a comforting hand on my shoulder. "For the record, I believe in you. I only ask that you believe in us. We are not characters from a game. We are flesh and blood, like you." He looked at KM, who was rolling along quietly, scanning satellite feeds, military communications, and emergency broadcasts. "Not that flesh and blood are necessary for life, eh, amigo?"

I placed my free hand on his, patting it. "Thank you, Scalar. I needed to hear that. All of it."

Scalar snorted softly. "Why do you think I said it?"

"Ol' Bill's not one to run at the mouth fer no reason," Clem chimed in from a few feet behind us. "I'm thinkin' that's the most I've ever heard him say at one time."

Scalar nodded. "You should listen to Señor Clem. His cow man wisdom is surprisingly accurate."

"Cow*boy*, not cow*man*," Clem grumbled.

"El Scalar, *not* Bill," the warrior replied.

And that was how it went for the next two miles or so. We talked, licked our wounds, and kept Becky dancing in the right direction. It was pretty genius, how we finally did it. We sang "Follow the Yellow Brick Road" and got her to skip with Kyle and me. Steve continued to poop himself, which was incredibly concerning, because I swear, by that point he'd pooped out the equivalent of Pharaoh's body weight.

Thankfully, once we crossed under the Highway 101 overpass, our clothes changed, and along with them — we hoped, anyway — our luck.

30
Mike Ferrari, P.I.: Rise of the Centurion

The last thing I remember before finding myself in an entirely different world was watching some giant pus wad with tentacles vaporize Mr. Pan, Stan, and that loudmouth Packard Campbell in Laboratory 311. Becky and Brad made it into the glass-walled control room with the lab tech, my classmates, and me. Oh, I should probably reintroduce myself. I'm Jamal Stone, one of the unfortunate students caught up in the whole 'rip in spacetime' debacle.

Becky was crying, and I'm pretty sure Brad's pants were wetter than when I'd seen them last. Then, without any sort of warning, Becky collapsed. Most of the kids, including Brad, stepped back, but Fuun — that was the tech's name — and I dropped to our knees to see if she was alright.

After removing her helmet, we found that Becky was breathing but completely unresponsive. Her eyes had rolled back in her head like one of them crazy folks at a faith healing. Wen Lim handed me a button-up sweater and I placed it carefully under our friend's head.

I turned to ask Brad where they'd been, if they'd been exposed to anything obviously suspicious, and if he was feeling okay. When I turned, the world around me blurred. I thought that maybe whatever'd affected Becky was also affecting me. In a way, I was right.

I closed my eyes and shook my head, trying to clear away the sudden wave of vertigo that overtook me. Imagine my surprise when I opened my eyes and found that I wasn't in Laboratory 311 anymore. I was kneeling on a bike path on a beach. Fine, sun-bleached sand spread out on either side of the path. As I looked around in a bit of a stupor, I saw the ocean was only about forty feet away. Catamarans, speedboats, and parasailers were making the best of the calmest stretch of shoreline I'd ever seen. Big, colorful towels and umbrellas decorated the beach in both directions for as far as I could see. Of all things, I could hear an old Duran Duran song playing on a vintage cassette player a few feet away. Not that it really matters, but I think the song was "Rio". Hey, I gotta set the scene for you, right?

A distinct, but non-threatening fog hung over the ocean several miles out and obscured the overall view. There were no thunderheads in the sky, so I wrote it off as a byproduct of dew point equilibrium.

A teenage girl wearing a yellow polka-dot bikini ran past me and caught a Frisbee with the tip of her index finger before looking me up and down, smiling approvingly, and running back to her friends. Her hair was like something out of a Cyndi Lauper video, pure '80s. I watched her and her friends for another moment, grinning like a fool when she glanced back at me and smiled again. Then, out of the corner of my eye, I spotted something coming at me fast. I turned just in time to see Brad

barreling down on me like I was holding a football or

something. He plowed into my midsection, knocking the wind out

of me, and sending us both tumbling into the sand.

I'm not weak or anything, but I spend most of my time in

the school research lab, where Brad spends most of his time on the

football field. So, I ain't gonna lie, when he hit me, it hurt like hell.

I picked myself up and began dusting the sand off my

clothes, careful to avoid what I believed to be more than just a few

bruised ribs. I was about to ask him what the *hell* he was thinking,

when a group of guys on mountain bikes — who weren't wearing

helmets, by the way — powered through the spot I'd just been

standing in. One of them shouted at us and flipped us off as they

passed. "Stay off the bike path, dorks!"

I extended my hand and helped Brad to his feet before

continuing brushing off my clothes.

Brad, always the quintessential jock, was wearing mirrored, wraparound sunglasses, faded, torn jeans, a bright yellow tee shirt, and a red and gold letter jacket with a big red 'M' patch sewn on one side. I didn't have to be on the football team to know what our jackets looked like. That wasn't one of them.

"Bro, where the hell are we," I asked. "And why are you wearing some other school's jacket? That ain't like you."

Brad looked down at the M on his lapel and frowned. "I was hoping you knew what happened," he said, sounding shaken. "One moment we were in that glass room, hiding from the monsters from the rip… the next, we were here. I mean, I was over *there*." He pointed at the sand on the other side of the bike path. "And you were just kneeling in the middle of the bike path, ogling girls and waiting to get run down by those jerks on the bikes." He looked at me funny, tipping his head like a dog trying to understand what their human is saying. "You should look in the mirror before calling me out for what I'm wearing, nerd."

I looked down and realized the clothes I was wearing were definitely not the ones I'd worn on the field trip. From the black, wingtip dress shoes, to the light gray slacks and jacket, to the white dress shirt and skinny black tie, I was in the fashion Twilight Zone. Brad held out his sunglasses, clearly wanting me to *actually* look in the mirror. What I saw in the reflection shocked me almost as much as magically finding myself on a beach with Brad. It was me I was looking at, but the six-inch tall, angled flat top with the faded sides was not a hairstyle I'd ever considered, let alone worn. "What in the Kid and Play," I muttered.

"We're not in Kansas anymore, nerd," Brad whispered.

"No... we're not," I replied, at least as stunned as he was. "And you can cut the nerd crap, I look pretty damned fly in these threads. You're the one wearing some other school's letter."

Brad took off the strange jacket and deposited it next to a set of unattended beach towels.

"Oh, and I wasn't ogling girls, Brad. She peeped me first, *bro.*"

~

There we were. Brad and I, still trying to get over what we'd just seen in Laboratory 311, wondering what had happened to Becky and the others, and clueless as to what our next move should be.

"What would Packard do," Brad muttered quietly.

That was the last thing I would have ever expected to hear come out of Brad's mouth. "Did I just hear you right? What would *Packard* do?"

Brad shrugged, looking really uncomfortable with what he'd just said. "Back in the lab, when the shit hit the fan, he came up with a plan out of nowhere. When we lost Mr. Pan and the map, the nerd got us to safety. And when Stan knew more than the rest of us about the weapons and stuff in the ammunitions room, he let Stan take the lead. Maybe he's one of those natural-born leaders or something?"

I wanted to laugh at him, but I really had no argument that would have been a good counterpoint, so I just returned the shrug. "Well then, in your opinion, what would he do?"

Brad pondered the question before pointing at a row of palm trees separating the beach from a public parking lot with his chin. "First, he'd get us out of the sun in these hot clothes. I mean, I'm hot in just a tee shirt and jeans. You've got to be roasting in that suit."

I was sweating pretty badly. "Good call. But I'm giving that one to you, Brad, not Packard. I don't care what you say, he ain't no natural-born leader."

Brad looked at me sideways as we made our way to the trees. "He's dead, Jamal. So, we'll never know now, will we?"

As scared and confused as I was, that hit home in a big, ugly way. Brad and I were alive, and maybe we had Packard to thank for it. "You're right, man," I told him. "I should be more grateful."

"I know you're scared," Brad said, sitting down on a low brick wall, perfectly shaded by one of the tallest palm trees I'd ever seen. "I was so scared, I pissed myself." He absently touched the crotch of his acid-washed jeans as he spoke. "But we're here now, wherever *here* is. I think we need to do two things. One, we need to figure out how we got here, which is your job, Mr. Brainiac. Come up with a theorem or something. And two, we should look around and see if any of the others are here too."

I nodded. "Not bad. Is that what Packard would do?"

Brad shook his head. "I don't know ner- uh, J... but it's what *I* think we should do."

I couldn't help but smile. "Looks like bein' a quarterback gave you some leadership skills after all."

~

Brad's first ask wasn't all that difficult. Not for me, anyway. I spoke science like Brad spoke sports. As my dad told me when I started taking college level physics courses — *the highly advanced ones*— "You got a big brain, son. Use it to make the world a better place." My dad was an auto mechanic, and a damned good one, too. But he always felt like he'd failed us by not being more. What he never really understood was that his support and belief in me, even when he didn't understand a word of what I was saying, was way more important than any material things or expensive family vacations. I mulled over our circumstances before committing to an answer. "The rip. It's the only thing that makes sense. Think about it. Fuun said it was a hole in spacetime itself. Look around, bro. We're straight up in an episode of *Miami Vice*. Look at our damned clothes, our hair, the boombox." I turned and pointed at the parking lot. "I'm willing to bet there ain't a single car here newer than the mid '80s. It's like a classic car show up in here."

Brad nodded. "Makes sense," he conceded. He scanned the beach before turning around. "Let's go see if anyone else from the lab came through the rip with us." He began scanning the parking lot and parts beyond.

"The sun's gonna be goin' down soon," I told him. "People are starting to pack up and clear off the beach. We got maybe an hour or two of daylight left, tops." I joined him in his visual search for anything familiar, or grossly out of place. "If we don't spot something soon, we should find shelter."

When Brad didn't answer, I glanced over at him curiously. He'd stood up and was staring at something southwest of us. The sun was in our eyes, so it was hard to make it out completely, but a group of about ten people were walking towards the beach.

Brad took a few steps forward, unconcerned by the harsh rays of the late afternoon sun. "Is that *Packard?*"

The group was odd, to say the least. A classic, black convertible flanked the group on one side. It was bomb, but I was never a big car guy, so I couldn't tell you the make or model to save my life. On the far side of the group was a brown horse, just trotting along like it belonged there. What looked like a rabbit, at that distance, sat on the horse's saddle, chill as could be.

In between the car and the horse was a group of people. As they got a little closer, I counted nine of them. One of them was a massive brother with dreadlocks. When I say massive, I'm not even exaggerating. He must've been taller than Shaq. Dreadhead wore neon yellow parachute pants and a hot pink muscle shirt that exposed arms the size of oak trees. Next to him was another tall dude, sporting an afro that would have made Jimi Hendrix jealous, but he was dressed like a preppy. Khaki pants with a salmon-colored polo shirt and an ice blue sweater tied loosely over his shoulders made him look like he was ready to attend a tennis match at Wimbledon.

Another tall brother, though not nearly as tall as the first dude, walked close to the horse. He was dressed pretty normal. Black pants, probably jeans, and a black tee shirt made up his ensemble. If it wasn't for his low trimmed mohawk, he would've barely stood out at all. Like I said, though, nothing fancy.

In stark contrast to mohawk, was a lanky, older dude who also maintained a close pace with the horse. He wore a bright red, one-piece flight suit with a thick yellow belt wrapped around his waist. His hat was wild. It had three tiers, large at the bottom, smaller at the middle, and little more than the circumference of a soda can at the top. It looked a lot like a cheap plastic wedding cake on his head. Red, mirrored sunglasses that looked like those things they give old people after cataract surgery completed his crazy '80s outfit.

Behind the group was another tall dude. Maybe even taller than dreadhead, but being behind the others, it was hard to tell for sure. All I could really see was the upper part of a yellow and brown outfit that looked like Michael Jackson's and Liberace's wardrobes got tossed in a blender.

Up front was a young, slightly overweight guy, wearing shorts that were far too short to look comfortable and a teal blue tee shirt. Over the tee shirt he wore an unbuttoned white outer shirt covered in multicolored geometric shapes with the collar popped up. His hair was shaggy and styled into a pink-tipped fauxhawk.

At the front of the group was, uh... how do I put this delicately? It was a small child, dressed as a pimp. The kid wore a red velvet suit trimmed with zebra print. He carried a walking stick in one hand and wore a matching red velvet cowboy hat.

The rest of the crazy group aside, it was the two in the lead who interested me most.

The first was a girl with nearly shoulder-length auburn hair. Her mop was trussed up in a little ponytail that stuck out from the side of her head, held in place by a frilly black and hot pink ribbon. She wore a blue tee shirt that had the neck cut away, so it hung off her shoulder playfully, and what looked like an orange tutu over a lime green miniskirt. Under the skirts were a pair of leopard print leggings and, I kid you not, purple legwarmers.

The second person was a young man with light-brown hair ending in frosted tips. He was fit, and wore aviator sunglasses, a white suit over a pink pastel tee shirt, and white shoes with no socks. They'd gotten a good bit closer by then. Getting a better look at the dude's face made my mouth go dry. I reached over and put a hand on Brad's shoulder. "I don't know how it's possible, bro, but that *is* Pack. Becky too."

As we watched them approach like those cool people who walk away from explosions without looking back, the group stopped just short of the parking lot and scanned the landscape before them. They had to be as blown away by the whole scenario as Brad and I were.

"Come on," I told Brad. "Let's go let 'em know we're here and find out what they know!"

31

Epilogue

or

The Devil Went Down to George's

When we crossed underneath Highway 101, and through a thin curtain of fog, a few things happened. Our clothes changed to reflect the new game grid we'd just entered, which we expected based on our previous experiences. Steve stopped pooping and immediately requested a fresh strip of the bed sheet we'd been using as a stretcher. He ducked behind some bushes and cleaned himself up, just to be sure. Becky stopped dancing. I was particularly happy about the last two. As much of a grouch as Steve was, I would never wish Warca levels of the 'rhea on anyone, especially not someone I actually cared about. And as far as Becky went, Kyle and I were getting really tired of skipping.

The moment Becky lost the urge to trip the lights fantastic, she staggered over to KM and leaned against her. She looked exhausted. "Why do my legs hurt so badly," she asked, looking like she might not want the answer.

"You don't remember," I asked.

She shrugged. "No."

"Heh! You've been dancing like crazy since the first round of the *Hiromon* tournament. We lost and got booted from the field. It was pretty bogus," Cool informed her. He smiled broadly as he realized Ferradillo was still with him after crossing the barrier between game worlds.

"I'll explain later," I told her. "Maybe you should sit inside KM and rest your legs?"

"My seats are quite comfortable," Knightmare added.

"That's alright, thanks. I just need to catch my breath." Becky practically slumped against KM's fender, then she rolled over, laid on her back on the not-so-comfortable hood, and looked skyward. As Pigmoset bounded from KM's back seat and hopped onto his partner's chest excitedly, Becky pointed up, her eyes widening with fear. "Pack? What's that," she gasped.

The rest of us looked at the quadrant of sky where she pointed. Not a single mouth remained closed.

Scalar was the first to speak. "Madre de Dios! What is it, Packard?"

It took me a moment to get the words out. The memories that flooded back when I saw it made me feel ill. If my friends thought the gladiators in the coliseum or the chimeras on the field were bad, they had no concept of the creatures that were materializing overhead. "That's DORADO IX-XXII," I told them. "It's a space station from the *Crawlspace* game. The monsters up there are way worse than anything we've come across so far."

Kyle practically gagged. "Worse? Worse than dragons, Mesoamerican death gods, and killer human-spider-snake hybrids? What the hell is up there, bruh?"

I looked at him, meaning to speak, but my mouth wouldn't move.

"That bad, eh," Clem muttered. "Well, at least it's up there and we're down here."

"For now," I replied. *"For now."*

~

We left the *Crawlspace* conversation for another time. While Becky rested her legs, I told everyone about the game we were heading into. Hey, I learn from my mistakes eventually. I never wanted to enter another game unprepared, ever again.

Of course, my friends, except for Gunner and Cool, who never received new clothing, had many questions and comments about their new duds. Pharaoh and Scalar complimented each other on their stylish, and dare they say, handsome attire. Steve, being a bit of a bad boy, was thrilled with his, uh… pimp suit. Kyle, though displeased with what he was calling his short shorts, found the rest of his outfit to be more than adequate. Becky was a pretty good sport no matter what… just don't *ever* mention the saloon girl dress.

My familiar white linen suit and boat shoes were a welcome change. When I checked my waistband, I found my silver plated ASP 9 mm pistol. The only one who didn't appear pleased with his change of clothing was Clem. He was less than thrilled with the jumpsuit, and the bright colors weren't at all his style, but what peeved him the most was his hat. Once again, the Nanops replaced his beloved cowboy hat with something less suited to his tastes and delicate sensibilities. It took a few minutes of explaining, but I was eventually able to convince him to keep the hat on, as it was a status symbol in the new game world, worn only by the great and powerful Emperor Devo. All he had to do was tell people that he *was* Devo, and he would be revered in the world of Miami like no other.

Alright, you caught me. I lied a little bit, but hearing Clem announce to the locals that he was Devo would be pure comedy gold.

Sorry, squirreling again. '80s duds, Emperor Devo... oh yeah. So, the game itself, I explained as we finally left the overpass behind and walked towards the Bay, was a detective, mafia, shoot 'em up, action thriller. My character was a field operative for the legendary private investigator, Mike Ferrari. In the game, called *Mike Ferrari, P.I.: Rise of the Centurion*, we took on various clients who would hire us for jobs ranging from pursuing a gang of international car thieves, to taking on the Cuban mafia in an all-out turf war between rival factions.

The world we'd entered was alive with dangers, and we'd have to watch each other's backs every step of the way.

Our top priority was to find Mike Ferrari and fill him in on what was happening. He'd know what needed to be accomplished — *that was how the game always went* — and we'd sign on to assist him.

KM informed us that, as expected, she'd lost track of all networks within the region. "Networks seem to be vanishing from every location with high levels of Quantum Nanop activity." She was silent for a moment, processing data, testing outcomes, and crunching numbers at mind-boggling speeds. "Gunner, I have seen you check your phone several times since we were in Rotgut. Is it safe to assume you have not been able to locate a network?"

Gunner nodded and sighed deeply. "Yeah. I know Hal and Irene are in tech-free zones, but I feel bad abandoning my security team like I did." He looked at the sun. It was sinking into the west. Yet another day had gotten away from us. "I'd just like to be able to check in and let them know I'm alright, that *we're* alright."

"Understandable," KM agreed. "I may have a possible solution. If we approach the shoreline, we might be able to connect to a network."

"Yeah," Becky agreed. "Cell signals, just like radio waves, bounce on water, right?"

"Correct," KM replied. "I detect active cellular networks on the other side of the Bay. It is possible, even though they're almost twelve miles away, we could catch a signal from the water."

"Like skipping stones," Cool asked.

"More or less," KM replied, sounding amused by the comparison.

I patted her fender. "Where to, then?"

"I'm still in charge," she asked, genuine surprise marring her otherwise even tone.

"Like I said, I'm learning."

Becky smiled at me. I'm not sure what it meant, but at that moment, knowing Knightmare was pleasantly surprised meant more to me than Becky looking impressed. I smiled back, but continued to focus on KM.

"I like you better in this world than in my own," Knightmare said finally. "I hope that is okay to say."

I was fairly certain her words were meant as a compliment, but I wasn't entirely sure. "Of course, but why do you say that?"

"In my world, I'm a tool. You call me your partner, but you would never put me in charge of anything." More silence followed. I was about to respond when she continued. "Here, you're a different person. Literally. I mean something to you here. At least, I believe I do."

Kyle cut in before I could respond. "I was thinking something similar, bruh. You're a better person here than in our- I mean, in my world. Over there, I say you're my best friend, but the truth is, you're my only friend. And that doesn't say much. The Packard over there is a real dick to me most of the time, but *you... this* you... you treat me like a real friend. Or is it like a brother? I know I met this version of you over there, but my Packard, he overshadows any other good memories there. This might sound weird, but to me, and maybe some of our friends too, you were the NPC. In our worlds, you were the visitor. You were the anomaly." Kyle looked like he was going to tear up. "Anyway, I'm glad, and really proud to be here with this version of you." He looked around at the others, settling on Cool and Clem briefly before returning his gaze to me. "With all of you."

Of course, Cool and Becky had to hug him before I could thank him and tell him that I too was proud to be there with him.

Then I turned to KM and told her, "I'm sorry if I ever made you feel like anything less than an equal. You do matter to me. You're my friend, and a great one at that."

~

Before any more hugging could take place, KM got us moving. She guided us another mile or so along what had once been Oyster Point Boulevard. The street now displayed signage for 17th Street in South Beach, Miami. A few minutes later, and more than a few sideways looks from the locals, we stopped at the edge of a large parking lot that ran along the coast for several hundred feet in both directions. Beyond the lot was a short brick barrier lined with tall palm trees that served to keep the beach sand off the pavement. It was far more effective as a bench where beach goers could stop and sit while they knocked sand out of their shoes.

After the wall, a twenty-foot-wide strip of grass provided a great place to walk one's dog or set up a romantic picnic.

Beyond the grass was Miami freaking Beach. I was simultaneously in awe and sickened by the sight. The coastline, which was straight and calm for as far as I could see in either direction, was once the home of the Oyster Point Marina, several restaurants, and even a tech firm's multi-billion dollar headquarters. The Nanops had erased and rewritten everything that had once been there, including the actual landscape. My stomach lurched when I looked around and realized that all the people around us, the people who believed they belonged there in that false Miami, were made of repurposed people, the people who actually belonged in my world.

My friends weren't the NPCs.

The people walking around, talking about the humidity and wondering where they would get drinks later, the people driving cars and riding bikes, the guys who wondered if the Dolphins would ever see another Superbowl; they weren't real. The stern woman in a mauve muumuu who shook her head at the yellow Pinto blasting Billy Idol, the teenagers in that Pinto, and the old guy letting his dog take a crap on the sidewalk without cleaning it up; *they* were the NPCs.

It suddenly occurred to me that they were like the horses we'd borrowed from Kincaid's ranch. If they tried to leave Miami, they'd probably just reset and go back to where they'd started. They were like the display furniture in an open house, put there to complete the illusion that the world around us was real, that it had meaning beyond a simple game.

If anybody was lamps, it was them. I didn't know if Becky would appreciate my observation, so I kept it to myself.

"I could drive onto the beach if I reformed my tires into all terrains," Knightmare told us. "However, I don't see any other vehicles driving on the sand. I believe local law enforcement frowns upon such activity. Perhaps it would be best if I parked here amongst the other automobiles. You may leave the chimeras with me, *if* you can guarantee Shartle will not have another *accident.*"

I agreed that her suggestion was a good one and apologized, for the tenth time, for Shartle's mess in the back seat. Once the chimeras were all inside, including Moreau, who'd been riding like a boss on Whisper's saddle, I asked KM to raise the top, but to please leave the windows down.

As the top lifted into place, I heard something completely unexpected on that strip of Quantum Nanop manufactured beach.

I heard my name.

~

I turned towards the beach and scanned it again, looking for anything out of the ordinary. Eagle-eye Becky saw them first.

"Pack! Over there!" She pointed towards the low brick wall, north of where I'd been looking.

Two young men were running towards us, waving and calling my name. It was when they hollered Becky's name that I recognized one of the voices. I'd heard him yelling for Becky under extreme circumstances in the past. It was Brad, my sometimes friend from *String Theories*. As soon as I recognized his voice, it dawned on me who was running with him. It was Jamal Stone, the brainiac who was supposed to close the rip in spacetime in Laboratory 311.

Spoiler alert — depending on how I play the game, *sometimes* he seals the rip and *sometimes* we all die.

Anyway, aside from Irene, he was the smartest guy I'd ever met. Smarter than my dad even. So, somewhere between my dad and Irene on the smart scale.

While I wasn't always either of their biggest fans, and they probably weren't mine, I was ridiculously happy to see them both alive and dressed in some pretty choice threads.

Becky and I ran towards them, waving back like they were our long-lost family. I suppose, in a way, they were.

When we reached them in the middle of the parking lot, we all exchanged hugs. Then, in a moment as unexpected as finding them was, we were all squished together in a group hug that was as painful as it was embarrassing. I had to twist my face to keep from touching lips with either Brad or Jamal, and Becky was clearly doing her best to avoid a lip lock with any of us.

"Cool! Please stop hugging us," I pleaded, hoping my breath wouldn't kill any of my friends... but especially Becky. I hadn't had the benefit of a toothbrush in a couple of days, and I was sure at least one of them would notice.

Cool released us and stepped back, thankfully retaining his human form. Jamal and Brad were probably confused and scared already. Easing them into accepting our lovable, shape-shifting Elastic Giraffe was the best course of action. I studied him for a second before returning my attention to my two wayward friends.

They were sizing up Cool as they straightened out their clothes. Given the locale and era, he had reshaped himself to look like his favorite '80s icon and one of the greatest singers of all-time, David Hasselhoff. Apparently, from the blank expressions on Brad and Jamal's faces, The Hoff hadn't been as big a deal in their world.

"You guys already know Becky," I smiled. "So, please allow me to introduce you to my old friend, Cool."

"Any friend of the Pack Man or Becky is a friend of mine, dudes," Cool said happily, extending his right hoof, which he'd formed into a metallic hand, for a handshake.

Jamal and Brad each shook hands with Cool tentatively, exchanging confused looks.

"I'm sure you both have a ton of questions," I told them. "I have answers. M-maybe not all the answers, but a lot of them."

They looked to Becky for a sanity check, but all they got from her was a shrug and a nod. "We're figuring out a lot of this as we go, guys. It would be best if we all talk together, with our other friends, too."

Jamal looked at the others, who still stood by the brick wall. "Please tell me those guys are wearin' masks."

"I'm not gonna lie," I told them. "Those aren't masks. This isn't your world, and it isn't theirs either. We're all here because of, well, something like a science project gone wrong." I pointed at Cool. "Cool's not from this world either."

"I'd already picked up on that," Jamal said flatly. "It's the rip, ain't it? That's what's causing all this? 'Cause last Brad and I knew, you were dead. Tell me I'm wrong…"

I hadn't actually considered a connection between the rip and what the Nanops were doing in my world, but it made some sense. As for having been dead… "No, you're not wrong. I died. Becky saw it happen, too. But here I am, alive and kicking. I do have an explanation for that. As for the rip, yeah, I think it might be connected."

Becky looked at me sideways. "That does make sense, doesn't it?"

I nodded, raising my eyebrows. "Jamal's the brainiac," I said, motioning for them to follow me. "If anyone can help figure out what's going on, it's him."

When we reached the others, I started making introductions, but was cut short by Gunner's phone ringing. He held it up and gasped.

"Good call, Knightmare," he said. "It's only one bar, but I'm getting a call."

My heart leaped. "Is it my dad?" I hadn't realized how anxious I was to hear from him.

Gunner shook his head and mouthed 'George' as he answered the call. "George." He listened for a few moments. "George?   George, you're not making sense. The Nanops are doing *what?*" Another pause. Gunner looked worried. *No.* Worse than worried, he looked panicked. "Wait, what… is everything… are you… What's happening there? H-hold on!" Gunner held the phone away from his face, scanned the screen, then tapped it. A video, accompanied by loud, chaotic audio, popped up on the screen. From where I stood, it was hard to make heads or tails of what I was looking at, but I do know that I heard several loud pops, followed by what sounded like George screaming.

Gunner was glued in place, clearly afraid to move even an inch for fear he might lose the call. Cool stretched up and over his shoulder, and watched, horrified, as the next fateful moments unfolded.

Gunner shouted at his phone's screen as absolute pandemonium erupted on George's side. "George! George, listen to me! George? Oh my god, George-" As abruptly as the call came through, it dropped.

Gunner stood there in stunned silence, staring at the screen in disbelief, seemingly trying to will it to ring again. His voice dropped to little more than a whisper, and if I didn't already know what he was saying, I might not have been able to make it out. *"George..."*

The big man's shoulders drooped like... aw, hell... I'm sorry. I don't have a clever analogy that would afford him the dignity he deserved at that moment. It was bad, and he looked like he'd just been gut punched.

Cool, not understanding who George was or what had just happened, stretched his head over to KM and looked in the back seat, calling out George's name. When George didn't resurrect next to the Lanier, Cool returned to us, looking confused. "Uh, what just happened, dudes?"

"George is dead," Gunner muttered, barely loudly enough for anyone else to hear. "I just watched him die. The Nanops... they killed him."

He let his arm drop and let go of his phone. Steve, who was standing in front of him, caught it and held it up.

The E.L.V.E. wrinkled his face when Gunner didn't take the phone from him. "Who's George," he asked.

"Uh, George is Irene's husband," I replied absently.

"Okay, then. Who's Irene," Steve insisted.

Becky stepped forward and took Gunner's arm. "Are you okay? Maybe you should sit down."

Gunner looked down at Becky's hands and shook his head. "No, kiddo. Thank you, though." He looked around, trying to get his bearings. He looked like he was going to be sick.

Becky held his arm tightly. "I really think you should sit down. You look like you're no-"

"I'm alright," Gunner replied gently. "I have to go." He looked around again, seeming determined but confused. "I need to tell Irene." His voice broke when he said her name. He sighed and nodded, as if he'd finally decided on something life changing. To him, it probably was. "Can Knightmare take me to where I left my truck, to see if it's still even on the highway? If it's not, then I need her to take me to Arete. George is dead, and she deserves to know." He looked at KM, and then back at me. "Will you let me take her for a while?"

I didn't even have to think about the answer. "Of course! Jesus, I don't even know what to say, Gunner."

Gunner shrugged. "Nothing to say, kid. I'll fill her in on what's going on here, too. She needs to know."

Clem took off his Devo hat and held it over his chest, looking like he was attending a funeral for the '80s itself. "I didn't know Irene's husband, but he must've been one helluva man fer her to have chosen him."

"That's very kind of you, Clem," Gunner said, sounding genuinely touched. "I'll be sure to tell her you said so."

Becky, who had not yet released his arm, pulled herself towards him, hugging him for all she was worth. "Can I go with you, Gunner? You shouldn't be alone."

Gunner shook his head. "No, I appreciate the offer, but unless you know anything about quantum mechanics, I, uh..." Gunner sighed again. It was one of those deep, hopeless sighs. "I'll be okay."

Jamal stepped forward. "Hold up, man. I know you don't know me from Adam, and you've clearly just experienced a very tragic loss, but if you need someone with a background in quantum mechanics or quantum physics in general, I'm all ears. I literally just popped into this world with Brad, Becky, and Packard, and we left a mess behind in our world." Jamal looked at Becky and me for support. "I'd like to help, and if I can, I need to get back to my world and fix things there, too."

Gunner offered a half-smile and quietly dismissed Jamal's offer. "Thanks kid, but Irene's got people at Arete who know what they're doi-"

Becky spoke up immediately. "No disrespect, Gunner, but you need to consider his offer. Jamal is the smartest guy you'll ever meet. He's been helping the experts rewrite the textbooks since he was about thirteen. He's seen all of this from the other side. Don't discount him because he's a kid. I think Irene will need him. Especially after you give her the news about her husband. We don't know how she'll react to that. Jamal will be able to keep his head in the game, where she might not be able to focus."

"If he's so smart, what's another word for thesaurus," Steve muttered before pocketing Gunner's phone.

Ignoring Steve's comment, Gunner studied Jamal, then looked at me.

"Becky's right," I told him. "Not to mention, the world he comes from has an understanding of physics and nanotech *light years* beyond ours."

Jamal shrugged. "Y'all'd probably think I'm crazy for wanting to go back if you knew where we came from. But I'm afraid that if I don't get there somehow, all my other friends, my family, everything will be in danger. If you've got someone who's already working through this, I'd like to lend a hand." Then he looked at me and frowned. "You just said in *my* world, not *our* world. Is that why you're dead over there and alive here? Is *this* your world? Are you not the Packard I know?"

Damn, his mind was quick. "Yeah, something like that. I wish I had more time to explain, but if Gunner's going to Arete, he needs to leave soon." I turned back to Gunner. "Are you sure you're okay, big guy?"

Gunner tried to smile. "I'm more worried about Irene." He let his attention drift over to Jamal. "So, you're from one of Packard's game worlds, eh?"

Jamal gave me a weird look.

"So much to explain," I sighed. "Gunner, will you be up to filling Jamal in on what's been going on?"

"Perhaps you're forgetting about me," Knightmare interjected. "I would be more than happy to fill your friend in on what's been going on here."

Gunner patted KM's fender. "Thanks. I'm not feeling all that talkative right now."

"It is understandable," KM replied.

Jamal looked at KM for a moment, and then back at me, the wheels turning behind his genius eyes. "AI?"

"The most advanced in any world I've ever been to," I told him.

"Yeah, that's gonna require more explanation," Jamal parried before turning to KM. "What's your name?"

"My name is Knightmare, with a K, after the Medieval warriors."

"That's badass. Nice to meet you," Jamal replied. "My name's Jamal. So, can I come with y'all? And do you mind catching me up on everything I'm in the dark about?"

"I would be delighted," KM told him. "That is, if Gunner wouldn't mind us talking."

Gunner looked Jamal square in the eyes. "How are you under pressure, kid?"

Before Jamal could respond, I had to put in my two cents. "He's got almost as cool a head as Pharaoh. I've watched him rewire a supercollider with monsters exploding around him, without even breaking a sweat. You need cool, he's your guy."

"Uh, dudes, speaking of, uh… Cool…" Cool gestured to himself, clearly not used to referring to himself in the third person. "If things are as bad as what I saw on your phone, Gunner, you're gonna need protection. I know Knightmare can handle herself, but she can't go inside buildings. I'm pretty much invulnerable to, like, everything, so I think I should tag along."

I felt like we were breaking up the band, but I knew he was right. "That's a great idea, Cool."

"Thanks, dude," he replied, more subdued than usual. "I just want to do my part. Gunner's headin' into danger, so it's the least I can do."

Gunner didn't even argue. He just sighed again and looked at KM. "As long as you're okay with it, KM."

"Thank you for asking," she replied. "You are part of my family now, just like Packard. I want to help in any way I can. Let's go inform Irene of the sad news, and if need be, protect her."

"I have no doubt it's going to come to that," Gunner said firmly. He looked at Jamal and Cool. "Last chance to back out, gentlemen."

Jamal stepped closer to KM, indicating that wild horses couldn't drag him away. Okay, bad analogy, since I'm pretty sure Whisper could drag him wherever she wanted, and he wouldn't be able to stop her.

"I'm in," Jamal said, without an ounce of trepidation in his voice. "One hundred percent."

"Same, dude," Cool replied. "Ferradillo, too!"

"What about me," Brad asked, suddenly feeling very left out.

Becky took his hand and I put an arm around his shoulders.

"We'll fill you in," I told him. "And Steve, give Gunner his phone back."

Steve pulled the phone out of his pocket and held it out to Gunner. "I already tried to give it back."

Gunner put up his hand, declining the offered phone. "Keep it with you. You might need it. I've got a radio in my truck and there are plenty of phones at Arete." He looked at me, trying to smile again but failing miserably. "Try your dad when you get some bars, but remember, the battery's pretty low already."

I thanked Gunner and asked Steve to keep the phone for me. He rolled his eyes dramatically and put the phone back in his pocket.

We spent a few minutes clearing the chimeras out of KM's back seat, then we added Jamal and Brad into the Lanier's database, promising to explain that, too, of course. A command decision was made to keep the Lanier with KM. Even though Pharaoh was strong enough to lug it around with us, it was likely safer with our departing friends. In truth, it was better off being at Arete in an emergency.

"My guess," I said as Pharaoh put the Lanier back on the floor of the back seat, "is that we'll find other checkpoints as we continue on. There are checkpoints in every game, so it stands to reason that at least some of them will be recreated here."

The final decision made before we went our separate ways was to keep Angus with KM, Gunner, and the others. He informed us that he'd had enough of 'the adventuring' for a lifetime, and that without Dirk, he would be content to lounge in silence at

Arete. I made a quiet bet with Cool as to how long the 'silence' would actually last.

Steve made a face at Angus and told him, "I won't miss you at all, you big old windbag."

"I'll mish ye too, ye wee fairy," Angus replied, making Steve turn his back to us and kick the sand like a pouting child.

The next few minutes were monopolized by hugs, wishes for safe journeys, and even a few tears.

Even Clem had to wipe his eyes as he said his fare-thee-wells to Gunner, Cool, and KM. He even introduced himself to Jamal without saying anything offensive, which made me proud, and gave me more relief than you might ever understand. "It's a damn shame we didn't get to know each other, young man. Hearin' Becky and the Marshal talk of ye, I'm sure I'd appreciate yer company. Should we meet again, I'd be Devo."

"Clem. His name is Clem," I told Jamal. Sighing heavily, I turned to Clem. "You're only Devo to the *locals*. To our *friends*, you're still Clem."

"Damned if this ain't confusin'," Clem lamented.

"Good to meet you, Clem," Jamal replied, shaking Clem's hand firmly.

That was what finally got Gunner to smile. "If we don't cross paths again, Clem Pickett," Gunner said softly, "it's been an honor."

Clem, looking as dignified as a man with red, puffy eyes could possibly look in that equally red jumpsuit and hat, nodded. "The honor's been all mine, lawman." And for his third miracle of the day, ol' Saint Clem reached out and embraced the very man whom he'd threatened to shoot a few days earlier.

Of course, I wouldn't be me if I didn't at least try to get the last word in. "Hey, Gunner. When you get to Arete, please hug Irene for me, and give her my love and condolences."

The formalities finally over, Gunner, Cool, and Jamal piled into KM and literally drove into the sunset.

I turned to my remaining friends. "It's time we found Mike Ferrari."

To Be Continued in:
indGame: Book 3
Open World